Binds
That
Tie

Kate Moretti

Binds That Tie
A Red Adept Publishing Book

Red Adept Publishing, LLC
104 Bugenfield Court
Garner, NC 27529
http://RedAdeptPublishing.com/

ISBN 13: 978-1-940215-26-6
ISBN 10: 1-940215-26-9

First Print Edition: March 2014

Cover and Formatting: Streetlight Graphics

PROLOGUE

SHE HADN'T MEANT TO KILL him. She remembers it as still photographs in motion, like a flip book: the struggle, reaching for something—anything—on the mantel, the surprisingly soft thump as the leaded crystal connected with his skull, the heavy finality of his body slumping on the wood floor. She remembers how she'd thought bone should be harder, stronger, like steel, and how it seemed too easy to knock out a man. She remembers Chris's face, long and white, as he stood in the doorway and stared at the body in the living room. His mouth opened, the baseball bat hanging like a failed punch line at his side. He said something—she doesn't remember what—and she shrugged, thinking he was being melodramatic.

She remembers reaching for the phone and telling Chris to get some water. She'd seen that in the movies, that cold water would wake an unconscious person. She remembers Chris's hand on her wrist, lowering the phone back into the cradle with a barely audible click. It's incredible how such a small sound could have such a resonating effect, cleanly dividing their lives in half. After all, it was just a click, like the soft closing of a door. Or the dry-firing of a gun.

CHAPTER ONE

MAGGIE

THE CLACK OF FINGERS TAPPING the keyboard kept beat with the top-forty Muzak playing at low volume. The combination comforted Maggie, the tap-tap-tap of a tinny bass-line beat. Sometimes, when a song came on the car radio that Maggie heard at least twice a day, she mentally added the clicking, like a calming metronome.

"Riley Martin is here. She wants you, not me." Linda Crawford rapped her orthopedic shoe gently against Maggie's chair, her lip curled.

Maggie studied her coworker, the only other nurse in the pediatrician's office. Linda was shaped like a beach ball, with a mound of permed blond hair and a permanent sneer. She was in her fifties, and a chronic shoulder injury gave her the wafting odor of IcyHot. Maggie wasn't surprised most of the kids asked for her instead. She stood and took the file from Linda's outstretched hand. Quick, easy last appointment of the day.

In the examination room, Riley, a towheaded, spectacled five-year-old, sat giggling on the table. Her father, tall and broad, stood next to her and held her hand. Maggie saw the unabashed love of fathers for their little girls every day, but she'd learned to push down the quick stab in her center. The most staid of men folded like circus performers at the prodding of a child, but the girls, more than the boys, had that ignition effect. The girls, more than the boys, seemed to take that for granted.

"Hi, Riley. Gearing up for kindergarten?" Maggie donned a pair of rubber gloves and opened the file, scanning for due vaccinations.

"Yes. But Markie isn't going with me to kindergarten. Daddy says I have to leave him home." A tired, well-worn brown rabbit sat in her lap, and she rubbed the petal-pink silk on his inner ear.

"Ah, well, you know what? I heard rabbits are really very smart. I don't think they even need kindergarten!" Maggie gathered a pre-filled syringe, tapped it once, and met Mr. Martin's gaze over Riley's head. He gave her a wry grin as she swabbed Riley's arm with alcohol. "Just a DTaP today, no big deal. It's not even a real shot, just a little booster. Riley, tell me, are you going on vacation this year?"

Riley launched into a long-winded description of Disney World, and while she was talking, Maggie snuck the needle into her bicep. As Maggie pushed the plunger down gently, Riley gasped.

Maggie laughed. "You barely noticed it! It was the smallest pinch. I told you, just a booster!" She pinched Riley's chin and slipped a Band-Aid over the puncture wound.

As Maggie removed her gloves and tossed them in the trash, she caught Pete Martin's eye. He gave her a wink. She smiled back, but as she left the exam room, she rolled her eyes. Pete Martin was over six feet tall, with salt-and-pepper hair and a quick, easy smile that he showered on women all over town.

She tossed Riley's folder in the To-be-filed bin. Penelope, one of the young, blond twenty-something receptionists, snatched it up. She was sucking on a lollipop, filling

5

the office with the syrupy, juvenile perfume of a grape Blow Pop.

"Riley didn't ask for you. Pete did." She twisted her mouth and raised her eyebrows, and Maggie couldn't help but laugh. "Oh, come on. I swear, Fridays are like well-visit Dad day."

Maggie shook her head as she turned off her computer for the day. The wall clock above her desk read 3:55. She heard Charlene's words in the back of her mind. *Pretty girls know they're pretty.* Her mother's voice had a tendency to sneak into Maggie's consciousness at inopportune moments, a measured timbre with a cultivated borderline British accent that Maggie abhorred. Whenever Charlene spoke, Maggie wanted to grab her by the shoulders and shake her. *You were born and raised in New Jersey, home of the worst accent in America.* "Good night, Penelope."

"I'm not far behind you." She waggled her fingers in Maggie's direction and packed up her bag. "Have a good weekend!"

Maggie waved to Linda, hunched over her computer, and stopped in the doorway of Dr. Tantella's office to say good night. He was so engrossed in the mounds of paper on his desk, he gave her a noncommittal grunt and a quick dismissive flick of his wrist.

As she opened the door to her black Volkswagen and climbed into the driver's seat, Maggie thought about Penelope's words. She'd heard it before, though not usually so matter-of-fact. Penelope, with her soup-can blond curls and rounded doe eyes, had probably heard the same things growing up and viewed Maggie as a sort of kin. Maggie wondered if Penelope had a Charlene whispering in her ear. *Shhh, don't protest, just say thank you.*

The worst part was, Maggie often found her mother was right. Pretty girls *do* know they're pretty. Even if they're never told or they never see it in a mirror, the world teaches them. People give them free coffee and appreciative smiles, hold open doors and lend them quarters at the vending machine. She tied her long blond hair in a ponytail and started the car. She was digging in her purse for gum when she heard a rap on the window. Her head snapped up, and for a second, all she saw was the white, straight-toothed smile of Pete Martin. She pressed the button to roll down her window.

"I just wanted to say thanks for being so nice. To Riley." His voice, smooth as butter, filled the car as he leaned in her open window. He smelled sharp, like citrus.

Maggie's finger twitched over the *up* button. "No problem. She's a lovely girl."

"Last appointment of the day?"

"Yep, headed home. Have a good night."

"Well, we have to bring Riley's brother in next week. Will you be in on Wednesday?"

"I'm here every Monday, Wednesday, and Friday, Mr. Martin."

"You can call me Pete, you know."

"Dr. Tantella insists on last names. It draws a line, I guess." She gave a shrug and a polite, thin-lipped smile.

"Okay, then I'll see you next Wednesday." He backed up and held up his hand in a friendly half wave.

Maggie rolled up her window and watched him jog back to his car. *Yes, pretty girls know they're pretty. They know because the world tells them.*

——<♦>——

"CHRIS!" MAGGIE CALLED AS THE door slammed behind her.

The house was empty. He'd been avoiding her, staying later at work, not returning her text messages. In the quiet, when he wasn't there to crowd her thoughts or flip her emotions, she acknowledged that she didn't blame him. Only in his absence could she admit her role in their growing divide.

The irony was, in his absence, she loved him. She loved

the way he'd pause in the kitchen doorway, leaning against the molding, to watch her cook dinner—when she did. She loved the gentle slope of his neck into his shoulder and the muscle that had formed there from years of manual labor. She loved his dark, curly hair and green eyes, a striking contrast to his wicked, toothy smile. The devil's smile, Maggie's sister had always called it. Because when he flashed it, he could do "whatever the devil he pleased."

Maggie loved the slow way he moved through life, his mind chronicling what he didn't say, the way he never rushed to fill silence. His shyness was often mistaken by strangers—or Charlene and Phillip—for stupidity, but she knew better. In his absence, she loved him. In his presence, she found that she struggled to like him anymore.

Forgiveness is a skill one learns only by being deeply hurt. Charlene had murmured that as she folded Phillip's golf shirts into an aluminum Rimowa. The memory startled Maggie.

She picked up her cell phone and texted Chris. *Coming home for dinner?*

Not *when;* she knew better. It was Friday, and Maggie felt restless, a pulsing in her chest, and a thickness in her throat. She wandered the house.

Before she could change her mind, she sent him another message. *Do you want to go to Anabelle's?*

Then she waited. Anabelle's, on their side of the Susquehanna, in Harrisburg city, was a small Italian BYOB they had discovered years earlier. It had only ten tables and one waiter who took their order with a mere head nod, never writing anything down. They'd often wondered if he could speak English. They'd fallen in love with the atmosphere, but through the years, they'd gone back for the cannelloni. They called it *their place.*

She opened the fridge and closed it. Unloaded the dishwasher, folded a load of whites, and at eight, she texted Mika. *Where are you guys?*

Unlike Chris, Mika texted back immediately. *At the hut, come meet us!!!!*

She noticed her texts to Chris had gone unread. The pulsing edginess in her chest bloomed into anger. She wondered where and what he was doing. *Tracy.* The word stuck in the back of her throat. Until Tracy, she hadn't known words could taste like anything, but *Tracy* always tasted like whiskey—a thin, caustic Wild Turkey. Bottom shelf.

Maggie grabbed a black shirt with a plunging neckline and matched it with a pair of skinny jeans. Wardrobe of the non-mom, because that's what she was and probably would be forever. Not a mom. Her belly was flat from not bearing children. Her skin, never stretched, was a smooth expanse of peach. Painted toenails, impeccable manicures, bikini waxes, and expensive haircuts were the things that had replaced child-rearing.

⬅◆➡

HELEN AND MIKA WERE BOTH single, so their Friday and Saturday nights were for finding dates. Maggie and Mika had been freshman roommates, a haphazard pairing that rarely worked. In their case, it was kismet—two similar souls. Mika was shorter and slighter than Maggie, but they both emanated the cool chill of pretty girls.

They had tried to join the same sorority their sophomore year, but neither girl was selected during rush. Later, Mika, who'd always had more grit than Maggie, found one of the sisters drunk at a fraternity party and convinced her to say why. Apparently the bubbly, friendly blondes of Zeta Omega had thought them *snobs.* Maybe that was true for Mika, whose confidence never seemed to falter. She drifted through life as though she was doing the world a favor by being there. But Maggie just never knew the right thing to say, choosing instead to say nothing.

Maggie joined Mika and Helen every other week,

although lately, when she and Chris got a movie and made popcorn, she found herself thinking about what the girls were doing, which guys they were talking to, or what numbers they were getting.

By the time Maggie got there, the Hut was jumping with throngs of sweaty twenty-somethings dancing to pulsing, loud music. The rough floor, in dire need of a refinish, was slick with spilt beer, and the air smelled like wet wood. The walls were adorned with neon beer signs, framed newspaper articles about local high school football heroes, a large mounted buck's head, and random state license plates. The tension in Maggie's shoulders released, and she closed her eyes. *Sometimes a girl just needs the comfort of her favorite dive bar.* She found Mika at their usual table. Helen was in the bathroom.

Mika warned, "She's in rare form tonight."

"Why?"

Mika shrugged. Helen had been a transplant to their all-girls college, and she'd become Maggie's biology lab partner. Helen was too smart for her own good and, like them, found herself nearly friendless at twenty years old, a by-product of being raised alone by an iron-fisted grandmother. Helen drank too much and slept with strange men on a regular basis, a practice that started in college and continued longer than it should have. They made an unlikely threesome.

Maggie looked around the room and made eye contact with a tall, broad-shouldered man next to the pool tables. He smiled slowly, and her heart thumped. *This is why I come here. To feel loved.* Instantly she pushed the thought down. *Well, that's silly.* Her phone buzzed in her back pocket, and when she pulled it out, Chris's text showed on her locked display.

Just got this, sorry. Went out after work with the crew. Should I come home now?

She made a disgusted sound and tossed the phone into

her purse without unlocking it. The text would show to Chris as unread. That seemed to be their pattern: half-hearted overtures that fell flat between them, the failure itself compounding resentment. *How long can you chip away at something until it finally breaks?*

Maggie tapped the table and then shoved herself up. "Do you want another drink?"

When Mika shook her head, Maggie turned, colliding into someone. She looked up, meeting the stranger's gaze. He gave her the same slow, sexy grin. *Now that's a devil's smile.*

"I'm Logan," he said. Instead of shaking her hand, he touched her arm on the pretense of leaning in to make himself heard over the music. He smelled like vanilla and something earthy, like musk.

Chris always smelled of cologne. *Well, when he doesn't smell of perfume.* She wrinkled her nose at the thought.

"Something I said?" asked Logan, raising his eyebrows.

Maggie shook her head, vowing to put Chris out of her mind for a few hours. She motioned for Logan to accompany her to the bar. She held up two fingers to the bartender. He pushed two beer bottles, slick with sweat, across the scratched wood top. She took a long pull from hers, and Logan watched her. She liked how she felt, showing off for a man.

Logan gave her a lazy grin and tossed his credit card down on the bar. "You're married?" He held her left hand and gently tapped her diamond ring. His hand was warm and soft, and it lingered, his thumb running up and down her palm until she pulled away.

"Yes... but he's... we're..." She couldn't explain what she didn't understand. "He cheated on me. We're not the greatest anymore."

"When did this happen?" Logan asked.

It struck her as funny that they were having an incredibly intimate conversation at full volume, trying

to be heard over the thrumming beat. "Two years ago."
She shrugged. *Eh, no big deal. My husband slept with his
secretary. Of all the fucking clichés.*

"I'll bet he regrets that." Logan leaned in.

His dark hair tickled her cheek, his breath a sugary
combination of beer and peppermint. For a moment, Maggie
thought about what it would be like to kiss him. About how
that beer and peppermint would pop on her tongue, sweet
and bitter. About how hard his chest would feel naked
under her nails as they formed half-moon indentations in
his skin. *Does he have chest hair like Chris does?*

"If he did, he didn't show it." She waved her hand
around in a circle. *Change the subject.*

But Logan didn't change the subject. "Why would
anyone cheat on you?"

The pick-up line was contrived, and she rolled her eyes.
"Why wouldn't they?"

"Oh, you're beautiful. But I think you know that."

"Don't you know? For every beautiful woman, there's
a man out there who's sick and tired of putting up with
her shit."

And that was how it all started.

—◈—

THE TEXTS CAME AT ALL hours of the day and night. With each
trill of her phone, she'd smile. Chris never questioned her,
either because he didn't care or because he assumed it
was Helen or Mika.

At first they were generic: *I miss your laugh* or *I want
to see you* or *I want to kiss you.* Later, after she'd started
confiding in him: *I hate that you're alone again tonight* or
does Chris know how lucky he is?

That night at the bar, they hadn't kissed. Flirted, yes.
Technically, had Maggie cheated on her husband? No. But
she felt like a kid again, sending notes in junior high.
Back before cell phones, a folded note would make its

way across the room, and she had known it was for her. Scrawled in boyish handwriting was *Meet me after school.* Memories of fumbling kisses, with her back against the rough brick school, and the inexpert thrusting of tongues that made her gag.

Now the boy was Logan, and the idea was tantalizing. She thought about that constantly, the initial contact of a first kiss and the soft give of his lower lip between her teeth. She thought about the deep white scar under his chin. *Where had he gotten it?* She wanted to run her fingernail along the raised flesh as her lips grazed the hollow between his neck and his ear, his breath hot on her cheek.

She saved all the texts in a file on her phone but deleted them from her incoming messages, just in case. She didn't even remember giving Logan her number, but both Helen and Mika had denied having any part in that. Maggie chalked it up to having too much to drink.

When the first one had come, it said, *Hello, beautiful. I'm not sick of you. In fact, I can't get you off my mind.*

Her palms had sweat, not with excitement, but with fear. *Who the hell wrote that?* Then, with a flash, she remembered and wrote back. *I'm spoken for, you know. Not very gentlemanly.*

He'd replied, *I'm not having very gentlemanly thoughts about you.*

And much later: *Can we meet up again?*

That one gave her pause because she had no plans to avenge Chris's affair. After a year of marriage counseling, they had decided to move forward, not back.

Dr. Deets's words came back to her. "You can't change the past, but you can change how your past impacts your future."

She remembered the family counselor's small, almost childlike frame folded into an oversized red leather chair, his thin legs effeminately crossed. His relentless throat clearing and nasally, know-it-all drone had made Maggie's eye twitch. He talked about control and loss of control. She waved him off and refused to go back. *Pompous. Arrogant.*

The idea of seeing Logan again sent a current through her spine and down her legs.

Maybe? Let's just chat for now.

Tease.

She would wonder later what would have happened if she hadn't played with him. But she was having too much fun.

———⟨◆⟩———

"RIGHT, HONEY?" CHRIS WAS LOOKING at Maggie, his hand on her knee. His voice brought her back to the present.

He and Maggie were at the nursing home, visiting Chris's mom, Gale, like they did every Sunday. Five years earlier, Gale had been the victim of a stroke that left her mostly paralyzed and mute. Chris's dad had already died in a car accident, so his mom was all he had left.

"What? I'm sorry." Maggie shook her head, loosening the cobwebs.

Gale slumped sideways in her wheelchair, her white hair a patchy halo of fuzz that barely covered the crown of her head. She always wore the same white dressing gown and peep-toed bedroom slippers, her toenails a shocking shade of pink that never seemed to fade or chip. Maggie spent a large part of every visit analyzing her toenail polish. What was it that made it so resilient? The lack of any foot activity? That must have something to do with it. She couldn't figure out who painted them. The nurses? Seemed unlikely with their proficient manner, clipped sentences, and clicking pens.

Chris laughed heartily, phony and loud. "Your head is in the clouds lately! I was telling Ma that we'd talked about trying for another baby."

Her head snapped up. "What? We never said that.

Chris, she can't hear you anyway." She regretted saying that when his face transformed and hardened with... What? Anger, embarrassment?

Then he said softly, to her, not his mom, "We did say that, a few weeks ago. Remember?"

Chris had come home from happy hour one Friday night, half-drunk on whiskey and talking a mile a minute. If she hadn't known him, she would have sworn he was on something. He insisted that he could tell that that time would be different; they would get pregnant and the baby would live. She nodded while she made dinner, sick to death of the conversation. He pressed against her backside, his hand sliding up the front of her shirt to clumsily fondle her breast. As if sex was in their rotation. The initiative was whiskey fueled, and that pissed her off. She shrugged him off until he stomped away, angry at her, angry at the world.

"Now isn't the time to talk about this." Maggie blew out a breath, and Gale moaned softly from her chair—not out of pain or need but because that was just what Gale did.

When they got up to leave, they mechanically kissed her cheek good-bye, and the nurse wheeled her away. Back to her room or maybe to dinner. They didn't ask, and no one told them.

"We did say we would try again soon," he said about five minutes into the drive home.

He'd rested his right hand on the console between them, and Maggie stared at it, thinking about how she used to love his hands. Large with square, neatly trimmed nails. For a second, she remembered how his hands used to feel on her body.

"We didn't say that, Chris, you said that. You were drunk and wanted to get laid. Which is disgusting that you would use a baby to get laid."

"Okay, well first," he began, his jaw working, "it has been a ridiculously long time. Second, I had no intention of 'using' a baby. Yes, I was drunk, but the alcohol made me say what I really want."

"You really want to try for another baby?" Maggie was incredulous. Hadn't that fight ended over a year ago, when they'd lost the fourth one?

"Yes. I do."

Maggie listened to the steady hum of the wheels on the highway. As they pulled in the driveway, he opened his mouth. Maggie held her breath, the air in the car thick with unmet expectations. Her phone trilled. She picked it up and looked at the screen.

What are you wearing?

She smiled and typed back. Chris glanced over, but the spell was broken, the wall resurrected. Maggie tapped his hand lightly before climbing out of the car.

"Pizza?" she asked, and he nodded. That was their Sunday ritual.

CHAPTER TWO

CHRIS

NOT A DAY WENT BY that Chris didn't think about how he'd paralyzed a man. The man's name was Derek Manchester, and Chris had had at least four inches and thirty pounds on him. At the time Chris put him in a wheelchair, he was a hot-headed boy. Chris liked the girl on Derek's arm, and in the brash way of college fraternity boys everywhere, Chris decided he was entitled to her. He hadn't known Derek before that night, and he knew little about him after that night, but he'd spent an inordinate amount of his life consumed with him.

Chris had smiled and flirted with the girl for the whole evening, across the crowded bar, before making his move when Derek went to the men's room.

"Why are you with that jerk?" He had expected her to swoon. She didn't.

She'd lifted one shoulder and gave him a small, teasing smile. "He's not a jerk. Well, not all the time." She giggled, touched his bicep, and bent her head forward, her long black hair tickling his arm.

He'd moved in, leaning to whisper in her ear, and he heard Derek's voice behind him.

"What the fuck do you think you're doing, man?"

Chris had smiled as he turned around, a slow, cocky smile, and shrugged. *Stealing your girl, you asshole.* The blow to his left cheek caught him off guard, and he staggered backward. *The motherfucker hit me.* He shook his head, and when his vision cleared, the rage set in. Derek backed away slowly, his face still menacing. Chris advanced and swung, controlled and powerful. One right hook, and in the freakish way the world works, he connected with the soft spot directly under his jaw. Derek's head turned lightning quick at an unnatural angle, and he dropped like a ragdoll to the floor. When the bartender shouted, "He's dead!" Chris repeated like a mantra, *It was just one punch!*

But he wasn't dead. Chris had broken his neck. The doctors called it a million-to-one shot, or at least that's what his fraternity brothers had told him when they came to visit him—that one awkward visit after he was expelled but before he went to jail.

Maiming. That was the charge. As if he was a feral cat.

He had done his time—his maiming charge—and was out in less than a year. Not quite a year of his life in exchange for Derek's whole life. With one punch to the wrong part of the jaw, Chris traded his plan of being an engineer for a chance with a girl with long black hair and a nose ring.

When he drove his truck into the lot of Carmichael Construction every morning at five-thirty and made his way to his trailer, with his little desk and small filing cabinet, he did it with his head bent low. His back was hunched by an invisible backpack heavy with a lifetime supply of guilt and resignation.

Certain days of his life, he had been genuinely happy, but Derek was always there, fraying the boundaries of his mind. On his wedding day, Chris tied his bow-tie and looked in the mirror, alone for the first and last time all day. He found himself thinking not of his lovely bride, tucked into the room next door, but of Derek Manchester. Would he ever tie a bow-tie? Marry a beautiful woman? Or any woman?

Those thoughts were Chris's lifetime sentence.

Chris sat at his desk on Monday morning, shuffling estimates from one side of his desk to the other, squaring the edges of the pink copies. They were estimates he had given weeks ago but had yet to receive a call back. He had some pride in his job. He built things—sometimes big things like parking garages, sometimes just a roof over a family's head. Mostly it was corporate, the "moneymakers" as Ed Carmichael liked to say. Chris was Ed's foreman, his "right-hand man." That meant Chris worked, and it seemed as though Ed did not. But Ed's name hung on the sign, so most of the time, Chris took it with a resigned shrug—like he took most things.

He made his way across the trailer to the other desk. His notepad had less than five pages left, and Tracy used to keep the new ones in her top drawer. Since he'd let go of Tracy, he was stuck being a foreman and a secretary— one man in a trailer with two desks.

"Shoulda kept your pecker in your pants, then," Ed had said when Chris tried to ask for a new secretary. He'd hooted as if he told the funniest joke on earth. Chris hadn't laughed.

The phone rang, and Chris picked it up, punching the *Line 1* and then the *Line 2* button. "Hello? Hello?" He wasn't sure if he was on line one or line two, and he muttered *hell* under his breath. *How hard is it to use a damn telephone?*

"Hi, it's me." Maggie's voice was low and soft, and for the first time in a long time, she sounded... happy. Affectionate.

His breath caught. "Are you okay?"

"Yeah, why?" The softness in her voice seeped out.

"I don't know. You don't call me at work. Usually, anyway. What's up?" He was shooting for lighthearted,

19

leaning back in his chair.

"Nothing. I wanted to know if you wanted to go out to dinner tonight. We haven't done that in a while, and I have off tomorrow..."

"Um, we can. But I don't have off tomorrow." He pushed his fist against his forehead. *Jesus Christ, it's only dinner. Shut up!* He never knew setting up a date with his wife would be so hard. He remembered their first date happening easily, but lately, their conversations had come in fits and starts, a stutter step on repeat.

"Well... We can do it Friday, I guess. It was a dumb idea."

"No! It's a good idea. Why are you awake?" It wasn't even six a.m.

She sighed, a puff of frustration. "I had a nightmare, and I can't get back to sleep."

Early morning nightmares had always plagued Maggie. Her arms and legs would tangle in the sheets, punching and kicking, as she yelled profanities at imaginary intruders. Between her nightmares and Chris's insomnia, it was a wonder anyone ever slept at all in their house. At least a baby would have given them something to do at night. The thought flitted across his mind, stabbing and painful.

"Do you want to talk about it?" He glanced at the clock. He had twenty minutes to load up the truck before the rest of the crew arrived.

"No, I'll let you go." Her tone was clipped. "See you tonight, okay?" She was gone, just like that—his ethereal wife. He hung up, knowing he could never quite catch her, but also that he could never stop trying.

―◆―

TWO GUYS SHOWED UP LATE. Ed called Chris's phone every twenty minutes, demanding information that was in Chris's trailer, a mere fifty feet from Ed's office yet miles away from Chris. When Chris got back to his desk, he sat and listened to seventeen voice mails, taking careful notes on a pink "While You Were Out" pad. He delivered Ed's in person, trying not to appear as insulted as he felt. After locking up the trailer for the night, Chris climbed into his truck and headed home under the same grayish pink sky he'd seen when he drove in. *Is it dawn or dusk?* And then he realized that the answer didn't really matter either way.

———— ◁◇▷ ————

"HI!" MAGGIE'S VOICE HAD AN uncharacteristic perky lilt, and her face was sunny.

She leaned into him, up on her tiptoes, and kissed his cheek, initiating physical contact for the first time in months. Her lips felt cool, and he touched his face. His fingers came away sticky with lip gloss. The knot in his gut uncoiled.

"Are we still going out?" She turned back to the sink to finish drying dishes.

She was dressed up to go out, and he placed a hand between her shoulder blades. Her back was hot, and he fought the urge to grab her waist and pull her against him.

"Do you want to?" Chris imagined her smile. He studied the molded curves of her back, the rounded dip into her bottom. He envisioned her legs under her fitted jeans, lean and strong. He inched closer, closing the gap between them, until he breathed in the scent of her hair—a heady floral aroma he couldn't name but was intimately familiar with.

"I think so. We should, don't you think?"

He didn't have an answer because he didn't know the right one.

She faced him and continued talking, apparently not needing his answer. "I want out of this purgatory."

Chris studied the tile floor, the twelve-by-twelve squares like a Minesweeper game. He chose to stand still, waiting for the detonation. She cleared her throat.

"Does that mean you want out of the marriage? Or you want out of the way we've been?" he asked neutrally.

"Either way, I kind of don't care anymore. But I can't keep hating the man I'm living with. The man I'm *married to*."

He was shocked by that word: hate. He hadn't known that was there. She stepped into his space. With her hands resting on his shoulders, she leaned into him, pushing her lips against his. Her body was soft and warm, and the unexpected touch ignited him. All thoughts of his day, Derek Manchester, and Ed Carmichael vanished. Vestiges of frustration were buffed out and made smooth by Maggie's mouth on his. All he could think about was how good she felt and how much he'd forgotten that.

"Except..." She breathed, her hands lifting his shirt and seeking out his skin. "I don't think I actually hate you. So, that's a problem."

He pushed her back against the sink. She eased him back with her hand and gave him a small, sly smile. In that instant, she looked like his old Maggie, before all the babies, before his mistake, before anger etched her face. She clasped his hand and traced circles in his palm, sending shivers down his spine. He closed his eyes, exhaling.

"Let's go upstairs," she whispered.

AFTERWARD, THEY LAY ENTWINED, THEIR skin cool and clammy. He twirled her hair, a strand of silken gold, impossibly pure and clean against the backdrop of his stained palm. She sat up, rupturing their cocoon. He tried to pull her back. She resisted, her head turned away from him.

He felt his control slipping. "Why? This feels so good. Please don't shut me out again, like you always do." He hated the whine in his voice, but he refused to go back to the tundra.

"This doesn't fix everything," she said. Her voice held

no malice, none of her usual contempt. Her words were simply out there, true and plain as fact.

"No." He knew that was true, but their current détente had the fragile feel of a cold war. One wrong move, and everything could blow the hell up. "But it's a start. Right?"

"Yes..." Her hair fell over her face, rendering it unreadable. As if it was ever really readable. "I don't know how to erase it all, Chris. Even now, two years later."

"We can't erase it. Like Dr. Deets said, we have to move forward."

"It's like my mind won't let me forget. I start to, and then I think about her. About Tracy. Even now, she's here." Maggie shifted away from Chris, tucking the blanket up around her chest.

"Okay, what do I have to do? How long do I pay for it? Forever?" He pounded the mattress with his fist.

"Well, what if I can't get over it?"

Her face was open, and to him, that was a step forward. He held her hand, softly thumbing the spot between her thumb and forefinger. He studied her long thin fingers, adorned with a delicate solitaire diamond and a plain band. "Then, I guess, I live with that. That's my cross to bear."

He felt the burden of more guilt suffocating him in the dusk of their bedroom. They sat like that, holding hands, for a while. Chris wondered if they got up and continued about their life, would they ever get back to that place again?

Way back when, before all the babies, before Tracy, he could lie in bed for hours next to Maggie, her legs wound around his. One gray February day, probably seven years ago, they had declared one day *Naked Tuesday*. Both Maggie and Chris had played hooky from work and burrowed under the heavy down quilt, emerging only to grab food and smuggle it back to the bedroom. Chris remembered Maggie diving under the warm blankets with a box of Ritz crackers, squealing from the frigid apartment air. That day seemed a million years ago, as if it had happened to two different people.

Then, fleetingly, his mind went to Derek, as it so often did.

Maggie looked up, met his eyes, and smiled. A real, genuine smile. "Did you still want to go out?"

CHAPTER THREE

MAGGIE

M AGGIE HAD AN INCOMPETENT CERVIX. When the doctor told them that, Maggie tried to make a joke and roll her eyes in Chris's direction. No one had laughed.

Instead Chris said, "What does that mean?"

"Well, the cervical tissue is too weak to accommodate a pregnancy. Once the uterus gains any substantial weight, puts any pressure at all on the cervix, the cervix dilates, resulting in a miscarriage or a preterm birth. It generally happens in the second trimester, but it can happen as late as the third."

"But what about the first one, then?" Maggie asked.

She remembered her first miscarriage—was it possible that she sometimes forgot it?—the blood and cramping at eleven weeks, the long night in the hospital, the almost laissez-faire attitude of the nurses. *Sometimes things happen, honey.* The deflation she'd felt. It wasn't really sadness, but frustration at having to start over with the calendar and the ever-romantic sex on schedule.

"That may have been related. First-trimester miscarriages aren't typical in cervical incompetence, but then again, we don't know all that much about it." The doctor cleared his throat in tacit apology for not having all the answers.

Maggie stared at her hands, turning the words over in her mind—*incompetent cervix*. Two little words that meant she could never have babies.

"Can we do anything about it?" Chris's voice cracked, and it occurred to Maggie for the first time that Chris would hurt, too.

She'd been so focused on herself—her body, diagnoses, doctors' office visits, procedures, pills—that she'd almost forgotten him. She leaned her head against his shoulder.

"We can perform a cerclage. That's a surgical procedure where the opening to the cervix is stitched closed. There's some controversy about whether it's effective, and it comes with some risks. We can also try bed rest. Anecdotal evidence suggests that's as effective as a cerclage. And we can always attempt to halt early labor with intervention. Steroids work well for some people."

"You're saying these things—sometimes it works, or anecdotal evidence, or tend to work for some people... None of that means it *will* work, right? None of that means you can fix me?" Maggie's voice edged up higher, and she covered her mouth with her hand.

All her babies—all three of them at the time—were sacrificed for nothing, really. The doctors couldn't learn anything about it or give her a drug to fix the problem. She'd spent a year feeling so angry because she didn't know why all of her miscarriages were happening, but that anger paled in comparison to the rage she felt after learning the problem had no solution.

"No, unfortunately, there is no easy 'fix,'" he said.

Chris put his arms across her shoulders and pulled her into his chest. The doctor waited until she sat up, sniffling, and then handed her a tissue.

"Okay," she said, "so what do I do?"

"Well, we can keep trying. We'll handle problems

as they arise and do our best. I won't tell you to stop trying to have a baby. Women with cervical incompetence have healthy children all the time. The body is amazing. Sometimes it just figures it out."

Maggie nodded, numbly, not sure at all that she did know. She wasn't sure she could keep going through that, but she couldn't give up.

⸱⸱◆⸱⸱

MAGGIE WAS AT HOME DOING much-needed house cleaning with her ear buds on. The iPod was cranked at full volume and tucked into her back jeans pocket. She needed a day off, a day away from Linda's endless good intentions and sound advice.

Dear, you'll be sorry you didn't try harder now. Linda only knew about one of the four miscarriages, and she'd waved it off as incidental, the way one waves a fly off potato salad. *Everyone has them. You need to move on. You know, I had two? It's God's way.*

Maggie had grown weary of hearing the variations on that—*God's way, the body's way.* She sang loudly, forgetting how good it felt to just let go and be happy. As she passed through the kitchen, she glanced at her phone, sitting face up on the counter, and noticed the waiting text message. She pulled the ear buds out of her ears, tucked them into her front pocket, and unlocked her phone.

What about tonight? Wanna meet up at the Hut?

The message made her feel both flattered and a bit sick.

This has to stop, Logan. I told you I can't cheat on Chris. Maggie hit send.

She jumped when her phone rang a minute later.

"Who said anything about an affair?" His voice was like silk.

They'd never spoken on the phone, and she'd forgotten how nice he sounded. He had a deep voice, a rumbling that was more like a growl, with a slight Carolina accent. Her mind wandered to where he'd grown up or what his childhood had been like, but she dismissed the thought. She would never know. It had to end. Now.

"Oh, come on, don't be coy. Of course it would go that way." She giggled despite herself.

"No, we can be friends, beautiful."

"Men and women, especially those who meet in dark bars, secretly, at night, cannot be friends."

"That's bullshit."

"Logan, I'm serious. The flattery feels good. I've needed it, but it's time for me to focus on my marriage. I've got to try, okay?"

"I thought you did try. You said you'd been to counseling." He seemed a bit pouty, and that was much less attractive.

She grimaced into the phone. "We did. But we're married. For better, for worse, and all that. Please?"

"Well, I don't get that. You were on the hunt that night at the bar. I can tell. Your marriage won't last the year."

She was taken aback by his spite. Logan had never seemed hot tempered, and she was turned off by his about-face.

When she didn't speak, he continued. "Well, when it's over, give me a call. Maybe I'll be around."

"Oh, come on, Logan, don't be like that. We had fun, no one got hurt; it's not like you're in love with me or anything. It was harmless flirting."

"Would your husband think so?"

Little alarm bells went off in her head. "Good-bye, Logan." She sighed. Before she could say anything else, he hung up. She yanked up the laundry basket. *Men. Geesh—and they say* we're *sensitive.*

SHE LOVED THE SMELL OF a clean house—the combination of Pine Sol and laundry detergent and a lit coconut candle. The soft whir of the ceiling fan in the living room was a soothing balm. She'd read somewhere that happiness was derived from accomplishment. Cleaning had cleared her head, allowing her to *think* for the first time in ages. She examined her deep-down buzz, the undertone to her whole day, and declared herself *happy*.

For months, she'd nurtured a pulsing hate, an unexplained animosity toward Chris she couldn't decipher. It had woken her up at night, sweating and scared. She didn't want to be a lonely, miserable wife—the kind that goes to Longaberger basket parties, drinks too much sangria, and trashes her husband in shrilly laughter—but she didn't want to be alone, either. She thought about the night before, about Chris's hands on her waist, her stomach, her breasts, his mouth hot on her bare shoulder. The panic in his eyes when she'd sat up, breaking the spell, gave her a tender pang.

She'd decided earlier in the week to try some of Gale's old recipes. Years ago, right after they'd married, his mom had written down all Chris's favorite dishes in a wire-bound journal. It had stayed tucked in the cabinet, shoved between editions of *Betty Crocker* and the *Joy of Cooking*, and had been used about an equal number of times. She pulled it down, blew the dust off the top, and flipped through it, finding the recipe for chicken pot pie. *Small gestures*, Dr. Deets said in her head. For the first time since they'd paid for counseling, she felt like following his advice. Was that what forgiveness felt like? Maybe. *Tentative forgiveness*. And maybe if she could *tentatively forgive* for a while, she could stop seeing the ghost of Tracy at every marital crossroad.

She browned chicken until the air became thick with the

29

smell of garlic and *mirepoix,* and she carefully cultivated a roux. She remembered liking to cook way back when and being good at it. She found satisfaction in watching the dish come together, the different spices melding into one flavor that would pop on her tongue. What did they call it? *Oh yes. Marrying.* Her cell phone trilled with an incoming text.

I'm thinking of you.

Well, stop. Find someone else to think about. Someone who's not married, if you know what's good for you.

What are you wearing?

Good-bye, Logan. She took her phone over to her purse, turned the ringer down, and tucked it into the pocket so she wouldn't be tempted to look at it.

⤙◆⤚

CHRIS'S EYES WIDENED IN SURPRISE, but he said nothing. She tried not to be irritated. Silence had been his weapon of choice for so long. Or shield, depending on how she looked at it. She'd set the table with real plates and silverware, white starched cloth napkins, and glass wine goblets half-full with a rich cabernet. No candles, though. She felt a bit uncomfortable with the over-the-top gesture of candles. *Baby steps.*

The whole setup was a stark contrast to their habit of eating on tray tables in front of the television, like an elderly couple. The feeling of courting her husband made her feel lighter somehow. For the first time in as long as she could remember, her belly didn't ache with emptiness and her chest wasn't tight with anger. She couldn't explain the about-face, but she felt compelled to act on it.

Chris led the conversation, haltingly at first. He told Maggie about his day, of Ed and the latest snafu at the site. She let him lead but didn't brood over silences, and she tried to keep up her end of the chatter. She felt a bit silly, as if she was on a first date. As smooth as a subway ride, the conversation started and stopped. She told him about Helen and her boyfriend breaking up, then about her sister and her sister's kids, then about her parents' latest cruise plans. She waited for a lull in the conversation.

Ice tinkled against the side of her glass as she took a sip of water. "I've been thinking about what you said about trying for another baby?"

Chris's head snapped up, his fork poised midway to his mouth. He slowly set it back down on his plate.

Maggie rushed on. "Not now. I don't think, anyway. But I don't think it's a horrible idea. Not anymore, anyway."

"What changed your mind?" Chris turned his fork, staring at his plate.

"I don't know. I just... feel better. Lately, I guess. I don't know if that makes sense or not, but well, there it is."

Chris nodded, making a face like *well, okay then.* He gave Maggie a small smile, and they finished their dinner in unusually comfortable silence. Maggie stood to clear the table, lifting her eyebrows when Chris also stood to help.

"What? I never do this?" His voice was challenging, a throwback to old patterns.

Maggie bit her tongue, clamping down on a sarcastic response. "I didn't say that, *you* said that." She smiled to alleviate misinterpretation.

His body relaxed, and his hands, with a plate in each, sagged. She turned her head so he couldn't see her smile, victorious over her win. As he walked past her, he gently nudged her back with his elbow, as if to say *sorry.* Those were the capricious conversations of unhappily married couples. What were the conversations of happily married couples? She couldn't remember.

That night as they fell asleep, she felt Chris move across the bed. His hand slipped, soft as a ribbon, around her waist. He pulled her into him, tucked into the bow of his body. She couldn't remember the last time he'd held her like that as they fell asleep. She vaguely remembered

31

being first married, appalled to discover he didn't actually like to fall asleep like that. They'd had a fight about it—about spooning at night. She'd thought that it was a huge problem, that her own husband didn't even want to sleep next to her. The dramatic arguments of newlyweds—before there were any real problems and all they could do was invent them.

She lay there for hours, listening to Chris breathe as her mind spun with thoughts of him, her babies, her friends, and Logan. She felt a pang of regret for ending things with Logan so abruptly, so coldly. She knew she'd miss the musical scale of an incoming text to tell her she was beautiful, desirable, *loved. Chris should be saying those things, not a stranger.*

Disengaging Chris's arm, she tiptoed out of bed and crept down the stairs. Pulling her cell phone out of her purse, she hit the button to activate the backlight.

Thirty-two new text messages. Thirty-two? That seemed crazy. She punched in her code to unlock her phone. Her heart raced as she scrolled through them, not even reading them completely. She was stunned that he texted her thirty-two times in one evening. When she got to the last one, she blinked twice and shivered with the cold chill of fear.

You're a fucking bitch, Maggie.

CHAPTER FOUR

MAGGIE

MAGGIE HAD A DEEP-DOWN-IN-HER-GUT HEAVINESS that brought with it fear and foreboding. The fear manifested itself in odd ways: she jumped when she heard the mail slot open and shut with the daily delivery; she called in sick from work two days in a row; she could have sworn she saw Logan in the supermarket, but then he seemed to vanish into thin air in the produce aisle. What she wasn't imagining were the daily ten or twelve missed calls and the countless text messages that rushed in like a river. *A woman-made river that will drown me.*

By Friday, she was fed up. She called the cell phone company and asked them to change her number.

"Did you want a new phone?" the voice on the other end chirped.

Maggie's mind gave her blond hair, blue eyes, and a normal boyfriend. Not a husband or a psychotic stalker she invited into her life while she was bored and lonely. "No. I just want a new number."

"Are you sure? Because it costs you nothing to upgrade, and your phone is a little bit out of date..." She giggled as her voice trailed off.

Maggie banged the phone face down on the counter without hanging up. She missed the big, corded phones, back when people still had landlines for harmless chatting, not psychotic text messaging. Those were the days when she could slam the phone down on someone. No matter how hard she pressed the 'End' button, it remained disappointedly static to the recipient. A phone slam was the best she could do, and she smiled before picking it back up again. "I'm sorry," Maggie said. "I dropped the phone. What did you say?"

"Are you sure you don't want an upgrade?" The blonde was persistent but far less giggly. *Thank God.*

"No. Just a new number."

"Well, I see you're on a family plan. I'll have to change both numbers. Is that okay?"

"You can't just change mine?" She realized then that either way she'd need a story. Another lie to Chris. She sighed. "Okay, I'll take the upgrade. What do I do?"

The blonde explained the process in excruciating detail, until Maggie felt as though she wanted to claw at her face. The blonde's voice was still coming through the earpiece, tinny and distant, when Maggie walked to the bathroom and dropped her phone into the toilet.

"WHAT'S THIS?" CHRIS GESTURED TOWARD Maggie's phone, his brows knitted in confusion. Components of Maggie's disassembled phone were intermixed with kitty litter in various Tupperware containers.

"I dropped my phone in the toilet today. This is how Google suggested I fix it. It's either genius or idiotic, I can't tell."

"How did you do that?" His voice was unnervingly disapproving.

Maggie had to stop herself from snapping at him. "It was in my pocket, I forgot, I had to go." She waved her hand like, *how else would that happen?*

Chris nodded and shrugged, seeming to accept the innocuous explanation. Of course he did. Why wouldn't he?

Maggie rushed to change the subject. "Did you call my sister today? It's her birthday."

"Oh, I forgot. We can do it now, together. We can use my phone." Chris smirked at her.

A little dig, but just for fun. Maggie exhaled a tiny wisp of relief.

<hr>

ON SATURDAY, CHRIS LEFT FOR Home Depot to buy topsoil for the garden he insisted on planting. He wanted to grow sugar snap peas, peppers, tomatoes, herbs, and who knew what else; Maggie had tuned out the details.

Maggie offered a stream of protests in her head but nodded and said, "Whatever you want." She acquiesced because she was truly trying to be a better person, a better *wife*. And because she was too anxious about Logan to protest something as harmless as a vegetable garden.

Chris had been gone for less than five minutes when the door shook with heavy thumping. Maggie looked out the peephole. Logan stood with his arm resting against the door jamb. His head was tipped down, his face in shadow. The first ripple of gut-clenching fear, swallowed up by a wave of reckless anger.

Okay, this ends right now, asshole. She flung the door open. "What? Logan, seriously, this is ridiculous."

"Ridiculous?" When he lifted his head, his expression was hostile, the contours of his face darkly drawn.

Anger bubbled up her throat, pushing out the fear. "Yes. Ridiculous. This has to stop. We met once, twice if you count *right now,* which I don't. We texted; we had some fun. Game over."

"Do you always treat people like this?"

"I don't even know what that means." Maggie sighed,

tired of him. His games seemed so silly.

"Do you use people and throw them away when you no longer need them?"

"I don't think I used you." She stopped. That was a lie. "You know what? I did. I'm sorry. I really am. I didn't mean to, and that's the truth. I didn't say, 'Oh, here's Logan. Let's see if he can make me feel better about my marriage or my life.' I guess I made a mistake, and I'm trying to fix it."

"Are you sorry you used me? Or sorry I won't let you get away with it?"

His words pricked a small hole of fear in her bravado. "I'm genuinely sorry I used you. I started down a road and then thought better of it. I thought I was making a mistake, which I was." She stepped forward, put a hand on his arm, and lowered her voice, trying to instill reason. "Do you want this? Would you want to be with me, really, if I'm not free? I'm married, for god's sake... Even if it doesn't last, I don't know up from down right now."

"Why is your phone off? I tried to call you." He slumped a little.

Maggie pitied him. *He's clearly a tiny bit off his rocker.* Could he really fall that hard for a woman he had only the most surface of relationships with? It was almost laughable. He was acting as if they were star-crossed lovers, and her patience was waning. "I dropped it in the toilet, and I got a new one. I think you should go." She stepped back into the hallway, putting distance between them, and put one hand on the door to shut it.

He pulled himself up to his full height, over six feet, and slapped the door. "What if hubby and I had a little chat?" His smile stretched wide, and Maggie felt her legs go numb.

"What? Why?" She kept her voice low to keep it from shaking. She couldn't let him know that thought terrified her. She and Chris had made progress, but Logan could certainly set them back. They'd survived Tracy; would they survive Tracy *and* Logan? Not likely.

"Well, maybe you're playing us off each other, right? I think our whole relationship has been about *you*. Maybe he feels the same way. Is your whole marriage about you too?" He stepped out onto the front porch and hopped from one foot to the other, almost jaunty. He laughed. "I hate bitches like you, you know that? You're so wrapped up in your damn self, and you love the guys that follow you around like we're all dogs or something."

"I don't think—"

"You won't get away with it, Maggie. You won't." He leaned forward, his face within inches of hers, and she saw all his pores, his eyebrows in need of a trim, and his mouth, pinched and angry.

She couldn't believe she'd ever thought him good-looking. She firmly closed the door and threw the deadbolt. She sank to the floor, folded against the door, and struggled to control the shake in her hands and bring her breathing back to normal. She had the sensation of being pressed down from all angles. Logan's words trampled each other in her mind. *You won't get away with it,* and *I hate bitches like you.* As if all women were alike—because to men like Logan, they were. She knew nothing of his upbringing, very little about his life before her, but she knew an irrationally angry man when she met one, a man who hated women with the hatred of a little boy who probably wasn't loved as a child. How had he even found out where she lived? She realized she wasn't dealing with a jilted boyfriend or a somewhat frustrated lover. Logan was a bona fide lunatic—off his rocker, screw loose, playing with a short deck, a couple of fries short of a Happy Meal. That knowledge pushed into her lungs with a heavy, wet certainty until she was drowning, unable to breathe.

Time seemed to stop. She had no idea how long she stayed with her head resting against the door jamb. A chill descended, and she realized the tile floor was cold, so she pushed herself up. The doorbell rang again, and she felt the blood drain from her face. "Please, please leave me alone—"

When she flung open the door, Chris stood in the doorway, his arms laden with brown plastic bags. "God, Maggie, are you okay?"

She waved in a weak attempt to be casual. "Fine, fine!"

She snatched a few bags from Chris's hand. She strode in front of him, as far as she could, into the kitchen and plunked everything onto the island. She forced herself to act natural, tying her hair back in a ponytail to avoid eye contact. He eyed her suspiciously, so she kept her back to him as much as possible. The effort to appear blasé was taxing.

She mumbled something like, "Be right back." She slipped out of the room and scurried up the steps to the safety of the upstairs bathroom.

As she gripped the sink, she studied her face in the mirror. She'd been sleeping restlessly, and her eyes were sunken and gray. Her skin looked flat, pasty. *God, I need this to be over.* She considered just telling Chris the whole story. They could start over, fair and square, together at the bottom. She dismissed the thought because the idea of sinking to Chris's level flattened something deep inside her. What she'd done wasn't as bad as what Chris did, not that he'd ever see it that way. The sooner she could get Logan to go away, the better. She just had to figure out how.

That night, they rented a movie. She laughed in all the right places, but her head wasn't in it. At the end, she wasn't even sure of the plot. She found herself thinking about Helen and Mika, probably at the Hut, and wondered if Logan was there too. Her heart skipped when it occurred to her that he could talk to them. Would they cover for her?

She hadn't been out with Helen and Mika since she'd

met Logan. That Saturday night should have been her night out with the girls. It was hard to believe it had only been two weeks.

"Are you okay?" Chris asked at bedtime. He brushed his teeth while Maggie applied lotion to her arms and legs.

"I'm fine. I'm just tired," she replied distractedly. Her sense of foreboding had not gone away, and she was on edge. She ran through her conversation with Logan every time she closed her eyes. *You won't get away with it. You won't.*

Chris kissed her good night, a resurrected addition to their routine, before he rolled over and turned off the light. She teetered on the brink of sleep, and the night became timeless, filled with overlapping visions and half-dreams, where Logan gave her red, writhing babies wrapped in pink and blue blankets.

<hr />

SHE BOLTED UPRIGHT AT ONE. She flopped back, flat on her back, staring at the out-of-date popcorn ceiling, and willed her body to relax back into sleep. After a half hour, she crept out of bed, tiptoed down the stairs, and scrabbled into the kitchen, fumbling for the light. She filled the tea kettle with water—a childhood insomnia remedy prepared by muscle memory. Hot honey water with a touch of milk. It smelled like Charlene's shoulder, a pointed pillow of baby powder and day-old lipstick.

She took her steaming mug into the living room and hit the power on the television. *Infomercial, sitcom rerun, infomercial, made-for-TV movie.* She finally settled on a *Law & Order* rerun. She'd already seen that one, which was odd, because she'd only watched the show two or three times. Her eyelids grew heavy, and she hit the power button on the remote. She was reaching to turn the lamp back off when she heard a soft knocking.

Her heart hammered, and she set the mug down with

a clang, a startlingly loud sound in the still house. The knocking continued. She tiptoed to the front door and looked through the peephole, although the act of looking was superfluous. She knew who was there. She swallowed back the bitter, sick taste in her mouth, closed her eyes, and instructed herself to breathe. Her mind raced. *Let him in? Try to talk to him on the porch? Yell for Chris?* If she ended up out on the porch, she would no longer be in control and it was possible that Chris wouldn't hear her yell if things went too far. *Too far like what? What is he going to do? Kill me? Well, that's ridiculous.*

She cracked open the door. "What are you doing here, Logan?"

He held up his hands, a gesture of surrender. "I just want to talk to you, I swear."

"At two in the morning?"

"I saw your light on. I was driving by after the Hut."

She smelled the beer on his breath, mixed with something sour. "Okay, so talk." Conscious of her thin pajama shirt, she pulled her robe tighter and tied a knot at her waist.

"Not out here. Could you let me in?"

"No way. If you want to talk, talk."

Next door, at Mrs. Jenkins's, the porch light clicked on, flooding Maggie's porch and hallway with light. Panicked, Maggie grabbed Logan's arm and dragged him inside. She eyed the staircase. It was fourteen steps up and possibly five additional paces to their bedroom. She had left the door ajar, not wanting to wake Chris with the click of the latch, a minor decision, so innocuous at the time, that it seemed almost laughable.

"Five minutes," she whispered and motioned him toward the living room. She wasn't sure if she was making a huge mistake, but she couldn't think of another way. Any other option would involve Chris. *No, this is better. In and out, and then... then what?* Would he come back?

When would it end? *It ends when Chris finds out.* Standing in the living room, she faced him, unsure of what to do with her hands. She clenched them in tight fists at her sides and then self-consciously crossed her arms across her breasts. "Go. Talk."

"Maggie, I wanted to say I was sorry. For this afternoon. Okay?" He swayed, almost unnoticeably.

That was when she realized that he was *very* drunk. Although she hadn't noticed it before, the room was moist with the stench of liquor and thick, manly sweat. His eyes fluttered shut, once, twice.

"Fine, Logan, it's fine. Don't worry about it, okay?"

"Can we still be friends, Maggie?" He moved toward her.

She stepped back. "Yes, of course we can be friends. We'll forget everything. I'll see you at the Hut sometime, and we'll just forget this whole thing happened."

Something seemed to click then, like a switch. Logan smiled, cocking his head to the side. Maggie smiled back, hoping it looked genuine. He advanced, still giving her a joker's grin, and Maggie realized he wasn't being friendly.

"I won't forget it happened, Maggie. I don't like when people dismiss me. Do you know I'm good with women?"

"Sure, I can see that."

As she nodded, he strode forward, slowly but purposefully, and she kept moving backward, like some choreographed fight out of *West Side Story.* She would have laughed if she weren't so completely terrified, if her heart wasn't thumping lightning quick and erratically, blood roaring in her ears. Before she realized it, her back was inches from the fireplace. Logan placed a hand on either side of her head and leaned forward, trapping her between his arms. He traced her jaw with his finger, like a lover. She shivered and swallowed.

"Logan..." Her voice was soft and pleading, and she hated that. She wanted to be strong, to be the kind of kick-ass girl who would swing and kick wildly. *This is my fucking house!* But the fear choked her, and instead she sounded youthful and stupid. "Please let me go. This is getting out of hand."

"You owe me, Maggie."

"What do I owe you?" she spat, incredulous. Her fear was usurped by anger for a brief, foolish second. *This is my house!*

"At least a fuck." He grinned and bent to kiss her neck.

She remembered the night in the bar, when his hair had tickled her cheek, and her insides turned and slid together. She felt like vomiting. "Logan, my husband is upstairs sleeping. I owe you nothing. Please leave. *Please.*" She turned her face away.

"You owe me what you promised me," he insisted, kissing the other side of her neck and forcing her head in the opposite direction.

Fear gripped her, rendering her breathless. *Oh my god, he's going to rape me. In my own living room.* She thrust her knee up, sharp and quick, between his legs. He staggered backward, releasing her with a low moan. But she was too scared, too meek. Before she could get away, call for help, anything, he recovered and lunged back at her. His left hand pushed her right shoulder against the wall, and his right arm crossed in front of her neck.

"You're a fucking bitch, Maggie." He banged the mantel, his voice loud with rage, and the hit echoed in the quiet house.

A surge of anger flooded her. "You've already said that. Can't you come up with something better?" Her hatred was palpable, and she struggled against his grip.

He pushed harder against her windpipe, and she coughed, trying to get a breath. He brought his elbow up and jammed it into her chin. Her teeth clashed together until she tasted blood. Her lungs were bursting.

He released his left hand, pressing down harder with his right, and she couldn't catch her breath. His thick arm wrapped around her like a serpent, and his fingers clawed at her thigh. He reached up her nightgown and pulled at her underpants, tugging until she felt the fabric give, a quick painful slice across her left thigh. She squeezed her eyes shut until red and blue orbs danced in her vision. She strangled out a scream, but he covered her mouth, his palm moist and smelling like fetid garbage. She gagged.

Her left hand reached up behind her. The fireplace mantel only reached her shoulder, and that struck her as odd, though it never had before. She gripped something cool and solid and, for a second, mentally cataloged the mantel. It was the Lenox crystal vase, a wedding present from Mika. She brought it down, hard and fast, and screamed, hoping she had the strength to knock him out.

He moved lightning quick for a drunk and caught the vase in mid-swing. "Are you trying to fucking kill me?"

His face was a mask of rage Maggie never knew was possible on a human being. Maggie cowered, hating how she couldn't seem to stop her tiny mewling sobs. The vase lay unbroken at her feet.

"You'd *kill* me?" he said. "For what? To keep me from getting what I deserved? Or to keep me a secret from your husband?"

Maggie felt as if her body was one giant bruise. She closed her eyes, forcing herself to focus.

Logan stepped backward, and his eyes narrowed. "I think it's time we ask *him* what *he* thinks of all this." He pivoted, striding across the room.

Maggie was left staring at his back, and she felt a bubble of panic rise up, choking her. *He's going to wake Chris.* Would he kill him? Would he tell him? She didn't have time to ask herself which option she'd prefer.

"Logan, *no!*" Without thinking, she picked up the vase and chased him, two skittering steps to his one. She caught up with him in the living room doorway to the hallway.

Without thought, without careful consideration of her

options or the consequences, she squeezed her eyes shut and swung the vase like a baseball bat. Right before the vase connected with the back of his head, she wondered if that was going to be the thing that angered him enough to kill her.

CHAPTER FIVE

CHRIS

THE SCREAM THAT HAD ROUSED him from sleep didn't startle him. He'd grown accustomed to Maggie crying out in her sleep. His stomach muscles clenched, and he waited for the inevitable kick or punch of his wife battling invisible monsters. When there was no impact, he opened his eyes to see the large expanse of white sheet. He groped for the baseball bat under the bed and stood, crossing the room in three large strides. He listened at the top of the stairs for something, anything. Nothing but gaping silence in an inky stairwell. He inched downward, his back hugging the wall, and in the hallway, he had to decide to go right toward the living room or left toward the dining room. He stayed close to the wall, traversed the front door, and headed right.

"Maggie?" Fear constricted his chest, his deep breaths doing nothing to ease the lightheadedness. The air in the house had changed, and he was certain that someone other than Maggie waited in the living room.

Maggie stood in the middle of the room, her robe off her right shoulder and belted loosely, haphazardly, to the side. She didn't look up when Chris stepped into the living room. "It didn't even break..."

That's when he saw the man lying at her feet. His body was bent unnaturally, like a kid's Tinkertoy construction—all angles and corners. The man's arms were outstretched, his fingertips almost grazing Chris's toes.

Chris jerked backward. "Maggie, what the hell... Who is this?"

"I have no idea." She dropped the vase to her side and stared at Chris as though she didn't recognize him.

He peered at Maggie, uncomprehending, until he noticed the blood flecked across her cheeks. "Maggie. What happened? I heard you scream."

She shook her head like a confused child thrust into an adult situation. "He broke in. I was watching TV. He tried to... to force himself... He backed me against the mantel. I hit him with this." She gestured with the hand that held the vase. "But it was so weird. I just wanted him off of me. I didn't even think I hit him that hard."

It was just one punch. Chris felt a surge of hopelessness. They seemed unable to catch a break, their lives an endless loop of consequences. He tiptoed over to the man, as though not to wake him, and craned to see his profile. For a split second, Chris was sure of one thing: Derek Manchester was dead in his living room. He heard the bartender say "He's dead!" over and over in his mind, all the while protesting, *It was just one punch.*

"We should call 9-1-1." Maggie's voice was a thin, reedy whisper as she sidestepped toward the kitchen. Her voice trailed off as she saw her footprints. She stared dazedly as though she hadn't felt the blood on the soles.

"Maggie, listen to me." He still clutched the baseball bat. He stood over the man and jabbed his index and middle finger into the side of the man's throat. He did not expect to find a pulse.

"Just get your phone. We'll call the police—"

"Goddamn it, give me a second to think." Chris pinched

the bridge of his nose. He studied the man at his feet, his head aimed toward the door, his arm raised as though grasping for something. Chris slowly turned around and reached out, reenacting the man's fall. "Maggie... The guy was running *away* from you."

He turned and watched his blood-speckled wife stare out the window, her gaze fixed on something in the distance. She either hadn't heard him or was pretending. Chris knelt next to the man and, with his index finger, parted the dead man's black, wet hair. He had a horizontal fissure on the back of his head, thinner than Chris expected. Beneath the skin, Chris spied a sliver of white bone, and he rocketed to his feet, his dinner in his throat.

"He tried to attack me. I defended myself." Maggie's chin jutted out, and her eyes dared Chris to argue.

"Okay, that may be," Chris said slowly, choosing his words carefully. He was trying to both assess the situation and prevent an argument. "But he was running away from you. Do you see that? Can you see that?"

"Why can't we just call the police and tell them the truth? He broke into our house and tried to rape me. He pushed me up against the mantel, and I fought him off in self-defense."

"But the wound is on the back of his head." Chris shook his head. "Why did you hit him?"

"He was coming after you! I was protecting you!" Maggie's chin quavered, and her eyes filled with tears.

It wasn't that Chris didn't believe her. He didn't know his wife as a liar, or at least not a good one. Whenever she lied, she'd absently touch the right side of her face, pull on a lock of hair, or scratch her ear. She could never figure out why she lost at poker. He waited, biting the inside of his cheek.

She held his eyes and scratched her elbow. "Isn't there a law that if someone breaks into your house, you are allowed kill them? I thought I read that once..."

"He broke in? How? Through the front door?"

"No, I... I heard a knock, and I answered the door. He shoved his way in."

"You answered the door at two in the morning? Without waking me up?"

"Can we please just call the police?" Maggie pushed her hair up, leaving a dark red streak up her cheek and painting her blond hair, like some kind of lurid shade of Manic Panic.

Chris tossed the bat, finally, onto the couch and stepped over the body. He gripped Maggie's shoulders and studied her face. Her cheeks were freckled with blood. She had a bruise on her clavicle that hadn't been there the night before.

"Listen to me. *Please.* Just listen. If you call the police, they will pick apart your story." He had to convince her, somehow. "They'll want to know why you would open the door. Did you know him? Why would he be coming after me? What did he want? Did he want money? Did you refuse? What did he say to you? What did he do to you? Why did you hit him? Did you mean to kill him?"

Her eyes went wild, and she jerked her head side to side.

Chris continued. "Can you answer all those questions? Why did he say he was coming after me? Nothing about this makes sense. They'll push, probe, and work this into some kind of angle. They'll go after one of us simply because the wound is *on the back of his head.* He was *walking away from you.* Legally, forensically, that's not self-defense, Mags. Can you see that?"

"So, fine, we answer all the questions. I don't know why he was coming after you. I answered the door because I thought it was Mika, coming home from the Hut. What's our alternative?"

Chris had been thinking about that, their alternatives. "Alternatives" was such a benign word, like ordering fries instead of garlic mashed potatoes, or *alternatively* getting a vodka martini. One didn't frequently think in alternatives when it came to handling a dead body. Except. *Except.*

He didn't know how to explain the truth. Maggie's unfettered-by-guilt vision of the world, her absolute trust in authorities, was a clash in their perspectives that Chris had always been aware of but had never thought of as important. He studied Maggie and her seeming innocence, her *prettiness,* and he had a horrible thought. *They'd come after him.* Chris with his checkered past and his dirty fingernails, his *penchant for violence,* the way people assumed he was stupid.

"They'll think I did this, Maggie. They'll think you're defending me." He squeezed the back of his neck.

"Chris, this isn't Derek. This has nothing to do with Derek. It's a different thing entirely."

He recalled the detective—whose name he'd long since forgotten—a brawny man with a ruddy complexion. He was a rookie at the time and brash in his insistence at the trial. Chris could only turn his words over in his mind. *Christopher Stevens is a violent kid who will be a violent man.*

Derek Manchester was local, a bright kid with a brighter future. He had been pre-law, following vaguely in the footsteps of his uncle, a cop. Chris pictured, for a moment, the detective, years older and perhaps wiser—but probably not—sitting with his immobile nephew at their next visit. *Well, the Stevens kid finally did it—back in jail. For murder this time.*

The number of witnesses who'd seen Derek hit Chris first didn't matter back then. Just like it wouldn't matter how a dead man had ended up in his living room. Once they saw the felony, the glaring neon light on his record, they would treat him the same way Derek's uncle had. It would be one for the win column—another scumbag behind bars. He was low-hanging fruit. Nothing Maggie or Chris could say would matter.

He chose instead to be resolute. "We're not calling anyone."

━━━━◁◇▷━━━━

HE CHECKED HIS WATCH: TWO a.m. He had three hours, maybe four. He pictured the site, prepared for the pour, and wondered if he could dig through the stone, bury the man, replace it, and get out of there in time. He hoped they hadn't tied the rebar yet. He didn't have a choice, but he had to move. He retrieved two pairs of the rubber gloves Maggie kept for handling meat from the kitchen utensil drawer. He used to mock her for that, using gloves to stuff chicken.

Maggie sat in the corner, in the rocking chair, speaking only when spoken to. Anger flowed off of her in waves, but he forced himself to focus on other things. He retrieved a tarp from the garage and spread it out on the living room floor, the corner draping over the body.

Chris's mind put together the plan, ideas like jigsaw pieces sliding into place. Carmichael frequently used Ludlow Cement when they needed concrete work done—foundations, sidewalks, pavement. Carmichael needed steps poured the following week, but they were waiting on Ludlow to finish a job—the foundation of a restaurant behind the strip mall off Route 322. He thought about the messages he'd recorded for Ed, the cement company setting the pour date at the restaurant for Tuesday, maybe Wednesday. Four days away. Too far? He didn't know. The connection between Chris and the site seemed tenuous enough. He envisioned the orange construction fencing around the hole, the mounds of excavated dirt, and hoped it was enough to shroud him.

He flipped the man onto his back, expecting a noise, a groan, or an exhaled burp of air—he'd heard of the dead speaking. Thankfully, the man remained silent, his face white and expressionless. Chris studied the man's unruly eyebrows, milky bloodshot eyes, straight Roman nose, and a thick, raised scar under his chin. He felt only passive guilt, the way he felt when brushing hastily past panhandlers—like he knew he should do something *more right*, but ultimately, it wasn't his fault they were homeless in the first place.

The man's eyes looked in two different directions, a startling dichotomy. The multidirectional gaze gave Chris pause. One eye gazed out the window at the neighbors' houses, where normal people slept. For a moment, Chris considered what it would be like to be one of them. *What if I had just handed Maggie the phone and gone back to bed?* He thought about that for a moment, aching to be stretched out on clean cotton sheets and drifting into a dreamless sleep. *To what end? One or both of us ends up in prison.*

He forced back the rising bile in his throat as he dug through the man's pockets, removing his cell phone, wallet, and his keys. Chris placed them on the mantel, next to the vase. After a moment, he picked up the vase and tucked it next to the man, into the crook of his arm as though it were a cat.

He talked to Maggie as he worked. "Self-defense isn't a get-outta-jail-free card. Did I ever tell you about Bedgar?"

Maggie didn't answer him, but she didn't have to. Chris had never told Maggie anything about prison. He'd never talked about it, period. She used to complain that he wouldn't tell her everything about his life *before*. As though she had cut a deep, uncrossable chasm through his life. How could he tell her that *before* Maggie, his life had nothing: a lonely, timid, hermitic mother, a brief escape into college, a senseless bar fight, a year of desolation. *After,* well, after was a love seismograph—sharp, ecstatic peaks and equally deep, despairing valleys, all intermingled with the apathetic flat line of the everyday.

"Bedgar was what we called this guy, Ben Edgar. He was the nicest guy, very soft-spoken. His story was a bit crazy." *Grunt.* "He and his girl were out for their ten-year anniversary. They polished off a bottle of champagne and were stumbling home. This was in Philly, I think. Anyway, they got cornered by this drifter, a drug addict, who was all out of his mind and yelling nonsense. Bedgar had a gun—he had a license to carry, too, but as it turns out that doesn't matter all that much if you're drunk." Chris looked at his wife.

She rocked stoically, her gaze focused out the window. In the bluish cast from the streetlights below, she looked ghostly fragile—a beautiful apparition.

Chris had no idea if she'd even heard him, but he kept talking while he dragged the dead man to the corner of the tarp. "So he pulls out his gun, just to threaten the guy, and somehow the gun goes off and kills the drifter. So the police show up and issue breathalyzer tests to Bedgar and his girl. It turns out, you can't fire a gun drunk. The cops search the dead guy, and he's got nothing. No knife, no gun, no weapon of any kind. So they make a big stink over Bedgar being drunk, dig into his past, and I guess he'd been in rehab or something—a known alcoholic with a DUI record. Either way, they make Bedgar into some kind of poster child for gun laws, enforcing background checks and firing under the influence, that kind of thing. They throw the book at him—murder two. It was crazy. Bedgar got a lawyer, probably one step above a public defender, though, and they argued self-defense. The cops called it *unreasonable force.* Meaning, Bedgar coulda stopped that guy any number of ways. Hell, he could have just walked away, not that he knew that at the time."

Maggie remained silent. The living room was eerie with the swoosh of the thick plastic as Chris wrapped it around the man, the *alive* smell of fresh blood, the *snap! snap!*

of the bungee cords. Chris had rolled the man into a long cigar. Sweat dripped off his nose onto the tarp.

"Maggie." He jumped to his feet, and her gaze snapped away from the window. He threw her a pair of rubber gloves. "You have to help me move him into the truck."

"You're crazy, Chris." She shook her head. "I killed him. I'll tell them that."

"Shut the fuck up, Maggie, and help me *now*."

Her face changed from impassive resignation to fear. He had never spoken to her that way, but regret was for much, much later. Regret was for the rest of his life. She grabbed the end of the tarp between her thumb and her forefinger, pincered delicately, and Chris rolled his eyes.

"You're going to have to gimme more than that, Mags."

She hoisted her end off the ground. There was more blood than he realized. He would have to come back and clean it up. His mind catalogued things to do with incredible clarity, a focus he didn't know he had.

On the front porch, they both looked left and right in unison. The row homes were dark and silent, brick and vinyl sided, with well-kept trees and late model economical vehicles, but there were no people. He took one step forward, and Maggie stopped.

"Chris, we can undo this. Please think about this. If someone sees us now, we're dead. We can't fix it. This is our last chance. We can bring him back inside, undo everything, and call the police. We'll still be okay." Her voice was plaintive.

"I don't have a choice," he said. "*We* don't have a choice. If we hurry, we'll be fine." He backed down the steps, almost before she was done talking, and she scrambled after him, the rolled tarp bouncing between them. Chris gave her a pointed look.

They heaved the body into the bed of the truck, a graceless, awkward transition, and the man fell with a resounding thud. Chris left Maggie on the sidewalk and circled around the back of the house to the garage. The one-car garage bordered the alley, but they both parked in the street. For the first time, Chris wondered why. He selected a shovel and a pick axe from the wall of hanging tools. Then, on second thought, he tossed a coil of rope over his shoulder, just in case. He walked back around front and set the tools in the bed of the truck as quietly as he could. Chris climbed in the driver's side, and before he shut the door, he turned to Maggie. She stood wordlessly on the sidewalk, her hands clenched in front of her. She stared at the truck bed.

"Maggie," he said sharply.

She turned to meet his eyes. He opened his mouth to say something profound, something to make her understand, but then he closed it again. Maggie had spent the past two years of their marriage disagreeing for argument's sake alone—protesting *anything* Chris proposed simply because he proposed it. On the most intense night of their lives, he expected her to simply trust him? Agree with him? *Doubtful.*

"Figure out which one is his car," he said.

"What?" She shook her head.

"But don't set off the alarm. Keep your gloves on if you use the key fob and don't touch the car itself. Just figure out which car is his. Hit the unlock button on the keys until you see the lights. Then re-lock it and go back inside. *Keep your gloves on.* Do you hear me? Don't touch anything without gloves, okay?"

"What? Why?"

"Just do it. I'll be back in an hour, maybe two." He slammed the door, shaking his head. As an afterthought, he rolled down the window. "Maggie, do you trust me?"

"I... I don't know. This all seems too crazy."

"Can you trust me? I'm asking you to trust me."

She hesitated, her eyes darting between the house and Chris's face. "Yes. I trust you."

"Then don't call the police. I'll be back." He needed to move quickly. He needed to think of everything.

CHAPTER SIX

CHRIS

C HRIS CUT THE LIGHTS ON the truck right before where he believed the turnoff was. The sound of gravel underneath his tires told him he'd hit the mark. He inched forward about five feet before rethinking it, and he turned on the fog lights. Low and dim, they cast a bluish-white haze over the dirt road into the site. He glanced over each shoulder. *Not a car in sight. Good.* He gunned the engine to get out of view.

He pulled the truck behind a mound of excavated dirt, accidentally running over a section of orange construction fence. He reached into the cab of the truck and hefted out a heavy-duty battery-operated lantern. When he flicked the power switch, it seemed dangerously bright, but he pushed aside any creeping doubt.

Chris wasn't a praying man; he saw the interior of a church at weddings and funerals. But as he stood in the deadly silence, the air thick with danger, he bowed his head, hands resting lightly on the truck gate. *Please, God, let this be enough.* His desperation bubbled up in a brief spurt of anger. He clenched and unclenched his fist, fighting the urge to punch the hard, unforgiving metal. He couldn't shake the feeling that he was being tested, yet again. When he grabbed the shovel, took a deep breath, and turned around, he half expected to see the slouched figure of Derek Manchester, his wheelchair wheels glittering in the lantern light.

Chris surveyed the area. The edge of the strip mall parking lot lay one hundred yards to his right. The parking lot lights were muted by a line of arborvitae, providing a row of privacy. To the left, he saw nothing but a barren field slightly illuminated from the Route 322 street lights. He could envision the large wooden For Sale sign in the center, invisible in the darkness.

The lantern light swayed, drunk as a boozy carnival clown, throwing eerie shadows to his left and right. His neck tingled with the sensation of being chased. In his other hand, he carried the shovel like a heavy, swinging scythe as he trudged forward to the foundation pad. The area was large enough for a six-thousand square foot restaurant, and he exhaled with relief at the sight of a sea of gray gravel. The steel rebar cages sat stacked off to the side, ready for another day. *They're a day behind. Does it matter?*

No, because he didn't have a plan B. Plan B involved the police and the inside of a prison cell. He dug his toe into the gravel and calculated at least six inches to get through. He eyed the field of undisturbed dirt as far as he could see, and he considered burying the man there. Years could pass before they found him. But what if they decided to plant something while they waited for it to sell? What if they started excavation on an unknown project earlier? *No, this is a sure thing. Buried in cement. Like a mobster.* He laughed at the thought, and the humid spring night swallowed the sound. He checked his watch: quarter after three. Less than two hours ago, he had been sound asleep. *Stop dicking around.*

He picked a spot about twenty feet from the edge

closest to where the truck was parked. It might be better to dig in the middle, but he'd have to drag the heavy tarp that far. The first shovelful was heavy and simultaneously paltry in volume, but the second and third seemed to be both bigger and lighter, somehow. He was getting into the swing of it. He built a knee-high hill of gravel to his left. He cleared a seven-by-four foot section in less than—he checked his watch—forty minutes. So far, so good.

Chris shifted so he could pile the dirt on the other side of the rectangular clearing. He tipped the first shovelful of dirt to his left when he was blinded by the headlights of a car driving east on Route 322. He killed the lantern light and crouched. The mound of dirt at the edge of the site blocked the truck and the street. When the lights passed, he stood again, turning east. In the distance, the street lamp reflected off the top of the car—a rectangular light bar, unilluminated, yet still threatening. *Cops. Fuck.*

Chris's heart raced, and he huddled down again. If they had seen him, they would have investigated. That thought provided a balm to his fear, and he stood back up and returned to his task as quickly as possible. The cop sighting was a trigger. *Get in and get out.* He dug with violent fury.

An hour in, his shoulders hummed with pain he barely acknowledged. He had intended on going down at least four feet, but that was impractical given the amount of time. With the gravel and the cement on top, a shallow grave would have to make do. He pulled off his work gloves and flexed his stiff fingers. A long blood blister snaked across his left palm. His fingers swelled from the pain. He slipped off his wedding ring and tucked it into his right pocket. He opened and closed his hands once more before picking up the shovel and returning to his task.

After another hour, he'd hollowed out a plot with two hills on either side: one of gravel, one of dirt. Chris sank down on his haunches, exhausted. He rested his elbows on his knees, his forehead against his palms. The blinking light of his phone clipped to his belt caught his eye. A voice mail. He dialed his mailbox and punched in his code.

"Chris, I'm nervous, are you all right? I found the car. I didn't touch anything. Call the house, okay?" Maggie's voice was thin and tremulous.

He was still holding the phone to his ear when he saw a red and blue flash from the street. His heart fell before he could formulate the thought *the cops are here*. As if his body had always known he'd get caught, but his mind had to catch up. He flicked off the lantern again and sat in darkness, fighting back nausea. The cruiser parked at the mouth of the dirt road, facing east.

Is it the same car? He couldn't tell. Why was the cop sitting there, lights flashing, with no other cars in sight? Was he radioing for backup? *A suspicious vehicle parked at the future Texas Roadhouse.*

Chris wanted to check the time on his phone, but he was irrationally afraid of activating the backlight. How long had the cop been there? Five minutes? Ten? The red and blue lights switched off, the car pulled back out onto Route 322, and peeled off like an adolescent with a hot rod. *Fucking cops.*

Chris was energized by the near miss; his hands shook with the rush of adrenaline. He felt jerky and took a deep breath. *Get done and get out.* He backed the truck up until the tires almost touched the wood frame of the restaurant site. He dragged the body to the edge of the truck bed and then, getting behind it, rolled the tarp cigar onto the gravel below. It hit the ground with a whispered thud, the loose dirt absorbing the impact.

He grabbed the tarp by one end. Through the layers of plastic, it was impossible to tell if he held the man's head or feet, but Chris couldn't be bothered to care either way. He dragged the body ten feet, and paused to take a deep breath. Carrying the body of a man easily his height and weight was more work than he'd expected. When he reached the hole, Chris dropped the end of the tarp. He felt nothing except a tight panic in his chest. A steady mantra of *get done and get out* ran through his mind.

He shoveled dirt with manic quickness. The dirt skittered along the tarp to either side, until finally, *finally*, it inched up the sides and covered the tarp. Chris dropped the shovel and jogged back to the truck for the tamper. He pounded the ground above the plot. He shoveled in more dirt, tamped, shoveled, and tamped, until all that remained was a small pile displaced by the man buried three feet under. That dirt was easily transported to the edge of the foundation site where it blended in with other, less sinister dirt.

With renewed vigor, Chris replaced the gravel in half the time it had taken him to shovel out the dirt. He squinted at the patch to ensure it wasn't visible. In the dark, with nothing but the lantern light, he couldn't be sure. All he could do was hope. He tossed his tools in the bed of his truck with a metal-on-metal clang and jumped in the driver's side.

He turned right, toward the first hint of light on the horizon, orange and pink on a gray-black canvas. The rising sun dotted his nighttime activities like a period. He contemplated turning back to ensure that his crime remained invisible with the light of day. *A useless endeavor. Just keep moving, get done, and get out.*

He stopped in front of their house and stared at it in the harsh shadows of early morning. When they'd first bought it, it had been in foreclosure, the windows boarded up, the siding slipshod, the front porch cracked. They had made it theirs with sunshiny yellow window boxes, planted geraniums and impatiens—right out of *Gardening for Dummies*. Maggie had planted and scrubbed and painted, chirpy and bubbling with excitement.

Chris had asked her, "Can you be happy here? In a

thirteen-hundred-square-foot two-bedroom duplex?" He'd always compared the life he could offer with the life she'd left behind.

There was no comparison, she'd insisted. But Charlene and Phillip had set up a camp in a small part of his brain, a duet of doubt he couldn't shake. But Chris loved his house. He loved what they had done to it together. Back when things were good, when they were peacefully sliding along, complacent in their happiness.

The peace Chris had felt when pulling into his parking spot out front had vanished. The house looked sinister. The dormers cast a furrowed, disapproving brow, and the red front door gaped accusingly. He thought about *not* stopping. He could put the truck in drive and head west, toward Washington or Oregon, somewhere wet and cool and rich with green, the color of life. His legs were leaden.

Instead, he retrieved the tools from the truck bed, hung them back up where they belonged, neat and orderly. As though the whole thing had never happened. The garage looked exactly the same. The space was filled with office file boxes: *Taxes, Chris Legal, Maggie College.* A square box filled with other labeled boxes.

But everything was different. That night would never fit into one of Maggie's stacked crates. There was no cardboard container for *The Night We Killed Some Guy,* labeled with thick black Sharpie in Maggie's perfect cursive.

With a jolt, he dug into his right pocket, pulling it inside out. He searched his left pocket the same way. With a thudding pulse, he scanned the garage floor, even sinking down on his hands and knees to study the dusty cement under the shelving unit. But it was no use. He swallowed thickly. His wedding ring was gone.

———◆———

MAGGIE WAS WAITING FOR HIM in the living room in the same chair she'd sat in earlier. She was staring out the window at the coming dawn. She didn't look at him when he let himself in. Her beauty struck him at odd moments and always had. He could be mad as hell at her, and she'd turn to him with her mouth open and her eyes glaring, and the room would seem to cave in upon itself. Her voice would mute, and he would be struck by the thought, *You're so goddamn beautiful.* It was always the moment he lost the argument.

Half of him wanted to shake her. *Tell me the truth about tonight.* The other half of him wanted to kiss her. *Make it all go away. Help me make the whole night disappear.* He didn't have time to ask her for help. He was racing against the sun.

"Keys?" he asked curtly, hurriedly.

She gestured toward the end table next to the couch. The man's keys, phone, and wallet sat in a pile.

"Did you touch them? Without gloves?"

"We have to talk about this," she said softly, still looking out the window.

He loped to the kitchen and donned another pair of rubber gloves. "We're not having this conversation now. Come show me his car before people start waking up." He struggled to keep the snap out of his voice—he needed her to obey as quickly as possible. An argument would only delay things.

She followed him outside, her face a mask. She barely looked at him, wouldn't meet his eyes. She pointed at an old Honda Accord, midnight blue, parked six spots away from their front porch. The street remained deserted, but the light gray stillness of early morning foreshadowed imminent activity.

Chris remembered that it was Sunday. *Maybe a bit more time then.* But soon people would pass by: the church-goers, the Sunday paperboy, dog walkers, and octogenarians out for their "morning constitutional." In the darkness of their porch, he pulled out the man's wallet. His eyes focused on the address, straining to see it, and skipped over the man's name. The scumbag lived on the other side of town in a section of rundown row homes.

"Maggie, get in your car and follow me, but stay well behind, okay?" He relayed the address. "Don't forget it, but don't tail me there."

Before he could second-guess himself, he climbed in the driver's side, turned on the ignition, and tapped the rearview mirror into place. He left the side-view mirror and the seat alone, his knees scraping the underside of the dashboard. He put the car in drive and pulled away, leaving Maggie standing on the curb. She looked lost, her shoulders wilted and round. He shook off the image and pulled into the street. He didn't look back.

CHAPTER SEVEN

MAGGIE

MAGGIE LAY IN THE DARK with her eyes shut, in the confused half-sleep where the time of day seems arbitrary. She sat up, blinking, and tried to see through the tightly shut blinds to the world outside. *Chris, where is Chris?* She had no idea. For a moment, she found herself wondering why she felt so sick. Then it all came flooding back: Logan's flat, black eyes, the odor of something richly biological. Beads of sweat popped up on her arms at the memory of all that blood. It belonged inside the body, and to see it out, covering her floor, her hands, the soles of her feet, felt pornographic. *Had it really not even been a day?* Hard to believe.

The bedroom door creaked open, and Chris stood in the backlit doorway. He picked his way across the room and sat on the edge of the bed. Neither of them spoke.

"Who was he, Maggie?"

When he'd asked earlier, in the thick of things, it had been so easy to lie. In the quiet stillness of their bedroom, the truth seemed eminently important. She feared another lie would sit between them like a parasite, leeching the life from their relationship. The truth, or some version of it, would have to come out for them to move on.

"I knew him from the Hut." She wasn't lying. That counted, right? "I met him there with Mika and Helen."

Saying their names gave an unreal quality to the conversation. Could she ever tell them about last night? No. *No one could ever know.* The realization dawned on her that she and Chris had distinctly separated themselves from normal people. They would always be different. Damaged. *They were people who had killed someone.* She had more in common with a convicted murderer or rapist, someone with little regard for human life, than she did with Mika or Helen.

"God, Chris, what have we done?"

The question fell between them on the bed.

"What we had to do."

They sat in silence. Maggie wanted to shake him. But she didn't because doubt festered in the back of her mind. It was easier to blame Chris for his decision to bury the truth. *Except, except...*

Chris broke the silence. "How did he know you? Where we lived?"

Maggie considered the shades of truth and their alternatives. "I don't know." And that was actually true. She'd never given him her address. Who, besides Mika and Helen, would know about Logan? Mrs. Jenkins, her next door neighbor, could have easily seen his visit to their house. Or cell phone records. But those would only come out if...

She grabbed Chris's arm. "What if we get caught?"

It was incredible that she hadn't thought of it before. She had thought *she* could get caught—she'd spent an enormous amount of energy hiding the truth from Chris—but she hadn't considered that *they* would get caught. As if it wasn't an option, as if no one would miss Logan. He had friends; she knew of at least one, a guy he called Tiny. Maggie remembered him from the night she'd met Logan.

Tiny had a gleaming shaved head, a large flat nose, and a distended upper lip. An indistinct neck tattoo climbed up behind his ear. He would miss Logan. Would Tiny know he was coming to their house? Her heart raced.

"We won't get caught. He was never here, Maggie. Come downstairs, I need you to look, to make sure I've thought of everything." His shoulders slumped a bit, the burden rounding his back.

"What about his wallet? His keys? His cell phone?"

"I threw his wallet and cell phone into the Susquehanna at different spots on the way to his house last night. His keys are under the floor mat of his car."

"What? Chris, that's so stupid! That's going to be a red flag!"

"I don't think it will matter." He sighed heavily. "That can't lead them to us."

"What about your truck?"

"While you were sleeping, I took it to the car wash. I power washed the bed. I doubt there's anything left there. Please just come downstairs and help me look." He motioned for her to follow him.

She waved him away. "I'll be there in a minute."

She stared at his retreating back and listened for his heavy footsteps on the stairs and the finality of that last step fading into the living room. She could imagine him stalled in the middle of the living room, waiting for her, unable to go to the kitchen to make a pot of coffee or sit on the couch and read the newspaper. Normal, boring things. Things they would routinely do on a Sunday afternoon. Was it really only Sunday?

She swung her legs over the side of the bed, and her feet hit the floor. The feeling of being pushed down upon by unseen forces descended on her, of moving underwater. Just like the weeks after each baby, and just like after she found out about Tracy.

IT HAD ALSO BEEN A Sunday. Six months after they'd lost Christina, the only baby they'd dared to name and the most heartbreaking. At twenty-eight weeks, they'd been well over halfway to full term, and Maggie had been hopeful.

She had been so *angry*. She knew it, but she couldn't do anything about it. Every conversation seemed to end with an awful, biting hostility—when she bothered to speak at all. But that Sunday, Maggie had woken up, for the first time in months, with a faint lightness. She rolled over to wake Chris, wanting to see him for no reason that Maggie could pinpoint.

The bed was empty. She checked the clock. Eleven thirty. She supposed he had grown tired of lying around until early afternoon. He had moved on easily—he'd even gone back to work after a week. *A week!* Maggie was still on sabbatical. The office had begrudgingly agreed to give her an indefinite amount of time off, and sleeping until eleven thirty had become part of her daily routine.

She padded to the kitchen and found a note on the countertop. *Had to run to work. Be back around two.* The kitchen was piled with dishes, including pots that had been used on Thursday for Chris's dinner. They were crusted with macaroni and cheese and a film of grease from boiled hot dogs. Instead of being angry—she recognized that perhaps the day before, she would have been angry—she rolled up the sleeves of her pajamas, pulled the dishes out of the sink one at a time, and ran the water. Hot, almost scalding, water left her hands raw and red, and the pain felt good.

She removed the grill on the stove and furiously worked at six months of cooked-on food with a scouring pad. *How hard is it to not over-boil milk?* She smiled at the thought. *Smiled!* And it felt *good*. The marble countertops had a film on them, substance unknown. An organic base layer was covered in bills, junk mail, coupons, flyers, and hospital paperwork—the detritus of six months of life.

When she stopped, searching for something else to do, the kitchen sparkled. She took a deep breath, pride filling her lungs. She realized her pajama top was soaked and went upstairs to get dressed. She checked the clock— twelve thirty. Was that all? Overcome with the urge to see Chris, to show him the kitchen, she called his office. It went to voice mail. *Go see him.* Leave the house? She'd done it a few times. Not recently, though.

Driving felt foreign, a language in which she was no longer fluent, and she braked too hard at stop signs or too late in traffic. When she pulled into the parking lot at Carmichael Construction, she barely noticed the two cars in front of Chris's trailer. Later, when she replayed the morning on an endless loop, she would recall the two vehicles with acrid clarity.

She opened the door with a resounding creak and called, "Chris!"

Maggie had heard people say they "couldn't believe their eyes," but for the first time in her life, she understood what that meant. Her first thought at the scene in front of her was that it was an elaborate practical joke, a skit put on just for her, and they would all crack up in *you should have seen your face* laughter. Tracy straddled Chris, half-standing and topless, her breasts hanging low and pendulous like some National Geographic special. Her cutoff jeans were pushed down on her hips—thank God she still had them on—accentuating a soft bubble of belly fat.

They had turned to gape at her. His mouth hung open, covered in the trashiest shade of fuchsia lipstick Maggie had ever seen. Tracy made no move to cover herself, and the three of them stood frozen in some French farce. Maggie laughed then, covering her mouth. She wasn't supposed to laugh at finding her husband with a half-naked woman, but her gut feeling was one of superiority. *Come on. Tracy?* Would it kill her to bleach her roots before they reached her ears? She drove a Camaro.

"Maggie, why are you here?" That was Chris's solitary sentence. It wasn't even a protest; it was an accusation. *At her.*

For what? Interrupting them?

"Oh, did I disturb you? Then by all means, please, carry on. Use protection." She left them, closing the door.

She hesitated on the unfinished wooden step of his trailer for ten minutes, waiting for him to come after her. But he didn't. When she couldn't wait anymore, she walked back to her car, wondering where she would go. Everything was gone. On the way, she picked up a solid steel rod that had been lying on the ground. It was heavy, about four feet long, maybe an inch in diameter. With calm precision, she raised it over her head and brought it down on the windshield of the Camaro. The glass splintered but did not shatter, no matter how many times she hit it. And no one came out to stop her.

<hr />

SHE HADN'T THOUGHT ABOUT THAT day in a while. She crept downstairs and paused in the doorway. Chris crouched with his back to her, studying the floor. A suds-filled bucket sat next to him.

"Blood?" she asked.

He turned to face her, and she was startled by the lines on his face, etched seemingly overnight.

"I think I got it all. But it's a hardwood floor, so... I guess you never know."

She bent down behind him. The floor glistened, and the smell of Murphy Oil Soap stung her nostrils. She saw nothing. She inspected the mantel. It was freshly scrubbed without a trace of blood. She realized the room looked as though the night before had never happened.

She tucked her face into the hollow of Chris's back, replacing the citronella odor with his smell—the earthy, musky, familiar scent of his skin. He made no move to return the gesture, and after a moment, he stood. He motioned for her to follow him. They walked outside and inspected the truck, the garage, and the front porch. Maggie didn't see a drop of blood or a single knickknack out of place.

"Coffee?" she asked and wandered into the kitchen. Her stomach rumbled, although the thought of food made her sick. The digital display on the microwave blinked three thirty. She'd slept most of the day, and Chris had worked.

"I'm going to take a shower," Chris replied.

Maggie gasped. "Chris! Your clothes! My pajamas!"

Her pajama shirt had been spattered with Logan's blood. After Chris left, she had balled up her pajamas and shoved them in the trash can, just needing it all to be over. She showered under water as hot as she could stand it, scrubbing until her skin was raw.

"It's all in the river." He didn't turn around, but he raised his hand in the *no more questions* gesture of exhaustion. He really had thought of everything.

Maggie took a deep breath. *Maybe we'll be okay.*

When Chris disappeared upstairs, she retrieved the back of her cell phone, which was still sitting in a Tupperware of kitty litter. She located the memory card and picked it out. It was about the size of her pinkie fingernail, and that amazed her. All her secrets in that tiny device. She tiptoed to the downstairs powder room and flushed the tiny electronic device. *Good-bye, secrets.* She snuck back to the kitchen, listening for the telltale creak of the shower shutting off. Minutes later, she heard Chris's footsteps on the stairs.

When he appeared in the kitchen doorway, for the first time, he looked scared. "This will be okay, right?"

His need was so uncharacteristic, so foreign, that she

didn't know what to say. She feared that anything she said would drive him further into himself. Between the night before and that morning, she'd grown accustomed to his assurance. She needed his confidence. His fear gripped her, a tight clawing around her throat. She couldn't be the rock. She nodded slowly. She had no idea if that was true, but the lie felt convincing, even to her.

The doorbell rang, jarring only in its normality. Their doorbell rang regularly with kids selling things or Jehovah's Witnesses. She met Chris's eyes and knew he felt the same rising panic she did. He loped across the living room and parted the curtains. Time seemed to stand still. Maggie knew what he would say before he turned around. Before she saw his face, ashen and wild-eyed.

"The police are here."

CHAPTER EIGHT

CHRIS

"**D**O YOU HAVE A SECOND to speak to us, Mr. Stevens?" Two uniformed officers stood on the porch, one behind the other. The one in front was tall and had a barrel chest that tapered down to a narrow waist. He had a close-cropped marine cut and the jutting jaw to match. He carried a cup of coffee and a manila folder tucked under his arm.

The second cop was a wiry wisp of a man with round, wire-rimmed glasses and cherubic cheeks. He was probably told he had a baby face all the time, and he probably hated it. The second cop gave him a friendly smile. Chris pushed aside the oppressive dread, opened the door wide, and tried to make his face impassive. *Cooperate and they'll leave.*

He cocked his head to the side. "Sure, can you tell me what this is about?"

"I think we should just come in. It shouldn't take long." The big guy did the talking.

Chris motioned them into the living room and gestured toward the couch. Chris sank into the recliner, but when the two cops remained standing, he popped up again. His palms were damp, and he wiped them on his jeans until he caught himself fidgeting. He dropped them to his side as the first cop pulled two photographs from the file and held them out.

"We're looking for this man. Have you seen him?"

For a quick second, Chris allowed himself the delusion that the visit had nothing to do with the dead man. That they were looking for someone else—a neighborhood drifter, a suspect in a rash of break-ins—*anyone else*. Chris took the pictures and studied them individually. The first one was a snapshot of a man at a picnic table, grinning widely with his hands folded in front of him. The second picture was a blurry close-up of his face in profile, his eyebrows knitted together in anger. Both pictures showed the same man, a man Chris recognized as being dead on his living room floor a mere twelve hours earlier.

Chris studied the pictures, flipping back and forth between the two, his eyebrows knit in concentration. "I don't think so. Should I? Who is he?"

"Is your wife at home, Mr. Stevens?"

"She is, but she's been up all night with the stomach flu. She's sick as a dog, in bed. You can call me Chris, by the way."

The cops glanced at each other, their expressions unreadable.

"I can go get her if it's important..." His instinct was to talk, to fill the silence with enough words to make them go away. From television, crime shows, he knew that was purposeful. He'd watched a ton of that stuff, and he knew the drill, whether it was real or not. Yet there he was, falling into the same traps. *Just stay cool and shut the hell up.*

He shifted his weight from one foot to the other. He wanted them to sit. If he could get them all on the same level, maybe he could say the right things. With everyone standing around, he didn't know what to do with his hands, and his arms felt too big for his body. Beads of sweat popped on his forehead, but he knew enough not to wipe them away.

"We have it on more than one authority that he was coming to your house last night," the first cop said, maintaining eye contact.

Chris glanced at his name tag, a flat, rectangular strip of metal with DAVIS engraved on it. He realized then that the cops hadn't introduced themselves. *Weren't they supposed to do that?* If they were there out of courtesy or friendliness, they would have given their names. Chris pretended to study the pictures again. *Whose authority?* "I'm sorry, officers, I don't know this man. I have no idea why he'd come to my house."

The second cop's eyes scanned the room and paused on the mantel. Chris's heart pounded as the cop ambled across the room. He plucked a framed photograph from the mantel. Maggie and Chris were on their honeymoon, sitting against the stern of a boat with open smiles and endless amounts of hope. They had just returned from a day of snorkeling, their hair still damp and faces shining. Chris loved that picture. If he'd had the opportunity to return to any moment in his life, he might have picked that one. Maggie's hands rested on his right thigh, and he remembered the way she had pressed her body into his, her skin cool from the water. He heard her laugh as the shutter snapped.

"Pretty girl. St. Barts?" the cop asked, tapping the picture and leaving a fingerprint in the thin layer of dust.

Chris shifted subtly to read his name tag. *Lupikino.* Chris nodded.

"Odd coincidence. Us too. In fact, on that same charter. It's the only way I knew."

"Yeah, well, most popular charter on the island." Chris waved dismissively. *Stop being an asshole to someone with the power to put you in jail. Again.*

The cop replaced the picture facing in the wrong direction—toward the window instead of toward the center of the room. He picked up the frame next to it. "Is this the same woman?"

Chris felt impatient. *Was he going to have to explain every picture in the living room?* "Yeah, Maggie was going through some kind of phase. She dyed her hair dark for our wedding and honeymoon." He shrugged.

The picture the cop was looking at had been taken the previous Christmas in front of the mantel, prior to a night out with Mika and her new boyfriend. Chris and Maggie stood side by side, smiling and happy. Chris didn't have to see the picture. On nights when Maggie had gone to bed early, leaving Chris to drink beer in the blue glow of the television alone, he'd sometimes studied it. Maggie's smile had looked impossibly genuine, wide, almost laughing, and he could never figure out if it was real.

"This was taken here, in this house, right?" he asked.

"Yeah, like Christmas or something. Not that long ago," Chris said.

"December twentieth?" Lupikino read the date stamp, framed as a question. He studied it, tilting the picture back and forth. He placed it back on the mantel.

Chris resisted the urge to adjust it.

"Mr. Stevens?" Davis jumped in. "Do you know the name Logan May?"

Chris's attention snapped back to Officer Davis as he turned the name over in his mind. The name meant nothing to him, but he knew with sinking dread who he was. Chris had never wanted to know his name. He'd avoided looking at that line on the driver's license or the mail on the front seat of the car. A man without a name stayed buried with greater ease, of that he was sure. Chris shook his head.

"Have you ever heard your wife mention him?"

"No, I don't think so." Chris cleared his throat. "So what's this about? Why was he coming here, to our house?"

"We were hoping you could tell us, Mr. Stevens. Last night, May got in a physical altercation with a patron in the parking lot of the Tiki Hut. He's looking at assault and battery. The other man is in Harrisburg Hospital in stable condition, but he's pressing charges."

"Then I guess I'm glad he didn't come here," Chris joked, but neither officer laughed. His smile felt pasted on.

"Well, the problem is, we can't find May, either."

Chris shrugged. "If I beat up a man in a bar parking lot, I might hide out for a while too."

"Is that what you did, Mr. Stevens?" Lupikino had a soft voice, unassuming. He was still studying the mantel and the pictures on it when he asked the question.

It took Chris a minute to comprehend. *They know about Derek. What else do they know?* "I'm sorry?"

The cops exchanged glances.

"When you had your little altercation, what, fifteen years ago? Is that what you did?" Lupikino repeated the question, each word dropped like carefully considered pebble.

"No, I didn't hide." Chris squared his shoulders, stood up straight, and pushed out his jaw. "I did my time for that, and I can't justify it for the rest of my life." That came out more obstinate than he intended.

The second cop raised his eyebrows, tilting his head. "No, I don't imagine you can. But our issue is that two different witnesses claimed May was on his way here. And they don't know each other. So now we have what we call a substantiated story. You see how that works?" The softness of his voice belied the condescension.

Chris had the distinct impression he was in a trap, but he couldn't see it. He felt the familiar anger bubble up. *They think I'm stupid.* Except if he was smart, wouldn't he be able to see what they were doing? Maybe they weren't actually doing *anything.* That thought was a balm to his fear. They hadn't actually accused him of anything.

"Yeah, I see that. But I have no idea who he is or why

he would come here." Chris's voice sounded weak and whiney, even to his own ears. He took a deep breath.

"Mr. Stevens, do you have a bathroom I can use?" Davis asked, shaking his empty coffee cup. He gave Chris a friendly smile, which looked out of place and sinister on his militant face. "We've been out for a few hours, tracking down May, and I, uh, had a coffee."

"Yeah, sure. You can call me Chris."

He led Davis through the kitchen, running a mental inventory of the countertops and table. He noticed nothing suspicious or out of order. As they passed the island, Davis lightly tossed the folder on the marble top. Chris pointed him toward the powder room. When the door clicked shut, he inched over to the island and gently opened the folder. The pictures of Logan sat on top. He pushed them aside, trying to touch only the edges. Underneath, a picture of a blond man was clipped to a stack of paperwork. The sound of a cough came from the living room, and Chris jumped back, blood rushing in his ears.

He pivoted and skip-stepped back to the living room. Lupikino was still standing next to the mantel, but he was hunched over, looking down the mantel from the side. When he saw Chris, he straightened.

"What happened to the vase?" He lightly rapped the mantel with his knuckle where the vase used to be.

Chris felt his throat close. "Vase?" His voice cracked, and he cleared his throat. Fear skimmed across his back. His shoulder blades tensed as though pulled taut with a string.

"In the picture from December, there was a vase on this mantel. What happened to it?"

"Oh, uh... Maggie broke it cleaning one day, I think? She was upset about it. It was a wedding present from her friend. I think it was expensive." He was babbling, but he couldn't seem to control his mouth. "Maybe I should wake her."

"Nah, don't worry about it. She's sick and all." Lupikino waved him off, suddenly flippant. "I think we got what we came for. As soon as Davis is done."

"I'm done, I'm done," Davis said from the doorway.

Chris turned, startled.

"The phone?" Davis asked, gesturing toward the kitchen. "In the kitty litter? Have you tried it yet? Did it work?"

"Uh, I'm not sure. Maggie dropped it in the toilet, and that's what they told her to do. She got a new one, but we haven't decided what to do with it yet." Chris babbled and felt his control slipping and wiped his palms on his jeans. *Jesus Christ, just get the fuck out.* He was being potshotted from all sides—no single blow hurt, but the effect was exhausting.

"Someone told me to try rice. My wife did that, dropped it in the toilet. But rice? It didn't work at all." He shook his head. "Why do all women seem to drop their phones in the toilet?" He looked at Chris as though he expected an answer.

"Well, the mechanics of it and all..." Chris waved, like *obviously.*

Davis casually tapped the file against the heel of his hand. The silence in the living room grew heavy, and Chris tapped his thigh.

"I think we've got everything we need for now," the second cop said to Davis, who nodded in agreement.

"We'll be back if we have more questions, though. And hey, thanks for being so cooperative." Davis was almost affable.

Chris was confused by their about-face. Or maybe they had been friendly in the beginning and he read them wrong? He couldn't tell. "Well, I wish I could have told you more."

They walked to the front door, and Chris opened it, anxious to be alone. Davis walked out first.

The second cop turned around as if he'd just thought of something. "Oh, Mr. Stevens, you know oil soap is pretty much the worst thing you can use on your floors."

Chris's head snapped up. "I'm sorry?"

"Yeah, well, the problem is, as the water evaporates, the oil builds up and leaves your floors dull. They don't tell you that, but there's no benefit in putting oil on hardwood floors. You'll end up refinishing your floor twice as often."

Chris nodded, not sure what to say or if it mattered if he said anything at all.

"The best thing you can use is vinegar and water, but you really shouldn't have to ever wet mop hardwood at all."

"Uh, okay, thanks, officer. I'll pass it along to Maggie. She does all of the cleaning."

"Yeah, I used to be an altar boy. I cleaned a lot of church pews, and some smells you don't forget." He tapped his nose and gave a small, sociable wave before he followed Officer Davis out to the car.

Chris parted the curtains and watched them pull away from the curb. They drove impossibly slow until they *finally* turned left at the end of his street and disappeared. Chris waited, making sure they weren't coming back. When he turned around, Maggie was standing in the living room, her face a stony mask of indignation, her arms folded tightly across her chest.

"We're in deep shit, Chris."

CHAPTER NINE

MAGGIE

THE FIRST TIME MAGGIE SAW Chris, he was wearing a dress. It was technically a kilt, but Maggie was unprepared for the sight of six strapping men milling around the front of the church in black-and-red-plaid skirts, their white knees peeking out between a sandwich of wool skirt and black knee socks. She stopped and laughed.

Maggie's cousin, Stacey, elbowed her in the ribs. "Don't let Miranda hear you laugh." Stacey's mouth was turned up in shared amusement.

"How did I not know about this?"

"Well, the two of you aren't the picture of sisterly love lately."

She had a point. Miranda and Maggie had a somewhat tumultuous relationship. They shared months, even years, of varying degrees of closeness pocked with weeks of discord. Their arguments were sparked by a word, a phrase, a failure (mostly on Maggie's part) to identify a need (mostly of Miranda's). Maggie found Miranda exhausting. Miranda found Maggie selfish and oblivious. Yet in their weakest moments, they called each other, convinced no one else would understand them.

In the months leading up to the wedding, Miranda had been high pitched and panicky whenever Maggie called her, so Maggie avoided calling her. Her lack of attention to Miranda's big day festered resentment. Not that Miranda had the gall to bring that up, *considering.* But it meant that when Maggie showed up at the church on that brilliant July Saturday, she had no idea there would be men in skirts. *Sorry, kilts.* Jake had his back to her, and she felt the blood course in her ears. She hadn't seen him in months.

"McHale, you look a bit ridiculous," she said.

Jake turned and grinned broadly, pulling Maggie into a vise-like hug. He felt solid and smelled like pine. Maggie pushed her nose into his lapel and inhaled.

Jake released his grip and nudged her with his elbow. "You think this was Miranda's idea." It was not a question, but a statement. He looked smug. "But nope, this was me. I'm a McHale. We all get married in kilts. Family tradition."

Maggie raised her eyebrows. She didn't know that. How strange that she and Jake had never talked about wedding traditions.

"Hey, you know what they say about men in kilts?" he said.

Maggie had no idea what he was talking about it.

"Ah, you'll figure it out. Maybe tonight—look at all these guys." He laughed and winked.

She slapped his arm and walked away. Some days, she loved Jake enough to want to tell him to run. Did he know how much work Miranda was? She suspected he did based on a drunken night they had spent on their patio. Miranda was long in bed, and Jake had given a long, rambling, whiskey-fueled diatribe to the one person who could understand. Except the last thing she wanted to do was *understand.*

She moved through the old-lady crowd, assaulted by Emeraude, and into the significantly emptier hallway.

She pushed open doors and peered into darkened rooms. She found Miranda at the far end of a pink-carpeted room standing alone before a full-length mirror. Maggie's breath caught. *Beautiful.*

Miranda wasn't beautiful in the classical way. She was curvy to Maggie's angular thinness, dark to Maggie's blond. Her eyes were a bit too small, her nose a bit too big, like a gag gift from some unknown Mediterranean relative. But she was fun, bubbly, and outgoing with a zillion friends. She was brash and bawdy with a speckling of men who followed her around. Until Jake.

Maggie hugged Miranda from behind, resting her cheek against her veil and breathing in her big sister Miranda-ness. Miranda patted her hand, and ill will faded away. Like it always did.

The ceremony was beautiful, and Maggie felt uncharacteristically teary. While everyone else watched the bride, Maggie watched the groom. When Miranda walked down the aisle, the look on Jake's face told Maggie he'd never doubted the work would be worth it. He'd labor the rest of his life to keep that smile on Miranda's face. And Maggie's gut stirred with a familiar yet unwelcome emotion that she'd worked for two years to bury. *Jealousy.*

The open bar meant Maggie was drunk before dinner. She moved among the crowd, offering smiles and small talk. She'd never easily fit in with other women. She was perhaps a bit too pretty, or maybe just too aloof. The giggling, perfume-laden conversations in the bathroom left her cold, and she was always a little too friendly with their men. Or more accurately, their men were too friendly with her. The other bridesmaids, save for Stacey, tolerated her with thin-lipped smiles. Maggie chose to hang at the bar, making small talk with the bartender.

"You know what they say about men in kilts, right?"

She turned and gazed into the greenest eyes she had ever seen. She remembered him from the church, quietly confident, not brazen or cocky, standing in the line of men on the other side of the aisle.

"Why does everyone keep asking me that?" She sighed. "No, I have no idea what *they* say about men in kilts."

"It has to do with what they're wearing underneath them," the bartender chimed in, refilling Maggie's glass and grinning at the groomsman next to her.

Maggie laughed then, a vague recollection of the adage clicking in her head.

"So the legend says that wearing nothing underneath showed the English that the Scottish were tough enough to battle unprotected. And sometimes they would flash them, just in case they didn't get it." The groomsman's smile was wide and wicked.

"I guess that only works if what's underneath is impressive." Maggie took a swig of her drink, watching him out of the corner of her eye.

He laughed. "Well, that's where the joke's on us, I guess." He ordered another round of drinks, and his arm brushed hers as he pushed the glass in front of her. He held her gaze and gave a little cock of his head, his lips curled in amusement.

For the first time, Maggie understood the phrase "he had a smile that reached his eyes." She studied his profile, his long straight nose, and had the urge to run her finger along his square jawline. *Probably the husband of a bridesmaid.*

But he wasn't. He was single and referred vaguely to a trip "away" with a lack of available women. *Christopher Stevens, the man with two first names.* Maggie was attracted to the funny, self-deprecating, secretive man in a way she hadn't been in a long time. She recklessly pushed her phone number into his palm before she hopped a cab back to her hotel. She lay on the bed with the lights on, watching the ceiling spin. She thought of her sister, locked miles away in a honeymoon suite, giggling and in love with the only other man Maggie had ever felt that way about.

When she woke up the next morning, the hangover pulsing relentlessly behind her eyes, her first thought was of Chris. Waking up thinking about a man, an *available man,* was so fantastic and freeing that she thought nothing of it when her phone rang at 8:17 in the morning. Chris's voice came through the earpiece like an electric current, and she jolted upright. She forgot to be coy, forgot to say she had plans, and agreed to accompany him on a tour of Philadelphia. In fact, she agreed to lead the tour, an audacious overreach of her abilities, given her knowledge of the city.

Later they would laugh about it. Chris would say he'd never suspected she'd only done the touristy stuff once, despite living there for a year, and that she'd never actually seen the Liberty Bell. Truthfully, she could have told him the Liberty Bell was a gift from aliens, and he would have nodded, paying little attention to her actual words. Later, when they were officially dating, he would confess how smitten he had been on that first date. He couldn't get enough of her voice, her movements, the gentle way she'd curve her hair behind her ear, the sweetly sexy floral fragrance of her skin. He never really noticed or cared that she'd bullshitted her way through the entire outing.

———<><>———

MAGGIE SAT IN THE DARKENED living room, shades pulled tight against the sunshine, holding the phone in her lap. Chris wandered around upstairs, restlessly opening and closing drawers and doors. They had both been climbing the walls since the police came. Three days of waiting. Every soft rumble of a parking car made them jump. On the second night, during dinner, heavy footsteps on the front porch halted their conversation, forks in mid-air, mouths open as if some celestial remote had hit pause. After the footsteps retreated, Chris went to the door and returned with a flyer.

"Apparently, Mrs. Jenkins is having a Pampered Chef party." His voice was wooden, without a trace of humor, as he dropped the pink paper into the trash can.

They were living scared. Maggie thought about how fear can fester in one's brain, spreading seeds of doubt like a blown dandelion head. She took a deep breath and dialed a number she knew by heart.

"If we needed you, would you come?" she asked in a rush. She relayed a highly edited version of the past days' events, one in which Logan had left alive. She sagged with relief at the response. "Thank you, Jake."

CHAPTER TEN

CHRIS

THEY CAME ON THE FOURTH day with heavy black suitcases and formal uniforms. Their black jackets, with shining white CRIME SCENE on the backs, glittered in the bright sun. Chris stood in the living room, self-conscious and uncertain, his hands shoved in his jeans pockets. A man and a woman spoke, their words tumbling over each other. They showed him court paperwork, signed and official, but spoke slowly and firmly, like grammar school teachers to a student.

"Chris, we'd like you to come to the station and talk to us." The woman was tall, angular, and attractive. Her strawberry blond hair was pulled tight against her head, and her face was all points and planes.

Chris didn't know where to look; his eyes settled on her forehead. He studied a crease on her forehead as she talked.

"You don't have to, of course," she said. "You're not under arrest. But we would appreciate some cooperation. We've had some developments, and we would like to talk to both you and Maggie."

"We'll go." Maggie stood in the doorway between the

kitchen and the living room, drying her hands on a dish towel, as if it was a normal Friday.

Chris met her gaze, and she nodded. *We'll go.* Because he had made all of the decisions so far, handing the reins to Maggie was both freeing and terrifying.

Maggie crossed the living room and extended her hand to the male detective. "I'm Maggie." She smiled uncertainly, but her face was open, almost congenial. Chris had seen her slide into the all-American girl role once in a while, and he'd always been intrigued by the incongruity of it. Generally, it worked. Maggie could be magnetic when she turned on the charm.

"Hi, Maggie. I'm Detective Renner, and this is Detective Small, my partner."

A man Chris had barely noticed stepped forward and shook Maggie's hand. As an afterthought, he shook Chris's hand too. The man was short. He had a wrestler's build with broad shoulders and red close-cropped hair with pale freckled skin. Detective Small was pinched and stern, but Renner seemed like an everyman.

Four technicians moved about the living room, placing their suitcases on furniture and spreading out tarps, creating workspaces. Chris watched their activity with a detached fascination. He felt a tap on his arm and turned to see Maggie, her head bent low, her hair falling over her mouth in an organic disguise.

"I called Jake."

The statement was so low, whispered and quick, that it took a moment to register. *Of course you did.* She'd done the right thing, no matter how it stung. Renner and Small were whispering over near the couch, and Chris caught Detective Small's eye.

She angled her head toward the hallway. "Are you guys ready? We can take my car."

Chris nodded to Maggie, and they followed the detectives out the front door. Detective Small gestured toward the unmarked Pontiac at the curb.

"We'll bring you back, don't worry." Detective Renner held open the back door.

Chris looked at Maggie. *Do we have a choice?* She shrugged and waved—*just get in the car.* Chris studied Renner and Small, trying to figure them out while Maggie clambered into the back seat. Maybe if he could appeal to Renner on a *hey buddy* level, they'd be back home in an hour. Detective Small seemed biting and hostile. Renner made a joke from the passenger's seat. Chris didn't hear it, but he could tell it was a joke by the way Renner laughed. Small glared at him instead of laughing.

As the car pulled away from the curb, Chris watched his truck through the rear passenger's seat window. The front and cab doors were open, and two technicians were crouched over in the bed. He looked away.

"Both cars were included on the warrant." Detective Small met Chris's eyes in the mirror.

This is a fucking nightmare.

Maggie laid her hand over his, cool and dry. While she stared out the window, ignoring the truck search, she tapped his knuckles three times. The long-forgotten gesture brought the sick to the back of his throat. They used to do that all the time, anything in threes—three taps on a door, three pulses while holding hands, three taps of her foot on his at night. It always meant *I love you.* He pulled on her hand, but she wouldn't look at him, staring stubbornly out the window.

—◄◆►—

THE POLICE STATION WAS AS corporate and vanilla as an office building. Detective Small led Chris to one conference room while Detective Renner led Maggie to another. Chris was unprepared for splitting up, and he hesitated in the doorway.

"It's standard procedure, Chris," Detective Small

reassured him, but her tone was clipped and efficient. She slicked the smallest flyaway hair back into place before leading him into a small room with a round table and four chairs.

She took the chair farthest from the door and gestured for Chris to sit opposite her. She opened a file and, with barely a glance, spun it around and pushed it toward him. She snapped a pen down on top of the paperwork. It read *Miranda Warnings.*

"This is a formality," she said. "Basically saying you're willing to talk to us, tell us your side of the story."

"Am I under arrest now?"

"Should you be?" She blinked twice, and he slowly shook his head, unsure if that was a rhetorical question. She said, "No, you're not under arrest. This is a conversation. This paper means you're willing to have it, but you don't have to. You're free to go at any time."

Chris signed the top paper and pushed it back to her. She clipped it to the front of the file. She leafed through the stack, holding the pen in her teeth, and a stiff curl escaped her bun, falling over her eyes. She looked human. Possibly even pretty. Young. Chris wiped his palms on his jeans and let out a slow breath. *This might not be that bad.*

He had no idea what Maggie would say. What were the chances they'd say the same thing? Would she sit stoically, her jaw set? Would she cry, break down with the truth? He had no idea what the actual truth was. It was like a black void in his mind. He knew the events in broad strokes. But he realized with a start that he didn't know the details. He didn't know nearly enough to get him through the interview.

Detective Small glared at him, and he realized he'd been bouncing his leg—a nervous habit he'd retained since childhood. She clicked the pen, wrote in the file, studied her notes, and twisted her mouth in a puzzled frown. She shook her head and noted something. *Click,*

click. The silence stretched out over minutes that seemed like hours. Chris watched her with interest. *Write. Study. Click. Frown.*

On Thursday night during dinner, Chris and Maggie had talked about what they might say should it come to this. But they hadn't agreed on their stories. Chris wanted Maggie to say, no matter what, that she had been in bed, sleeping. She didn't wake up; she never heard anything. He would decide what to admit to when the time came. She had refused and insisted on telling the *truth.*

Chris had slapped the table, stinging his palm. "Maggie, don't you get it? Not only did we kill someone, but we buried him. As of yesterday, he's under two feet of concrete. We'll be in jail for the rest of our natural lives. The truth is no longer an option."

She laughed bitterly. "It never was! We're going to live in fear for the rest of our lives. Because of you!"

"I'm pretty sure you had a hand in this, don't you think? After all, who *actually* killed him? And can we talk about who *he* is yet?"

That was when Maggie had left the room. She slowly put down her silverware and pushed back her chair so gently that it didn't even scrape on the tile. Chris had watched her back, ramrod straight, as she walked through the living room and into the hallway, turning the corner to go upstairs. He sat at the table for an hour, listening to her sob at the foot of the stairs. He couldn't bring himself to go to her—his fury had been ignited by voicing the one thing that was driving him crazy. He was sure she had lied. She'd known May a hell of a lot better than she'd let on, but to what extent, he couldn't ascertain.

"Okay, Chris, I need you to start with Saturday night. Not the bogus story you told the uniforms. I know that was bullshit, and so do you." Detective Small held her pen above a blank pad of paper. For the first time since they'd met, she met his gaze and gave him a slight smile.

Her eyes were light chocolate brown and surprisingly warm. Brown, flecked with gold. *Cute.* Could he sway her? Maybe. He used to be good at it.

He *knew* she was playing him, but he couldn't help relaxing. His knee stopped bobbing, and he opened his fists. "It's not bullshit. The guy—" He was interrupted by a soft knock at the conference room door.

Detective Small rose and crossed the room, opened the door a crack, and whispered to the unseen person on the other side. She returned to the conference table with an eight-by-ten photograph that she pushed across the table while tucking a stray lock of hair behind her ear. "*This* is how we know your story is bullshit. Well, this is *one* of the reasons we know it's bullshit."

Chris took the picture with shaky hands and a sick sensation in his gut. All he saw was a black smudge on a white background, nestled in the corner of an L-shaped ruler. It looked senseless to him. He tried out a tentative smile. "I'm sorry, but what is this?"

"*This* is a palm print from your house. Specifically, Logan May's palm print."

"How do you know that's his palm print?" The question just popped out. *Shit. Shit. Shit.* Chris knew it was a mistake. There were a hundred other questions he should have asked if Logan May had never been in his house.

She touched her eyebrow, giving him a sympathetic look. "Oh, Chris, what's the story here?" Her voice was soft, compassionate, and she leaned in close.

He could smell her hair. Something strawberry-ish. He rubbed his forehead and studied the photograph. They must have *just* gotten that print. How did they do that so fast? Weren't there always backups in the lab? That was how it worked on television. He weighed his options. *Give her one small thing, just to appease her. Explain it, and then it will go away.*

"Okay, yeah, he was at our house. I don't know why.

He was looking for Maggie." He put his palms up and met her eyes, holding her gaze.

She leaned back, folding her arms across her chest, and nodded once.

"He was drunk and"—Chris recalled the cop on Monday saying he had been in a fight—"he had a cut on his cheek. He looked kinda beat up. It was hard to tell. But he was going on and on about seeing Maggie. I think he had a thing for her." He shifted forward in his seat. He was warming up, like his words could all be real. He almost thought they weren't a lie, because it was so possible.

"So you let him in?" Detective Small arched her eyebrow.

"Well, I felt bad for him, kind of."

"A drunk man comes to your house at two in the morning, asking to see *your wife*, belligerent and argumentative, and you *feel bad for him*?"

His words repeated back to him sounded ridiculous.

"Well, he wasn't argumentative. He seemed upset or something. So yeah, I kinda felt bad for him. Said he didn't know Maggie was married."

"So you let him into your house?"

"Uh, yeah. I didn't want him to wake up Maggie, and he said he just wanted to talk to me. He sort of pushed his way in. I figured I could talk him down."

"Down, how?" Detective Small asked.

"Well, like calm him down."

"You said he wasn't angry."

"He wasn't. He was agitated."

"How does agitated look different than angry?"

Chris took a deep breath and wiped his hand on his jeans. Her questions were pissing him off. "It just does. He didn't seem angry. He seemed bothered. I wanted him to go away. The fastest way to do that was to calm him down."

Detective Small considered that. "Okay, fair enough. So what happened after you let him in?"

"Uh, we talked. I guess he liked Maggie. He didn't know

she was married. He was pacing all over the living room. He was going on and on. I think he was off his rocker or maybe on drugs. I guess that's how his palm print got on the mantel."

"I didn't say it was on the mantel."

"Uh, well, I remember him touching it?"

"Are you asking me?" She cocked her head to the side.

"No. I remember him touching it. I was guessing that was where you found it."

"What else did he touch?"

"I don't know."

"So you specifically remember him touching the mantel but not anything else?"

"Um, yeah, sure."

"Huh, okay, fine." She rolled her eyes and twirled the pen. She leaned forward, resting her elbows on the table. "What about the vase?"

"I'm sorry? What vase?" Chris didn't have to fake surprise. He was genuinely stunned. *What does the vase have to do with this?*

"The vase that used to be on the mantel. In *this* picture." She pushed the print of him and Maggie across the table.

They'd removed it from the frame, and he pushed back a surge of anger at that. *His life, dismantled.* "Maggie broke it while cleaning. Like a month or so ago." He shrugged.

"Interesting."

"Why is that interesting? You never broke anything dusting, Detective?" He was getting snotty, but he couldn't help it. He'd lost any chance of winning her over already.

"Five minutes ago, Detective Renner asked Maggie about the vase. She said she didn't know anything about it. That maybe you broke it that night by accident."

"No, I didn't break it that night."

"Are you sure?"

"I think I'd remember that."

"Hmmmm. Well, I think she'd remember if she broke

it... um, what did you say?" She flipped back a page in her notes. "Oh, dusting. Right. Okay, so then what happened?"

"When?"

"I mean, what happened after he was pacing all over the living room. And you felt so bad for him."

"Uh, he left."

"He left?" She snapped her fingers inches from his face. "Like that? Just up and left?"

"Well, no. I told him to go. Said that whatever he thought he and Maggie had going was over. He needed to go home."

"When he left, did you watch him walk to his car?"

"No, I shut the door and kind of leaned against it for a while, thinking about whether or not I was going to wake Maggie."

"And did you?" *Click. Frown. One eyebrow arch.*

"No. I didn't even tell her he was there."

"Why not?"

"Well, it didn't seem... important. Until the cops showed up and started asking questions. Then I told her." Chris drew a circle on the table with his index finger.

"What did she say?"

"She was plenty ticked I didn't tell her in the first place. But ultimately, she said he'd had a crush on her and she rebuffed him whenever she saw him at the Hut. But Maggie..."

"Maggie what?"

"Well, she's too nice. Guys tend to think her nos mean they still have a chance. Or maybe they just hope? I've seen it before."

"Oh? How so?"

"Uh, about three years ago, a widower at the doctor's office, a dad of one of the kids, was really into Maggie. Showed up places, drove past the house, called the office and hung up when she'd answer, that kind of thing. She eventually called the cops because her 'gentle talks' hadn't done anything. A cop went and talked to the guy. When he asked him why he'd been harassing Maggie, he said it was because she listened to him. That's how she is. She listens to people—makes them feel important."

Chris had ultimately ended up feeling sorry for the guy, and he'd never doubted that Maggie was telling the truth. In a weird way, he could relate. She could, when she wanted to, make Chris feel like the only guy on earth. Chris rested his forehead on the heel of his hand. He was so damn tired.

"Was he bleeding?"

"Who? The widower?"

She shook her head, eyes closed. "No, Logan May. That night. Was he bleeding?"

"Uh, just on his cheek."

"Did he use the bathroom?"

Her question caught him off guard. If she was asking that, did that mean they had found evidence that he was in the bathroom? *I have no fucking clue what he did before I found him. I have no fucking clue why he was in our house.* "Yeah, he had to piss. Right before he left, he used the bathroom." He answered on a whim, with little thought.

"Which bathroom?"

"The downstairs one." A complete guess.

"Chris, was your wife cheating on you?"

"What? No."

"Is your marriage happy?"

"Yeah, sure." He answered automatically but choked back a laugh. The honest answer was ridiculously complicated.

"Do you love your wife?"

"Yes." Not a lie.

"Does she love you?"

"Yes." Did she? He'd spent the past two years wondering the same thing.

Detective Small smiled, opened the folder, selected a sheet of paper, and passed it across the table. It was a list of phone numbers, incoming and outgoing, CALL and TXT in alternating rows. With sinking dread, Chris realized where the conversation was headed. He was powerless to stop it. Worse, he didn't have the answers. The person who did was separated from him by a thick cement block wall. A wall he felt angry enough to charge through. Blood coursed through his veins, pulsing in threes. *I love you. Yeah, fucking right.*

Detective Small spoke, but her words were superfluous. "This is Logan May's cell phone records. There are hundreds of texts over the last month back and forth between Maggie and Logan. Let's try again. Was Maggie cheating on you?"

"It would seem so, wouldn't it?"

"Did you know?"

"Not until right now." Chris gritted his teeth. He honestly hadn't allowed himself to think about that possibility until *that moment.* Which, in retrospect, made him a fool. Or an idiot. Or both.

"So when Logan knocked on your door at two in the morning, you had no idea he was your wife's lover?"

Chris *knew* that question was designed to piss him off. He stood, knocking the chair over. The crash brought a uniformed officer rushing through the door. Chris leaned forward with his palms flat on the table, breathing heavily through his nose. "I want to call my lawyer."

CHAPTER ELEVEN

MAGGIE

Philadelphia, 1996

THEIR APARTMENT HAD BEEN BEAUTIFUL—TWELVE-FOOT ceilings with the ornate woodworking of a converted Victorian. Jake and Maggie occupied the entire bottom floor, a coup in University City. Maggie curled up in front of the old fireplace most nights, waiting for Jake to come home from class. She shivered because of the draft and because a working fireplace was illegal in Philadelphia. Jake was buried in his second year at Penn law. He'd drag in at eleven at night, worn thin. Maggie, in her third year of nursing school, would rub his shoulders before they ate peanut butter sandwiches and talked case law or patient histories.

Like the night they lit all the candles they owned, and Jake framed them in front of the faux fireplace. Maggie lay with her head on Jake's belly, and they traded legal puns, trying to come up with the worst one. *Do they serve drinks at the sidebar? Oh, aren't you good at re-torts!* They practically choked laughing until Maggie licked peanut butter off the corner of his mouth. That was the night they ended up kicking over a candle and almost burning down the building.

The flames had licked at the fringe of the carpet and Maggie shrieked, yanking the throw blanket up to her bare shoulders. Jake struggled, completely naked, with the old, greased-over fire extinguisher until half the living room was covered with white foam and they were crying with laughter. Years later, Maggie would feel empty and sick whenever she tried to eat a peanut butter sandwich.

For months, Maggie ignored the signs, the waning interest, the later nights when Jake came home and mumbled about being "tired." He was snoring, facedown in their bed, before Maggie could scramble after him. He began missing dinner most nights of the week, claiming he'd grabbed pizza or Chinese after class but before study group. Maggie didn't know how to stop the downward slide into the end of things, but she felt it coming.

She'd jerk awake at night, panicky and scared, and she'd touch Jake's back underneath the covers, feeling for warmth that seemed to exist only in sleep. During the day, he emitted the cool chill of lost interest, with his thin plastic smile. He said, "What?" whenever she spoke first, as though he was surprised she was still there.

She tried to ask him about it. "Are we okay? Can we talk?" And the worst question, the one that made her cringe when she thought about it—which she purposefully almost never did. "Do you still love me?"

Jake gave her a kiss and a flash of brilliant smile, seemingly so genuine, and said, "Ah, Mags. I love you to death, you know that."

She didn't want to be needy. She hated the whine in her voice and her unintentional pouting, like an insolent toddler. But she'd open her mouth to speak, and his eyes would wander to the television, to the stove, to the waitress, anywhere but Maggie's face. She felt pregnant with dread.

The Friday before Valentine's Day, Miranda stayed for the weekend. Miranda with her loud, infectious laugh and bawdy sense of humor, her thick, dark hair, voluptuous curves, and penchant for men. Miranda was a stark contrast to quiet, cool Maggie, and the house vibrated with energy. Jake stayed home for the first time in months, and the three of them got drunk and laughed until tears streamed down Maggie's cheeks. She'd forgotten how funny Jake was. They'd both been so wrapped up in their classes that fun had plunged to the bottom of their *To Do* list.

Miranda talked about things Maggie did not: sex and men, dirty jokes, all her comments dripping with innuendo. Miranda commanded the attention of all men—young, old, married—especially married. Miranda relayed stories of horrific dates: the guy who talked obsessively about his car, the guy who filed his canines into points like a vampire, and the guy who barked when he orgasmed. Jake ate it all up, literally slapping his knee at one point. Maggie thought about how much fun they were having, how much she loved Jake, and how glad she was that Miranda could bridge their widening divide. That night, in bed, Maggie had climbed all over Jake, turned hot by the lingering sound of his laugh and desperate to preserve the high. *Love me.*

On Saturday, Maggie was on call for her obstetrics rotation, and as the three of them got dressed for dinner, her pager beeped. She called the hospital, and the head nurse informed her that Amelia, a young nineteen-year-old who reminded Maggie of herself, had gone into labor. Maggie sighed at the long night ahead of her and waved Jake and Miranda out the door. In retrospect, she'd ignored the signs. She'd been so naive.

The night was catastrophic. Amelia labored for hours with disaster after disaster: a plummeting fetal heart rate, a placental hemorrhage, and an emergency C-section to stanch the bleeding. The baby slid out blue and silent.

The NICU worked for an hour, but the infant never drew a breath. Amelia remained unconscious from blood loss, and after fifteen hours, the head nurse sent Maggie home, tearstained and heartbroken.

"We all remember our first loss," she said.

As if that would make it better. As if that would bring the baby back, or wake Amelia up, or quiet the screaming in Maggie's head. Ragged, whipped, and sick with grief, it was two in the afternoon before she pushed open the heavy wooden door of their apartment. She'd forgotten that Miranda was even visiting, and she was momentarily taken aback by her shoes in the front hall. When she remembered, everything had a dreamlike quality: the soft *fop!* of her nursing clogs on the hardwood, the starched scrubs between her fingers as she pulled them off, and in the shower, amidst the curling steam, the slick soap as she scrubbed traces of crusted blood from her neck and forearms.

"Miranda!" she called as she toweled off, padding to her bedroom.

Jake was gone, but she'd expected that. Saturdays were for study groups, long coffee-fueled sessions at the library. Maggie sometimes showed up with sandwiches or Indian. *Not today.* She pulled on her ratty blue fleece bathrobe and curled into bed, her body aching for sleep. Behind her closed eyelids, all she saw was a blue and frighteningly still baby boy, arms and legs akimbo.

She groped blindly on the floor for a book, needing distraction. Her fingers brushed something soft and slippery. *What the hell?* A purple satin thong. She studied the tag. Two sizes bigger than anything in Maggie's drawer. She bolted upright and looked toward the guest room, as though she could see through the walls. *Couldn't be.* But she'd cleaned the day before in preparation for Miranda's visit, and the thong hadn't been there.

Maggie climbed out of bed and hazily made her way

down the hall to the guest room. She pushed open the guest room door without knocking. Miranda lay face up in bed, her dark hair splayed out on the pillow. One curvy, tanned leg was wrapped around the blankets, seductive even in sleep, and her upper body was wrapped in a man's sky blue button-up dress shirt. Maggie recognized it as Jake's Christmas present the previous year.

She silently closed the door, her stomach flipping and a sour taste in her mouth. The front door opened, and Maggie heard a soft, jaunty whistling. She followed him, like a ghost in her own home, still clutching the purple satin panties. Jake, his back to her in the kitchen, pulled doughnuts out of a paper bag and two Styrofoam cups of coffee from a carrier. When he turned, Maggie was struck by two things: the relaxed bounce in his step and his small smile.

"Maggie!" He nearly dropped the carrier, and a splotch of coffee hit his shoe.

"Breakfast in bed, then?" She tilted her head, still holding onto the hope she was wrong. Her face and neck were hot.

His face changed, like a shade pulled down over an open window, and she knew. She'd known from the minute she found the panties under the bed.

"Oh, Jake," she said softly.

She offered him the panties, but he had no hands with which to take them. She carefully draped them over his arm and stumbled back to their bedroom. She wondered if he would follow her; he usually did. He had never been one of those men who didn't chase his girl. But then again, they had rarely fought. He hesitated in the doorway.

Maggie sat woodenly on the bed, staring at her hands. "It's true, right?"

Jake said nothing.

It was all so *fucking civil*. Later, Maggie would wish she'd made a scene. Screamed, shouted, threw things.

Anything. But what she did was pack a small overnight bag while Jake stood in the kitchen and waited, as if she was heading out on a weekend trip. He never put down the coffee. Jake made a half-hearted attempt to stop her, to deny it. She shook her head and held up her hand, fighting nausea.

"It was coming anyway, Mags, you know that, right? Couldn't you feel it?" He hovered over her shoulder, finally set the stupid coffee down, and reached out to touch her. His hand was heavy and awkward and anything but comforting.

He gave her his best *Jake* smile, and like a desperate fool, she let him touch her. What sickened her was that she *wanted* it, wanted him to touch her. No amount of anger usurped her love, like the pathetic girl lusting after the popular football player. She left and let her sister slip into her place, as placidly as though she'd gifted Jake to her.

She spent a month crying on Mika's couch, two hours away in Harrisburg, blowing off her classes and her rotations. Then she called her advisor and dropped out of school altogether. It wasn't just the Jake thing. Whenever Maggie closed her eyes, even at a red light, she would jolt upright at the flash of purple-blue skin, loosely folded around soft, infant bones. Some people weren't cut out to be nurses.

Her advisor returned her call and offered her an associate's degree. Maggie had completed all the requirements, and she took it without hesitation. She could still get a job in a clinic or a practitioner's office, but she wouldn't advance. That suited her. The very idea of setting foot in a hospital pressed into her lungs, making it hard to breathe.

She avoided contact with Miranda and Jake, save for the day she returned to the apartment to gather her things. She noticed the small touches: the pink toothbrush in the bathroom that wasn't hers, the *Glamour* magazines strewn across the coffee table, a bottle of Dior Poison on the dresser—a cloying scent that had gagged Maggie her whole life.

Weeks later, Miranda finally called her—not even a face-to-face visit, but a goddamn phone call. She'd sounded almost flippant about it. "Jake said you were practically over this. I don't want this to ruin us, Maggie. You're my sister, please, you can't leave me."

"So are you guys a couple now?" Maggie tasted bile.

"No! Maggie, no, we would never do that to you. Jake is a wreck."

No, she didn't know that, but it made her feel better. He'd miss her eventually. Miranda wouldn't rub his shoulders or bring him homemade chicken soup when he was sick and stuck studying in the drafty, stone halls of Penn Law. Jake needed maternal, and Miranda didn't *do* maternal.

"We're just friends," Miranda insisted.

Months went by. Miranda made sporadic phone calls, carefully avoiding any mention of Jake. Then almost unnoticeably, she started sentences with "Jake and I" or "we," as though they'd always been a *we,* and Maggie silently screamed.

But she never screamed out loud. Not once.

CHAPTER TWELVE

MAGGIE

"**Y**OU'RE NOT UNDER ARREST YET, but you can count on it.**" Jake sat at their kitchen table, a small tape recorder next to him and a fresh legal pad in front of him. His sleeves were rolled up, folded twice, and a mug of coffee was perched at his elbow. The top binding of the notepad had STEVENS printed in block letters with thick black marker, officially naming Chris a client.

The fat black print felt offensive to Maggie, an intimate reproach. In some ways, meeting with Jake was worse than the police. The police had come and gone, leaving the house in a disarray Maggie had no energy or will to straighten.

"First, I need to know what you told the detectives." Jake clicked on the tape recorder, his hand poised above the pad to write down all of Chris's lies in indelible ink.

Maggie listened to Chris recount the story he'd told Detective Small, and she concentrated on breathing. Her hands ached with a deep down, bone-chilling cold. She squeezed her fingers, willing blood back into them. She closed her eyes and listened to the deep timbre of Chris's voice, the rise and fall she knew by heart, the familiar telltale catch in his voice. She'd heard it a million times. *I'm out with the g-guys tonight. I only s-slept with her once.* At the click of the STOP button, her eyes popped open.

"One question," Jake said without looking up, writing furiously. "Is that the truth?"

"Yes," Chris said without hesitation.

Maggie blew out a breath. Chris glared at her, and she glanced away, to the refrigerator. Pictures of Miranda and Jake's blond and blue-eyed kids stared back at her, tacked up next to a six-month-old bank statement and a "Honey Do" list, faded from the sun. The first line, written in Maggie's hand, was *Running. When was that written?* Before things got bad. Running for what? She'd never run in her life, not for fun or exercise.

"Maggie?"

Jake and Chris were both looking at her, and she shook her head.

"What did you tell the police?" Jake repeated.

"That I was sleeping all night. I didn't hear anything."

Jake met her eyes. His eyes were blue, swirled, crystal clear, and Maggie felt like drowning in them. "Is that the truth?"

Under the table, she felt the insistent pressure of Chris's toe on her bedroom slipper. *A plea, not a warning.* "Yes."

Chris motioned Maggie into the living room, leaving Jake to sift through his notes at the kitchen table. She followed him.

When he was out of earshot of the kitchen, he turned around and crossed his arms. His jaw jutted out belligerently. "Maybe we should hire someone else."

She shook her head. "Jake is the best. We know this. And he's our brother-in-law."

"Yeah, but he's not local. He doesn't know the police procedures here—"

"Stop." Maggie held up her hand and looked away. "Now's not the time for your manhood to be insulted.

God, you throw a fit when I talk about Tracy, and here you are—"

Chris's face grew dark. "Jesus, Maggie, I wasn't even talking about that. Besides, now's not exactly the time to have the faithful conversation."

"What does that mean?"

Chris laughed, a hollow bark that didn't sound like him. "Are you joking? I saw the phone records."

Air rushed out of her lungs, and she couldn't breathe. *Detective Small showed it to him. To piss him off enough to confess to killing Logan.* They were dead; the police had more than enough to charge Chris. She'd singlehandedly supplied them with a motive. She wanted to kick things, punch large jagged holes in the drywall.

"Chris, it's not what you think." She almost laughed at that. Her "defense" was so trite and banal.

He'd never uttered those words about Tracy. Most of the time, it's *exactly* what it looks like, and the truth can be so indefensible. She moved to touch him, and he pulled back, quick with fury. She wanted to grab his arm and say, "Wait a minute, why do you get to be angry?"

"Well, first, I'm not sure we're not on even ground now, at the very least," Maggie said. "I mean, I never actually slept with him, so aren't you just throwing stones at my glass house?"

"Don't. *Everything* about this is your fault. *Every single thing.* If I get out of this, I won't stick around to see how it all works out for you, got it?"

Before she could stop him, he stormed back to the kitchen. The men's voices intermingled, rising and falling over each other with jovial familiarity. Maggie picked up on the undercurrent, the halting cadence or delayed laugh as they danced around the obvious. People thought it strange, even impossible, that they remained so superficially friendly. Maggie had learned that most people expected certain behaviors based on movie and television scripts—

an intriguing plot, climax, and peaceful denouement in a hundred and twenty greasy popcorn minutes or less. Real human behavior was messier, more flawed and less explainable. The best she could ever surmise was that Chris kept up the friendly front *for her.* She'd never questioned Jake's motives. She followed their voices back into the kitchen.

In the doorway, Chris pushed past her, tossing back a mumbled apology for the inconvenience. Maggie bit back a laugh. Jake rummaged through the fridge for the makings of a turkey sandwich for the road. He would head back to Philadelphia, and they would remain in Harrisburg and everyone would wait.

The front door had barely clicked closed when Jake said, "Are you both lying to me?" His voice was mildly disgusted, and he avoided eye contact.

She tried to shrug off his disappointment. Maggie pulled one leg up on a stool and rested her cheek on her knee. She needed to confess, yet the idea terrified her. *Was she afraid of Chris or the truth? Or both?*

"I never ask that question, you know?" Jake still didn't turn around. The muscles in his back worked as he gripped and released the countertop. "I don't need to know the answer to do my job. Any good defense attorney will tell you that. Having an innocent client, it's so much pressure. What if you lose? I hate having innocent clients, I really do." He turned then and crossed the kitchen in a few steps to put away the sandwich fixings. For a moment, the kitchen was filled with sounds—the clattering of the deli drawer, the soft closing of the refrigerator door, almost like a kiss. He stood there with his hands on his hips and twisted his mouth. "I don't need to worry about that here, though, do I?"

Maggie shook her head, closing her eyes. They faced off—him looking at her, her *not* looking at him—until his phone vibrated in his pocket for the fourth time since he'd arrived. *Miranda.* He checked the display and typed a quick text. He pocketed the phone, and they made eye contact before she looked away.

"Your sister wants to know if you're okay," he said.

"Then *my sister* can call me."

"Ah... Maggie, we'll talk, okay?"

"Can't you stay? Why do you have to leave?" She felt abandoned.

He shifted his weight. "I just... have to. Remember, call me *first* when the cops come." He kissed her cheek, paused with his hand on the doorknob, and turned to her. "Listen, if I take Chris's case, I can't do it for free. I'll need money. You should start thinking of a way to get it."

Maggie yearned to call him back, tell him everything, soak his shirt while his arms held her upright. She listened for the whoosh of tires pulling away from the curb, and only then did she cry.

—⋖◇⋗—

THE HOUSE WASN'T IN COMPLETE disarray, like in the movies. No toppled chairs. No upended sofa cushions. There was a subtle imbalance in every room. The hall rug was skewed to the left. The knickknacks from the mantel mingled on the easy chair in a jumbled pile. Fine black powdery streaks marred every flat surface, as though the technicians had tried to wipe up after themselves with all the diligence of a teenage boy.

Maggie plugged her iPod into the surround-sound system and cranked it up as far as it would go. The house vibrated with the bellowing notes of an Italian opera, a haunting soundtrack to her task. Maggie sought escape. Leoncavallo's *Pagliacci* coursed through her, the thundering aria edging out rational thought. She scrubbed and straightened and restored order to their possessions with an ease she wished she could apply to their life.

The living room was the biggest mess, and her throat

closed up when she stared at the floor where Logan had fallen, his gray, pallid skin like wax against the dark wood floor. She saved the bedroom for last. The mop water sloshed gray and foamy with fingerprint powder, so she lurched down the hall, lugging the heavy bucket to the kitchen.

As she walked into the living room, she stopped short. Detectives Small and Renner stood between her and the kitchen doorway. Small had been leaning in toward Renner, trying to be heard over the stereo, but they straightened up quickly, apologetic when they spotted her.

"What the hell are you doing?" She set down the bucket, hard, and the dingy water sloshed onto the wood floor. "You can't just come in here like this." She marched over to the stereo and stabbed the power button.

Renner held his hands up in surrender, his face sympathetic. "We know. We knocked for ten minutes and heard the music... Your door was unlocked."

She didn't want their pity and felt the room tilt. *I'm barely keeping my shit together.*

"Is Chris home?"

She shook her head. "He's at work."

"Can you call him? We'd like to speak with him."

"Is he under arrest?"

Small and Renner exchanged glances, confirming everything Maggie needed to know.

CHAPTER THIRTEEN

CHRIS

H E WAS DRIVING ON ROUTE 322 when his phone rang. He checked the display: *Maggie.* With a disgusted sound, he buried the phone under an old sweatshirt in the passenger's seat. He couldn't stand the thought of her lies. *It's not what you think.* The classic line of cheaters everywhere. He may have even used it himself.

She'd never been a liar, honest to a fault. It kinda killed him the way his wife had learned to lie with such ease. Weren't people supposed to suck at new things? Like no one knitted a sweater on their first bout with a knitting needle. They started with potholders or something. But not Maggie. She went right for the afghan of lies. And they were woven together in some big, deceptive knot. Everything was such a disaster.

He turned up the stereo and angry hard rock vibrated the truck's ancient speakers. As he approached the gravesite, he lifted his foot off the gas and craned his neck to get a better view of the construction site. The tall wooden frame atop the foundation created the impression of progress. Almost as if he could stay out of jail long enough to see the whole restaurant built, he would be in the clear. Faulty logic with a pinch of superstition, but Chris couldn't shake the sensation that the whole mess was temporary. The Jeep behind him blared a short, impatient beep, and he gunned it.

Ed's office was dark when Chris pulled into the lot at Carmichael, and he let himself into his own trailer. The orange light on Chris's voice mail blinked. When he punched in his code, an electronic voice informed him he had twenty-seven new messages. He hung up. *That's what you get for calling out from work for a week.*

He sank down in his chair, not really having anything to do. He couldn't stand to stay in that house with Jake and Maggie and watch them exchange looks about him, quick and surreptitious, as if he wouldn't notice because he was the dumb one. He needed to get away from her and her crazy family and the whole insane situation.

Could he tell the truth? With everyone closing in on him, could he throw his hands up in surrender? *Listen, Maggie actually killed him.* He imagined saying the words and watching Detective Small's pretty little mouth drop open. Would she believe him?

He crossed the trailer, sank into the fabric-covered office chair, and hit the power button on what used to be Tracy's old Dell computer. He punched in the username and password carefully printed in bubble-round handwriting underneath the keyboard tray. The screen churned to life. *Tracy. That was a mistake.*

He spun the seat around, waiting for the computer to boot up. Tracy's only appeal had been her readiness, her adoration of him. He wasn't as dumb as everyone thought—he knew she'd spent months seducing him slowly. He didn't sleep with her because she finally won or because he had been all that attracted to her. He'd just stopped giving a fuck, and one day, she seemed better than all his other options.

She had been willing to touch him, and he'd gone

months in Maggie's frigid shadow. Maggie used to touch him constantly, a simple skin-on-skin contact that had always grounded him. Her cool fingertips on his sun-hot forearm or a feather-light kiss on his neck, his cheek. After the miscarriages, Maggie radiated coldness and sterility. Then Tracy came along, all warmth and dazzling smile. Not beautiful but not horrible, and she had a fun laugh, infectious and free. He remembered her hands, with her long acrylic nails, as she massaged the knots out of his shoulders, her palms hot on his back.

Her chair smelled of something cheap that had lingered and turned tangy with age. Perfume and menthol cigarettes. The stench made him sick. He rose and kicked her chair back before replacing it with a ladder-back wooden one that sat off to the side. The computer hummed, and he navigated to Google. He typed "obstruction of justice" and "conspiracy to commit murder" in the search box. He clicked on the return links, one after the other, and studied them at first. Then he clicked the windows closed almost immediately after they opened, his eyes scanning the page. *Ten years in prison... Carrying a sentence of at least five to ten years.* Over and over again. The addendum *depending on the offense* offered no consolation. Wouldn't burying a body and lying about it constitute the worst kind of offense?

Chris logged off and punched the power button on the computer. He replaced Tracy's chair and, in three steps, banged out the trailer door. He yanked open the truck door and heard the musical notes of his cell phone, muffled underneath the sweatshirt. When he checked, *Ed* appeared on the display. He rolled his eyes. Ed had been calling him all week, at all hours, despite the fact he'd called out. Sometimes he answered, sometimes he didn't. He hit the answer button with his thumb.

"Hey, you need something?" For the first time in his life, Chris hoped the answer to that question was *yes*.

112

"Uh, yeah, we need another five-foot girder. Any chance you could drop it off? There're a few in the warehouse."

He agreed and clicked the power button. He trudged the dusty thirty feet to the warehouse and retrieved the beam. His phone rang while he walked back. *Maggie. Again.* He hit Ignore. When his home screen flashed, he counted five missed calls, all from Maggie. *Jesus.* He clipped his phone onto his belt and tossed the girder into the back of his truck. The corner clipped the wall of the truck bed and hit the rear window. The glass splintered like a spider web. *Damn it!* That would need attention. Eventually. He climbed into the driver's seat and pulled out his cell phone. His home screen showed he had a text message.

Detectives Small and Renner are here. They need to talk to you. Come home.

⬥

Jake had beaten him home, and Chris fought back the white-hot anger that surged whenever Jake was around. Jake met Chris in the hallway, and over his shoulder, Chris watched Maggie and the detectives in the living room. What did they do before he got there? Talk about the weather? *I hear it's going to be a hot summer.* He bit back a laugh.

"We're going to have to go to the station, Chris. You're under arrest. They have a warrant," Jake said softly, his expression inscrutable.

Chris wanted to shake him. *Dude, remember college? I know you. You might fool them, but you don't fool me.*

Jake used to be the fuck-up, not Chris. Pre-Derek, Chris was going places while Jake smoked pot. Even after graduation, the only thing Jake had going for him was law school and a gorgeous girlfriend. Somehow while Chris languished in prison, Jake had morphed. As though Jake had gotten the life Chris was *supposed* to have.

"Jesus. Now what?" Chris raked his hand through his

hair, the full weight of the situation boring down. "Do I need bail?"

Jake shook his head, and his words came out in a jumbled rush. "The warrant is for murder. There's no bail. I don't know how to say this, Chris, but you're going back to jail."

Chris sagged against the wall. Most of his memories of what was about to come were spotty, but what he did remember was sharp with terror. Dark, dank hallways and stoic guards with gloved hands searching his body and calling him by a number. Then later, the black peering eyes of other inmates through iron bars.

Jake placed a hand on his shoulder. "If there's anything I need to know, now would be the time to tell me."

"How can they arrest me for murder? Did they find the guy?" There was no way; he'd just driven by the construction site.

"No, they were nice enough to fill me in a bit. I don't have all the evidence yet—the first thing I have to do is file a discovery motion. But according to Detective Renner, they don't currently have a body. That's why if there's *anything* you've left out, now is the time to tell me."

"How can I be arrested for murder if they don't have a body?"

"It'll be hard for them to make it stick," Jake said. "They must have a lot of circumstantial evidence against you. But even if they have all the forensic evidence in the world, a conviction without a body is a tough sell. I can beat this, but I need honesty from you. Should I find us a place to talk? Is there a big hammer coming down? If so, tell me *right now.* Before we take the drive."

Chris studied Jake. *Always has been a cocky son of a bitch.* But as long as he could remember, Jake had always won when it mattered. Not just in law but in life. Chris flashed back to Jake's wedding and watching Maggie down drinks at the bar, soaking her anger in alcohol. He wondered if Jake had picked the good sister, not the broken one.

Maybe their underlying competition could help. Chris and Jake's long-standing rivalry ran as deep and ruinous as geological fault lines. When Chris had gone to prison the first time, Jake had come to visit only once, bringing with him their team's lacrosse championship trophy. Chris had only peripherally contributed toward that championship, and he had snorted. Jake had picked at his hands, stashing the glass-and-wood cup beneath the table, and mumbled something about trying to keep things *normal.* On the surface, the gesture had been insensitive, even cruel, but Jake was just doing what Jake did best: avoidance. Chris had always suspected a subconscious drive to hammer home a widely accepted truth: Jake was first, Chris was second. Jake seemed to rarely miss an opportunity to reinforce the perception.

If Jake could keep Chris out of prison, wouldn't that be another tie to bind? Another way that Jake bested him? *Don't worry, little buddy, I got this one. Owe me one.* That would be a lifelong debt Chris could never repay. They were Bonasera and Don Corleone. *Someday I may call upon you to do a service for me, but until that day, consider this justice a gift.* Maybe that was too dramatic.

Killington. The ski trip from hell. If Jake helped Chris, would that wipe the Killington slate clean? Truth be told, Chris wasn't comfortable holding any cards. Having Jake owe him felt about as comfortable as a Goodwill suit.

"Why do you want to do this?" Chris asked. "We're not the picture of family love."

Jake stepped back and shook his head. "We're still family, right? And we've known each other for what? Twenty years? Why *wouldn't* I help you?"

"I don't know. Ever since Vermont, everything has been

so screwed up with us. And now, here you are—"

"Where is your head, man? Why are you thinking about that? Vermont was six fucking years ago. Just yes or no, do we have to talk?"

Either Chris told the truth and did ten years for obstruction, or he bet on Jake. He met Jake's eyes. "No. It's fine. There's nothing else you need to know."

Jake ran his hand through his hair and scratched the back of his head. "Okay, fine. We'll talk soon after you're booked."

Chris and Jake walked back into the living room. Detective Small explained the warrant in a brisk, no-nonsense voice. Her eyes flitted over Chris's face, cold and contemptuous, and Chris could tell that she had written him off. It took all he had to keep from asking exactly how he'd screwed it up.

Jake checked his watch. "I need to run to the courthouse and do a few things. Chris, sit tight, and I'll be back as soon as I can."

Detective Small smirked. "Don't worry, he's not going anywhere."

"Get your paperwork straight, detective. We'll challenge the preliminary hearing. No games with discovery, okay? We want it in the ten days." Jake stood straighter and leaned in, his hands on his hips.

"No games? Really? You're going to challenge probable cause and force the ten days, *and* you expect no games?" Detective Renner snorted. With his hand on Chris's elbow, he guided him out of the living room toward the front door. In the front hall, Renner stopped and sighed. "Listen, we gotta cuff you. If we're bringing someone in, it's gotta be in cuffs, okay? If it wasn't capital, you could turn yourself in and it'd be a different story. But..."

Detective Renner was brisk and gentle as he clinked the cuffs into place. That act alone brought Chris back to a time he thought he'd moved on from. Somehow, he thought he'd become better than the guy nursing bruised knuckles in the parking lot of a crowded bar at two a.m. But he wasn't. He'd never be better than that guy. *You can't run from your past, I guess. Eventually, it sneaks up behind you and cuffs you.*

CHAPTER FOURTEEN

MAGGIE

Vermont, 2007

K ILLINGTON WAS JAKE'S IDEA. JAKE and Chris used to take ski trips together, back when they were fraternity brothers. They'd spend weekends cutting through powdery snow on snowboards and picking up giggly snow bunnies in pink snowsuits. Or so the stories went, anyway.

Maggie had skied occasionally, but after the second miscarriage, she balked at the idea of a weeklong party with her sister. Chris begged and pleaded, promising the getaway would bring them out of their funk. It would be a last hurrah before midnight feedings and expensive formula meant the end to self-indulgent, lavish ski trips. Killington would be a trip for adults only, complete with alcohol and warm fires and big sweaters.

"Well, that's assuming there will *be* midnight feedings." Maggie pouted.

"You'll be up to your elbows in dirty diapers any day now, Maggie. I swear on my life. This is our *last chance.*"

Miranda jumped on the bandwagon too, calling Maggie at all hours of the day. "When was the last time you and

I did anything really fun together? Like we did in high school or college? It's been years! This trip will be great."

"I know, M, but I'm telling you, I'm horrible company lately. I'm so focused on babies, babies, babies..."

"This will help. Give you some perspective. Besides," Miranda continued as though Maggie hadn't even spoken, "I need this. Jake and I need this. Things have gotten weird, and I don't know why."

"What does that mean?"

"Just please say you'll come, please?" Her voice narrowed down to a point, small and pleading.

Maggie could see her at home, curled up on her overstuffed easy chair in her cacophonous white living room. *Why even argue?*

So they went. They loaded up the SUV with skis and snowboards and boxes of hot cocoa and puffy nylon ski suits and bottles and bottles of wine. Almost nine hours later, they pulled into the gravel driveway of their cabin, rustic and surrounded by evergreens. Maggie was *finally* glad she'd agreed to go. Chris and Maggie would have Friday night alone because Jake had a big case and needed Friday to finish. Initially, Maggie had fought irritation at that—they'd begged her to go, only to bail on the first night?

But with the white landscape stretching as far as she could see and the tree branches glistening like spun sugar, Maggie exhaled. She leaned up on tiptoe and kissed Chris's stubbled cheek. He laughed, rubbing his face with one mittened hand. They unloaded the car and stocked the kitchen. Maggie giggled at the gleaming stainless steel Viking range in their "rustic" cabin.

"Jesus, how much did this place cost?"

Chris shrugged. "All I know is Jake said he would cover it. That Miranda was picky."

"Miranda, who doesn't cook, needed a Sub-Zero refrigerator and a scullery sink?"

She was still impressed, and she shooed Chris toward the living room, with its flat-screen television and home theater system. She spent that first evening buzzing around the kitchen, stirring and bubbling and simmering her way to a new Maggie. For the first time in months, happiness flickered inside her like the initial spark off a flint. She forgot about ovulation calendars and nursery themes and names. She lit candles, and they laughed over dinner, easy and blithe as though there were never any babies at all. They made love in front of the fireplace on a bearskin rug, like some kind of cheesy romance movie, and Maggie was happy. She was filled-to-the-brim happy.

The next day, Jake and Miranda showed up. They were obviously *not* filled-to-the-brim happy. They barely spoke to each other. The air crackled with hostility, a barely audible buzzing of high-tension wires. Jake dutifully emptied the trunk of suitcases and ski equipment, and Maggie chirped around him, exclaiming over everything in the cabin. Miranda stalked inside, the wooden screen door banging behind her. Jake and Chris exchanged man-hugs, a gesture Maggie had always found curious and slightly comical, as though the act of touching was obligatory, but only to a certain extent.

"I can't get over this place, Jake, seriously. You didn't have to do all this!" Maggie said. "You should *see* the movie collection, though. We could all spend the entire vacation watching anything you'd ever want to see."

"Well, I thought we would all relax in a little luxury. We won't be able to do this forever."

"Yes, luxury. Ask Jake how many hours he billed last month?" Miranda stood in the doorway, her arms crossed and her lip curled.

"Jesus, Miranda, it's hours billed, not really hours worked," Jake muttered.

"Close to three hundred hours," Miranda called as she stalked back inside the cabin empty-handed.

"You didn't seem to mind the fifteen-thousand-dollar paycheck!" Jake called from the driveway and then flushed.

Maggie shifted. She'd rarely seen Jake angry and *never* without composure. Maggie and Chris exchanged glances, and Chris coughed.

"Let's get inside." Chris clapped and picked up a suitcase. "Oh my God, what's in here?"

"Don't even fucking ask. Probably rocks, just so I'll have to carry it." Jake shook his head and strode through the front door, leaving Maggie and Chris by the car.

Maggie, Chris, and Jake wanted to hit the slopes right away, but Miranda insisted on staying in her room, claiming a headache and that she wanted to read. Which would have been fine except when Jake emerged from their room, Maggie and Chris were suited and hot and ready to go. He apologized and promised to meet them later. Everyone spoke in whispers.

"It makes no sense," Maggie said later on the lift. "I mean, we're the ones with actual problems. We have no money. We can't have a baby. Our life sorta sucks. But Miranda's miserable. For no reason! They haven't even tried for kids yet, I don't think!"

"I don't know. You can't judge someone else's life, I guess."

Chris patted her knee, and she leaned against him, content in the knowledge that at least they were better off than them. Later, Chris motioned to the slopes across the path—the black diamonds that Maggie couldn't even fathom attempting. She waved him on. She could take care of herself, and being alone was never something she'd much complained about.

She cut smoothly across fresh powder, lost in the silence of an almost deserted mountain and feeling a peace she'd long missed. *Chris was right. This is good for me.* She stood at the crest, adjusted her goggles, and just looked. The evergreens were topped with dollops of snow like whipped cream, and the fresh, unmarred snow glittered in the bright sunlight. She filled her lungs with frigid air and was about to push off when she felt hands grab her shoulders. She screamed, the echo mocking her. When she turned, she expected to see Chris but instead found Jake with a wide, laughing smile.

"I got you! You should have seen how you jumped!" He snapped his goggles on his face and flew past her as if there had been no fight or awkwardness earlier.

Maggie pushed off and raced to catch up to him. She remembered his agility in the snow, but she was confident she was—or used to be—better. She was smaller, lighter, her turns tighter, and catching him proved a breeze. She was plain *better,* and she felt a growing sense of pride. Time hadn't taken everything away.

At the bottom of the mountain, Jake bent over, panting. "Jesus, Maggie, you're going to die if you hit a tree at that speed!"

She laughed and pushed away from him toward the lift.

He called after her, "I mean it, you nut! It's reckless!"

When he caught up to her, she flashed him a grin. "You're just jealous. You're too old and too scared, that's all."

"Old? Scared? Okay, now it's on."

They rode the lift together, laughing and joking like the old friends they were. Maggie couldn't stop marveling at how happy she was. Sometimes she really did forget what Jake had done to her. She forgot about Philadelphia, about how she used to think that nothing would heal the stabbing pain caused by his smile. It seemed preposterous that she could forget, but that afternoon in Killington, she felt a rush of protective love for her old friend. They chased each other down the mountain in S-shaped trails until they finally retired to the lodge to wait for Chris, both too exhausted for even one more run.

The lodge was huge, dark, and wooden with a long

gleaming bar and silver and red vinyl stools. The walls were adorned with various antique ski equipment and local paraphernalia, including framed newspaper articles. Above a massive stone fireplace was a ten-point buck head. Maggie averted her eyes. Stuffed game always creeped her out. Something about their eyes seemed to still be *alive*, as though somehow the layers of foam and wire had trapped a living soul. They each settled on a swiveled bar chair and ordered whiskeys on the rocks.

"What's going on with Miranda?" Maggie asked, touching his arm. She rarely asked him about Miranda. It felt too weird, even a decade later when water should have long flowed under that bridge. But after their day together, she wanted to know. She felt compelled to *help* somehow.

"I don't know. I think she's tired of being alone. I can't tell anymore. I work constantly, but I'm a junior. She likes a certain lifestyle, and I can't keep up with it. I can't keep up with her." He traced an M in the sweat of his water glass, over and over, and Maggie stared, mesmerized.

"If she got a job, could you slow down?"

"I don't know. Maybe? Probably not. I'm a lawyer—and a young one. I'm required to bill a certain number of hours a month. She wanted on this train, but she doesn't like the speed." Jake ran a hand through his hair, expelling a whiskey-laden sigh. He nudged her with his elbow. "Enough. I had so much fun today. Don't ruin it, okay?"

"Okay. Fine. I have a dirty joke. Wanna hear it?" Maggie cleared her throat and, with a slurred bravado, told a long, intricate joke in a half-assed Irish brogue. She was laughing so hard, she could hardly choke out the punch line.

"Well, now I have to know. What's so funny?"

They turned to see Chris pulling off his hat and gloves and heading for the stool next to Maggie. Maggie felt off kilter. She forced a smile. She'd forgotten Chris was there. Jake recapped the joke, but the magic was gone. The punch line seemed stupid. Their discomfort dissipated as the three of them sat at the bar longer than they should have, telling jokes and drinking. Maggie thought of Miranda fleetingly. *She should have come.* But she knew her sister. Trouble was brewing.

The threesome stumbled back to the cabin, loud and raucous and hungry, their faces red from alcohol and windburn. Maggie marched off to the kitchen to attempt another culinary wonder, but she failed miserably. They consoled themselves over grilled cheese sandwiches.

"Oh, nice. Thanks for making me dinner." Miranda stood in the kitchen doorway, and all the energy seemed to suck out of the room. "I fell asleep waiting for you guys. Do you know what time it is? What the hell have you been doing all day?" She stomped back to her room, slammed the door, and Maggie's head buzzed.

Pain in the ass. All the time. This *is why I didn't want to come.*

Chris picked up his sandwich and gave a mock salute. "Well, this is where I retire." He winked at Maggie.

She heard him take the steps two at a time and the soft click of their bedroom door. In typical Chris fashion, he fled from confrontation. Maggie sat at the island, reluctant to follow Chris. Jake shrugged with good-natured resignation and left the kitchen. Maggie heard knocking on a door, followed by muffled voices that were soft at first and then increased in volume. The words were indistinguishable, angry and hate filled.

She pulled the bottle of whiskey from under the sink and filled her glass. She moved away from the kitchen, the voices growing faint and dull, and flipped the switch next to the gas fireplace. She curled up in front of the fire, watching the flames lick upward until her vision wavered. *God, I'm properly drunk. That's been a while.*

She must have fallen asleep because the next thing she knew, she was being shaken gently. When she turned her head, she peered directly into Jake's clear blue eyes. He sank down to the floor next to her.

"How's Miranda?" She was groggy and struggled to sit, pushing herself up.

"She'll live. She's pissed for sure."

"Then why didn't she come with us? Jesus. She's so much fucking work!" Maggie looked around for her glass.

"I know. I don't know what to do anymore. All we do is fight." He lowered his head into his left hand, his elbow resting on his knee, and gave her a wry smile. He took a gulp of whiskey and looked at the ceiling. "I think I'm drunk. God, it's been forever."

Maggie smiled and relaxed back on her hands. She studied Jake's profile, his straight nose and strong jaw, long lashes and full lips, and felt a stirring deep in her gut that hadn't been there in years.

With his eyes closed, Jake said, "Maggie, I was so dumb. Did I break your heart?"

Her breath caught at the conversation she'd wanted to have almost a decade earlier. *It's too late now, though. God, Jake, don't. Not after today.* "Everything worked out for the best, Jake. Life has a way of moving on, that's all." Her voice was soft. The alcohol had worked a number on her system. The room blurred around the edges, and the only clear thing was his face. Her heart thundered in her ears, and she couldn't think beyond *that moment.*

He turned his head and met her eyes. "Did I? I want to know. I've *always* wanted to know." He thumbed her jaw.

Her elbows gave out, and she felt weak. Helpless. "It's old news. We've all moved on." She gripped his wrist and lightly led his hand back down to the floor.

"Did I? It's a question." His gaze was intense, his eyes searching her face.

Because she didn't know how to answer, even though she'd known the answer for what seemed like her whole life, she shook her head. Jake's face was inches from hers.

Before she could protest, his mouth was on hers, a faint buzzing memory of heat and warmth. His hands pulled her against him. She couldn't think, couldn't process it, but she couldn't push him away either. She'd spent so much of her life wanting to touch him again. He smelled the same, felt the same, *tasted* the same, and her body moved of its own volition. Her hands moved up his chest and in his hair, and her teeth softly bit his lower lip.

He let out a soft moan. "Oh, God, Maggie."

In an instant, her name on his lips brought her crashing back to the present, back to reality. With both of her palms flat on his chest, she pushed him softly off of her. The sudden lifting of weight felt isolating. He lurched forward and buried his head in her neck, and she shoved him again. Harder. *This is insane. Enough.* She struggled to sit up and, just like that, noticed a shadow in the doorway. Tall and blurry, broad-shouldered. *Chris.*

"What the fuck is going on?"

CHAPTER FIFTEEN

CHRIS

L ONG AFTER CHRIS GOT OUT the first time, he'd walk down a city street and get a waft of warm air blown up from the sewer, triggering memories of prison, the combination of warm gravy and sour breath. City sewage had nothing on jail; it was potpourri in comparison. Prison smelled of something indefinable, more disgusting and fetid. Odd that the odor seemed so universal. Lying face up on a thin, lumpy foam mattress, Chris tried to pinpoint it. The toilets that were never flushed? The inmates who never seemed clean no matter if they'd recently showered? The chemical odor of drugs? Perhaps it was the pervasive smell of human corrosion, the dregs of society all contained in one place and rotting from the inside out.

He'd been stripped and cavity searched, fingerprinted, violated, and manhandled. He knew his current cell was temporary. He'd heard them announce shift change for the guards, and that meant he was stuck in purgatory until tomorrow. They never did any paperwork or official transfers on the off-shifts. An hour back inside and thinking like an inmate already. He was disgusted with the ease with which he'd assimilated back into the role of a prisoner. As if he'd never left, or perhaps that the prison and all the people in it had just been patiently waiting for his return.

"Stevens, up," a gruff voice called from the other side of his door.

When it opened, a scrawny kid stumbled in, propelled by a beefy hand. The kid sported a wild shock of red hair, a puffy juvenile face covered in freckles, and looked as though he belonged on the cover of MAD magazine. He also looked terrified, and his right arm crossed in front of his chest, gripping his left elbow. The door slid shut with a slam and Chris shook his head before he flopped back down on the bed. *Jesus, you're dead, kid.*

For a white Irish guy, Chris had done surprisingly okay on the inside the first time. His six-foot-three-inch, two-hundred-and-twenty-pound frame helped. He wasn't the biggest on the block, but he looked intimidating enough. Chris studied the redhead through slitted eyes. The kid huddled in the middle of the cell, his arms wrapped around his middle, looking as if he was about to piss himself. Chris felt a stab of sympathy.

"What's your name, kid?" Chris asked, forgetting his own rule and forgetting Jake's words. *Don't talk to anyone.*

"Smith. Smith Hamilton."

Chris's eyes flew open. "Are you fucking serious? Your name is Smith Hamilton?"

"Yeah. Why?" He furrowed his brow and wrinkled his nose.

Chris laughed. "Dude, you better make some shit up. If you walk around here looking like you do with the name Smith Hamilton, you're a dead man." He eyed him up and down. The kid looked a hundred thirty pounds soaking wet, and his forearm had a red, crusted scab from his elbow to his wrist. Looked like the worst case of road rash Chris had ever seen. "What'd you do, fall off your moped?"

Smith shrugged and grinned wickedly, revealing

moss-colored teeth.

Chris shuddered. "You're probably a dead man anyway."

"What do you mean 'dead man'? Like someone's bitch?" The kid looked terrified. His fingers worked at the thatch of raised skin on his arm.

"You watch too many movies or something? Just listen, okay? Don't talk to anyone. Ever. Mind your own business. Don't initiate conversations. If people talk to you, answer their questions and move on. Do what you need to do. Don't talk to the guards, especially. If they talk to you, try to get out of it before someone sees you. But don't be rude. You'll piss them off, and they look for reasons to be pissed at us. Keep your head down."

"What'd you do? Why are you here?"

Chris sat up and looked the kid right in the eye. "Don't ever ask anyone that question unless you want to get yourself hit. That question will get you labeled a snitch. Got it?"

"Pssst, Abercrombie, who's your friend?" The question was hissed from across the block, and Chris rolled his eyes.

Prison never changed. His last nickname was Letterman. With his black curly hair, green eyes, and dimples, Chris looked the consummate preppy. He crossed the small cell and stood at the door, looking out. He saw two eyes peering back at him from across the hall.

"I dunno." Chris shrugged, and the eyes receded into darkness.

Through the dim light, Chris made out the figure of a hulk of a man, bigger than Chris. He knew the guy had been there awhile. His cell was covered with lined papers scribbled with what he'd heard were Bible verses. Chris didn't know about anyone else on his block. Yet.

"Who's that?" Smith asked.

Chris shook his head. "Go to bed, kid. We're done talking. Maybe forever." Chris put his finger to his lips and rolled on his side, his back to the center of the room.

"Dude, it's like eight o'clock at night. Can you really go to sleep this early? Are they gonna turn out the lights?"

Chris pulled his pillow tight over his ears, blocking out the kid's questions and the fluorescent nighttime lights, and willed himself to sleep. He dreamt of a vampiric vision of Maggie, her wild blond hair swirling around her, and he woke up sweating. In the darkest hour of the night, he dreamt of Derek, a long, spindly arm stretched out in accusation. *Killer. Liar.*

THE LIGHTS FLICKERED IN THE early morning hours before coming on full blast.

Chris was pacing by the time the bang of night sticks on metal and the clanking of doors opening signaled morning. Wake-up time was five thirty, but not knowing the time on a regular basis was driving him crazy. He wanted a shower and a watch. The latter he could get at the canteen.

"Okay, ladies, time for breakfast." The guard opened the door and shoved in a tray containing two of everything: bowls, spoons, small boxes of Cheerios, and pint-sized milk containers. He was short and squat like a bulldog with the low-slung posture of an ex-wrestler. He had a thick, wobbling neck and an impressive paunch hanging over his standard-issue black belt.

Hamilton sat on his bed, rocking gently. Every once in a while, he'd hum under his breath. It was kind of making Chris crazy. The guard blinked twice at the kid, his mouth turning up in a smirk.

Chris grabbed the tray. "When can I get a shower? And maybe visit the canteen?"

Chris could tell the guard was a dickhead by the chiseled set of his jaw. The real *screws* had a look to them, like they enjoyed their job in ways they shouldn't. As if they knew they were exactly like the guys on the other side of the bars, and they get off on it. The kid pushed himself up and leaned close to Chris, hopping back and forth. Chris waved him back.

The guard shook his head, shutting the door as he answered. "You're not staying here, bud. You're a capital case. When you off someone, you don't get the princess treatment. Meth head behind you though, he'll get a shower around six."

When Chris turned back around, the kid eyed him suspiciously. "Dude, you killed somebody?"

"I'm not talking to you, kid. Eat your Cheerios. They're heart healthy."

CHRIS JUST NEEDED TO MAKE it to nine or ten o'clock, when he figured Jake would get in. The uncertainty was killing him. If wake-up was at five thirty, it had to be close to seven. They never came to get the kid for a shower, and Hamilton waited at the door, watching the rest of the block.

Chris shook his head. "Curiosity is a terrible thing in here."

The kid whirled around and glared at Chris. He seemed to resent Chris's unsolicited advice, and Chris had to wonder why he kept offering it. "What am I supposed to do?"

"When you watch the block, they think you're watching *them*. So you can use it later. Go lie down, take a nap, whatever."

"I can't lie down. When's my shower? Do you know?" Hamilton ran his right hand up and down his left arm, over the raised skin.

Chris cringed. His head was pounding, a deep thrumming behind his eyes brought on by the chemical smell wafting off the kid and a lack of sleep. Hamilton stood next to the cot. Chris turned his head and looked down, watching Smith's toes wiggle under his starched

131

canvas Keds. *Jesus, keep still for two minutes.* The cell door slid open with a metal-on-metal groan. On the other side stood the Dickhead.

He gave Chris a wide smile with lots of teeth. "Okay, Abercrombie, your lawyer is here."

Chris raised his eyebrow to ask *where'd you hear that?*

The guard shrugged, his smile widening. "What? I thought it was pretty good. It's a good thing you won't be here long. You'll be going up to the high security in a few days, I'd guess."

Chris held his hands out in front of him, his wrists together. He didn't feel like listening to the guy any longer than he had to. The guard cuffed him and held open the door. Chris followed Dickhead down the hall to meet Jake. When they reached the end of the block, the guard fished a key from his ring and swung open the door to a small conference room, motioning for Chris to enter first.

"You get an hour." Before Chris could reply, Dickhead pulled the door shut with a thunk. Loud metallic locks clicked into place, final and definitive.

Jake stood, crossed the room, and gave Chris a perfunctory hug. He looked as comfortable in jail as he did in his seven hundred-square-foot office or on an expansive golf course. Chris was convinced Jake had received the five-star treatment from Dickhead. Jake was a defense attorney, abhorred by prison guards everywhere, but he had the kind of face people liked. An everyman. A *good guy*. His shirt was appropriately wrinkled, the top button undone. Professional but not unapproachable.

Jake once said that everyone who learned of his profession would say, "Oh, can you help out my cousin? He's having some trouble..." He just looked like the kind of guy who would say, "Yeah, no problem." His smile was quick and inclusive, his laugh easy.

"How are you? How was the night?" Jake's brows knitted in concern. He pulled out a metal chair with a lime-green vinyl seat and sat opposite Chris.

Chris studied the mottled surface of the cheap, dirty Formica conference table. He wondered how many other guys had been in that chair, staring at that table. How many were still there? "Uh, I've been better, but then again, I've done this before." He shrugged.

"Did you talk to anyone?"

"Yeah, my cellmate. He doesn't shut up."

"Do you know his name?"

"Uh, yeah. Smith something. Hamilton. Smith Hamilton."

Jake wrote it down on one of his legal pads. "We'll try to get him switched, okay?"

"Fine. Now what?"

Jake opened a file. The legal pad with Stevens printed on the binding was filled with pages of notes. Jake had been busy. "Okay, yesterday, I went to the courthouse. We're going to challenge probable cause at the preliminary hearing. It'll be us, the prosecution, and a judge. No jury. They still don't have a body. I filed a discovery motion, meaning we should get the police file, as complete as they can make it, in a few days. We'll have about a week to put together a good defense."

"Great. What's the defense?" Chris liked efficiency. He rubbed his hands together. In two weeks, it could all be over. He could be home. His stomach lurched. *Home to what?* He pushed that thought away. Home with Maggie. Everything that entailed was still better than prison. *Maybe.*

"Well, right now, we're just hole poking. What some lawyers call the house of cards. It's a good defense, and sometimes the only one. The D.A.'s job is to make a case that we can't knock down. If we can knock down every card they have, the house comes down. Sometimes all it takes is the one *right* card, one at the very bottom."

"So am I staying here?"

"I'm gonna see about keeping you here until the

hearing. SCI Camp Hill is a medium-security facility, but with your charges, you should be in a high or max facility. I'm thinking we can drag out the transfer until at least after the hearing."

"After the hearing?"

Jake held up his hands. "If we need to. I can't guarantee anything, Chris."

"Okay, well can you pretend to have some kind of confidence? I didn't kill him," he said.

Jake eyed him and leaned back in his chair. "Then what the fuck happened?"

"I told you what happened."

"That story is bullshit. I know it, you know it, and the cops know it."

"It's the story we're going with."

"But not the truth." That statement hung in the air, heavy like wet wool. "Another thing you should know. They found Logan's blood. In your truck."

"How would that happen?"

"Are you serious? You tell me."

"What if I punched him?"

"Did you punch him?" Jake looked skeptical and lifted an eyebrow.

Chris wanted to laugh. "Sure, but he swung at me first. He missed. I hit him back because I was trying to get him to leave my house."

"Then how did the blood end up in the bed of your truck?"

"I have no fucking clue. I didn't watch him leave."

"According to the statement on file, you didn't touch him. Do you want to amend that?"

"I don't know. Should I?" Chris blew out a slow breath.

"If that's the truth, then yes." When Chris made no attempt to answer, Jake gathered his file and paperwork into a pile. "Listen, if you let me go out there, balls to the wind, I can't help you. I can't protect you if I'm vulnerable. If you lie to me and I go up to the judge with just my dick in my hand, that'll be what kills you. Do you get that? You're giving them just enough rope to hang you with."

"You want the truth? Fine, here's the truth. I didn't kill him."

"Who did?"

Chris didn't answer, and the air between them crackled.

Jake banged the table, his wedding band glinting in the fluorescent light. "Chris, goddamn it, this isn't about Killington or Maggie—"

"But it *is* about Maggie. Let me ask you this, hypothetically—what if I knew who killed him? What if I was a witness, not a suspect?"

"Then we go to the police, and we tell them the story." Jake held up one finger. "Chris, if you tell me something right now, it has to be the story we go with. This whole conversation is covered under privilege, but what I *can't* do is put you on the stand to lie. That's called the subornation of perjury, and I will lose my license for that. So you are free to talk to me, but if we're not marching into the D.A.'s office with the truth, I cannot put you on the stand. You'll basically lose the right to testify on your own behalf. Is that clear?"

Chris considered that. He wasn't sure that testifying on his own behalf was an option anyway, but it seemed foolish to take that away. "Okay. What if I ask you a question, hypothetically?"

"Hypothetically? Fine, what's the question?"

"Say someone buried a body and lied about it. But didn't kill the person. What're the charges?"

Jake held Chris's gaze. "A year. Maybe two. Could this someone prove they didn't kill the person?"

"Maybe. Beyond a reasonable doubt? No."

"They don't need reasonable doubt. They need probable cause. They need *prima facie*."

"Then yeah. Maybe. If we talk out of hypotheticals, what happens then?"

"Well, I can't put you on the stand knowing that you're lying. Which, right now, hypothetically, I don't know that," Jake said.

"So in the scenario, the 'witness' goes to jail anyway. A year, maybe two you said. That's still jail, though."

"Yeah. Probably."

"But without a body, it's probable that everyone just walks away."

"Possible, not probable. There's a difference."

"It's a gamble."

Jake nodded. "Yeah. It is."

———◆———

WHEN CHRIS RETURNED TO HIS cell, Smith was gone. Chris lay on his cot, staring at the ceiling, and missed the chatter. He hovered at the door until he saw a guard. It wasn't the Dickhead. Someone softer, round, and fleshy. Chris suspected he was new. Not first-day new, but somewhat unfamiliar with how things worked. His eyes darted back and forth.

"Hey, what happened to the red-headed tweaker?" Chris asked.

"Bonded out. He's probably cranked as we speak."

Chris nodded and faded back, away from the door. He'd broken about five of his rules.

Prison was one lonely fucking place.

CHAPTER SIXTEEN

MAGGIE

S HE HEADED EAST ON I-81, marveling at the vast, green
Pennsylvania countryside. Whenever she returned to
her hometown of Haverford, her calm slipped away, replaced
by tight anxiety, the sensation of failing expectations, and
an irrational feeling of suffocation, like trying to breathe
through fabric.

When Maggie had called, Miranda answered the phone,
sounding irritated and impatient. "Hold on, ISAAC, WILL
YOU PLEASE! Hi, Maggie, what's up?"

As though Jake hadn't been staying at Maggie's house.
As though Chris wasn't in jail for murder. As though it
was a normal Saturday afternoon.

"I'm coming out. I mean, can I come out? I'm going
crazy. I want to see my niece and nephew," Maggie said.

"Sure. Doesn't Jake or Chris need you there, though?"

"The hearing is eight days away. Jake doesn't need me
for anything. And Chris... I went to visit him. I might not
again. I'll tell you when I get there."

"How are you holding up?"

The background quieted, and Maggie could tell she'd
gone into another room. Most likely the laundry room, just

off the kitchen, where Miranda frequently sat against the closed door to have a quiet conversation. Maggie craved the craziness of Miranda's house, the inability to have a complete discussion or even a coherent thought. She couldn't stop the movie in her mind, the one where Logan crumpled to the floor and the blood on her hands left red handprints on his white T-shirt.

"I've been better, but I guess not as bad as Chris."

"Have you talked to Mom and Dad?"

"Once. I called and told them the whole story. Mom was... surprisingly empathetic. Dad seemed to expect it. Like Chris had finally fulfilled some kind of expectation."

"Oh, Maggie, you're imagining that. You've always been so sensitive. Chris, too."

Maggie's dad, Phillip, was as tall and imposing as Chris, but he had the dignity of a self-made millionaire, which he was. Not to mention he was silver haired and tan from winters spent yachting in various Caribbean locales. When Maggie and Chris had gotten engaged, they made the drive east to tell Maggie's folks.

Her father had looked Chris up and down and asked, "What do you do again?"

When Chris had replied that he was in construction, Phillip's eyes flitted to his daughter, a glance so brief that only Maggie caught it. He smiled then, because he was a gracious and polite man, and so very slick.

He'd said, "Welcome to the family, Chris. Every man should be so lucky to have a handyman as a son-in-law."

Maggie had snapped back at him, "He's more than a handyman, Dad. You couldn't do half of what he does."

Phillip had laughed, an unfamiliar sound to Maggie's ears. "So sensitive, honey. I meant it as a compliment."

Rich men knew how to make insults sound like compliments, and Maggie seethed, confident that any protest would be treated with utter disregard.

Years later, when they'd learned of Chris's stint in

prison in college—how they'd learned, she never found out—her father merely shook his head and waved, which could have meant any number of things. To Maggie, the gesture meant *I should have known.*

Maggie had ended the call with Miranda with a vague promise to finish the conversation later, when she arrived. Truthfully, talking about Phillip and Charlene gave her a headache, and she was already dreading the entire weekend.

Maggie loathed visiting her parents, and she fulfilled the obligation only as frequently as required. Her childhood memories felt stiffly starched, as if they'd been sanitized and dubbed together like a Tide commercial. As if the less-than-pristine bits lay on a cutting room floor somewhere. Miranda claimed to have wonderfully happy memories of them as kids and always spouted off incidents that Maggie could never recall.

Maggie had some flashes of beach vacations, exotic locations and bright, bright sun with blue water, and staying in houses with cold marble floors. Her father's silver hair, glinting and plasticky, his eyes hidden behind dark glasses. Her mother saying, "Shhhh, don't yell, you'll wake your father," as they made silent sand castles. Her mother, preening and fluffing around her father as though he were an exotic bird. Maggie and Miranda were unwelcome appendages, interruptions to their carefully calculated life. Maggie remembered watching her parents kiss and wondering what it felt like to kiss glass.

Maggie pushed the thoughts of her father down where she always pushed them. Somewhere deep inside her was a pit of memories as sharp and cutting as the day they'd happened. She spent the rest of the drive thinking about Chris, about their situation. She couldn't get Logan's eyes out of her mind, his black, flat eyes staring up at her from the living room floor. She couldn't shake the sensation that when Chris had wrapped Logan in a tarp, he'd thrown in a piece of her soul. Until the day she died, she'd only be pretending to be a real person. Pretending to be whole.

⸻◆⸻

SHE PULLED INTO THE CURVED driveway two and a half hours later, circled the outdoor fountain, and put her late-model Volkswagen in park. Her childhood house had been sold years earlier, replaced with a formidable brick structure that didn't look like anyone's home. She felt a surge of gratitude toward Chris, followed by a disappointment so pervading, she felt it in her limbs. *He would have been a good father.*

Maybe a year or two earlier, at Jake and Miranda's, Chris had raked all the leaves from the street into a pile almost as tall as she was and then threw himself backward into it while Rebecca and Isaac shrieked with laughter. Later, on the drive home, Maggie said she thought it was odd that the kids had never done that. They were seven and five!

Chris had shrugged and said, "Well, who would show them that? Jake? He'd have to be home first."

The image of Jake, in his thousand-dollar suits with his omnipresent cell phone, jumping into brown, rotting vegetation, wouldn't stick. Chris, though, would have been so alive, so in love with his kids. She imagined him showing a boy the intricate workings of an engine, his hands stained black but steady. He would pass along his love of all things mechanical, his need to fix things and build things, his quiet study of how things work. She fought back tears, swallowing the tightness in her throat.

Before she could get out of the car, Phillip, in a dark, tailored suit and yellow tie, opened the screen door and stepped out onto the porch. He held up his hand in a formal wave, and she slowly climbed out of the car.

"Maggie." A simple statement with so many possible meanings.

As always with her father, Maggie was left to *look* for significance. Normal people had conversations and their intentions were obvious, or at least decipherable, but her father spoke in a code she'd spent a lifetime trying to decipher. She'd read somewhere that the tribes along the banks of the Amazon River all spoke in a different tongue with their own words, customs, and traditions. Their intertribal fights were as deadly as full-blown wars. But they also had a common vernacular with less than a hundred expressions, a universal way for the leaders to communicate. Over half of the words were centered on peace. *Love. Family. Food. Eat.* It was, in effect, a truce language. If Maggie and Phillip had a truce language, it would have one word. *Money.*

"Phillip." She nodded once before he enveloped her in a stiff, distant hug.

"You should come by more often, Maggie Bell. Not just when you need something."

His use of her long-buried nickname, short for Margaret Isabel, brought her up short. She stared at his face, which seemed to be all straight lines, his jaw and mouth rigid.

He looked down at her and smiled, a small and unexpected gesture. "What? You think I don't know why you're here? Come in, your mother is anxious to see you." He walked ahead of her, and she double-stepped to keep up.

"Maggie, honey!" Her petite mother hovered in the foyer, her blond hair up in an elegant chignon. Everything about her, from her "casual, Sunday skirt" to her designer flats, oozed sophistication and style. Although her face was fine lined, she was dolled up, her makeup settling in the cracks around her mouth. She held Maggie's face in her cold hands, and her black, spidery eyelashes blinked frantically. "Are you okay?"

Maggie didn't answer, and Charlene led them into the dining room. She poured herself and Maggie a cup of tea from a scrolled teapot adorned with blush-pink roses and delicate gold leafing. Maggie hated tea and always had. She left her cup untouched.

"What do they think Chris did?" Charlene asked.

"They think he murdered a man." Maggie's voice sounded flat, even to her ears.

"Did he?" Phillip's voice boomed behind them.

"No, of course not, Phillip." Charlene turned to Maggie, her eyes wide. "He didn't, did he?"

"Mom! No, of course not."

"Well, why do they think that? What happened?"

Maggie sank down in the dining room chair and relayed the official story, the one where Maggie slept while Chris and Logan had a middle-of-the-night conversation and Logan left alive.

Charlene shook her head. "My goodness, what a mess. I wonder what the boy wanted with you." She cocked her head to the side, and Maggie shifted in her seat. She was uncannily sharp. Maggie had forgotten that.

"I don't know. I didn't know him, except to say hello. I certainly didn't know he was *stalking* me." She was improvising; there were too many details they'd never discussed.

"How much do you need?" Phillip asked. He hadn't moved from the doorway, and during Maggie's recounting, he hadn't even leaned against the door jamb. In another lifetime, he would have made an excellent Queen's Guard.

"Um, we have to pay Jake. His usual retainer is fifty thousand dollars. He said he'd do it for twenty-five."

"Twenty-five!" Phillip's forehead creased. "Not a bad price tag for a criminal defense."

"Phillip!" Charlene's voice was sharp.

He lifted one shoulder, his frown deepening, and strode out of the room. Charlene patted Maggie's hand, her skin soft and cool, her heavy gold bracelet clattering against the table. Maggie fought her desire to pull her mother's hand against her cheek, to wrap herself around Charlene's arm and nuzzle it like a child.

"Do you need more?" Phillip walked back in waving a check, filled out in the perfect penmanship of a man groomed in Catholic boarding schools. He held out the check to Maggie. "I always have more, Maggie Bell. You can always ask."

She nodded, feeling too sick to speak, and pinched the check as though it were foul. She pressed it into her purse with her forefinger, not even glancing at the amount.

Later, when she stood to go, her mother looked startled and uncertain, her eyes darting between Maggie and Phillip, willing one of them to speak. Maggie kissed their cheeks, said she'd call, and let herself out the front door. She climbed into her car, the seat burning from the midday sun, and sat in the driveway with the vague sensation that she'd just narrowly escaped.

———◆———

WHEN MAGGIE WAS EIGHT, SHE counted on her fingers the times she'd seen her father smile *at* her. Not at something else while she happened to be in the room, but legitimately *at* her. *One,* when she'd made the Junior Mathletes team at school—even though he'd never come to a match. *Two,* when she'd told a joke at dinner—she couldn't even remember the joke—and he genuinely *laughed*. *Three*, when she was seven and had asked Phillip what he did for a living. That also made up their longest-running solo conversation to date. *Four,* the week Charlene had pneumonia, and they all worried she would die, Maggie had begged Phillip to sit with her in bed, like her mom always did. That time it was sort of sad, more like the faint, faded memory of a smile. She still counted it.

Number *five* had been that New Year's Eve. Her parents threw glamorous parties—glittering, low-lit affairs with heavily perfumed women and tuxedoed men. Her mother, in gold lamé, laid out pink party dresses for the girls, identically hideous with satin and ruffles. Miranda squealed, clapping her small, dark hands while Maggie had to be prompted at every step.

"Maggie, please, we need the white lace stockings, not the pink ones. The pinks don't match, see?"

The girls would make an entrance, amid sighs and polite clapping. Maggie hated the parties. She found them dull, and the stench of intermingling colognes and perfumes gave her a headache. She'd curl up under the dining room table, hidden beneath the sheer tablecloth, and she'd watch the crowd. Mostly, she'd watch her father.

Phillip circulated and, like a choreographed ballet, small circles would open to him. He laughed with the men or lightly flirted with the women, his palm low on their backs. Maggie watched with seething jealousy, searching his face for clues. The women soaked up the smiles he bestowed as if he had millions of them tucked inside the breast pocket of his two-thousand-dollar suit.

The wait staff served small, dainty pickings piled on glinting, silver trays. Maggie shrank back against the middle leg of the dining room table, watching the parade of shoes—shining, and sparkling, open toed with perfectly painted nails, black wing tips and Italian leather. The room emptied as the crowd migrated to the ballroom.

Maggie's eyes grew heavy, and she slept intermittently under the table, awakening to the sound of soft giggling. She peered through the gauzy tablecloth. Phillip leaned back against the wall, his arm encircling a woman Maggie did not know. His hand rested on the small of her back, his fingertips dancing up the length of her spine. Maggie pressed up against the center leg of the table and watched a red, spiky heel move up and down her father's calf. Maggie inched toward the edge of the table and dared to look up. Phillip was giving the woman a smile Maggie had never seen, a secret smile. The woman leaned in and nipped her father's ear. Maggie put her fist in her mouth to keep from screaming.

Later, when the clock struck midnight and everyone cheered, Phillip kissed Charlene with the same mouth that had kissed the woman in the red dress. Maggie shrank back against a row of books and watched Miranda skip around the room, waving a noisemaker. Maggie met Phillip's eyes and he waved her over, his mouth turned up in a happy grin. Maggie turned to see if someone was behind her. There was no one. *Five.*

——◁◆▷——

SHE PULLED UP IN FRONT of Miranda and Jake's, and Isaac and Rebecca came running out to greet her. Her nephew and her niece never failed to put a smile on her face. Miranda stood in the doorway and waved the kids back in. It had been a while since they'd seen each other, and Maggie studied Miranda with a critical eye. Her sister looked worn. Heavier. Tired.

When Maggie reached the porch, Miranda enveloped Maggie in the way that only Miranda could. It wasn't the cool hug of affectation that Maggie usually got from her mother or the detached half pat she'd get from Phillip, but a real down-to-your-bones *hug.* Maggie pulled out of the hug, rubbing her thumbs under her eyes.

"God, Maggie, are you okay? I don't think I've seen you cry since we were kids. You're always like the ice queen." Miranda whistled to the kids, who ran up the steps and thundered to the back of the house toward the playroom.

Miranda lived in a new McMansion a few miles from their parents. Her house was a mini-version of Phillip and Charlene's, and Maggie almost laughed. *How could Miranda not see this?* It was uncanny. The brick, the sterility, the lack of decorating. *I'm the ice queen?*

Miranda led Maggie into the kitchen, alternately chattering and yelling commands back toward the playroom. Maggie glanced around the industrial kitchen—all stainless steel and poured-concrete countertops, like out of some kitchen makeover show. Maggie thought of her kitchen with its chipped tile floor and wooden countertops, her dying spider and aloe plants, her hanging brass pot racks and dusty cookbooks. Miranda poured Maggie a cup of coffee, and Maggie took it gratefully. She blew across the top of her mug as she settled onto a stool at the marble-top island.

"Mom made me tea!" Maggie curled her lip.

"Of course. Have you ever seen her not drink tea?"

"Ugh, I hate tea!"

"She doesn't care. She'll make it anyway."

They laughed softly, in shared connection. Maggie had missed her sister.

Miranda touched Maggie's hand. "What the hell is going on?"

"Oh God, Miranda, I have no idea." The real story, the truth, ached to be released. Then she thought of Chris, the look on his face as he was led away, and she stopped. If Miranda told Jake, it would hurt Chris. Maggie had done enough to him. "I was asleep, and this guy I'd talked to at the Hut showed up, looking for me. He claimed he didn't know I was married or something, which seems weird, but the details are fuzzy. Chris said he let him in, which was stupid, but you know Chris—he can be stupidly nice! They talked, and the guy left. Then he was just... pffttt—gone. No one can find him. But I guess they have something because they arrested Chris for murder. I mean, murder! Can you imagine?"

"Jake left here the other day like a bat out of hell," Miranda said. "I didn't know what to think. He hasn't been home for dinner in weeks. You called, and he was out the door. He told me later, but geez... what a mess!"

"I just can't stay there in that house. I went to see Chris in prison, which was *awful*. I can't go back. The hearing is in ten days—well seven now—and will probably last a few days. Jake says everything goes so fast with a judge and not a jury. If he wins, then Chris comes home and it's over."

"And if he loses?"

"If he loses... there's a trial, I guess. But Chris will be in jail for months at that point. Oh God, Miranda, he'd die. He's so miserable. I couldn't even stand it."

"He'll win, Maggie." Miranda patted Maggie's hand. Her palms were warm and dry. "Jake almost never loses."

"Almost never? What about the ones he's lost?"

"Oh, well, they were probably guilty."

THEY DRANK WINE, BOTTLES OF it, long after the kids went to bed. Even with the hearing and Chris and everything going on in Maggie's life, the conversation centered on Jake and Miranda. Maggie lay on the couch, her feet dangling over the armrest, as she swirled her wine and Miranda prattled on.

Jake was never home. Miranda was alone all the time. Jake was up for partner in two years, and then it would be easy street with *giant* paychecks. But until then, it was all Miranda, all the time. Alone with the kids, taking care of everything while Jake worked. Jake, Jake, Jake.

Maggie would have, in the past, gotten frustrated at the one-sided conversation. But that night, she reveled in it. Focusing on someone else felt good. Chris and Maggie had been so insular lately, and with all that'd happened, their world had shrunk down to two people. Well, three if she counted Jake.

As Miranda ranted, Maggie tried to picture Jake alone in her house. Would he pry? She tried to envision him in her bedroom, pawing through her silk and lace. The idea was ludicrous. Then again, lately everything had felt ludicrous, like a clown at a funeral.

"But he'll be partner in two years, and you'll be on easy street. Everything is so temporary," she interrupted Miranda's monologue.

"You don't get it. I'm alone *all the time*. I'm a single parent. I doubt Jake even knows what grade Isaac is in. I'm sick to death of it. I've been doing this for twelve years. I'm done. We talked about splitting up."

"You did? When?" Maggie sat up and a spatter of wine landed on the arm of the white leather sofa.

Jake and Miranda had always seemed split-proof to Maggie, which was silly because no one was exempt from divorce. But somehow, despite their brawling and Miranda's demands and Jake's absenteeism, Maggie had always envisioned them together, old and rocking and still fighting. Or she'd never allowed herself to think of Jake as free. The idea sent her head spinning.

"A few months ago. The only reason we haven't is because Jake doesn't have time to meet with the lawyers. Ironic, right? I'm too bitter to care anymore." Miranda waved haphazardly.

"How can you not care?" Even in her darkest days with Chris, she'd always cared.

"Oh, it's not hard to be apathetic. It's much, much harder to give a shit."

Maggie laughed because that was so *Miranda*. For the first time since she'd arrived, Maggie actually saw her sister hidden under the layers of bad hair and baby belly and shapeless cotton clothing.

"Besides, shouldn't you love your husband?" Miranda continued, running her thumb along the edge of her glass.

"Don't you?" Maggie held her cold fingers against her wine-warmed cheeks. The question shocked Maggie, who was still pulled toward Chris. When the lights went out and she was alone in her room, she still thought about the way the corner of his mouth lifted to the left when he smiled. Or how he countered her busy impatience with a slow plod and how most people mistook his deliberation for stupidity. Did those things amount to love? What if those things were all that was left? Did Miranda still admire the way Jake's hair fell in front of his right eye as he leaned over a legal pad?

"I have no idea if I ever even did," Miranda said. "I mean, I don't now, that's for sure. Look at me. Do I look like a woman who gives a shit?"

Maggie had to admit she didn't. Years ago, Maggie had watched Miranda sing "Cry Me a River," Julie London style, at the Swansons' swanky Christmas party when she was barely eighteen. Weeks later, Maggie was visiting sixteen-year-old Wendy Swanson when Wendy's father jokingly referred to Miranda as *jail bait.* He'd ducked his head, his neck flushed, when he realized Maggie was still in the room.

"When we go places, to Jake's functions or whatever, do you think I don't see the other wives wondering how Jake got stuck with me?"

Maggie cringed as she remembered wondering the same thing when she'd studied her sister's haphazard ponytail or oversized, stained T-shirt. "Oh, Miranda, I think that's just your insecurity talking—"

"I wonder all the time what would have happened if I'd left him alone. Would you have married him, do you think?"

Why didn't the room cave in, the walls unable to support *the thing they never discussed*? Not Killington, because Miranda didn't even know about Killington, but the boyfriend-stealing-sister thing that had happened in college. The thing that had altered their lives and ended with Miranda marrying her sister's ex-boyfriend. Maggie lay back down on the sofa, avoiding Miranda's steady gaze. Miranda's eyes glittered in the soft lamplight, and Maggie realized how long Miranda had wanted to ask her that question. Maggie felt wrung out, raw and open from the murder and Chris and the hearing. The weight of one more thing might crush her. *Not tonight. No way am I discussing this now.*

"Miranda, that was what, almost fifteen years ago? I think we can safely assume we've all moved on." She stood and crossed the living room into the kitchen, where she rinsed her wine glass in the sink.

"Do you think so?" Miranda paused in the doorway between the kitchen and the living room. In that moment, she looked lost. Almost pathetic. "Jake talks in his sleep. He has no idea I've heard him. I'm not even sure he knows he does it. But every once in a while, dear sister, he says *your* name."

CHAPTER SEVENTEEN

CHRIS

"WELCOME, MR. MCHALE FROM PHILADELPHIA." Judge Wallace Puckett nodded over his bifocals in Jake's direction, speaking as though *McHale from Philadelphia* was Jake's last name. He held out his hands, palms down, and lowered them until they floated three inches above the bench. The assistant district attorney and Jake sat on their respective sides.

"A few things before we begin," Judge Puckett continued. "This is a preliminary hearing to find probable cause. There's no jury here. There's just little old me. Courtroom theatrics are mildly entertaining, but frankly, I've got a docket to keep. I've been doing this for thirty-five years. Probably since you all were in diapers."

Chris looked across the aisle at A.D.A. Janice Farnum, who looked at least eight years younger than Jake. Chris studied the judge. With his white hair and beard and heavy frame, he looked like Santa Claus.

Judge Puckett said, "I will not be swayed by flamboyance, but feel free to showboat if you're keen on irritating me. Let's save our drumroll moments for the actual trial, shall we?" With that, he glared at Farnum over the top of his rimless bifocals. "*If* there is one, Ms. Farnum. You might want to work on your poker face."

There was a faint din of laughter, and Chris turned to study the gallery. Maggie sat straight and tall directly behind the defense table. She avoided eye contact and watched the judge with a studied interest Chris knew to be contrived. Underneath his anger simmered a pull of attraction meshed with resentment so interwoven, he doubted he could separate the two. Would Maggie always draw him and repel him in equal measure? He could hardly remember a time before she had consumed him. Even with their fight in the prison visitor's room so fresh in his mind, the hatred he'd felt at being the one in the inmate uniform, he couldn't help but feel that his life would have been so much easier had she not been so beautiful. He marveled at the way that even then, with the hearing making his heart and his thoughts race, he still found a way to think about *her.*

He focused his attention on the smattering of people in the gallery: one young kid holding a notepad and pen who Chris figured was a freelance reporter, a few rumpled public defenders presumably waiting for their own clients' hearings, and a fifty-ish woman reading a paperback. Chris studied Janice Farnum. She couldn't have been more than five feet two and a hundred pounds. She looked like a child, her birdlike face overshadowed by large, round glasses. Chris couldn't have been less intimidated if he was being tried by his ten-year-old niece. He tried to remind himself that, without a doubt, she held *all* of the cards in Jake's house-of-cards analogy. Chris needed to maintain some kind of reverence.

Jake had given him a description of the A.D.A. and the judge in their last meeting before the hearing. "Janice is young, still in her twenties, and ambitious, I've heard. She's very smart, but her biggest issue is overconfidence."

"How do you know? You don't even practice here," Chris

had asked, and Jake shrugged. Chris laughed. "Leon, of course. I can't wait until I'm out of here and can meet the notorious Leon."

Leon Whittaker, an investigator at Jake's firm, was renowned for being able to gather dirt on anyone. The good, decades-old stuff, too. Rumor was that Leon had files on every political figure in Harrisburg, from the governor on down. He was also, according to Jake, a bit of a conspiracy theorist.

"Yeah, we'll all go out for a beer," Jake said. "Now, listen, Judge Puckett. He's mostly fair and honest. He doesn't mess around, but he used to be an assistant district attorney. Which means he could have a slight bias toward the left side of the aisle."

"Oh, great. Well, at least he's fair, you said?"

"That's what I hear. We'll find out. If Leon's right, this whole thing will be over in no time."

<hr />

"OPENING STATEMENT, MS. FARNUM?" JUDGE Wallace leaned back, removed his bifocals, and rested his hands on his considerable girth, taking the relaxed posture of a man about to watch a long, leisurely game of cricket.

Janice Farnum, her legal pad in hand, approached the podium halfway between the tables and the judge's bench. She adjusted the microphone as low as it would go; a squeal of feedback made Chris wince.

"The People intend to show that on the morning of June second, Logan May visited the Stevens home at roughly two fifteen a.m. From that point on, no one has seen or heard from Mr. May. He vanished without a trace."

Her loud, deep voice clashed with her diminutive stature, like stripes and plaids. Chris had expected high and soft, girly almost. He stiffened his spine.

"The evidence will show irrevocably that Logan May was inside the Stevens residence. While in their living

153

room, he bled quite heavily. You might ask, why would Logan May visit the Stevens home on the morning of June second? The evidence will indicate that Logan May and Maggie Stevens, Christopher Stevens's wife, were engaged in an extramarital affair."

Janice reread her legal pad. She flipped a page up and back. Janice's slow, deep intonation reminded Chris of being a child and listening to horror stories on an LP in his darkened bedroom. He used to run his index finger along the grooves, slowing the voice to a distorted bellow, heightening the terror. Chris tapped the table in front of him until Jake gave him a sidelong look and nudged his arm.

"In addition, we have statements from Mr. Stevens. Not one, not two, but *three* separate statements. With *three* different accounts of the evening. In the first statement, Mr. Stevens maintains that he never saw May on the morning of June second. In the second statement, he remembers, *oh yes, I saw him*, but we had a nice little chat and he went about his merry way. In the third statement, Mr. Stevens alters his account, yet again, and says they had an altercation that resulted in a fistfight. In all three accounts, May left the Stevens house unharmed and of his own accord. The People will show this is a lie."

Janice stepped down from the podium and walked around to the front of it. Judge Puckett surveyed the courtroom with a small smile. He clearly enjoyed his job and moments like that. Chris wondered if he'd wished for a bigger gallery, more interest.

"The People believe that Mr. Stevens murdered Mr. Logan May in a fit of rage over his wife's affair. Panicked over his prior violent history, he disposed of the body."

Judge Puckett tented his fingers at his chin. "So what you're telling me, Ms. Farnum, is you're attempting to try Mr. Stevens for murder, but you don't actually have a corpse."

Janice Farnum stopped mid-stride. She strode back to the podium and flipped through her legal pad. "*People of the State of California v. Scott,* 176 Appendix 2d 458 states that a defendant can be guilty of murder of a missing person where only circumstantial evidence exists to prove the act of murder."

"Yes, counselor, I'm aware of *People v. Scott.* It's just uncommon, that's all. And, I must confess, more interesting. Carry on." Judge Puckett stroked his beard. His eyebrows arched, and a small smile played on his lips.

"Through witnesses and forensic and physical evidence, the People intend to show sufficient probable cause to charge Christopher Stevens with the homicide of Logan May." Farnum retrieved her legal pad from the podium and returned to the prosecution table, visibly annoyed at the judge's interruption.

Judge Puckett turned to Jake. "Mr. McHale-From-Philadelphia, are you ready with your opening statement?"

Jake tossed his legal pad on the defense table in antithetic deference to Farnum's formality. He stood at the podium and leaned against it. *Let's just chat like guys,* his posture seemed to say. Judge Puckett nodded once.

"I studied *People v. Scott,*" Jake said. "In *People v. Scott,* the major issue is the circumstantial evidence. The question becomes: *Is the circumstantial evidence enough to warrant a murder conviction?* In this case, absolutely not. There's not even *corpus delicti* here. Every single piece of evidence the People have can be disputed and explained. There is not even a shred of evidence to support that Mr. Logan May is, in fact, dead."

Jake studied the podium, as if weighing his next words. "Let's start with the biggest a-ha the prosecution thinks they have—the defendant's lies. Well, *of course* he lied. Mr. Stevens knew the police would take one look at him and his record and see an easy way to close the case. Look, we all know the system. There's no jury here to impress. We have overcrowded jails, overworked cops, and the papers splash case closure rates on any slow news day. We're all cogs in that wheel. Chris—I'm sorry, Mr. Stevens—*knew* this. So he lied. The reason he rushed to lie is simple: he's been carrying the guilt of his past transgression around for over a decade. He thinks about it every single day. When the police showed up at his door, asking about a man that, yet again, he'd hit in the face—might I say these have been the *only* two fights Christopher Stevens has been in in his life—he was sent back into his worst nightmare. He panicked, and yes, he lied."

Jake eased back off the podium, expelling a breath, lightening the mood. He gave the impression of giving the whole opening argument on the fly. Chris stole a glance at Maggie, who watched Jake, rapt. He felt an unwelcome stab of jealousy.

"Ms. Farnum quoted *People v. Scott*," Jake continued. "Let's go back to that, and ask the question. *Is the circumstantial evidence enough to warrant a murder conviction?*"

"Yes, Mr. McHale, but we're not going for a conviction. Not yet. We're just looking for probable cause here. That's a whole other kettle of fish, don't you think?" Judge Puckett seemed to delight in interrupting his attorneys' opening statements, a practice that was fairly unorthodox.

"Oh, sure, Your Honor. You're absolutely right. Reasonable doubt versus probable cause. But with this overburdened system, do the People really want to pursue a case that they can't be convinced could result in a conviction? I mean, you said it yourself, your docket is your number-one concern. So let's pretend, for opening argument's sake only, that we're looking for a conviction. That we're examining reasonable doubt. As soon as I sit back down, we'll go back to probable cause."

Judge Puckett nodded, seemingly amused by Jake McHale-From-Philadelphia.

"Mr. Stevens's wife, Maggie, had a casual friendship with Mr. May. The prosecution will not be able to prove otherwise because proof doesn't exist. They had a mild flirtation, certainly not the steamy affair Ms. Farnum is insinuating. When Mr. May showed up at two fifteen in the morning, drunk and belligerent, Mr. Stevens did engage in an altercation. To put it simply, he hit him. He told Mr. May to get out. He gave the guy a bloody nose in his living room.

"There're fingerprints on the mantel. Well, *of course* there are. Mr. Stevens has said that Mr. May was in their living room. Witnesses state that Mr. May was headed there. Sure. We don't argue that he was unhealthily obsessed with Ms. Stevens. He sent her over thirty text messages the night he disappeared.

"The defense can explain every single piece of circumstantial evidence the prosecution claims to have. In addition, the defense will offer a more plausible theory to Mr. May's disappearance. One that the police and the district attorney never bothered to look into. Did they examine his friends? Look into his financial records? Did they care that Logan May was wanted for assault and battery at the time of his disappearance? That he had a history of assaulting women? Logan May had a plethora of secrets, Your Honor, that I guarantee will come as a surprise to the People. Why? Because they did exactly what Chris Stevens believed they would do in the first place. They fingered him. Then they made the rest of the facts fit. Does that add up to reasonable doubt? Absolutely. Does it equal a conviction? Not even close. It doesn't even satisfy probable cause."

Jake took his seat at the defense table, and Chris stole a quick look at Janice Farnum. She stared straight ahead at some unknown spot on the wall. Chris suppressed a smile.

"Don't get too confident, my friend," Jake whispered.

"You can say anything you want in opening statements. Janice is worried, though, and that's enough."

"Brief opening statements are always preferred." Judge Puckett leaned forward, scrawling something on a pad in front of him. He sat back and looked around. "Let's take a fifteen-minute recess and then reconvene for the first prosecutorial witness, shall we? Ms. Farnum, who will that be?"

Janice stood. "The People are going to call Mika LeBaron to the stand."

CHAPTER EIGHTEEN

MAGGIE

A T WORK, SHE COULD FORGET that Chris was in jail. She could stop seeing those obsidian eyes staring back at her from the living room floor, spidered with red broken blood vessels. She could stop replaying the movie of *Logan's Death*. She focused on the kids, their chubby, sticky mouths, their matted hair infused with lollipop pieces and bits of gummy vitamins, their sweet milk breath as she opened their mouths with tongue depressors. She was good at listening to ratty teddy bear heartbeats (*See, it doesn't hurt!*), always earning a grateful smile from a careworn mom. She administered shots with the efficiency of a military nurse but with enough high-pitched bubbliness to earn a tear-laden baby giggle. Those three to four days a week passed at a clip.

She was assembling records, oddly one of her favorite jobs. She made sure those multicolored tabbed folders were placed in the right bins—prescriptions needed, signed, needed to be signed.

"How are you managing, dear?" Linda asked from behind her. Linda's hands were on her ample hips, her gray hair held back with a purple glitter barrette, probably purloined from her granddaughter's collection. Her head tipped slightly, a universal symbol for macabre curiosity disguised as concern.

Maggie turned her back to Linda and busied herself with squaring printouts. But Linda never took hints. Maggie wasn't dumb. She'd seen the furtive glances, the squirreling away of a newspaper—a flash of Chris's forlorn face on the front page. The office girls avoided the subject, avoided talking to Maggie entirely, which was fine with her. She mostly thought they were airheaded anyway.

"I'm fine, Linda, just getting through it."

Linda inched up, her body heat oppressive. Maggie resisted the urge to swat at her.

"Do you need someone to talk to?" Linda's voice sank low, sugary and fake.

Maggie tried not to roll her eyes. Did Linda expect her to fall to pieces, crying about an abusive, murderous husband and missing boyfriend? Even if Maggie were meek and fragile, which she was *not*, did women really do that? Confide their deepest, darkest secrets at the drop of a hat? No woman Maggie ever knew, that was for sure.

"I'm okay, but thank you, Linda." Maggie turned, pasting on a bright smile.

As Maggie brushed past her, Linda grasped her forearm, a grandmotherly gesture that seemed too intimate. "Do you believe him, honey?"

"I'm sorry?"

"We were thinking of you. And your safety, if he comes home. Do you think he didn't kill that boy?" Linda didn't waver or step back or break eye contact, and Maggie was struck speechless by her gall. Linda said, "It's hard when you're young and in love. You don't always see that people aren't good for you. And he's so good looking! That would be hard to see past. The paper—they said he'd been in prison before. For assault?"

Maggie had no words. She just stood frozen, staring at

Linda's stupid glittery barrette. Linda pushed something into Maggie's hand, a crisp ecru piece of perforated cardboard—a homemade business card with a phone number. *Safe Havens. Ask for Lisette. Code word: basement.* A battered women's shelter? Maggie wanted to laugh out loud.

"I don't think you really need it, but you know, just in case." She gave Maggie a big smile and a pat on the arm, as though she'd just given her a gift card to Starbucks. As Linda walked back to the billing office, envelopes in hand, she hummed softly.

<hr />

MAGGIE ARRIVED HOME AROUND FIVE to discover Jake and a man she'd never met seated at her kitchen table, which was covered in paperwork. They'd stacked files on either side of the table, creating a private cave. She was a pariah in her own home. Maggie cleared her throat.

"Maggie, hi." Jake glanced up, his eyes flicking over her, dismissive. He looked neither happy nor disappointed to see her. He gestured to the bearded stranger. "This is Leon Whittaker. He's my investigator at Harbinger."

Harbinger and Whiteside, the firm where Jake worked, had several investigators. Maggie knew from talking to Miranda that Jake would only work with one, though. Maggie was taken aback by his bedraggled appearance. Leon was small and scrawny, and frankly, he looked like a bum. The kitchen reeked of cigarettes.

"Are you guys smoking in here?" Maggie wrinkled her nose.

"Who are you, Miranda?" Jake didn't look up from his notepad.

Maggie felt stung. She waved her hand in apology. "Sorry. Hi, Leon, nice to meet you."

His smile was no more than a flash. His mannerisms were jerky, and his eyes shifted around the room, flicking

161

across Maggie's face then back to Jake.

"What are you... investigating?" Maggie felt on guard. *Would Jake investigate her as an alternative to Chris?* Her naïveté concerning the law was astounding, even to her.

Jake sighed and kicked back the chair closest to her, gesturing for her to sit. "Leon here has a gift. He can find out anything about anyone. I don't know how, and I don't ask." The two men grinned at each other. Jake's teeth were straight and perfect; Leon was missing an incisor. "But for the past two days, Leon has been investigating your little boyfriend."

"Jesus, Jake, he's not my boyfriend." She closed her eyes and shook her head.

"No, of course not, Maggie. He's dead. But what matters is, did Chris kill him? No, scratch that. What matters is, can Leon convince a judge that Chris didn't kill him?"

"How do you know he's dead?"

Jake held up his index finger, a small smile on his lips. "Leon?"

Leon grabbed a sheet of paper and turned it so it was right-side-up before her. "This is May's bank account. No activity since June second." His deep, gravelly voice defied his squirrely appearance. He pointed at sequential piles. "That's May's credit card statement, cell phone bills, landline phone records, even his E-ZPass statement. Nothing since June second. His car hasn't moved. His neighbors, his friends, his boss—no one has heard from him." Leon finalized the list with a swiping motion across his throat.

"Leon's job is to take apart May's life, piece by piece," Jake said. "I want to know everything about him: his hobbies, his family and friends, his ex-girlfriends, his boss, his current girlfriend. Did he have one?"

Maggie shook her head. "I have no idea. We didn't talk... about that kind of thing." She felt on thin ice.

Jake cocked his head to the side, scanned the table,

and snapped up a paper. "What exactly did you talk about, oh... a hundred and twelve times in one month?" He pushed the cell phone bill across the table at her and folded his arms, his face unreadable.

The black-and-white numbering of her "affair" was obscene coming out of Jake's mouth. Suddenly, all the justifications she'd leaned on for the past few weeks seemed paper thin. She didn't feel embarrassed; she felt, for the first time, a gut-level shame. She shook her head and pushed the paper away with her index finger. Leon pushed himself back and snuck out the back door. Through the open screen, she heard the flick of a lighter and smelled the acrid odor of cigarette smoke. The scent reminded Maggie of the Hut, and her stomach lurched.

"Maggie, what have you guys done to each other here?" Jake murmured, and Maggie shook her head again. He placed his hand over hers on the table. His touch was warm, and Maggie felt herself coming undone. He said, "Please. Not for the case, not for Chris's lawyer, but something big is going on, and I'm worried. About both of you."

Maggie opened her mouth to speak but found that she couldn't. *Dear sister, he says your name.*

The screen door slammed, and Leon loped across the kitchen. He settled back in his chair, oblivious to the moment. Maggie withdrew her hand and wrapped her arms around her waist, as though holding herself together.

"Boss, I had an idea." Leon shifted through the papers.

Jake broke eye contact and turned toward the center of the table.

"You see this? Something about it hasn't sat right with me." Leon lined up nine bank statements across the table. He wrote October through June across the top of each one in scrawled, childish handwriting. "Look here, there's a $1,500 cash withdrawal every month on the twentieth."

"So what? It's rent," Jake said dismissively.

"No, I don't think so. First of all, who pays rent on the twentieth? Secondly, fifteen hundred bucks for his piece-of-shit apartment? Not to mention, who pays rent in cash? I'll look into his rent, see how much it was, but I'm willing to bet this is something else. We have all his bills. His car was a joke—no payment. Insurance was bi-yearly. He had no big bills. No credit cards, nothing. No ex-wife, no kids. You know what this looks like to me?"

"He was paying someone off," Jake finished, and Leon looked deflated for a moment.

Maggie choked back a laugh.

Then Leon brightened, waving March's statement. "Guess what else? No withdrawal after February."

"So what does that mean?" Maggie asked.

He turned to her, his eyes twinkling, and he tapped his temple. "Well, darling, it means that for whatever reason, in March, he stopped paying."

MAGGIE WANDERED UP TO HER bedroom and left them huddled around the table, pondering the meaning of the stopped payments. She flopped backward on the bed and stared at the ceiling, turning over the past week in her mind.

Before she had left the kitchen, Jake murmured, "Go see Chris, Maggie." She nodded but didn't share that she'd already been there.

Before she'd called Miranda on Saturday, she'd made an appointment to visit the county jail. She drove to SCI Camp Hill, checked in at the desk, went through the violating and humiliating more-than-a-pat-down search of her person and her belongings. She swallowed her dignity because Chris was there because of her. She stared at the gray block walls, the dingy beige-and-gray tile floor, the grimy windowsill of the visitors' area, and waited. When Chris arrived in what looked like scrubs and tennis shoes, he nodded as though she were a fellow inmate. Negativity pulsed off him.

Maggie spoke first. "How are you?"

He shrugged and leaned back in his chair. The visiting rooms Maggie had seen in the movies had partitions with phones and Plexiglas. That room looked like a doctor's office waiting room, though. She studied the table in front of her, smudged with dirt and a sheen of some unknown, sticky substance. The room was crowded with about ten tables of the same size. At each table sat an inmate, dressed identically to Chris. Maggie was conscious of the stares and unasked questions.

Chris eyed her up and down and snorted. "Are you trying to get my ass kicked?"

"No. What does that even mean?" she snapped.

"Jesus, you don't get it. You could have at least left the jewelry at home."

The only jewelry Maggie wore was her engagement ring and diamond-studded wedding band. Her hand glittered under the fluorescent lights. Self-conscious, she pushed it under her left thigh. She closed her eyes and took a deep breath. "Chris, I'm sorry you're here. I'm sorry about everything. What should I do? Should I tell Jake the truth?"

Chris shook his head and gestured to the many cameras around the room. "Watch what you say here. And no. What we have set up with Jake is fine. What you're talking about? If we go forward with that, I'll be here for two to three years, without question. And you might be joining me. At least this way, there's a free and clear shot. Do you get that?"

She nodded, but his eyes still glittered angrily. *This is completely unfixable.* The realization settled, heavy as a stone, along with a small amount of relief. They would finally, finally end.

"I didn't sleep with Logan," she blurted in a hushed voice.

Chris closed his eyes and shook his head. "I'm not having this conversation here. Or now."

"Why not? I have no reason to lie anymore. At least here and now, you have a shot at believing me. We've ruined each other. We've ruined everything. If we talk about this two weeks from now, when you're home and we're trying to figure out our lives, you'll never believe me."

"Maggie, please."

"You act like you're not culpable. Like this is all my fault. You've even said it, back at the house. You said, 'This is all your fault.' But it's not. If we had called the police instead of doing what you did, what *we* did, they would have believed us. They would have believed the truth. You have to see—"

"The only thing I see is that I'd be in the same place," Chris said. "Cops don't care about the truth. They care about closure rates. They don't care *at all* about guys with criminal records and violent histories."

"You're wrong. I was wrong to let you do what you did, but you have to see—"

"No, *you* have to see. Do you know how many people in the prison system *didn't do it*? Not just claiming their innocence, but are victims of the system? There's no room in *this* world to trust. You can't trust anyone here, and I'm not about to move back into a nine-by-twelve cell. At least not permanently."

"This is crazy. If we take Jake and go talk to someone, either the police or the district attorney, I'm sure we can figure it all out somehow. Please just think—"

Chris banged his palm on the table. "Damn it, Maggie! We are so different, you and I. You live in this fantasy world where people do the right thing, whatever that is."

Maggie sat back and saw, for the first time, the ways that Chris's previous prison sentence had run like invisible fault lines beneath their relationship. His *hardness*, his lack of empathy for her, stemmed not from lack of love but from a worldview so different from hers. His was shaped into hard, square edges by cement block walls and iron bars. Her new understanding, dawning at such an inopportune time, made her feel thinly connected to Chris, like a wispy tendril of smoke from one of Leon's cigarettes.

She reached out, wanting to touch him for the first time in what felt like forever. "Trust me this time, okay? Please, let me do the right thing for *us*."

"You sit there with your convictions that *somehow* you're better than me because you're on the right side of the bars. You wanna switch places? Trade in your Jimmy Choos for a pair of laceless Keds? How about you brush your teeth with a flimsy disposable toothbrush so you can't file it on the floor into a weapon you'll use to kill your cellmate? What do you say, Maggie? You take my spot. We'll see how long it takes to crack *you*." His voice shot up, above the din of the crowd. When he stood, two corrections officers flanked him.

"Okay, you're done, here." One of the guards guided Chris's arm behind his back and led him out the door he had come through not more than ten minutes earlier.

As Maggie watched him disappear, his head down, the frail connection she'd felt irrevocably broke. She was overcome with the sensation that she was married to a man she no longer knew.

CHAPTER NINETEEN

CHRIS

AGGIE'S BEST FRIEND, MIKA, MADE her way down the center of the courtroom, her head bent low. She avoided eye contact with everyone, especially Chris and Maggie. Chris had always gotten along well enough with Mika, but he'd sensed throughout the years that she felt Maggie had settled. Maybe it was the way she'd roll her eyes and glance sidelong at Maggie when Chris made a corny joke. Or the night he'd teased her about her revolving bedroom door, and she'd snapped, "Why? Because I didn't marry the first guy who nursed my broken heart?" When things were good, he'd talked himself into believing he was paranoid.

He had the sinking sensation that nothing good would come out of Mika's testimony. The bailiff swore her in, and Mika fidgeted in the witness chair. Janice approached the podium, her face open and friendly, and asked Mika to state her name. As if they were simply having a casual conversation, Janice established that Mika had known Chris for ten years and was Maggie's best friend. Mika relaxed in her chair, focused only on Janice.

"Do you like the defendant?" Janice asked.

Chris held his breath. He knew the answer, *he knew it,* and he knew why. One night, one mistake, a few drinks, and a slip of his temper. It would come out. He felt naked.

Jake jumped to his feet, and Chris started. Jake said, "Objection. Relevance. Your Honor, what does that matter?"

"Relax, counselor, it's only a hearing. I'll allow it."

Jake sat, leaned toward Chris, and whispered, "Be cool."

Janice nodded to Mika. "Go ahead, Ms. LeBaron. You may answer."

"I... I used to. Maggie is my best friend, and Chris had an affair when she needed him the most. They were going through... something. Maggie was a mess. Chris didn't know how to handle her or what to do. He... slept with his secretary." Mika said the last part quickly, almost inaudibly.

Chris sucked in his breath. He hadn't known it would cut like that—the nakedness of their secrets and his failures out there for the world to see as front-page news. He watched the court reporter, her hands poised above her stenotype, her face blank. *She must hear so much worse all the time.* The thought didn't make Chris feel any better.

"Had you ever seen them fight?" Janice asked.

Five years earlier, before Tracy, Chris and Maggie had gone out to dinner with Mika and her current boyfriend, whose name Chris no longer remembered. Chris had drunk more than usual, and after dinner, they all went back to Mika's apartment. Mika's boyfriend sat next to Maggie on the couch, a little too close. He filled her wineglass when it was empty, his fingertips brushing hers as he passed her wineglass. Maggie seemed to delight in the attention.

Chris had huddled in the corner, glowering and growing angrier with each tinkling laugh. The way Maggie touched his bicep, her long glossy hair falling over her face, made his blood surge white hot under his skin. With Chris, Maggie had been withdrawn and quiet. Chris had spent weeks staring at her back—in bed, at the sink, in the living room. Whenever he'd tried to really talk to her or touch her, she turned away. The isolation was driving him crazy, and when he tried to bring it up, she waved him off as though he was imagining things. Her dismissiveness killed him, made him feel worthless.

When Mika's boyfriend went to the bathroom, Chris had crossed the room. "Why don't you just sit *in* his lap, Maggie? Jesus, it's embarrassing." He spit the words at her like venom. He forgot about Mika, forgot about the guy—in that moment, the room shrank down to him and Maggie.

Maggie's eyes had widened in fear then narrowed. He felt his heartbeat, a throb in his head, his fingertips, all over his body, and he flexed and unflexed his fist.

"Oh, come off it, like you care." She had tossed her hair back over her shoulder and pushed her jaw out, her lip curling.

"What the hell does that mean?" He'd stepped closer, his face inches from hers. Maggie's eyes searched his, and his insides twisted at what he saw. *Fear.* To his knowledge, prior to that night, he'd never scared her.

"It's nice to have *someone* pay any attention to me at all. I'm practically invisible to you. I can't even believe you noticed."

"It's hard not to, when my wife acts like a slut." He'd spoken softly and didn't realize what he said until it was out of his mouth. Too late to pull the words back. *Fuck.*

"Get out." Maggie's voice had dripped with contempt.

Chris had shaken his head, disgusted, and turned and punched the wall. The drywall crumbled under his fist, splintering like a plaster spider web, and his hand pulsed with pain. His knuckles were scraped and bleeding. He stepped back, horrified at his outburst. He truly never did things like that. The room came into sharp focus. He turned to Maggie then Mika, looking like twins in their shock. He stormed from the room, the door slamming with a fury that shook the small apartment. His bubbling rage had been focused inward, a truth he'd never been able to get across to either Maggie or Mika. So he didn't try.

As Mika recounted the story, heat climbed up the back of his neck. Only Maggie knew how much he regretted that night. He'd gone back a week later, apologized to Mika, and fixed the hole in her living room. She had waved off his apology with a thin smile.

The incident had been a turning point, one of many in their marriage, and brought with it the knowledge that he could and should do better. He started bringing Maggie flowers after work. He would wrap his arms around her waist from behind, pulling her into him. The arch of her back curved perfectly against him, and her hair smelled like jasmine or something sweeter, almost almond. When he opened the front door in the evening, she turned to him again, her face tilted up and open, her mouth seeking his.

When he and Maggie were happy, he thought daily about how he couldn't believe his luck. Most guys complained that their wives were nags or that they couldn't go out with their friends. Maggie was never like that. She never inhibited him. She never made him feel stupid. He loved the way she'd stare at him in awe when he fixed a broken drawer or repaired a leaky faucet. She'd always say, "How do you know how to *do* that?" As though he was some kind of hero. She'd wind her arms around his back while he was still crouched under the sink and press herself against him. One time they even made love there, on the kitchen floor, with a wrench digging painfully into his back. When she was open to him, *really open,* he couldn't imagine ever living without her. As if she was his air.

After that night at Mika's, they laughed together, rekindled private jokes. His foot would find hers under the blankets at night, tapping three times—almost like in the beginning, when they were happy. They *were* happy again.

Three months later, they lost the second baby. Three months after that, they went to Vermont.

"Ms. LeBaron, do you believe that Christopher Stevens is a violent person?"

Mika paused and, for the first time, gazed over to the defense side. She stared at Maggie. From his angle, he couldn't tell if Maggie met her gaze. He couldn't bring himself to turn and look. He knew where Mika was going, and he was powerless to stop her. He wasn't accustomed to not having a modicum of control in his life.

"I think that Chris, when pushed to his limits, has a tendency to become violent."

"And jealous?"

Mika ducked her head. "Yes, Chris is jealous."

"Ms. LeBaron, did you see Mr. Logan May on the evening of June first?"

"I did. At the Tiki Hut."

"Did you speak to him?" Janice asked.

"He spoke to me. He asked me if I'd seen 'my bitch friend around.'"

"Did you know who he was talking about?"

"Maggie and Logan had a… flirtation. To my knowledge, she never saw him after the night they met. But they talked, or texted."

Jake stood again, his pen drumming on his legal pad. "You Honor, I object. This is all hearsay."

"Mr. McHale-From-Philadelphia, it's a hearing. Hearsay is permissible." The judge leaned forward, folding his hands in front of him in tacit admonishment.

Jake held his hands up, palms out. "I had to try."

Janice watched the whole exchange with obvious disgust. She turned back to Mika, shaking her head. "Ms. LeBaron, tell me about your conversation with Mr. May at the Tiki Hut."

"Logan was drunk. I'd never really talked to him, but I'd seen him around. He always creeped me out. He seemed so intense. Brooding. Never smiled. And he was always with this huge bald guy called Tiny. Helen, my friend, and I had a table. Logan came over and tried to sit down. Helen stopped him and said the seat was taken—we didn't want him sitting with us. He got mad because he knew no one was sitting there. He leaned in close to my face and said, 'Is it reserved for your bitch friend? I haven't seen her around lately.' I said, 'That's because she's married, asshole.' Then he kicked the chair over and left. He sat at the bar with Tiny."

"Did you talk to him again that night?"

"We left the Hut right after that. It was dead, and he was making us nervous. He kept staring at us, like he was *so angry*. As we were leaving, he came up to me and grabbed my elbow."

"What did he say?"

"He said, 'Call the bitch and wake her up. If she's not coming here, then I'll go to her. We need to have a little chat.'"

The judge nodded in Jake's direction, and Jake stood. "No questions at this time, Your Honor. We may call Ms. LeBaron back at some point."

Mika was excused. As she walked down the aisle, she looked at Maggie and offered a small mouthed, "I'm sorry."

"Your Honor, the people call Officer Davis to the stand."

Judge Puckett checked his watch. "We'll hear Officer Davis's testimony today and then cross tomorrow. Is that okay with you, Mr. McHale?"

Jake half stood and nodded. "We're fine with that, Your Honor."

A uniformed officer Chris remembered from the first police visit was led through the back doors and to the witness stand. He was sworn in and sat stiffly in the witness chair. He didn't even glance in Chris or Maggie's direction.

"Officer Davis, you were on duty the morning of June second?" Janice asked. "What can you tell us about the scene at the Tiki Hut?"

"We received a call about a parking lot assault at about one thirty on the morning of June second. When we got there, approximately twenty people were standing around. A man had been beaten. He was lying on the pavement, unconscious. I radioed for a squad. The ambulance came, and the man was taken to Harrisburg Hospital. We detained all twenty witnesses and took statements until about three a.m."

"What did you learn?"

"No one seemed to know the reason for the fight, but a witness knew the suspect as Logan May, a regular of the Hut."

"Then what did you do?"

"We let everyone go and proceeded to Mr. May's apartment," Davis said.

"What did you find?"

"Nothing. He wasn't there. His car wasn't there, either. We figured he'd show up eventually. We hung out for a while, watching the place, but he never came back. Around four a.m., we went back to the station and compiled our report. The next day, when I came into work, we pulled Mr. May's phone records, hoping there was some activity to give us a clue as to where he went."

"What did you find?"

"Nothing. Not a phone call or a text. Nothing past two a.m. I saw about twenty text messages to the same number that night, and when we ran the number, it came back to Ms. Stevens."

"Then what did you do?"

"While I worked the phone records, my partner pulled up the credit card receipts of all the patrons of the Hut that night. There weren't that many; business must not be that good. We started making calls, asking standard questions about if they knew Logan May or they'd seen him. We got two leads: a guy named Randall Richter, who everyone called Tiny, and Mika LeBaron. They both knew Logan and independently stated that Mr. May claimed to be going to the Stevens's residence to talk to Ms. Stevens."

"Did you go to see Ms. Stevens, Officer Davis?" Janice asked.

"Yeah, we did, but first we ran a quick background on Ms. Stevens. We found out she was married to Christopher Stevens, and that threw up a red flag. Why was she texting Mr. May a hundred times a month if she was married? Then we saw Mr. Stevens had a felony record for assault some years back."

"Did you interview the Stevenses, Officer Davis? What did you find?"

"Well, things just seemed off, you know? It's hard to explain, but you see a lot of stuff in this job, a lot of people trying to deceive the police. You develop a nose for it. *Something* was going on at that house."

"Like what?"

"Well, Mr. Stevens seemed nervous. Stuttering, stammering, not making eye contact. We asked to see Mrs. Stevens, and he claimed she was sick in bed with the stomach bug. He invited us in, and the whole house reeked of cleaning agents. Specifically oil soap."

"Did that make you suspicious?" Janice asked.

"Not by itself, no. But it smelled as though they'd just cleaned the whole house."

"Okay, what else?"

"We asked Mr. Stevens about Mr. May—if he'd ever seen him or if he came to the house the night before."

"What did he say?"

"That he'd never met him," Davis said. "He didn't recognize May's picture, he didn't know his name."

"Did that make you suspicious?"

"Again, no, not alone. But Mr. Stevens was fidgety and nervous. My antenna was up. My partner noticed the mantel was askew. The rest of the house was meticulous, not a knickknack out of place. There was a photo of the two of them taken in front of that mantel, but there was a vase in the picture. No vase on the actual mantel, though."

"Did you ask him about the vase?"

"Yeah, he said his wife broke it cleaning," Davis said.

"Okay, so the house smelled of soap, Mrs. Stevens was sleeping, Mr. Stevens was acting strangely, and there was a missing vase. Then what?"

"I had to use the bathroom, which I asked to do and was granted permission. The bathroom was through the kitchen. On my way in, I saw a cell phone in a Tupperware of kitty litter. It looked like one of those smartphones. I initially looked at it because my wife had once dropped her phone in water and we tried to use rice to dry it out, but it didn't work. But when I picked the phone up with the corner of my pen and really looked at it, I noticed that the memory card was missing."

Janice walked back to the prosecution table and retrieved a small plastic bag. "Is this the memory card that was missing from Ms. Stevens's phone?"

Officer Davis took the bag and studied the card. "I can't say for sure, but it looks similar to a card for that phone, yes."

"Objection, Your Honor," Jake said. "The witness is not an expert on what SIM cards look like for each phone or even if this is Mrs. Stevens's SIM card."

Janice turned and spit her rebuttal at Jake. "Mr. McHale, would you like us to call in a representative to testify that this SIM card is for a Motorola smartphone? We can do that, but you're splitting hairs. I'd like to enter this into evidence, Your Honor. This data card was found during the execution of the search warrant of the Stevens' residence. It was found in the toilet. Specifically in the trap."

"I'll allow it, Mr. McHale" Judge Puckett said. "You may have your chance to rebut on cross."

Jake sat swiftly.

"Back to the issue at hand, Officer Davis, what else did you notice?" Janice asked.

"As we were leaving, my partner made an offhand comment about the use of oil soap. Chris said he'd pass it along to Maggie, that she did the cleaning. That was the biggest red flag to us. If she was sick in bed, how could she have recently cleaned the whole house?"

Judge Puckett leaned back in his chair, looking at Jake with raised eyebrows.

"After you left," Janice continued, "what did you do?"

"We went back to the station, wrote up our report. We thought Mr. Stevens was acting a bit strangely, but you never know. People get nervous with the police, even when they're innocent. My partner ran another check on Mr. May's vehicle. We'd put an APB out for it."

"And what did you find?"

"At three a.m. in the morning on June second, Mr. May got a parking ticket for parking in front of a fire hydrant."

"Where was the car parked, Officer Davis?"

"On Maple Street."

"Who else lives on Maple Street?" Janice half turned in Jake's direction with a faint, condescending smile.

"Christopher and Maggie Stevens."

CHAPTER TWENTY

MAGGIE

M AGGIE TURNED THE RUSTED KNOB and pushed open the door. She was hit with the smell of earth and must. The air was thick with dust that danced and sparkled in the shafts of light slanting in from the rear windows. The garage faced the alley behind the house. They never parked in there, but they used the space for storage. File boxes stacked five high contained the organized flotsam of a life half lived. How could two childless people accrue so much? Her bold handwriting labeled the side of each box: *2005, 2006, 2007, Taxes, Insurance paperwork, Chris Probation/Legal.* Stacked between *Cars* and *Bills* was the box she was looking for: *Keepsakes.*

She pulled it down, balanced over her head, until she could squat in the open floor space. She lifted the lid until a gentle resistance made her pause. *This is stupid. Why am I even here?*

She needed to get out of the house. The kitchen reeked of cigarette smoke because she'd given up and let Leon smoke in the house. Thin wisps curled and hovered above the kitchen table like a malevolent cloud, spreading into the living room and up the stairs. She swore she could smell it in her room with the door shut, a constant reminder of how fucked up her life had become. Jake's relentless presence was both comforting and unnerving. His ease in her home, making himself and Leon dinner like she wasn't even there. Half the time he didn't even ask her if she wanted anything. It was like living with an estranged spouse. *And yet.*

The *really* unnerving part came when she'd walk into the kitchen unexpectedly and catch his eye before the veil returned. Once in the hallway, they'd had a chance meeting in the middle of the night. Neither Jake nor Maggie had spoken, his bleary-eyed mumbling and a wave of his hand had been enough, but she chastised herself later for noticing the sloping curve of his bare back. She had to stop herself from trailing a finger down the dip of his spine. She'd spent a lot of her life shutting the door to Jake. Having him there, saving her mess of a life, felt as though the door had been flung open. Her life had been invaded the way a gust of snowy air blew into a fire-warmed house. She spent her nights thinking of Jake's mouth on hers in front of burning embers, his body warm and insistent, and the chilling timbre of Chris's voice cutting through the haze.

She'd written a letter to Chris, long rambling prose begging him to understand that she didn't cheat on him with Logan. She spilled the full story of how she'd met Logan, when, and most importantly, why. Why did she take such a risk with him? She was stupid, and she was sorry. Logan had filled an indefinable emptiness, previously filled with the hope of babies. If she was giving up on babies, she had a lot of free "thinking time," and Chris hadn't been around. Which was no excuse, she knew. But people would do anything to fill the hole created by vanished love. Even if that "anything" was an attentive man with a nice smile. Logan had made her feel whole, like her life wasn't a mess, like she was wanted or needed. She didn't love him, but she'd loved the way he made her feel.

She couldn't find all the right words to explain, and all she could do was pour out her heart. When she'd handed the sealed envelope to Jake to give to Chris, he'd taken it without an expression.

Two days later, she'd asked him, "Did Chris say anything about it?"

He'd shaken his head slowly, holding her gaze.

Were things ever good between her and Chris? She couldn't quite remember how that felt. Which was how she found herself kneeling in the garage in front of a box that held all the happy memories her heart had forgotten. She pawed through it greedily, a tactile inventory of love: letters, cards, little knickknacks that had been squirreled away.

At the bottom of the box lay a scrapbook, its pages falling out and the binding broken. The cover lay at a cocked angle. Chris had clumsily attempted to chronicle their first years with glue-streaked photos that had become faded and yellowed. Maggie hardly recognized herself in them. She passed her fingertips over her wide, carefree smile, her head tilted back in laughter. She was struck by the realization that in every picture, Chris's eyes were fixed on her while she gazed directly at the camera. His smile lifted on the left side, and she was shocked to realize she'd forgotten that his *big* smile—everyone has big smiles and little smiles—was crooked. She hadn't seen it in a while. She tried to pinpoint when he stopped looking at her like that.

In the center of the scrapbook was a dual-page spread of Valentine's Day, a year and a half after they met, and at once, the memory of the day came back.

It had been a surprise. Maggie rode in the passenger seat from Harrisburg to a train station in New Jersey blindfolded, bouncing in her seat like a child. At the train station, he removed the blindfold, kissing her cold lips as the wind whipped around them on the platform. When he told her where they were going, she squealed, jumping and clapping. She *loved* New York! Chris had always claimed to be indifferent because of the smog and the crowds. He preferred the solitude of nature, but Maggie reveled in the busyness of a city, the anonymity of being surrounded by thousands of strangers. Not only had Chris agreed to go, but he had planned it!

As he led her to Central Park, she had realized they were going ice skating. *Ice skating!* "But you can't ice skate!"

Chris had shrugged and gave her his best crooked half-smile. "How hard can it be?"

She had laughed as he wobbled like Bambi around the rink, which thankfully wasn't crowded—which was why one shouldn't skate in Rockefeller Center, she'd always said that. He held on to the side, and later to her, while she spun in the center, a childhood skill she thought she'd forgotten. Her face flushed as she watched him watch her.

He'd pushed off from the side and, using mainly momentum, cut across the ice straight to her, forcing other skaters to circumvent his slow beeline. His arms swung in small circles in an effort to keep his balance. When he finally reached her, he gave her one of his crooked *big* smiles. Standing in front of her, he cupped her face. "God, you're beautiful."

Later, they'd traded in their skates for a hansom cab. Maggie squealed again at the sight of the gorgeous white horse and red velvet seat. She'd never taken a horse-and-carriage ride, but she'd always wanted to. As she clambered in and Chris followed, she gasped.

"What?" His eyes grew wide and concerned.

"This is my date!"

When they'd started dating, in the ways of couples everywhere, she'd rambled about her perfect date—skating in Central Park, a hansom cab ride, and dinner at Tavern on the Green—because after a hansom cab ride, dinner at

Tavern is imperative.

"This is what I said I wanted! Oh my God, you remembered!"

Chris had shrugged with a shy grin. "Just get in. And yes, of course I remembered."

"Then we're going to dinner at—"

"Tavern. Where else?"

She had laughed because when she initially told him of her dream date, as clichéd and unoriginal as it was, he'd scoffed. *Why do you need an expensive dinner at an overpriced restaurant to call it romantic?*

As the horse clopped off down the street, she'd nuzzled up to Chris, kissing his cheek. The soft stubble scratched her chin, and she knew for certain that she would never love him more than she did *that second.* He patted her knee and nudged her away with his shoulder, distracted and distant. She chattered on and on about the horse, New York, skating, and what they should order. The streetlights glittering on the soft snow blanketing the park created city diamonds, wealth beyond measure. Chris fell silent, brooding in the way he sometimes did.

Exasperated, Maggie had thrown up her hands. "What is wrong with you? When I imagined the perfect date, I also imagined both people wanting to be there. Isn't this romantic to you?"

He'd looked pained and tugged on his ear. "Well, it is, but I didn't think this through, really." He pulled out a square box and set it gently on her thigh. "I wanted to get down on one knee but there's no room. Plus... we're moving..."

Maggie could scarcely breathe, and at the same time, her insides melted. He looked like a boy who'd lost his baseball, and she couldn't help but giggle, her hand clamped over her mouth. He slid the ring onto her finger, and she found that she couldn't stop laughing. She leaned forward and kissed him.

With her lips still on hers, he'd asked, "Are you going to say yes?"

She'd giggled. "Are you going to ask?"

"Will you marry me?"

"Yes."

Once they'd tumbled from the carriage onto solid ground, she'd whispered, "Screw Tavern. Let's get a hotel room."

"I already did."

They had stood kissing in the center of Union Square, his coat wrapped around her and her hands curving around his waist, tugging on the heavy cable of his sweater. They were vaguely aware of the sounds of the city, the drifting snowflakes, and the far-off music of a street accordion player. He led her to the Plaza, with all its brass and gold opulence, and she gasped. She'd never seen so much marble in one place, white and glowing under the lights of an enormous chandelier. A grand staircase led up to a brass balcony emblazoned with the world famous back-to-back double Ps. They were Scott and Zelda, or she was Eloise, or Holly Golightly. She felt flung backward in time to the twenties, infused with the glitz and the glamour of the Plaza's heyday. She wanted a cigarette holder and a gimlet.

"I thought you said romantic didn't have to be extravagant!" she'd teased.

"No, but it helps, right?" He'd flicked his credit card across the marble gold-veined counter with the casual disregard of a person accustomed to wealth, as if he'd done it a hundred times before. Only Maggie noticed the tremor in his hand.

In the elevator, she'd shifted on her feet, practically dancing with want. She impatiently ran her hands down his back, under his sweater. She kissed the back of his neck, his hair wet with melted snow, and he laughed and wriggled away, fumbling with the card key. When he flung open the door, she was temporarily stunned. The room was dominated by a king-sized bed with a gold-leaf headboard.

She'd shoved him back on the bed, yanking at his clothes as though she couldn't get to the warmth of his flesh fast enough. Afterward, they ordered room service and answered the door wrapped in towels, laughing and giggling like oversexed teenagers. They lay on the bed eating shrimp and butter, talking about their future kids and calling each other *Mr. and Mrs.* They said they'd go back there on every Valentine's Day. They pinkie swore they'd never become old married folks, they'd eat shrimp and butter together every year, and their kids would roll their eyes and call them disgusting. The idea of a warm, inviting, loving home, where affection was given freely and there were no limits on kisses, was foreign to Maggie. She wanted that the way a starving man wanted bread.

But the memory that stuck with Maggie the most was lying under the covers with a sleeping Chris and calling Miranda to tell her the news. Miranda's voice was steeped in relief and something Maggie couldn't discern. She'd handed the phone to Jake who said simply, "I'm happy for you, Mags." He always used to call her that.

But his voice had cracked on her name, and when she hung up, she felt the first pinprick in her balloon of happiness, the elation seeping out like a slow leak.

<hr />

MAGGIE RAN HER FINGERS OVER the pictures, the few they'd taken. A close-up of her hand shoved into the camera lens, a self-portrait of their kiss on the carriage—her left hand placed strategically on his cheek. Before they'd left their extravagant hotel room, she insisted on making the bed just as it was when they came in—not that she could remember it—and taking a picture. They'd always try to get the same room, she had declared with vehemence, and she even stuffed the list of phone numbers into her purse so they wouldn't forget. She traced the seven-ten with her fingertips and smiled.

They'd never gone back, not once.

She pushed up on her haunches and scanned the boxes, knowing and yet not acknowledging what she was looking for. She saw the carton in the corner, buried under four other boxes, labeled *Maggie College*. She studied the four boxes on top, gauging their weight, though it wouldn't have mattered if they were all labeled *Rocks*. She hefted the boxes around, like one of those kids' missing-square puzzle toys, until she could grasp the handles of *Maggie College*. She set it on the floor next to *Keepsakes*.

Maggie College mostly consisted of photo albums of crazy parties with her roommates, and she moved them aside. At the bottom, she found the netted red fabric of an old lacrosse jersey. She snatched the jersey up and heard the hard *thump* of something heavy hitting the bottom of the box. She closed her eyes and inhaled the faint scent of sweat and tears and, so faint it could have been imagined, Jake. She was transported back to college, cheering from the sidelines as her boyfriend jogged onto the field.

For the first time in weeks, her shoulders unclenched and her heart loosened. For a moment, she was sure that when she opened her eyes, she'd be in the thick of a cheering crowd and the biggest fear in her simple life would be an unwanted pregnancy. She kept her eyes closed and lay down, using the jersey as a pillow. Her tears fell freely then, and she mourned the Chris she'd never again know and the Jake and Maggie that never were.

She mourned the decisions she'd felt forced into but accepted as her own, from giving Logan her phone number to bringing the vase down on his head. As her sobs subsided, she felt a strange peace, a heavy resignation. The only one way off the train, out of that mess, was to confess everything to Jake and accept responsibility for her role. She pushed her face into the red nylon, drying her cheeks, and sat up. The garage seemed different, otherworldly. She'd entered as one person and would leave as another. Maybe when she walked back into the house, Chris would be there and Jake would be gone. A *Twilight Zone* episode, a skipped-track reality.

She folded the jersey and peered into the box. Maggie blinked in disbelief at the thing lying diagonally at the bottom. What she was seeing was illogical, but her mind clicked with recognition. After all, it had been her favorite wedding present, a gift from Mika—a leaded crystal Lenox vase.

CHAPTER TWENTY-ONE

CHRIS

JAKE TAPPED CHRIS'S ARM ONCE and, without looking at him, pushed himself up from his chair. He took the podium and adjusted the microphone in one smooth motion. Officer Davis eyed him warily, his right eyebrow slightly arched.

"Officer Davis, one of the first things you did was run Logan May's cell phone records? Why is that?" Jake asked.

"Yes, we did that before we even visited the Stevens residence. We were hoping we'd see some activity that could help us could locate Mr. May either using triangulation or a leadoff of who he contacted."

"And who did he contact?"

"Well, that was the funny part. No one, except for Ms. Stevens."

"What about who had called him?" Jake asked.

"Pardon?" Davis cocked his head to the side.

"Did you look at incoming calls?"

"We did. But they wouldn't indicate if Mr. May was alive or not. All the calls on the record were one or two minutes, indicating that they were unanswered."

"But did you track down who had called him?"

Jake asked.

"You mean each individual number?"

"Yes, Officer Davis. Each. Individual. Number."

"No, we ran the numbers and came up with names, but there was no suspicious activity."

"'No suspicious activity.' What exactly does that mean?" Jake tapped a pencil on the podium, making a light steady beat on the wood.

"Well, uh, just no one who seemed suspicious." Davis looked annoyed, his prominent lower lip twisted as he spoke.

"Did anyone who called Mr. May have a record?"

"Not on the day he disappeared," Davis said.

"What about the other days?"

"Well, we didn't run the criminal records of every phone call he'd ever received."

"Why not?"

"What do you mean, why not?" Officer Davis leaned forward and adjusted his microphone. On the *not,* his voice boomed through the courtroom. He looked at Judge Puckett for help. "Look, what is that med school expression? When you hear hoofbeats, don't look for zebras."

"Right. So you found a few dozen calls and texts to Maggie Stevens and a husband with a violent record."

"Well, yeah. It would be shoddy work to not check it out. So we did, and then all the lying started."

"We'll get to the lying, Officer Davis, bear with me. What about all the other callers? Did you *ever* check them out?"

The officer sat back in his chair and narrowed his eyes. Chris fixed his gaze on the back of Jake's head. He found himself, for the first time, watching Jake with awe. Jake leaned against the podium, casual and off the cuff. His blasé attitude somehow increased the tension.

"Not all. No. It no longer seemed pertinent," Davis said.

Jake let the statement hang in the air, and he shuffled papers. The silence stretched out, a long, tight triangle between Jake, Janice Farnum, and Officer Davis.

Janice stood. "Your Honor, is Mr. McHale done with his questioning or are we going to sit here all day?"

"Is that an objection, Ms. Farnum? Because I don't think there's a grounds for time wasting," Judge Puckett snapped. He looked over his glasses at Jake. "Although it's my job to move things along here. So, Mr. Philadelphia, please *move things along.*"

Jake snapped up a piece of paper, as though he'd finally found it, and Chris almost laughed. He had no idea if whatever Jake was looking for had been truly lost or if it had been a ploy.

"Officer Davis, do you know the name Marcus Walton?" Jake asked.

The officer sat a little bit straighter, and his jaw jutted out. "Yes. I know of Marcus."

"Who is he?"

"Marcus Walton is a bookmaker."

"How do you know him?"

"What do you mean how do I know him? I'm a beat cop downtown. It's my job to know the criminals," Davis said.

"So Marcus Walton is a criminal."

"He's done a few rounds in county, sure."

Jake sighed. "Officer Davis, I can pry this out of you one sentence at a time and we can annoy the judge, or you can tell me what you know."

Judge Puckett leaned forward and peered into the witness box. "I'd just talk, Davis. I'm hungry."

There were a few snickers from the gallery.

"Okay, yeah, I know Marcus Walton," Davis said. "He's the biggest bookie in Harrisburg. Probably in the tri-county area. He's in and out of jail. He never seems to get caught with enough to do any serious time, but he's got a band of guys who break legs and whatnot for him. He's also got someone on the payroll who moves cocaine around for him. We don't know who, exactly."

"So, not a nice guy then." Jake waved his right hand in a circle.

"No, not a nice guy." Officer Davis shifted in his seat. He crossed his ankle over his leg and changed his mind when his knee banged the banister.

"Did you investigate Mr. Walton when looking into Mr. May's disappearance?"

"No, of course not. There was no connection between Walton and May."

Jake snapped up the stack of loose papers and strode toward the witness box. He handed the paperwork to Officer Davis and pointed at specific pages with his pen. "How many times do you see the highlighted number?"

Officer Davis flipped through the papers, his lips moving as he counted. "Seventeen."

"Seventeen times in how long?"

Davis flipped back and forth between the stack of pages. "It looks like two months."

Jake handed him another sheet. "According to the report in front of you, who does AT&T report having that phone number?"

Officer Davis stared at the page.

Chris wiped his palms on his pants. *Come on, answer the damn question.*

"Marcus Walton," Davis said.

"I'll ask you again," Jake said. "Did you investigate Walton when looking for May?"

That time, Judge Puckett let the long silence sit undisturbed.

Officer Davis narrowed his eyes, and Chris was pretty sure he'd lost all of Davis's sympathy. "No. We didn't."

Jake walked back to the podium and shuffled through more paperwork. He pulled out a second stack of documentation and approached the witness stand. Officer Davis slumped slightly.

"Can you tell me what this is, Officer Davis?" Jake asked.

"It looks like a bank statement." Davis thrust the paper back at Jake, but Jake made no move to retrieve it. Davis's hand hung out over the top of the witness box, waving the page like a white flag.

"Can you tell me the dollar amount in the blue highlighted rows?"

"Fifteen hundred dollars, cash withdrawal."

"And the withdrawal date?" Jake asked.

"Of what month?"

"Every month, Officer Davis. Do I have to spell it out for you? It's the same day every month. What's the day?"

"The twentieth."

"Do you know why he withdrew this every month?"

"I don't know. Rent, probably."

"Officer Davis, what day do you pay your rent?"

"I own a house, Mr. McHale."

Jake let out a puff of air, rolling his eyes.

Janice stood again. "Objection, Your Honor. I've let a lot go here, given that it's a preliminary hearing, but for God's sake, what could the relevance of this be?"

"Well, it seems to me that Mr. Philadelphia is making the argument that Mr. May wasn't paying rent. Is that right?" Judge Puckett asked.

Jake nodded but tossed a quick sideways grin at Chris. "Yeah, but I was hoping *I* could make the argument, Judge."

"Oh, right. The grandstanding I abhor. Carry on, but make it quick."

Jake retrieved the paperwork from Officer Davis and returned to the podium. "The question still stands, Officer. What day do you pay your mortgage?"

"The first of the month," he answered reluctantly. "But that doesn't mean anything. It's not impossible that it's rent."

"No, you're right, he could have made arrangements with his landlord." Jake approached the witness chair with yet another piece of paper. "What is the amount on the copy of this cleared check?"

"Eight hundred and seventy-five dollars."

"And what is the date on the check?" Jake asked.

"The thirtieth of April."

"And what's on the memo line?"

Officer Davis studied Jake, his face a mixture of hate and defeat. "'May rent.'"

"So what is the fifteen hundred for?"

"We have no idea," Davis said.

"Did you look into it?"

"No."

Jake picked up the same two stacks of paper, one in each hand, and approached the witness chair. He handed them both to Officer Davis, who still held the paper from earlier.

"Officer Davis, can you please look at the blue highlighted time on the phone bill? Can you tell me the date and time of the call?" Jake asked.

"February twentieth, 3:17."

"Okay, thank you. Please look at the bank statement. Can you tell me the date and time of the blue highlighted item?"

"February twentieth, 3:25."

"So does it seem like a fair assessment that Mr. May received a call from Mr. Walton and then, eight minutes later, withdrew fifteen hundred dollars from the ATM?"

"It seems possible, yes. But the two could have no connection at all. I'm sure in that eight minutes, Mr. May did many things that weren't connected to the call from Mr. Walton."

"But what was that expression, Officer Davis? Something about hoofbeats and zebras?" Jake tapped his chin, his eyes toward the ceiling.

"I get the point, Mr. Philadelphia. Move it along!" Judge Puckett bellowed.

"Officer Davis, you testified that Mr. Stevens seemed fidgety and nervous. How so?"

"He just *looked* like he was lying. Looking at the ceiling or the floor, fidgeting in his seat. When my partner asked him about his honeymoon picture, he practically jumped out of his seat. Then we found out later he *was* lying. More than once. Why would he lie if he wasn't guilty?"

"Are you asking me, Officer Davis? Because I think if I had a record and thought the police would try to use me to close an easy case, and I'd got into a fist fight with a guy who'd gone missing, yeah, I think I'd lie."

"Objection, is that a question?" Janice's voice boomed through the room.

"Mr. McHale, is that a question?" the judge asked.

"No. Apologies, Your Honor." Jake turned back to Officer Davis. "Let me rephrase this. If you thought you had no way out, you had a record, you'd been in a physical altercation, would you lie?"

"No, I would never lie to the police. It's our *job* to investigate. If there was a legitimate reason for Mr. May's visit and he left there alive, then Mr. Stevens should have communicated that. We're not in the business of accusing innocent people, Mr. McHale. We would have looked into his answer, substantiated it, *investigated it.* Just because he was at their house doesn't mean we would assume the defendant was guilty."

"But, Officer Davis, that is exactly what you did!" Jake leaned forward, pointing at Officer Davis. "You never bothered to investigate anyone past my client. You said, 'Here is a man with a violent record. Here is a man with a motive. Here is a man with a troubled marriage.' Those facts alone incriminated Christopher Stevens."

"Objection, Your Honor. Is there a—" Janice stood. The volume of her voice matched Jake's deep resonance.

"Yeah, yeah, withdrawn." Jake took his seat, tossing

his legal pad on the defense table with a roll of his eyes. To Chris, he gave a surreptitious wink.

"Officer Davis, you may step down. Ms. Farnum, after lunch, who is your next witness?"

"The people will call Detective Small to the stand."

CHAPTER TWENTY-TWO

MAGGIE

HATE WAS AN EMOTION SHE was unfamiliar with. But lately, her blood rolled through her veins as though it was boiling, making her hot and uncomfortable. She found herself gripping objects—a pot or a spoon, a pen, her sunglasses—with a manic tightness, her knuckles white and her fingers stiff. She'd walked through a doorway and banged her elbow, and she turned and slapped the door frame. When the bruise came, it wasn't on her arm but her palm—ugly purple splotches, like the hate was seeping out.

She'd taken the vase from its hiding spot in the garage. She noticed the small chip on the lip, a smear of deep brown along the edge. It fit perfectly in a shoebox that used to hold a pair of soft camel leather Max Azria boots that Chris had bought her for Christmas.

She shoved the box to the back of her closet and stuck the boots under a pile of sweaters. Her mind hummed with possibilities and questions. Why hadn't the police found it during the search? Why had Chris kept it?

The vase was supposed to be wrapped in the tarp under two feet of earth and cement and a burgeoning Texas

Roadhouse. But Chris had removed it—why? There was only one answer: *in case.* In case Chris was found guilty, or got in trouble, or whatever he'd thought about at the time; his get-out-of-jail-free card was the vase. The vase with her fingerprints. She thought back to that night, about Chris setting objects around the room like a game of chess, Logan's body skewed sideways on the living room floor as she sat, numbed and apathetic, on the sofa. He'd worn gloves the entire time. Was that planned?

When Maggie thought about it, hate flushed her face and blurred her vision. Not that Chris would want to get out of jail or that he would want to use the vase as evidence of his innocence, but that he was so willing to leave Maggie to fend for herself. She'd been saying from the beginning, "Let me tell the truth."

He had been adamant, and she'd thought it was to protect her. Well, truthfully, protect both of them. They were in it together. But if Chris owned up to burying the body, that surely carried a lesser sentence than murder. *Murder!* That's what she would be charged with. *Like a common criminal!*

On the third day of the hearing, Maggie didn't want to go to court. The stress of the hearing, her anger at finding the vase, pushed down on Maggie's chest like a fifty-pound weight. She'd been waking up at two in the morning, sometimes three—when she could sleep—to vomit her fear into the toilet.

Jake stopped in the hallway that morning, glancing at the front door and back at Maggie. She lay curled on the sofa, a warm, hours-old tumbler of whiskey in one hand. He seemed to be weighing his options —be late to court or save his sister-in-law's life.

He sighed and rested his briefcase against the railing. "Maggie, it's not a jury, but it still matters. The judge is human. If you're not there, that's akin to saying you believe Chris to be guilty."

Jake sat on the edge of the couch, his elbows on his knees, his hands laced together—the unabating defense attorney. A faint rhythm pulsed behind Maggie's eyes from the sleepless night and the liquor, and she struggled to sit up. The dark gray morning cast a bluish glow, and she studied Jake's profile—the soft pulse at his throat, the curve of his ear along his hairline. When he turned to look at her, his normally veiled eyes held such compassion, she thought she might fall to pieces.

"I can't, Jake. I can't go sit in that room and stare at the back of his head. I think I'll punch him—how will that look?" She tried on a wry smile, but her face felt stiff and unnatural.

"Do you want to talk about it?" He glanced almost imperceptibly at his watch.

Maggie sighed. "No. Yes. But not with you. I can't with anyone." She traced patterns in the throw blanket, large swirled stitches with her index finger, mesmerized by the motion. When Jake's hand moved over hers, the warm softness felt like a woman's palm to Maggie. The untouched smoothness of a lifetime of office work and manicures—callous free and velvety—made Maggie wince inwardly. It felt obscene.

"I can't turn it off, Maggie."

Her heart stopped, she swore it did. She mouthed, "What?" Fear of the answer trapped her voice in her throat.

He tilted his head. "The defense attorney in me. I can't turn it off. If what you're feeling will hurt Chris's case, you can't tell me. But it affects me, too. I want to make sure you are okay. Are you okay?"

She nodded even though she wanted to shout, "No! I am not okay!" She was fairly certain she'd never be okay again.

The world felt sideways: her husband an enemy, her sister barely an ally, her parents strangers. Even Mika had vanished. The only one there and just as he appeared to be was Jake. Maggie rested her cheek on her knee and rocked. The swaying motion provided comfort, like the hushing of a colicky child. When Jake tipped her face up and stared into her eyes, Maggie felt the slip of reality. She leaned forward and kissed him.

His mouth moved under hers, almost as though he were speaking. The cold metal of his watch slid along her collarbone as his hand curved around her jaw. His fingers worked gently through her tangle of hair, and his suit jacket made a soft swoosh as he moved closer.

Jake found common sense first. "Maggie, Maggie." He pulled away and stood. He stopped halfway across the room. "That never happened, okay?"

"Jake, wait, please come back?" She sounded pathetic, her voice small and desperate.

He didn't turn around. "Please, if you can, come to court. For *Chris*." He ducked through the doorway, his footsteps clipped and official on the tile floor. The soft click of the front door, the whispering finality of isolation, echoed back to the living room.

AT ELEVEN, MAGGIE DRAGGED HERSELF off the couch. Court would break from eleven thirty to one. Jake wanted to abandon her too? That was *fine*. She would, and could, stand on her own two feet. She would be *just fine*. She was the *ice queen*, after all. She never asked anything from anyone. Never mind that at the moment, there seemed to be no one to ask.

On impulse, she picked up her phone and dialed Mika's number. The phone rang four times and went to voice mail. She hung up without leaving a message. She pressed the pads of her thumbs into her eye sockets, staving off a persistent headache.

By the time she climbed into the car, she had to temper the instinct to keep driving. To take the interstate west and stop when she hit Nevada or California. Or maybe stop somewhere in the great Midwest, a large expanse of country whose states she couldn't identify on a map. To become anonymous, *invisible,* like she'd felt her whole life.

She had tried to explain the feeling of isolation to Chris once, the way it bloomed from her center as though it was a physical part of her body.

He'd laughed at her. "No one who is beautiful is invisible."

She'd countered, "Oh yeah? Walk down Fifth Avenue."

Beautiful women were everywhere, and yet she'd never felt as lonely as she did on the crowded streets of Manhattan. There was a difference between being seen and being *seen.* Frequently, the only time a person was *seen* was when they allowed it. To be *seen,* a person had to reach out, invite someone in. Maggie wore anonymity like an old comfortable bathrobe.

When she was little, maybe ten, Charlene had taken her and Miranda to an amusement park. The other moms wore jean shorts and fanny packs. They talked, smoked cigarettes, and drank Snapple in tight circles. Their baby strollers bumped together while gooey baby hands slapped at each other across oversized food trays. Charlene stood back with a frozen smile, ever polite. Her short blond bob was sleek and shiny, a stark contrast to the closed circle of frizzy ponytails.

Maggie remembered being embarrassed by her mother's Ann Taylor, sailor-inspired ensemble with gold buttons and tasseled shoes, a small nautical pin on her lapel. It was not an outfit for an amusement park. Miranda rode the carousel, choosing a horse on the edge so she could grab the rings. Maggie pressed her back against a stationary bench, terrified that her sister would fall and get sucked under the spinning platform. She envisioned Miranda's body bloodied and maimed to the brass soundtrack of carnival music. She felt frozen with fear.

Later, Maggie approached the wide-open clown mouth at the Fun House with all the trepidation of a gangplank

199

walker. She studied herself in the mirrors—her fat self, her skinny self, her upside-down self—looking for *something*. She pretended to laugh just to see if it was as fun as all the other kids made it seem. She stumbled through the rolling barrel, feeling along the sides for support. On the other side of the barrel, before the giant wooden slide, was a roped-off hallway and, at the end, a closed metal door. She slipped under the velvet rope and gave the door a quick pull. It gave way, opening with a whispered creak. She hunkered down in the supply closet, between buckets and mops, and felt a surge of overwhelming relief. The door shut behind her, and the sickening smell of sugar and popcorn abated. She rested her head against the wall and slept.

When the police banged open the door, hours later, Maggie startled awake. "We found her! She's here!"

Maggie only remembered her mother's face, frozen in a silent *Oh!* and the feel of her arms, thin and spidery, wrapped around Maggie from behind as she kissed her hair and thanked the police. Maggie was sure her mother had said the appropriate phrases, asked the standard question. *I was so worried! Why did you hide? Are you okay?* But the only thing Maggie could remember her saying was, "Do you know they shut the park down looking for you? I have never been so humiliated."

At the time, she didn't know what *humiliated* meant. For years, she thought it meant *scared* or *worried*. In fifth grade, she opened her vocabulary book to discover it simply meant *ashamed*.

"So THE BIGGEST ISSUE, AS I see it, Detective Small, is that you and your partner never found Mr. May's body. Is that right?"

Maggie snuck into the courtroom, hugging the back wall, and made her way to the front. She had missed

Detective Small's testimony. Jake was at the podium for cross-examination already. Maggie sat behind Chris and was surprised to discover the hate had waned. She studied the back of his head. His hair was longer and curled above his green shirt collar. She didn't know anything about his life in prison. He still hadn't answered her letter, and he'd never made an attempt to call her. Their lives were out of control, and her moods swung wildly. Not even an hour earlier, she could have easily driven away, the hate choking her out. Now, she sat on her hand to keep from twirling a silky black curl around her index finger. She lightly tapped his shoulder, but he made no move to acknowledge the touch.

"No. We have yet to find the corpse." Detective Small was composed and professional, almost cool, and not the least defensive. Really a perfect witness. Her hair was pulled back into a glossy knot, blond and streaked. Her face was small and pinched, as if all her features were crowded into too small a space. She was pretty in a kindergarten-teacher way.

If Maggie had to bet money, she'd guess that Small didn't drink. Maggie could smell the whisky wafting from her own pores.

"*If* there is one. Do you have the murder weapon?" Jake asked.

Maggie gave a little gasp, and her heart raced. For a brief, senseless second, she wondered if Jake had rifled through her closet. Too late, she realized that she had nothing to do with the line of questioning.

"No, but we have a missing vase."

"So you have a *possible but missing* murder weapon?" Jake asked.

"We don't know, Mr. McHale. Mr. Stevens changed his story so many times, we think this is yet another lie. He claims his wife broke it. During questioning, she stated he must have broken it the night of the altercation. No one can find it." She sucked her teeth.

"Your Honor, I'd like to request that be stricken from the record citing spousal privilege. Maggie's statement to the police cannot be used against her husband."

"Mr. McHale," Detective Small continued, speaking over Jake's objection, "that doesn't change the fact that it was yet *another* lie. Or an inconsistency, at least. One in a string of many—"

"Detective Small, please answer the questions with information from only Mr. Stevens's statements. *Not* Mrs. Stevens's. Is that clear?" Judge Puckett leaned forward.

She sat back, her mouth set in a firm line.

Jake asked, "Do you normally arrest a suspect without a body?"

"It is done, Mr. McHale. But no, not normally. In this case, there was overwhelming circumstantial evidence."

"Right. Tell me about the circumstantial evidence."

"Well, there was Mr. May's handprint in the Stevens's living room. In Mr. Stevens's initial questioning, he claimed he had never seen Mr. May before. When we brought him in for questioning, he changed his story and admitted that Mr. May had been in his living room. Later, he changed his story a third time, claiming he and Mr. May engaged in a physical altercation in his home."

"Either the second or third version accounts for the handprint though, correct?"

"Well, yeah, but there was so much lying, we don't know exactly what happened." Small smiled sweetly, all dimples and cherry Chapstick.

"Let's talk about the truck," Jake said.

"We found traces of blood in the bed of Christopher Stevens's truck. It was swabbed and sent for blood typing and DNA. It came back as a blood type match for Logan May—B negative."

"B negative? What about DNA?"

"We were unable to obtain a usable DNA profile," Small

said. "The truck appeared to have been recently washed, and the sample was denatured. We did obtain the blood type, though."

"What does that actually tell us, though? Blood type isn't definitive evidence, is it, Detective Small?"

"No, of course not. B negative is the second rarest blood type. About one percent of the population in the United States share it."

"One percent of the population? What's the total United States population, roughly three hundred million people?"

"Something like that," Small said.

"So Logan May shared a blood type with about three million people. So one of three million people's blood was in that truck bed?"

"Well, it wasn't Christopher Stevens's blood, Mr. McHale. Mr. Stevens's blood type is O positive."

"Still, those are odds I wouldn't bet on. Did you examine the truck itself?"

"We did," Small said. "There were no fingerprints, blood, or DNA consistent with Logan May in the truck interior or anywhere else on the exterior. The blood traces were found in the back of the truck bed, closest to the cab. The rear window was cracked."

"Did you examine the window?"

"We did. It was a spider-web crack, like someone had hit it with an object. It was concave, as though the blow had come from the outside."

"Could you determine when or how this crack had occurred?" Jake asked.

"We could not. Over time and with exposure to heat and cold, the edges of cracked tempered glass will fracture, which is visible under a microscope. Pieces of the broken window were examined under magnification and appeared intact, indicating the break was fairly recent."

"But you could not determine if the glass was cracked two weeks ago, or say, with a baseball bat the early morning of June second?"

Detective Small looked surprised and then gave a small smile. "No. That we couldn't tell you."

Jake approached the witness box with an eight-by-ten photograph. "Judging by this picture, could you tell if the glass was cracked by a baseball bat?"

Detective Small slightly rolled her eyes but took the photo and studied it briefly. "No, we have no idea how it was broken."

"But it *could have* been a baseball bat?" Jake persisted.

"It *could have* been anything." Detective Small cocked her head to the side.

"Answer the question, Detective. Could it have been a baseball bat?"

"Sure. Of course. It could have been a baseball bat."

"Could you determine the angle of the object that hit the window?" Jake asked.

"We actually could. The center of the splinter was angled slightly down, indicating the object struck the rear window from about a twenty-five degree angle, give or take."

"So is it possible that whoever broke the window was standing in the truck bed?"

"It's *possible,* yes. Not definitive."

"So let me tell you an alternate theory. Logan May visits the Stevens' residence, intoxicated. Mr. Stevens answers the door, and Mr. May forces his way into the house, into the living room, where the two of them have a verbal exchange resulting in a physical altercation. Mr. Stevens strikes Mr. May and gives him a bloody nose. Mr. May leaves the house, retrieves a baseball bat from his car, and strikes the rear window of the truck, breaking it. In the course of doing so, he leaves traces of blood from his bleeding nose in the truck bed. Again, does the theory seem possible?"

"It seems far-fetched, Mr. McHale. I mean, where's this

bat?" Small tilted her head and gave a quick flick of her wrist, like the theory was too preposterous to be anything but dismissed.

"Where's the wallet? The phone? For that matter, where's Logan May?" Jake gave a quick snort.

Farnum stood. "Objection. These are speeches thinly disguised as rhetorical questions. I've let it go on far too long, Your Honor."

"Stick to the facts, McHale. Ask questions, please," Judge Puckett admonished.

"Detective Small, does the proposed theory account for the evidence, *yes or no*?" Jake said slowly, the floor creaking under his feet.

"Mr. McHale, why would Mr. May climb into the bed of the truck and strike the *rear* window? Doesn't it seem more logical to strike the windshield?" Detective Small's jaw jutted out, and she puffed a frustrated breath into the microphone.

"You can't account for the logic of a drunk man, can you? Does the alternate theory seem *possible*?"

Detective Small took so long to answer that Judge Puckett cleared his throat and Maggie suppressed a smile. "Possible, maybe. But it seems unlikely."

"Does that version of events account for all of your physical, circumstantial evidence?"

"Yes. It doesn't factor in motive and the excessive lying," she said.

"Talk to me about motive."

"Ms. Stevens was having an affair with Mr. May." Detective Small sat up straighter and crossed her legs, folding her hands over her knees.

"Substantiated?" Jake arched his eyebrows and cocked his head.

"We have over a hundred text messages in a month between the two of them. When we searched the house, we recovered the memory card from the trap in the toilet. From that card, we were able to retrieve the messages themselves."

Jake approached the witness chair with a ream of documents. "Detective Small, can you read the highlighted passages?"

Detective Small took the inch-thick stack and paged through it. "All of them?" She looked at the judge.

"Let's start from the beginning and see how far we get, okay?" Judge Puckett amended.

Detective Small took a deep breath. "May second.

"Logan: Why won't you meet me again? Come to the hut.

"Maggie: We'll see, okay? I might go out with the girls on Saturday, it's possible we'll make it there. I'll text you and let you know.

"May fourth. Logan: I'm starving, wanna get coffee?

"Maggie: Logan, its two thirty in the morning, why aren't you sleeping?

"Logan: Too busy thinking of you.

"Maggie: Go to sleep. Go think about someone else.

"May sixteenth. Logan: Come to the hut, everyone is here. I want to see you again.

"Maggie: Logan, I'm not coming down there, we're watching a movie.

"Logan: You and your cheating husband?

"Maggie: He's not cheating anymore. Fuck off, Logan. I'm getting tired of this.

"Logan: Sry, just got jealous.

"Maggie: I'm married.

"Logan: you sure don't act like it.

"Maggie: You're just pissed I won't see you again.

"Logan: Can you blame me? You've got one gorgeous ass.

"Maggie: Good-night, Logan.

"May thirty-first. Maggie: This has to stop, Logan. I told you this, I can't cheat on Chris."

Detective Small turned the last page and squared the stack, avoiding eye contact with Jake. Maggie sat back in her bench, her face hot and the blood in her ears. She couldn't look at Chris or Jake, which was fine because neither of them was looking at her. She lifted her head and met the eyes of Detective Small, gray and reproachful. Maggie kept in her seat only because slinking out would garner more attention.

Wait, Jake had those transcripts for how long? At least a week. She wracked her brain to remember when he said discovery was. The days blurred together. *When he kissed me this morning, what had he been thinking of?*

"So tell me, Detective, does that seem like a consummated affair to you?" Jake asked.

"I wouldn't know, Mr. McHale. It certainly could be."

"So is Maggie purposefully being deceitful in her texts on the off-chance that someone will read them? Even though she deleted them from her messages?"

"We don't know what happened before, after, and in between these text messages."

"The last one was received on May thirty-first," Jake said, "approximately thirty-six hours before Logan left the Tiki Hut for the last time. Are you contending that an affair was established in those thirty-six hours?"

"Mr. McHale, you're splitting hairs. What is this? The Bill Clinton school of defense? What is the definition of an affair? Everyone's answer will be different. That line is determined by each individual couple. Yes, I maintain that this correspondence would have angered a hotheaded man enough to kill his wife's lover, whatever the gradient of the affair."

Maggie sucked in her breath. That was a very, *very* good answer.

CHAPTER TWENTY-THREE

CHRIS

C HRIS LAY ON HIS BACK, staring at the chipped and peeling paint on the high ceiling. The flickering and buzzing fluorescent overheads and the lingering smell of dinner turned his stomach. In the day, during the hearing, he could shell himself—he felt like a Chris statue, devoid of emotion. At night, he'd wake in a sweat hearing Maggie's voice. *What if we get caught?*

During the day, he could sneak glances at Maggie and remain stoic. Her honey hair was pulled back, the pervading yet familiar jasmine scent of her perfume wafting to his table. His wife had become a stranger to him. But at night, he was consumed by all things Maggie. Sleeplessness became inevitable. When she shifted in her seat or sighed or coughed—things he could sense or hear from behind him and slightly to his right—did it mean anything? *How do you feel?* The question was so familiar to him after ten years of marriage. With the murder, it had taken on new significance.

The creak of the bed across the room and the final flicker of lights, followed by blanketing darkness, snapped him out of his reverie. His new cellmate was a quiet man, mid-fifties, and had the sweaty, fleshy smell of an alcoholic. He shook the bed violently, a metallic clattering on the concrete floor that combined with his primal howl. More than once, Chris had summoned the guard, sure the man would die from withdrawal. Their sole conversation, three days ago, had revolved around the one topic Chris had warned Smith to avoid: what they were in for. *Vehicular manslaughter.*

Chris had considered telling the man to hush, giving him the same lesson he'd given Smith, but he thought better of it. After the man's rambling, disjointed account of his accident, he seemed to revert inward and hadn't spoken a coherent word since. After lights out, while the block back-up lights buzzed and hummed, Chris studied the ceiling and thought of Maggie. The man shouted in his sleep about hallucinatory spiders. Chris had bought earplugs at the canteen.

The guard rapped on the bars in the morning, and after Chris was escorted by police car to the courthouse, Jake met him in the hallway. Suited men and women weaved around them, a veritable hub of activity: lawyers, judges, social workers, jurors, and criminals. Chris waited while they removed the handcuffs and snapped on a GPS bracelet. The entire act was demeaning, and the line between contributing citizen and society-draining leech became hair thin. Typically, Jake was perfunctory.

On the fourth day of the trial, Chris broke the mold. "How is Maggie?" He'd been in jail fourteen days by then— including one awful visit with her where his anger had smothered his desire to touch her hand, run his thumb along her palm.

Jake looked up and gave a barking laugh. "About time. She's a mess. But you know that. You've seen her."

"I... I didn't know how to ask, I guess."

"She asks about you every day, do you get that? She asks if you've read her letter. If you wrote her back and gave it to me, and maybe I forgot." Jake's voice was low, his mouth set in a firm, straight line, his fury and disgust suppressed.

Chris clenched his fists, hating his helplessness. Perhaps Jake loved Maggie even more than Chris did. They certainly had history. Chris *hated* how much he needed Jake. He needed Jake to fucking save him, as if he was a child. But *goddamn it,* Maggie was his wife. He didn't need Jake to tell him how to love her. "Fuck you, man. Just get me out of here, okay? And today, tell her I asked about her."

Jake snorted once and brushed past Chris into the courtroom. Chris followed him, watching the back of his head. His black hair was slick, his swagger cocky, and Chris wished he had a snowball.

The creases in her letter had worn dangerously thin, even ripped in some spots, from being folded and unfolded. He studied her beautiful handwriting, so perfectly spaced. It looked like a computer font called *handwriting* rather than actual human handwriting. He ran his fingers over the *L* in *love,* looking for confirmation. *Did she really "love?"* It frustrated the hell out of him, all the words he'd wanted to hear for years, all the *I love yous* and the *I'm sorrys* and just plain *warmth.* Energy that he'd been so long without radiated off the page, and he felt warmer and closer to his wife, twenty-five miles away in a jail cell, than he had in five years. It wasn't that he didn't want to reply. He didn't know how.

"All rise," the bailiff said.

The door to the back of the courtroom opened, and Judge Puckett heaved himself into his chair with considerable effort. His microphone squealed as he adjusted it. "Morning, all. I trust we're ready to begin?"

Jake and Janice replied in unison, "Yes, Your Honor."

"Then go ahead."

Chris was surprised. The judge had started the past

few days off chatty, talking about his coffee or his broken shower, his wife or a phone call from his son. He was generally amiable, a man who loved his job. That day, he seemed short and impatient.

"The People call Randall Richter to the stand."

Randall "Tiny" Richter was a hulk of a man. His bald head gleamed under the courtroom lights. His fitted navy blue suit stretched tight across his shoulders, and his top and bottom halves seemed mismatched. He had the overdeveloped upper body of a gym rat. He took his seat after being sworn in and grinned, revealing a gold-capped canine. Above his crisp white collar swirled the black and red ink of an indiscernible tattoo. Jake tapped his pen as he studied Tiny then scribbled on his yellow legal pad.

Janice approached the podium. "Randall, have you ever been in prison?"

"No."

"Ever been involved in selling drugs?"

"No." Tiny's sigh in the microphone sounded like the whoosh of the ocean.

"Do you have a job?" she asked.

"Yeah, I do auto detailing down at Rim's Body Shop. It's an art form."

"He's a delicate genius," Jake muttered under his breath, and Chris almost laughed out loud.

"Do you drink?" Janice asked.

"Sure, on weekends. I take care of my grandma on Saturdays, so usually I go out Saturday night but not Friday." Tiny smoothed the gleaming skin on the side of his head with his palm.

"And a Boy Scout," Jake whispered to Chris. He lazily pushed himself up. "Your Honor, I *finally* object. Relevance?"

"Your Honor, certain... um... prejudices may apply given Randall's physical appearance," Janice said. "We'd like to head that off by showing that Mr. Richter is, despite his style and look, an upstanding member of society."

Tiny appeared unruffled by the slight and rubbed his clean-shaven jaw.

"We have no problem stipulating that Mr. Richter isn't a thug, Your Honor," Jake said. "Maybe Ms. Farnum should check her prejudices at the door?"

"Everyone, please sit down," Judge Puckett snapped. "I'm not in the mood today. We get it, Ms. Farnum, move along. Mr. McHale, keep your insults to yourself."

Jake sat and shrugged at Chris.

"Mr. Richter, how do you know the deceased?" Janice asked.

"Objection!" Jake half-stood with an irritated eye roll.

Judge Puckett didn't even wait for cause. "Ms. Farnum, please!" His voice exploded into the microphone.

Chris jumped. Janice didn't appear to miss a beat. Jake sat back down, shaking his head.

"Mr. Richter, how do you know Logan May?" Janice asked.

"We went to high school together. We've been buddies since we were kids."

"Was Logan a good guy?"

"Yeah, for the most part." Tiny stretched his arms out in front of him, shaking his jacket into place, and Chris had the distinct impression he could rip the sleeves out if he tried. "He always had women falling all over themselves for him. I think he was a little bit of a player. But he'd never hurt anyone physically."

"Did he have a girlfriend?"

"Besides Maggie? No. He only had eyes for Maggie in the past few weeks. He was blinded by her. It seemed mutual to me."

"How so?" Janice asked.

"They texted all the time. Talked on the phone too, I think. He'd get all moony over her. He had a picture on his phone. She'd sent it to him. One of those self-portrait girl shots where she's looking all 'come hither' at the camera?

Not dirty or anything, but sexy, yeah. I got it, you know? She's a great-looking girl."

Chris clenched and unclenched his fist, stealing a glance at Maggie. Her mouth was set in a hard, thin line. He tried to remember if Maggie had *ever* sent him a picture like that. He wanted to reach across the bar and grab her arm. *You did this.*

"So what did Logan tell you about their relationship?"

Jake tapped Chris's shoulder and stood. "Objection, Your Honor. Hearsay."

Judge Puckett waved him down without even looking up. "Sit down, McHale. It's a *hearing,* not a trial. Stop with your games."

Jake sat, his face slightly reddened.

"You may answer the question, Randall." Janice glanced at Jake with a smug smile.

"Um, he said she was hot for him. That as soon as she could get away from her husband, he would get them a hotel room together."

"What can you tell us about the night of June first into the early morning of June second?"

"Logan and I met at the Tiki Hut for a few drinks," Tiny said. "When I got there, he was hammered. He was texting Maggie, and she wasn't writing back. I guess she hadn't written back for a few days. He kept showing me her picture and asking if a girl sent that kind of picture to him, then she wanted him, right? I kept saying I didn't know. No one ever sent those kinds of pictures to me. I tried to joke about it, but it just pissed him off. I tried to distract him by playing some pool. I let him win, and he seemed to calm down some."

"What happened at the end of the night?" Janice scratched the back of her head with a pen, and Chris envisioned it getting stuck, snarled in the nest of hair.

"Logan decided he was going to see Maggie," Tiny said. "He said he had to know what was going on. I guess I didn't blame him, and I said it was probably a good idea. Then some drunk jerk accused us of hogging the table, claimed he'd put quarters down on the rail and we'd taken them or something. I didn't really understand what he was talking about. He and Logan got into each other's faces, yelling and whatnot. One of the bartenders broke it up. It was close to two anyway, so I dragged him outside to leave. I only live a few blocks from the Hut. We were gonna walk to my place. I thought maybe he'd forgotten about going to Maggie's."

"Did you go to your apartment?" Janice asked.

"No, that guy—the one in our faces before—came running out yelling at us. I had no idea what he was saying; he wasn't making any sense. But the next thing I knew, he swung at Logan, and Logan went nuts. Dropped him. I never saw him like that. He was wild, throwing punch after punch, even though the guy wasn't fighting back. He was lying on the pavement, unconscious. I pulled out my phone and called 9-1-1. When I looked up, Logan was gone."

"Have you seen or heard from Logan since that night?"

"Nope. I've called and called his cell phone. Nothing. Popped into his apartment, fed his cat. No idea what happened to him, but as far as I can figure, he's gotta be dead. What else coulda happened to him?"

Jake half-stood. "Objection, Your Honor. Mr. Richter is hardly an expert on missing persons."

"Sustained. I'll strike that from the record, but, Mr. McHale, there's no jury." Judge Puckett lowered his voice. "But I tend to agree with Mr. Richter. Do you have any further questions, Ms. Farnum?"

"Just a few, Your Honor." Janice gave the defense table a half-turned smile. "Did Logan May gamble?"

"No. Not that I know of."

"Could he have gambled when you didn't know about it?"

"Sure, I guess," Tiny said. "But we've gone to the casino

a few times. I never even saw him play a slot."

Janice bowed her mouth in feigned surprise. "Really? Then what did he do there?"

"He always talked to the waitresses. They recently put in table games, you know, roulette and poker. That's what I like to do, but Logan couldn't be bothered. He liked to sit at the bar, drink, and talk to women."

"Had you ever heard him mention Marcus Walton?"

"Yeah. We knew Marcus a little bit. I wasn't a huge fan of the guy, but Logan knew him better than I did."

"Oh? And why is that?"

"Marcus was Logan's second cousin."

CHAPTER TWENTY-FOUR

MAGGIE

WHEN MAGGIE ARRIVED HOME, THE house was dark. She assumed Jake was out with Leon. In her bedroom, Maggie sank onto the neatly made bed and curled against the white and sage throw pillows on the deep cocoa Matelassé coverlet. Her bedroom was frequently her haven, a place that centered her. In the past two weeks, it had become the place she spent most of her time since her downstairs had been taken over. Hanging on the wall opposite the bed was a sixteen-by-twenty reprint of Andrew Wyeth's *Christina's World.* The painting depicted a woman lying in a barren field and reaching out to an old farmhouse in the distance. Chris had always hated it. He claimed it depressed him. Something about the woman's desperate yet half-hearted stretch toward her home.

Maggie stripped off her heels and stockings and padded downstairs to the dining room. She never ventured in there anymore. Groping the wall, she flipped the switch. Fast food bags and soda cups had been added to the piles of paperwork. A chair had morphed into a tie rack. A small collection of gray and blue Windsor-knotted silk ties hung off the back, and Maggie picked up the top tie. She caressed it and brought it to her nose. Spice and oak. *Jake.*

She eyed the thin manila folders labeled *Tiny, Mika, Detective Small.* The file labeled *Logan May* was thicker. But *Christopher Stevens* was the fattest. A separate folder stacked on top, perpendicular, was labeled *Evidence.* Maggie carefully opened the evidence folder. She paged through the tissue-thin pages, yellow and pink carbon copies of interview sheets, scrawled with official-looking signatures. She moved the *Evidence* file to the table and lifted the front cover of *Christopher Stevens.*

Her husband's whole life had been condensed and confined to a plain manila file folder. She saw a letter from Carmichael Construction listing all the guys on Chris's team and a report detailing the Derek Manchester incident. A glossy photo of Derek was clipped to the front. To her knowledge, Chris had never seen Derek as an adult. He slumped slightly to the left in a wheelchair but grinned into the camera. The combination of sandy blond hair and open smile with straight, white teeth made him attractive. She flipped through all the loose paper—bank statements, credit reports, dry cleaning receipts—until she came to a yellow legal pad filled with page after page of Jake's scrawled handwriting.

Maggie skimmed the notes, most of which were unreadable. Her name caught her eye.

Interview w C.S. 16JUN: Hypothetical: what IF witness, not the murderer? Charge for burying the body vs. Murder? Spousal privilege. Double check on options to testify—Will check. Maggie??

Maggie pushed the heel of her hand into her forehead. Confirmation that Chris was considering telling the truth. She scrambled for the missing piece. She'd been asking, *begging,* to tell the truth since the beginning, and Chris had been adamantly against it. Why? She checked the date. Ten days earlier, he'd approached Jake with the hypothetical situation. Could he testify against her? What about spousal privilege? *He had asked those questions.*

In the beginning of their marriage, Maggie had delivered lunch to Chris on his job sites. His face lit up at the sight of her, and he had confessed that he loved the envy of the guys on his team. Once she'd watched with intense interest as a stone worker split a large slab of limestone. Among the deafening whir of power tools and rumbling construction equipment, he quietly drove steel shims by hand with a hammer. His slow, careful, solitary work was a stark contrast to the guys guffawing at sex jokes. He'd given Maggie a shy smile, and she'd inched closer, watching the sweat drip down his neck in rolling beads. He drove the wedges, six inches apart, until the limestone split cleanly and evenly, like an apple sliced with a sharp knife. Maggie's mouth had watered.

He removed his glove and ran his bare palm along the smooth, newly cut surface. The muscles in his forearm flexed. "There are modern ways of doing this, I guess. But it's hard to argue with the Romans." His voice was low and sensual.

Later, Chris had commented on the interaction. "I'm not blind, Maggie. Men want to impress you. I'm just not a fan of you actually being impressed."

In the dining room, reading Jake's muddled notes, the implications came in waves. To Maggie, it felt like the final shim—that muted groan as the limestone broke apart in a clean, striated plane. Maggie was on one side, Chris on the other. She felt numbness spread down her legs and a cold, invisible fury ran like icy fingers up her spine.

"Maggie?"

She spun around. Jake leaned against the door jamb, his tie pulled loose and the top two buttons undone on his dress shirt. He swayed, and the pungent odor of whiskey stung her nostrils.

"Are you... drunk?" she asked.

Jake snorted softly. "Uh, yeah, you could say that." He

gave a soft laugh and shook his head. His unfocused eyes stared at the mess behind her.

"What's wrong? Are you okay?"

"I dunno, Maggie. You tell me."

Maggie slid the piles of paper back to the center of the table and leaned against the beveled edge. "I don't know what that means. Are we going to lose?"

"Oh no, we'll win. I'm pretty sure we'll win."

"Pretty sure?"

"I'm not worried, if that's what you're asking."

"Then... what's wrong?"

Jake met her eyes, a small smile on his lips. "Well, for starters, your sister moved out."

"Are you kidding?"

"Nope. Says she can't play third fiddle her whole life," he said.

"Who's first?"

"Law."

"Who's second?" Maggie wasn't sure she wanted the answer.

Jake snorted again. "She *says* you."

"That's crazy. We need you here right now to help us, but... this is not a normal situation. She *has* to see that." She held her breath. *He says your name.*

Jake reached out, his eyes holding hers, and her heartbeat thundered in her ears. He reached past her, the thin cotton of his dress shirt brushing her bare arm, and snapped up Chris's file. He stepped back, waving it. "This is privileged information." His breath was hot on her cheek. He sank into the chair next to her, his thigh pushing against her leg.

"You mean it's not covered by spousal privilege?" She hated her snide tone, but it had a life of its own. As she watched Jake rub his two-day beard, she realized she held no anger toward him. He was doing his fucked-up job. His loyalty, by definition and virtue of a paycheck, was to Chris. Chris's loyalty, ironically, also seemed to be only to Chris.

"What I don't get, Mags, is why you're so angry." He tugged at her hand, pulling her inches closer. His voice was soft and his hand was hot, as though he'd been holding a mug of coffee instead of an ice-cold tumbler of whiskey. "Because you did it. Right, Maggie? Chris didn't kill anyone. But *you* did. You're angry. And maybe, what? Scared?"

He laced his hand through hers, his thumb caressing the pad of her palm, and she felt liquid. She shook her head, mouthing, "No."

He pulled on her hand, and she let him until her face was inches from his. "Say it, Maggie. Tell me the truth."

When she kissed him, his mouth tasted like whiskey. He pulled her toward him, and she straddled his lap. The heat from his body rising through his trousers onto her bare thighs ignited her. She tugged at his tie and pulled open his shirt, running her hands up and down his chest. He peeled her shirt up and over her head. In one movement on the way down, he unhooked her bra. His hands ran down her sides, over her breasts, his thumbs sliding over each peak, and she nearly jumped with need.

He slid her skirt up to her waist, lifted her up onto the table, and kissed each inner thigh. The coarse sandpaper of his cheek scratched her skin, leaving it pulsing. His hands skimmed her hips, and he pressed his thumb, softly but insistently, through the flimsy fabric of her panties. He hooked his index finger around the thin film of lace and tugged them down. She watched his eyes, dark and hooded and clouded with want, as his gaze lingered over her body.

She fumbled with his belt, pushed his pants and boxers to his knees, and slid her hands around to his bottom, pulling him to her. His mouth found her breasts then her neck and her ear. His hand got lost in her tangle of hair as he tugged at the base of her neck. She wrapped her legs around him, and for a brief moment, she clenched her thighs and considered stopping. What was happening, or about to happen, would be a betrayal to both Chris and Miranda. But Miranda had never seemed to care much about betraying Maggie.

When Maggie felt him slide inside her, as quickly and easily as though they'd never been apart, she abandoned rational thought. All that existed was Jake, and for a moment, she pretended they were back in college. Before there were consequences, careers, babies, and murders. The act felt easy, freeing, and she moved with him. Her legs tightly flanked his hips, her feet moving slowly up and down the backs of his thighs, and she felt pulled closer to the edge. When his mouth once again found her breast, he laid her back onto the table, pushing aside all the papers and debris. The remnants of real life scattered beneath her, and Maggie arched her back and gasped. Pleasure came in undulating waves, and for those few seconds, Maggie felt only faintly tethered to reality. The most real thing on earth was the weight of Jake's body and the feeling of his back beneath her fingertips, the valley of his spine that she'd longed to touch again for as long as she could remember.

WHEN MAGGIE WOKE TANGLED IN the guest bed sheets, where she'd curled against Jake's back all night, the bed was empty. She checked the bedside clock: seven a.m. He was probably gone, preparing for his cross-examination of Tiny—court started at nine. She gathered the sheets tightly around her and drew her knees up to her chin. The low-level jitters she'd been living with for weeks seemed to have upped their game; her heart raced as if she'd had several cups of coffee already. She felt slick and sticky. The memory of Jake and his weight on top of her pulled tight and sharp in her belly. In a whiskey-induced haze in the wee hours of the morning, Jake's hand had found her breast and she complied, sleepy and wanton. They hadn't used a condom. Maggie had been off birth control for months. After they'd lost the fourth one, their sex life had dwindled. She'd read that the pill could worsen depression, so she'd quit. She never even told Chris.

She sat upright, mentally calculating. *Two weeks. No, four. No, six?* Pulling on Jake's blue dress shirt, she crept out of bed and down the hall, the hardwood cold against her bare feet. The house was still and silent, and she snuck downstairs to her purse. She pulled out her calendar and flipped back and forth through the pages. *Eight weeks?* Had she been that distracted? *Murdering a man will do that.*

She took the steps two at a time, her heart thumping in her throat. She dug under the bathroom sink, emptying the cabinet's contents onto the bathroom floor. She found what she was looking for in the back, behind an aging bottle of Calgon. The box with her remaining two pregnancy tests was yellowed and dusty. She had no idea if the tests were any good, but she remembered from nursing school that there was no such thing as a false positive. She tore the wrapper and, with shaking hands, removed the plastic stick.

As she took the test, she searched her memory for the how, the when. After she'd met Logan? The night she had seduced Chris felt like years ago, the memory as old and yellowed as the box in her hand. At the time, she had hoped that night would be a new beginning, a fresh start. She tried to fix her disdain with love, but she'd felt only the cool detachment of an intangible wish. The hope on his face had broken her heart; she hadn't felt that kind of hope in years. Then his face had looked crestfallen when she sat up and, out of her control, her mind handed her snapshots of Tracy straddling his legs, his lips on her breast. Sometimes, she didn't know what she'd seen and what she'd invented.

Maggie sat on the edge of the tub, balancing the capped stick on her knee, and waited. She pushed her left hand under her thigh, her diamond ring gouging into the sensitive skin, and stared at the oval window. In less than a minute, a purple vertical line. Almost instantaneously, a bright horizontal line developed, forming a formidable cross. Despite the test's age, Maggie had no doubts. Her middle-of-the-night vomiting came back to her in a rush. The feeling of cold sweat dripping down her back in court. All the things she had chalked up to anxiety.

Maggie was two months pregnant.

CHAPTER TWENTY-FIVE

CHRIS

JAKE FLIPPED THROUGH PAGES OF notes on his legal pad, and when Judge Puckett cleared his throat, he glanced up. "May I have possibly three minutes, Your Honor?"

The judge nodded and sat back in his chair, closing his eyes. When Jake stood, the judge made no move to sit up. Jake coughed.

Without opening his eyes, Judge Puckett said, "Are you ready now, Mr. Philadelphia?"

"Yes, Your Honor. I apologize for the delay, and thank the court for your patience."

"Proceed."

Jake approached the podium. "Mr. Richter, who is Emily Masterson?"

Tiny shifted in the witness chair. "She's... uh, Logan's ex-girlfriend."

"An ex-girlfriend? Amicable break-up?"

"No. Are any, Mr. McHale?"

"True. But do most involve a charge of attempted rape and a restraining order?" Jake snapped.

"Is that an actual question? I'm sure Mr. Richter isn't an expert on all relationships, Your Honor," Janice called from the prosecution table.

"I'll rephrase," Jake said. "Did Emily Masterson accuse Mr. May of attempted rape?"

"Yes, but it was bogus. He dumped her, and she was pissed."

"What about the restraining order? It's still upheld, by the way. They generally have a two-year expiration date. Which means that as little as a few months ago, Emily Masterson was still fearful of Mr. May."

"Your Honor!" Janice stood. "Objection. That's not a question either!"

"Mr. McHale, please keep your monologues to yourself." Judge Puckett yawned and nodded to Tiny to answer the question.

"Um, yeah, she had a restraining order against him," Tiny said. "I don't know all the details, but Logan said she was nuts. For a while after they broke up, they kept hooking up. Logan tried to get back together. Then this attempted rape bull. He tried to talk to her a few times—talk some sense into her—then she pulled out this restraining order, and he washed his hands of her."

"So Mr. May had a temper?"

"Well, yeah kind of. I never saw him beat up anyone the way he beat on that guy at the Hut, though. I've actually never seen him fight at all."

"Okay, let's talk about that night. Did the guy Mr. May attacked have friends with him?" Jake asked.

"Yeah, I think so. He was with one guy who hung with me while we waited for the squad. He was okay. A little pissed off."

"What happened to him?"

"What do you mean? Nothing."

"I mean, after the squad came and took his buddy away, where did he go?"

"Oh, no idea," Tiny said.

"Could he have gone after Logan?"

225

"I guess. He didn't seem all that pissed, though. He was like me, kind of. Friends with a hothead."

"But your buddy just put his friend in the hospital. Could he have gone to look for him?" Jake asked.

"Uh, maybe. I really have no idea. I didn't even get his name."

"Okay, Mr. Richter. Before Mr. May fled the scene, did you see him call anyone?"

"No."

"You didn't hear him speak to anyone?"

"No."

"Did *you* call anyone?" Jake asked.

"What do you mean?"

"I mean, did *you* call anyone after Logan fled the parking lot?"

"I called 9-1-1."

"Besides that," Jake said.

"Uh, yeah. I called someone."

"Mr. Richter, who did you call?"

Tiny leaned back against the witness box like a deflated parade float. "I called Marcus. I knew he could help me track down Logan. I went to Logan's apartment to wait for him. The police were looking for him, and I wanted to get to Logan before they did. But Marcus, he knew the cops, you know? He knows everyone in town. I needed him to know that if he saw Logan, he should tell him to come home."

"Was there another reason you called Marcus?"

"I don't know what you mean." Tiny's voice edged up a little higher, almost imperceptibly.

Chris found himself leaning forward.

"Okay, let's try again," Jake said. "Was beer the only substance in Logan May's body that night?"

"Objection Your Honor, this is beyond hearsay," Janice said. "Unless Mr. Richter *saw* Mr. May take another substance."

The judge stroked his chin and leaned forward. "Go ahead, I'll allow it."

"What was the question?" Tiny asked.

"Was alcohol the *only* substance in Logan May's system that night?" Jake said.

Tiny stubbornly folded his arms. His nose twitched. "No. Logan had done a few lines before we went out."

"So, cocaine then?" Jake clarified.

"Yeah. Cocaine."

"Did Logan do cocaine a lot?"

"Uh, I think so," Tiny said. "He was discreet about it, but I think it was more of a problem in the last year or so."

"How many times a week?"

"I'm not sure. Every time I'd seen him lately, I think he was high."

"Did you try to talk to him about his problem?" Jake asked.

"A little, but coke makes guys punchy. I've seen it before. Logan got a little hyper when I tried to bring it up."

"What do you mean hyper?"

"Uh, defensive. He denied being high a lot, but well, I'm not an idiot."

"Do you know how extensive his hobby was?" Jake asked.

"Not really. I asked him how much he was spending on that shit, and he said it was nothing. Like a few hundred a week. Which is a lot of money to me."

"Right. How did he pay for it?"

"Well, he had a job," Tiny said. "He worked at Jiffy Lube doing oil changes. It didn't pay that well, I don't think. But I didn't ask too many questions."

"Do you know the name Winston McInerney?"

"Uh, I don't think so."

"You might know him as Mickey Bricks."

Tiny inspected his hand. "Yeah, Bricks is one of Marcus's jerk-offs."

"Do you know him at all?"

"Nah, I steer clear of that guy."

"Did Logan?"

Tiny went back to his fascinating hands.

He took so long to answer that Jake had to prompt him. "Mr. Richter?"

"No." Tiny sighed. "Bricks was Logan's hookup. Logan was under his thumb."

"Did Logan owe Bricks money?"

"Yeah, I think so. He had a monthly payment schedule going. I don't know if he kept up with it. I think he was in trouble."

"How so?" Jake asked.

"He called me, like, a month ago, begging to borrow two thousand bucks. I let him but said not again. I don't *have* two thousand bucks. That was my grandmother's money."

"Did you tell him that?"

"Yeah. I did."

"And what did he say?"

Tiny sighed. He fixed his gaze on the rear of the courtroom and narrowed his eyes as though the answer would appear engraved across the door. "That if he couldn't pay him back, Bricks would kill him."

<hr />

DURING THE DAY, CHRIS SAT in court with heartburn and a sick, twisted feeling in his gut that only seemed to intensify as the day wore on. He had nowhere to go that was better than that hard wood chair in an oak-paneled courtroom. When Janice stood at the podium, he sat impossibly straight, his muscles aching with tension. Jake was conciliatory. He anticipated Janice's questions every morning and explained what his cross would be. He'd tap Chris's elbow during particularly damning questions, a reminder to relax. But the nights were always the same, and the final bang of the gavel seemed to coil his stomach tighter every day. Chris dreaded the nights with their emptiness.

After Tiny's testimony, Chris returned to prison, and for the first time, the knot loosened. Jake walked with him as far as he was permitted, and when Chris turned to say good-bye, he almost hugged Jake. He knew that it had been a "good day in court" in Jake's book. Jake had a bounce in his step and whistled periodically, until he caught himself and stopped because whistling while walking his client back to lockup was just cruel.

Chris wondered if Jake would stop and have a beer, call Miranda. Did they share victories like that? Chris was half-tempted to call Maggie. He missed having someone to share his day with. Such a silly thing he didn't know he could grieve for—the exchange of mundane details. *Did you call Visa? Wait till I tell you what Ed said.*

In the first airlock, as far as Jake was permitted to walk with him, he gave Chris a quick handshake and a gentle nod. Chris was guided by a guard back to his cell.

The beds lined opposite walls with four feet of space between them. Along the back wall, between the beds, was a toilet and a small stainless steel sink. Everything was stainless steel. Steel and gray. The walls, the floor, the bunks; it was so fucking depressing. Maggie had painted their house in bright, vibrant colors. Chris had forgotten to appreciate it.

His cellmate was curled on his bed, his back to the center of the room. Chris had learned his name was Carl a few nights earlier. As Chris shuffled in, the guard closed the door with a metal-on-metal groan.

Carl turned and spoke, his voice low and gravelly. "Hey, how'd you get a lawyer? I thought we all had PDs."

"Uh, well, he's my brother-in-law, so he's sort of obligated."

"Huh." Carl ran his hand across his forehead and winced. "I bet he's expensive?"

"Well, he's from Philadelphia, not here. I think yeah, probably. But don't worry, we're not paying him his full rate."

"Well, still. Awfully nice of him. At least he cares about you. That's more than most of us in here have."

Chris admitted that was true. Sunday visitations were a bit pitiful. The public defenders who routinely trawled the corridors were pallid with loose-skinned, drawn faces, receding hairlines, and polyester-blend suits in a wrinkled rainbow of khaki. Chris *was* grateful for Jake—his energy and his projection of the belief that he *could not* fail.

Chris wondered then, for the first time, if the truth mattered to Jake. It didn't seem so. It was clear that Chris not killing Logan was of no consequence to Jake— it wouldn't make him work any longer or harder for a dismissal. Jake's true motivations would never fit into a media-savvy sound bite of sanctimonious declarations about the *burden of proof* and *the presumption of innocence* complete with wide sweeping gestures.

When Chris had stood in the doorway of that ridiculously elaborate "cabin" in the mountains of Vermont and watched Jake kiss his wife—and watched Maggie push him off—he realized the only reason Jake had stopped was because Chris had interrupted them.

Maggie had begged Chris not to say anything or to make a scene. "Jake is so drunk. He has no idea what he's doing."

Chris had shaken his head. What would be accomplished by blowing it up into a bigger deal? No life-changing decisions would be made off a drunken mistake of a kiss, except to permanently mar the intricate façade of friendship they'd all spent a decade nurturing. For years, the dynamic among all four of them had been so wrong and yet so deeply ingrained that Chris barely knew to question it.

In the cold, cement hollow of his cell, it was so obvious that their whole relationship, the entire playact of friendship, was fucked up. But even with Chris in prison and Jake and Maggie residing under the same roof, Chris worked to bury the threat. It had been long accepted that *Jake and Maggie* had come first, then *Jake and Miranda,* and last, *Chris and Maggie. Jake and Chris* had fit themselves in among whatever relationship was pulling at the time. They shape-shifted as buddies, as *bros,* giving good-natured jabs with perhaps just a bit too sharp of an edge.

On Chris and Maggie's five-year anniversary, before any babies, before Chris knew to stop questioning the way things were, they'd drunk two bottles of champagne. Before Maggie became violently sick, they lay on their living room floor on a blanket. The remnants of an indoor picnic were scattered around them, their stomachs full of grapes and cheese and bread and pâté.

Chris had asked the question. "Do you still love Jake?"

The question had been met with a silence that swallowed Chris's heart whole. In so many moments in life, silence answered questions that words could not. Maggie was quiet for so long that Chris thought she'd fallen asleep. Despite *needing* the answer, he felt his eyelids droop closed.

Her fingertips had found his in the dark. She pulled his hand to the gentle dip between her breasts, and her heart thumped twice under his thumb. "No."

They had both pretended it wasn't a lie.

Chris saw the lie with the clarity of hindsight, as large and looming as the proverbial elephant. It had always been like that, though. Chris could only think clearly in Maggie's absence. He was logical; he could assess situations, even his marriage. But when they were together, she seemed to fill the room, suffocating him and demanding his attention, an unrelenting force.

Chris recognized the absurdity of that. Maggie had spent her entire life ducking the spotlight, kowtowing to a demanding older sister. On the surface, she commanded no more attention than a common housecat.

And the really messed-up part was he *longed* for her. He felt like the biggest chump. He pulled out that goddamn letter every goddamn day, as if he was some lovesick kid. How could he want someone and be so pissed at her at the same time? Pathetic.

The one time he'd jerked off in prison, quick and surreptitious under the scratchy green blanket—into a white government-issued sweat sock as if he was fourteen again—he was thinking of Maggie. Which was weird because his mental Rolodex at home—usually in the morning shower—consisted of women on television or movies, or the Starbucks barista who gave him free coffee with a smile, or sometimes even a girlfriend from freshman year who used to suck on ice then do a thing with her tongue. But that time, he'd imagined Maggie when she straddled him only a month ago, her skin reflecting the bluish moonlight. Her one hand cupped her breast, the other tangled in her hair, and her eyes were half open and her lips parted.

The problem was, having been away for almost two weeks, the drug of *Maggie's presence* was seeping from his system. In its place was the hard, black-and-white truth Chris could no longer avoid. The pressure Chris always felt when they were together, the soft cluck in her voice, the somewhat imagined rise and fall of her chest whenever he answered a question just *not quite right*—it was all a by-product of her quiet disappointment that he wasn't someone else.

CHAPTER TWENTY-SIX

MAGGIE

MAGGIE HAD BEEN AVOIDING JAKE. She muffled her retching into a trash can if he was downstairs, or she took her time in the shower until she heard him puff with frustration and stomp down to the first-floor bathroom. After a few days, it occurred to Maggie that Jake was also avoiding her. Sleep evaded her, and she stared at the ceiling at night, imagining she could hear Jake's soft snoring.

Pregnant! The whole thing was ridiculous. All she'd wanted for years was a baby. She used to cry at work after a "first doctor's visit" with the infants. She'd take their temperatures and examine their pink, scrunched baby feet, their toes like raisins. The parents would leave, crowing about their perfect baby, and Maggie would lock herself in the ladies' room, lifting her legs up onto the toilet seat to avoid detection. And now she was growing more pregnant each day, but her life was suspended while the rest of the world spun around her. She had a million questions: When should she tell Chris? Jake? What would they do? How would it work? What if Chris lost the hearing? Would he let her come forward? Would he ever answer her letter?

To make matters worse, she was consumed with thoughts of Jake. Blame it on hormones or call it escapism, but it was driving Maggie crazy. *Jake, Jake, Jake.* As if she didn't have better things to worry about. She was overly aware of when he was in the house and when he wasn't. She woke up every single time he went to the bathroom at night, and long after he'd climbed back into bed, she'd stare at the ceiling and feel his hands on her hips, her thighs, skimming the mound of flesh between her legs. God, a person could lose her mind that way.

The night after Tiny's cross-examination, when Jake had looked as if he'd been punched in the gut, when Miranda had moved out and Maggie couldn't decide whether she wanted to comfort him or slap him, she heard him pacing in the living room. She crept from her bed and paused in the hallway, cocking her head toward the sound of low talking. She inched down the stairs, the second step from the bottom groaning even though it never had before. She stood on the hall side of the doorway, cloaked in darkness, with a hand clamped over her mouth.

Jake, mumbling and broken, cried into his phone. "Please come home. I'll be back soon. This is all going to shit, and I don't know if I'll keep the case. I'm too close to it. I can't live without you. Please?"

When she allowed herself a peek around the corner, she saw him, or rather the outline of him, in the moonlit living room. He sat on the floor, his elbows on his knees, holding his head. She listened to his voice crack for an hour.

"I'm sorry. I'll do better, I'll be better." Near the end of the conversation, his tone lifted. "I love you, too."

She crept back up the steps and sat on the cold floor outside her bedroom door. Reality hit her hard and fast. Jake had two options: his estranged wife who wanted nothing to do with him, or Maggie, warm and real and, as far as he was concerned, willing. He still chose Miranda. Despite the pregnancy, Maggie felt rejected.

Maggie waited, with her back pressed against her oak-paneled bedroom door, for Jake to return to his bedroom. She had a fleeting fantasy of holding Jake while he cried on the floor, telling Maggie he loved only her. *Women need to be needed.* Charlene's voice popped in her head. The stairs creaked, and she stiffened.

"Maggie? What are you doing?" His voice was low even though they were the only two in the house. He knelt in front of her. "Are you okay?"

She shook her head, hot tears dammed in place by the bags under her eyes. *I'm pregnant.* She couldn't say that to Jake, or maybe she couldn't say it at all. She knew the confession would bring his final rejection. It would be the final *ker-thunk* of a deadbolt, locking *Jake and Maggie* in the past. She bit the inside of her cheek until she tasted the warm, tangy telltale iron.

"Mags, seriously, what's wrong?" He placed a large hand on her knee, his eyebrows knitted. "You're scaring me."

"Jake, who do you love? Do you even know?" The question popped out. She kept her knees pulled to her chin and watched his face.

He sat back, positioning his long legs on either side of hers. "Truthfully, no."

His candidness surprised her. Maggie nodded and reached out, needing to touch him. He grasped her wrist, a quick defensive move, and held it in an almost parental gesture of admonishment. Her face flushed.

"How is Miranda?" The question sounded snotty, which was an accident. She'd been trying for casual.

He tilted his head, twisting his mouth. "She's at your parents'. Can you imagine? With the kids?"

"Phillip is probably miserable. So much echo in those marble halls..."

Jake snorted. "It's for show. *I think.* I'm pretty sure Miranda doesn't actually *want* to leave me." He ran a hand through his hair.

Who did he love? She wasn't going to let him wriggle out of answering. Jake had spent most of his life dodging hard questions. *Everybody's buddy, Jake.* The hard conversations made that a tough reputation to keep. When one drew lines in the sand, people tended to get pissed. Jake avoided pissing people off like a cockroach avoids light.

"What do you want, Jake? If you could have anything, what would you pick?" *Who would you pick?* Maggie avoided the real question, which was a Jake move. Perhaps they weren't all that different.

"Ah, Maggie. It won't change anything. We're both stuck in the lives we're in, right?"

"Jake, that's the thing. We don't *have* to be."

"Yeah, we *have* to be." He chucked her under the chin. "Doesn't mean you're not the love of my life."

Maggie knew Jake was simply making his life as painless as possible, buffing the rough corners of his relationships down to a soft, easy curve. She resented his spinelessness, hated his weakness. She touched her chin with her thumb. *Too late, too late, too late.* In so many words, she had her answer. Who did he love? He loved Miranda. It was really that simple. She stood and the blood rushed to her head. She left him sitting on the floor in the hallway, and she let the bedroom door shut behind her with a hushed click.

⤙⬦⤚

MAGGIE GAVE UP ON SLEEP long after she heard Jake retreat to his room. The digital clock on her nightstand read 3:10 when she crept downstairs. The déjà vu of standing in her living room, her head cloudy from lack of sleep, in the middle of the night was overpowering. She stared at the mantel and envisioned Logan's bulky frame crumpled on the floor. She scooted to the kitchen, retrieved a glass of water from the tap, and drank it down in one gulp. The dining room was black. From the kitchen, the doorway loomed, dark and alluring. The pull of all those manila folders, all those notes was strong. How much did Jake know about her? About them? Likely, everything.

Maggie flipped the switch on the dining room wall and squinted in the bright light. The table was covered in papers, most contained within creamy yellow files. The pile seemed to have grown tenfold since she'd been in there four days earlier. She shuffled through the mess until she found *Christopher Stevens*. She took her time reading each document, each note. She painstakingly decoded Jake's shorthand, his doctor-like scrawl, until she knew everything Jake knew.

She realized two things: Jake didn't know about Tracy, and he didn't know about the vase. Chris had probably never told Jake about Tracy out of pride. The affair wasn't germane to the hearing, and it suited Maggie just fine to not air *that* particular dirty laundry in court. But the lack of references to the vase in Jake's notes meant that even if Chris had spoken to Jake about being a "witness" instead of a suspect, he hadn't done it with any level of detail. Yet. But it was coming.

Culpability was a funny thing. Although in most situations, the finger pointing went both ways, the truth was generally some variation of *it's complicated*. Maggie thought about Chris rolling up that fat, foul tarp, digging a hole in the dark, wiping sweat from his brow, heaving the gravel back on top, smoothing out Logan's very existence. Had he doubted himself? Impossible to tell.

She knew, deep down, had they called the police—had Chris listened to her instead of blindly forging his path, expecting her to trail behind him like the dutiful wife— their entire nightmare would be over. Maggie would be making pepper steak out of Gale's cookbook, and Chris would be banging through the front door, his work boots caking mud all over the house. She might have killed

Logan out of fear and desperation, but when it came down to it, who was more *culpable*?

Maggie's fingers trembled as she shoved paperwork back into folders, trying to reorder her mess. She thought of the baby. If it lived—and she barely allowed herself to think about the possibility of it living—would one of its parents be in prison? Would she take an infant to that dank, clammy visitors' room? She tried to envision herself with a wailing baby boy, a pacifier dangling from his onesie and a trail of white spit-up on his chin. Would she bounce him on one knee while she made small talk with Chris, dressed neck to ankles in an orange jumpsuit? *He can wave now, show Daddy how you wave!* They'd leave after an hour and stop at McDonald's on the way home so she could breastfeed him in a stall in the bathroom.

The alternative seemed so clear to Maggie. One of them was going to pay—they'd committed a crime and someone had to be held responsible. She tried to picture herself dressed in a women's correctional sea-green maternity shirt, her prenatal care reduced to a worn-down, burned-out doctor at the prison infirmary. Would anyone care if her baby lived or died? Not likely.

What you need, Maggie Bell, is a plan. She heard Phillip's voice, as clear as if he were standing in the room next to her.

When Maggie was sixteen, Phillip had taught her to drive. She gripped the steering wheel until her knuckles literally turned white. Later when she let it go, her hands had cramped and her palms were red and itchy. She sat in the driver's seat, panicked as she let her foot slowly off the brake and felt the car move underneath her. She slammed her foot on the brake so hard they both lurched forward, Phillip bracing himself with a slap against the glove box. She didn't know what was more nerve wracking: the lesson itself or the fact that Phillip was perched in the passenger seat, his back rigid as he barked instructions.

More gas, less gas, brake. Don't forget your signal.

When the session was over, Phillip had held out his hands for the keys. As she placed the key ring in his palm, his fingers curled around her wrist. "In driving and in life, always have a plan."

She'd nodded, trying to form her face into something that would look impressed at his wisdom, but as usual, she had no idea what he was talking about.

"Always think about what you would do if the oncoming car crossed the yellow line," he'd said. "Don't get complacent."

She could barely hear him over the thumping of her heart.

He'd pulled on her hand, drawing her closer. "In crises, people survive on a plan alone." He dropped her wrist as if it had scalded him and opened the car door.

The memory ambushed her. She'd thought of his advice many times in her life, and if she'd been asked, she would have said she was a person who generally liked to have a purpose. But she hadn't thought about that afternoon in a long time. She had stood in that misty parking lot, the fog settling low and heavy as the sun dipped below the horizon, until Phillip rapped on the passenger-side window and motioned for her to just *get in the goddamn car.*

Don't be complacent. She'd been drifting. They both had. With the baby—*the baby*—she had purpose. She flipped back through Jake's notes, fanning the pages like a deck of playing cards. She had no real idea what she was looking for. Somewhere in the first few pages, a name jumped out at her, the shadowy figure of a man who could be her salvation. *People survive on a plan alone.*

CHAPTER TWENTY-SEVEN

CHRIS

"I'M SORRY, I STILL DON'T understand. Why can't I testify?" Chris folded his arms and leaned on the long table in the courthouse conference room.

Jake was studying his legal pad, and Chris wanted to pound his fist on the table. Jake had asked for the early-morning meeting. He expected the prosecution to rest, and then, he'd explained, he would call his one and only defense witness: Leon Whittaker. Through Leon, he could tell the full story of Logan, his life, and his presumed death—one that had nothing to do with Chris or Maggie. It was, after all, a hell of a story.

Jake set down his pen and met Chris's eyes, drumming his fingertips on the tabletop. "Oh, you can. Never assume I said you *can't.* That would get me disbarred. You are absolutely free to testify on your own behalf—the Constitution says so. But you should know that if you testify, we'll lose."

"Why is that?"

"Because you're lying." Jake was matter-of-fact. He leaned back in his chair, folding his hands behind his head.

Chris stood, his vision clouding with white starbursts.

"I didn't kill him!"

"No, but you know who did."

"What?"

"You know who killed him. And so do I," Jake said. "If you take the stand, do you think they're going to stop at 'Did you kill Logan May?' No. Janice will find what is currently a nick, a tiny paper cut: the fact that you know who killed him. We're ninety-percent winning. But if you took the stand, she'd stick her finger in that paper cut and work it open to a full-on wound. We'd bleed to death. Got it?"

Chris grimaced. "That is a disgusting analogy."

"Like you're afraid of blood."

Chris snorted but said nothing.

Jake stood and motioned for him to follow. "It's show time."

<hr>

JUDGE PUCKETT FILED IN. EVERYONE stood then sat again. Chris had grown weary of the playact. The tradition and ceremony had long since lost its luster. The judge banged his gavel to indicate court was in session, and Chris counted to three in his head.

On cue, the squeal of feedback filled the room as Judge Puckett adjusted his microphone. "Yesterday, we heard from the last of the prosecution witnesses. We assume that at this point, the State rests?"

Janice approached the bench and handed a piece of paper to the bailiff. On her way back to the prosecution table, she dropped off what Chris assumed to be a copy. "Actually, Your Honor, a new witness has come forward. With the court's permission, we'd like to obtain their testimony."

"Objection, Your Honor. We weren't informed of this witness, and we've had no chance to investigate them or substantiate their claims." Jake rose, his voice booming.

Chris cringed, and he stole a look at Maggie. Her mouth hung open, and her eyes darted between Chris and the judge. She mouthed something Chris couldn't make out, and he shrugged, shaking his head. She let her head fall back.

"He came to us this morning, Your Honor," Janice said. "We'd like to at least hear him out—we're taking a chance, too. We haven't even gotten to interview him."

"Your Honor, this is ridiculous. I ask for a recess to at least—"

"Silence!" Judge Puckett pounded his gavel. He leaned back, his arms folded across his midsection, and rested his chin on his chest. He sat like that for what seemed like hours, and Jake cleared his throat. Finally, the judge looked up. "Okay, here's what we'll do. We can hear from the new witness. But first, Mr. McHale gets a two-hour recess to check him out. We meet back here at..." He twisted to check the clock on the wall behind him. "Eleven thirty. Eat an early lunch, folks, there's no break. And *no one* interviews him. We're all going into this blind, got it?"

Janice nodded and shot a glare across the aisle. Jake gathered his paperwork and grabbed his briefcase. At the sound of the gavel, he scrambled down the aisle, motioning for Chris to follow him. He ushered Chris into the conference room and gestured toward the plush leather swivel chairs. On the center of the table, Jake plunked down his cell phone. It was already ringing on speakerphone.

"Yo, what's up? What'd ya do? Oversleep?" Leon yawned.

"No, listen, Leon, we got a job to do and fast." Jake consulted the paper in his hand. "We need everything we can get on Mr. Smith Hamilton. We have two hours to do it."

"Two hours! The clerks at the courthouse take shits longer than that. I can't get anything in two hours, boss."

"That's what we've got, Leon. Let's make it work, okay?" Jake punched the end button and turned to Chris. "What did you say to him, buddy?" The menace in his voice belied the friendly moniker.

Chris held up his hands. "Nothing! I barely spoke to him. I told him not to talk to anyone!"

"Did you tell him what you were charged with?"

"No!"

"Then what is he going to testify about?"

"The guard made a comment." Chris snapped his fingers. "He said something about me being in for murder and not getting the princess treatment. Shit. I can't remember exactly."

Jake came around to the other side of the table and pushed his face toward Chris. "Listen, I'm serious. You gotta think. I want to know every little thing you talked about. He's listed as an informant, which means he's going to testify that you said something to him in prison. If I have any hope of defending you, I need to know what it is. Got it?"

"Jake, I'm serious. I said *nothing* to the guy. *Nothing.* Aside from my 'don't talk to strangers' speech. Fuck, I probably gave him the idea. I told him that asking too many questions would make other guys think he was a snitch. I thought he was new to the system, just a dumb kid."

"Dumb kids don't turn informant. Leon'll figure it out. He'll get the guy's history, record, that kind of thing. I'm going to run to the administration office and try to get some background. Stay out of trouble for two hours, okay?"

Jake opened the door and motioned to the bailiff outside the door. In a hushed voice, Jake recapped his plan. The bailiff nodded, which Chris took to mean he could stay where he was for two hours. Chris used his thumbnail to work at a nick in the finish of the shiny mahogany conference table. He watched the clock. While he'd never relished killing time, he'd rather be in the silent, air-conditioned courthouse than back in his cell.

The door creaked open. Maggie lingered in the doorway.

He tilted his head and gave her a small smile. He hadn't seen her one-on-one since that awful visiting day when he couldn't say the right thing no matter how he tried. He'd pounded the bench in front of him and watched her eyes grow wide in shock, and then he'd run away like a coward.

He scratched his chin and stared at the faux wood finish of the conference table. She rushed to the seat next to him, tucking her hair behind her ear. She smelled clean and flowery, fresh from the shower. He longed for home.

"What's going on, Chris? What are they talking about, surprise witness? Do you have any idea who it is? Do you think it's Mrs. Jenkins? I didn't think she was home that night—"

"Maggie, Maggie, stop." Chris held up his hand and looked over his shoulder. "No, it's my first cellmate. This little redheaded tweaker. Couldn't have been more than twenty. But the little fucker apparently got it in his head to become a snitch. Listen, I'm not worried. This kid hardly looks credible, and snitching is common. Jake'll ferret out the lies. It's annoying because it adds time to the hearing."

"What could he snitch about if he knows nothing?"

"Oh, these guys can make a story sound plausible enough. They get snippets from your conversations with guards or your lawyer. Then snippets expand into whole stories. D.A.s call them 'substantiated' if even the littlest fact jives. But don't sweat it; there's nothing. I was—I am—so careful about what I say. I learned the first time."

"Oh." Maggie chewed her pinkie nail, avoiding eye contact. "Well, listen. If it all comes down not in our favor, I'm going to the D.A., okay? This has gone on long enough."

Chris felt trapped. He couldn't make her see that no matter what happened, whether they told the truth or stuck with the story, he would likely do time. He imagined standing up in court, announcing the whole truth of the awful night. His shoulders drooped at the idea; his relief was palpable. Maggie sat in front of him, looking delicate and impossibly fragile in a soft pink fuzzy sweater. Her arms looked thinner than he remembered. He tried to picture her in scrubs and laceless Keds, and the image kept sliding away.

She placed her hand over his, and her faint pink nails traced circles on his knuckles. "What if we went now, together? As a team? We'll come out with the truth, back up each other's stories. They'd believe us now, don't you think?"

"Maggie, first of all, you have to be quiet. I have no idea who's listening here. I have no expectation of privacy. Secondly, no. Definitely not. I've explained this. If we tell the truth, I will do a certain two to ten years in prison. If Jake wins this hearing, they won't charge me with anything. I walk away. With or without this surprise witness, we're winning. Jake is a cocky ass, but he's a fantastic lawyer. We absolutely did the right thing."

"But... can't they charge you later?" she asked. "What if they keep digging? Can they arrest you again? Or me?"

"There's nothing for them to find. Anything they could find is out there already. It's been neutralized by Jake. Everything else is—" he mouthed the last word, "buried."

"I just keep thinking we forgot something." Maggie wrung her hands.

In his first gesture of tenderness in almost three weeks, he pulled her hands into his. "Maggie, I thought of everything."

—<‹═›>—

THEY SAT HOLDING HANDS FOR over an hour. It was the longest Chris could remember maintaining physical contact with his wife in years. She spent most of the time with her head bent low over the table, her blond hair falling over her face. Their knees almost touched.

"Do you remember the cemetery?" Maggie asked.

Chris felt his arms and legs go cold. He did remember the cemetery. On nights when he didn't dream of Maggie or Derek Manchester, he dreamt of the day at the cemetery.

The day had been a day for a funeral, cold and dark, the misty rain coming in spurts. Behind the cemetery was a large park with walking trails and beautiful views of the valley below, the rise and fall of hills, green and lush and new with life. Headstones dotted the landscape high atop the hill, haphazard and scattered like thrown confetti. It was late spring, after the fourth miscarriage, when leaving the house was still a struggle.

Chris had packed a picnic lunch and a bottle of wine and led Maggie through the cemetery to the walking path beyond. They walked for hours and talked for the first time in months. Chris opened the wine and they finished the bottle. It was a noir, Maggie's favorite. It made Chris's mouth cottony and his tongue thick, and he only drank one glass. They hiked up to the summit. The air cleared for a bit, the clouds opening to a cerulean sky that looked painted. They spread a blanket and lay side by side in the grass.

Maggie had been transformed. She laughed, she talked, she touched Chris—his hands, his arm, and later, her hands sought the bare skin underneath his T-shirt. When the sun set, streaking pink and gold and bathing the view in shades of orange, they packed up languidly. They had no place to be. They hiked back down the summit, their hands grazing, to the trail that would lead back to the cemetery and the car. The drizzle and the mist returned as they got closer to their car, as though bringing real life along with them.

Maggie's hand had slid from his, and he felt the void. A loud guttural sound that bordered on a shriek cut through the peaceful silence, echoing back from the hills. Chris realized it had come from his wife. She pointed, her hand covering her mouth, and when he followed her outstretched arm, the back of his neck tingled. Fifty feet away, next to a mound of freshly turned dirt, rested the smallest casket he'd ever seen. The coffin was mahogany and pewter, swirled with carvings along the lip.

To Chris, it had seemed that someone had aggressively selected the most regal, ornate choice as a balm to their grief. He thought of the day he'd held Christina, her small, malleable bones folding into her impossibly tiny body. Her face had been blurred by his tears, and they'd dripped down his nose and onto her hair. He turned away and tugged on Maggie's hand. She yanked her hand away as though she'd been seared and inched closer to the gravesite.

"Maggie!" he'd called, but she ignored him. He sighed and set down the cooler before following her.

At the casket, she had run her hands along the gleaming wood, her fingers leaving smudged trails. She circled the small wooden box, tears streaming down her cheeks. She made no move to dry her eyes or wipe her nose, and the pain in Chris's chest struck so deep, he turned away. He stared at the spot where upturned dirt met bright green grass, where death met life. He heard Maggie's keening cry, her deep, mournful moaning. She was on her knees, her forehead resting on the casket.

He'd reached out to touch her back, his hand inches from the narrow dip between her shoulder blades, but it hovered there. It was all so hopeless. They would go home, back to the way they were, and the Maggie from the park would be gone. He dug his toe into the ground. Two cemetery workers stood nearby, their shovels pitched into the dirt, their hands resting on the handles, their heads bowed in reverence. Chris felt his cheeks grow hot.

"Maggie, come on, honey. I think these guys want to do their job," he'd whispered.

She'd pushed herself up, swiping her forearm across her face and smearing snot and tears on her cheeks. She wouldn't meet his eyes. She brought her slender fingers up to her lips and rested them lightly on the wooden lid. Chris turned and began the walk back to the car. The Maggie from the summit was gone, buried along with a stranger's baby.

"That day was the last time I remember loving you." Her nails traced patterns in his palm.

He gaped at her. "What do you mean?"

"You *watched* me. You didn't even *try* to comfort me. I'm always alone." She shrugged as though that was expected, a normality.

Chris felt sick. He didn't want to have that conversation there and then. He had no ability to fix anything. "Maggie, please, I don't know what to say."

"That's always been our problem. You said you wouldn't be here to watch how it all unfolds for me. You said you want to leave me now, but to me, that moment at the cemetery? That was when you left me."

He touched her cheek. "I'm sorry."

She sat up straight, brushed the hair from her eyes, and met his gaze. "I think it's too late." She pushed her chair back and, without a backward glance, left the room. The door thunked shut behind her.

AN HOUR AND FORTY-FIVE MINUTES later, Jake and Leon spilled into the conference room, breathless, with wide, giddy smiles. Chris studied Leon's greasy hair and slight frame, his wizened face gnarled with creases, and his surprisingly sharp eyes. Jake waved at Chris and then at Leon, a hasty, silent introduction.

"*This* is why I practice law, my friend." Jake threw a file folder on the table, a star quarterback showing off his game ball.

Chris was caught up in the excitement but pushed aside a murmuring irritation. He needed Jake to win—so why was he irritated that Jake was winning? Because it was Jake? A twenty-year internal conflict raged inside Chris: hug him or hit him? He wanted to laugh. "Okay, I give up. What'd you find?"

Jake looked at his watch. "We don't have time. But basically, Janice should really do her homework. But you can't fault the D.A.'s office. They can't afford Leon." He motioned everyone up and toward the courtroom.

Jake led, followed by Leon and Chris in single file. The bailiff brought up the rear, herding them all from the conference room to the courtroom.

Leon tossed a grin at Chris, showing off his gapped incisor. "Does that mean I get a raise?"

"THE STATE CALLS SMITH HAMILTON to the stand." Janice stood at the podium, straight postured, with a small smile playing on her lips.

The rear doors opened, and the bailiff guided Hamilton up the aisle. He looked much like Chris remembered: young, skinny, redheaded, and freckled. *A kid.* His reedy voice as he was sworn in had a nasal twang Chris didn't remember.

"Mr. Hamilton, are you currently incarcerated?" Janice began.

"No, I'm, uh, out on bail."

"How do you know Mr. Stevens?"

"Uh, he was my cellmate. I *was* in jail for a week until my sister got bail money together." Hamilton had a nervous habit of picking at a scab on his chin. His face was pocked with acne scars. He fidgeted in the witness chair, his thumb and index finger pinching at his skin. He glanced at his thumb and flitted his fingers together, scattering whatever he'd worked free onto the ground.

"What were you incarcerated for, Mr. Hamilton?" Janice asked.

"Possession of a controlled substance."

"Are you currently awaiting trial?"

"I think my lawyer and the D.A.'s office are arranging a plea agreement, but I haven't talked to him this week yet."

"Okay, so during your incarceration, did Mr. Stevens talk to you at any time?"

Chris's thighs flexed, and he fought the urge to leap up and preempt the answer.

"Yeah, we talked a lot. He schooled me on the workings of prison. He was an okay guy, really," Hamilton said.

"But you're going to reveal what he believed to be private conversations?" Janice arched her eyebrow.

He shrugged, his face reddening. "Yeah, well, I was uncomfortable with the things he said, and I knew talking about it could help my personal situation a little bit."

"Are you receiving a benefit in order to testify here today?"

"Well, yeah, the terms are kind of unclear. It won't be anything big, maybe a reduced sentence in my plea agreement. I wasn't guaranteed anything."

Chris divided his attention between Hamilton and Janice, whose lips moved along with Hamilton's words. *No one interviewed him, bullshit.* Chris counted to twenty to calm the bubbling rage prickling the back of his skull. Jake touched Chris's knee. Jake's eyes stayed facing front, his face expressionless. Chris felt his admonishment: *Calm down.*

"What exactly did Mr. Stevens say to you?" Janice asked.

"Um, well, we talked a little bit about prison. He told me how to avoid getting beat up by the other inmates. He told me to be as quiet as possible, to avoid eye contact, to do what I needed to do, and that's it. That alliances can be used against you in prison. That... I was at risk because I'm so small."

"Did that make you angry?"

"Oh no, it was just the truth. Like I said, he was helpful." With that, Smith looked over at Chris as if to say

Sorry for spilling your secrets, buddy.

That infuriated Chris even more. The twitch in his thighs traveled down his legs until even his toes moved inside his shoes.

"What else did you talk about?" Janice smoothed her red puff of hair with no effect.

"Well, eventually, what we were in for. I told him about my arrest. He told me what he was accused of, sort of denying it, but I could tell there was something there."

"Did you ask him about it?"

"Yeah, later I brought it up again," Hamilton said.

"Why?"

"Um... boredom, I guess. I mean, there's not a lot to do in prison. I was curious. He didn't strike me as a dangerous dude."

"What did he tell you?" Janice asked.

"That his wife was cheating on him with some grease monkey she met at a bar. She thought he didn't know, and one night, the guy showed up at their house. The guy picked a fight with Stevens, and he hit him over the head with a baseball bat. *Bam*, the guy went down. Dead as a doornail."

Chris gripped Jake's arm. "That never fucking happened. Object or something, damn it!"

Jake waved him off.

"Did Mr. Stevens happen to tell you what he did next?" Janice tossed the defense table a cursory glance.

"Uh, yeah, said he panicked. He said, 'Do you know how heavy a dead body is?' I said I had no idea. I had to carry my dog after he died. He was eighty-seven pounds, so I can only imagine pretty heavy."

"Mr. Hamilton, did there ever come a time when Mr. Stevens confided in you what he did with the body?"

"Uh, yeah, he did. He said he buried it. Under four feet of dirt and cement."

"Did he happen to tell you the burial site?"

"Under the new Texas Roadhouse on Route 322."

The courtroom exploded.

Chris jumped up, clutching Jake's arm. "That entire story is a lie. Jake, you gotta do something."

Judge Puckett banged his gavel, and Chris turned to look at Maggie, who was ghostly white and stricken. She shook her head, almost in slow motion, her mouth open. Even Farnum looked bewildered.

Jake jumped up and shouted over the din, "Objection, Your Honor. This is completely unsubstantiated. There is absolutely no evidence that there even *is* a body, much less where it's buried."

"Everyone sit down. *Now!*" Judge Puckett ordered, and everyone obeyed. He turned to Hamilton. "Are you telling me that it's possible the body we're all looking for is buried under this Texas Roadhouse?"

"Yes, sir, I am," Hamilton said. "I don't know for sure, but I know what I've been told. I shoulda come forward sooner, but like I said, I liked the guy."

The judge leaned forward even farther, his glasses resting on the edge of his nose. He coughed, a low, chiding sound. "Listen, son, this isn't a game. Did Mr. Stevens happen to tell you how he buried a body under a restaurant?"

"Um, he was in construction or something. He buried it a few days before they poured the foundation."

The judge's pounding gavel sounded like the proverbial nailing of the coffin lid. Maggie's words from three weeks earlier floated up. *We're in deep shit, Chris.*

CHAPTER TWENTY-EIGHT

MAGGIE

THE SUN BURNED HOT FOR an end-of-June morning, and sweat dripped down the back of Maggie's neck. She shivered despite the heat and shifted her blazer, examining the fleshy button imprint on her forearm. Men in hard hats bumbled around her while analysts in black jackets cut through the throng, their shiny white lettering reflective in the sun. Maggie closed her eyes, took a breath, and expelled it while counting to six. She'd read somewhere that six was the magic number. *In, out. In, out.* She opened her eyes and checked her phone. No missed calls. *Jesus, is it only nine o'clock?* She craned her neck, searching for Jake's tailor-suited shoulders.

"This is going to be pretty cool, actually."

Maggie turned toward the sound of a smooth, feminine voice and swallowed thickly when she saw Detective Small standing behind her. Detective Small was wearing a black tank top and jeans. She looked like a college kid with her blond hair pulled into a loose ponytail. Her badge hung off her front jeans pocket, demanding the respect her casual appearance belied. She sidled up to Maggie and kept her focus on the scene before them. The black jackets had squared off, outlining the foundation and framed restaurant that would soon become a Texas Roadhouse.

Nothing about what was happening seemed "pretty cool" to Maggie. She pulled her arms in closer. Her insides slid together with a sharp swoop as if she was in free fall.

Detective Small shifted and continued. "They have these glass probes—they're not much bigger than a human hair, if you can believe it. They sample air pockets in the soil for something called ninhydrin-reactive nitrogen, which is a by-product of body decomposition. The techs have hand-held detectors that beep when there's enough pocketed nitrogen. All they have to do is drill very small holes, less than an eighth of an inch, in the foundation and thread the probes through. Amazing, really. It's completely new technology. I'm not sure we've used it before, which is part of the reason you see so many crime scene techs." She gave Maggie a blinding white smile. "It's their Disneyland."

Maggie gave her a weak smile. *I could save them the trouble.* "So what will that tell us?"

"If there's a body under there. If there is, we'll dig it up."

"Is it a hundred percent?"

Detective Small studied her, head cocked to the side. "Is anything? But through a few feet of concrete, it's better than a cadaver dog. If there's a body there, it should tell us. Doesn't mean we'll know who put it there, though." She clucked softly and scratched her cheek.

Maggie covered her surprise by adjusting her sunglasses. "Well, I think if there's a body there, you'd know who put it there by the testimony yesterday?"

"Oh, if I took everything at face value, I wouldn't be half as good at my job as I am." She gave Maggie a sardonic smile, turned, and left her standing alone against the tape.

Maggie reached out and ran her fingernail along the thin yellow plastic. She'd been unable to eat properly for days. Under the blazing sun, her vision wavered and her head swam. She hoped she didn't pass out. She checked her phone again. *Come on.*

Two techs had quartered the foundation, drilling two holes per segment—a total of eight sample sites. She thought of the childhood game *Mousetrap*. Once you gave that little steel ball its initial push, even if all the buckets and pulleys weren't in place, there wasn't anything you could do about it. Maggie rubbed her forehead. She needed to make decisions, and soon. It was coming down to the wire. *Him or me?*

The thing was, Maggie held Chris's trump card. Finding that vase had been like a light switch. In the resulting glow, she saw so clearly what had previously been cloaked in thick, black resentment: Chris would pick Chris. When it all fell out—and it would, she was sure of that—Chris would point to the vase, the fingerprints, the blood. Or at least he would have, had she not found it. Just his act of keeping it signaled a subconscious division in his mind that Maggie hadn't known was there.

She battled questions. *Who will I pick? Is it too late?* She thought about sitting next to Chris in the courthouse. It was too late for them, too late for loving Chris, too late for Jake, too late, too late, too late. Everything felt wrong, like she'd missed the last train and remained on the platform, cold and alone. *I am invisible.*

She had no desire to hear them shout with joy about the success of their new gadget, to see them jackhammer through the foundation, or to see that rolled tarp like a fat, stale cigar burping the stench of death. She turned to leave, and she slammed into Jake.

"Hey, I need to talk to you—"

He shook his head and put a hand on her elbow, gentle and firm. He bent toward her to be heard over the commotion, and her fingertips brushed his stiff shirt. He smelled like ironing.

She closed her eyes and leaned, ever so slightly, into him. She'd barely seen him since their night together. He hadn't come back to the house last night until after two—she assumed he was out with Leon. She hadn't offered to help, and he hadn't asked. Being so close to him, her mind handed her snapshots—his naked chest under her palm, his expression all tenderness and hope, the feeling of his fingertips tracing her face, and the sound of him gently snoring as she pressed her bare pelvis against the heat of his backside in the guest bed. She resisted the urge to kiss his cheek, to run her hand along his jaw.

Jake stepped back. "Maggie, I've got to talk to *you*. I can't, for the life of me, figure out where or how Hamilton got his information. Do you know anything?" He motioned her away from the crowd, toward the back of the taped-off square.

She shook her head, not trusting her voice to lie. "Jake, can you fix this? Can you—?"

He touched his lips in a *shhh* gesture and looked around. "Just wait and see what happens here. But I have a feeling I know what's going to happen here. I just don't know the *why*. Get me?"

They stood side by side watching the motion around the foundation. Four technicians knelt and carefully threaded their sample probes. Maggie studied the foundation, wondering which technician would hit the jackpot. *The body jackpot.* She bit her cheek to keep from laughing. She guessed the two in front, in the two sections closest to the dirt access road. Chris might have been too lazy to drag the body any farther.

They lapsed into silence, watching the virtually motionless playact. Just waiting. Maggie shifted her weight, a fluttery restlessness dancing in her stomach. She checked her phone again, and silently cursed.

The distant, tiny beeping of an electronic device was joined a moment later by a second squawk at a slightly higher pitch, like a harmonic orchestra. Jake looked at her, two small creases between his eyebrows.

"So it looks like it's a positive." Detective Small stood behind them with her hands on her hips, her toe tapping the loose gravel. "We'll have to get a warrant to jackhammer up the foundation. That might take a day or so."

"We'll get a continuance." Janice Farnum appeared behind Detective Small. "I'd venture to guess that if Logan May's body is under that slab, the probable cause hearing becomes moot?"

"Janice, relax, we'll cross that bridge when we come to it," Jake said. "Body or not, I still maintain that you guys barely did due diligence on who actually killed the guy. Oh, and before you put all your eggs in Smith Hamilton's basket, you might want to look into him."

"We *did* look into him," she said. "He's got a nonviolent rap sheet, drugs and weapons possession. He's never been used as an informant."

"He has an alias." Jake reached into the briefcase on a rock beside him and pulled out a file folder. "You'll never believe this—his alias was Hamilton Smith. He was an informant on three different capital cases: murder and rape in Detroit and twice in Chicago." He flipped open the folder and pointed at a page.

Janice's mouth opened, and she looked at Jake. She snatched the file from his hands. "That little—"

"Also, he was discredited in two of those three. In the third one, he left town before the trial ended, so he was never even cross-examined. His testimony was discounted."

"Well, we probably don't really need him now. If what they dig up here is truly Logan May, we have enough evidence to put Mr. Stevens in prison for a very long time."

"You have evidence that at least now there *is* a body. You still have very little evidence that Christopher Stevens is responsible. This dig"—Jake spread his arms—"actually doesn't even do that much for you."

"Hey, Small, can you c'mere?" one of the crime scene techs called from across the dirt expanse.

Small held up one finger to Jake and Maggie and jogged to the foundation site. Maggie couldn't see what they were looking at. Detective Small and two other techs had their heads bent together, crouched at the ground at the front base of the foundation. At that moment, Maggie's phone buzzed in her hand, and she jumped. She recognized the number and stepped away from Jake to take the call, but Small trotted back to them, her hand wrapped around something Maggie couldn't see.

"Maggie, when is your wedding anniversary?" Small asked.

Maggie hit decline, her heart a steady thump against her ribcage. "May 1, 2002. Why?"

Small handed a small bag to Janice Farnum, who looked at the contents. Janice smirked at Jake and held it out for him to inspect. "I think our case just got a little stronger."

Jake took the bag, and Maggie, with a cursory glance, knew exactly what it was: a man's gold wedding band, size ten, engraved with the date May 1, 2002.

CHAPTER TWENTY-NINE

CHRIS

"I'VE ADVISED MY CLIENT TO be forthcoming with his version of events," Jake said. "The truth, as it so happens, and I'd appreciate if that was considered from here on out."

Farnum snorted, and Detective Small lifted a corner of her small mouth in disbelief.

Detective Renner laughed. "*This* is the real story? Oh, okay, why didn't you say so?"

"Listen, do you want to hear it or not?" Jake spread his hands wide. "We don't have to tell you anything. Springing it on you in court would be fine, too."

Detective Small clicked on a tape recorder, and for a second, the only sound in the room was the whirring tape. Chris marveled at the high-tech instruments responsible for bringing him down, but in the end, it came down to a man and an analog tape recorder. Jake touched Chris's elbow, and he jerked his arm away. Jake nodded.

"I buried him, but I didn't kill him," Chris said.

Renner cocked his head as if to say, *Really? This is the big revelation?*

"That guy and Maggie had a thing. I didn't know it

until you guys showed me the phone bill, though. He came to our house in the middle of the night to talk to *her,* not me. *She* answered the door. They got in a fight. He pushed her against the wall and threatened to—" His voice faltered. He was suddenly overly aware of the dirt under his fingernails. "To rape her. She fought him off, and he said he was coming after me. She grabbed a vase off the mantel and hit him over the head. Leaded crystal, heavy as hell. I wasn't there. This is what she told me. She screamed, and I ran downstairs. When I got to the living room, the guy was on the floor. I knew he was dead. She wanted to call 9-1-1, I wouldn't let her."

Renner stopped for a beat. He almost looked surprised. "Why wouldn't you call the police? That makes no sense. If a man breaks into your home and tries to rape you, you're allowed to defend yourself. You're allowed to defend your spouse. It could have been worked out, depending on the scenario."

"I know. *I know.* I panicked. That's the truth, I swear. Maggie begged me to call the police. She *said* that. But I *knew* the police—you guys—would see my history and look at me."

"If Maggie backed up your version of the story, Chris, no one would have accused you," Detective Small said. Her feminine, lilting voice was a minor comfort.

Chris closed his eyes. He wanted a do-over button. "No, I know. I see that. *Now.* I'm telling you, I was so sure. So that's the truth. Maggie killed him, and I buried him. And she *will* back this up. She's wanted to tell the truth through the whole stupid hearing, and I wouldn't let her."

"Can you go back to the part where Maggie killed him?" Renner's tone was syrupy, almost sarcastic, and he crossed an ankle over his knee. He tapped a pen against his blank legal pad—he had yet to take a note. The gesture seemed too flippant.

Chris looked over at Jake, whose eyes narrowed.

"Why go back?" Jake asked. "You've got it on tape. If you wanna go back, then hit rewind."

"No, I just want to make sure. You said it was the vase, right?"

"Yeah, it was a big, heavy vase. Look, I don't know how to say this, but I saved the damn thing. I have it hidden in my garage."

"What the fuck, Chris?" Jake lurched forward, his face within inches of Chris's. "Are you kidding me? Jesus Christ, I've never worked so hard for my money." He expelled a breath and fell back against the seat. "Let's take a break. Go to the garage, get the damn vase. That should solve this entirely."

Renner and Small exchanged glances. They looked shocked and something else... *Weary.* Chris felt something click then, the knowledge that he was on the outside looking in. He grabbed Jake's elbow, his eyes holding Detective Small's.

Chris whispered in Jake's ear, "Something's up here, Jake. I don't think this is an all-on-the-table conversation like we talked about."

Jake nodded, and Chris felt the tumbling relief of being on the same team. He'd been half-expecting Jake to wash his hands of the whole mess with an *I've-done-all-I-can* speech.

"Where exactly is this vase, Mr. Stevens?" Detective Renner asked.

"Uh, in my garage. In a box labeled *Maggie College.*" Chris ran the back of his hand along his jaw line, rough with two-day stubble, and felt down-to-his-bones tired.

Detective Small barked out orders. "Renner, you go with Mr. McHale and Janice to the Stevens residence. Take a tech with you, please—you haven't collected evidence in years. Bag the vase, get it back here, and we'll process it. You have an hour."

Renner and Farnum scrambled from the room. Chris liked her take-charge attitude, the way Renner and

Farnum kowtowed to her. Jake palmed Chris's shoulder once before following them. Chris turned to watch them go, and with the whoosh of the closing door, he faced Detective Small again. She clicked off the tape recorder. She opened her file and paged through it, making small notations as she went. Her handwriting was scrawled and messy, slanting one way then the other.

His stomach uncoiled, and for the first time in weeks, he longed for sleep. He wanted to run outside and yell at the top of his lungs, eat an ice cream cone, net a basketball, anything. He tried to quell his burgeoning elation but found he couldn't. In less than an hour, it would be over. The truth would be out, and it couldn't be *that* bad. Even Renner had said it: *You are allowed to defend yourself.*

Maybe Chris would do jail time for the burial, maybe not. He'd bet Jake could get him out of that. Detective Small seemed to like him. It all seemed so stupid to him now. They should have just done what Maggie wanted from the beginning and told the truth. The room felt comfortable, airy and light. He envisioned himself home. What would become of him and Maggie?

Chris studied Detective Small with interest. Did she believe him? He couldn't tell. She sighed. Her lower lip puckered as she wrote, and because he was bored, filled with restless energy, he wondered what she was like in bed. How her small breast would fit like a tennis ball in his palm. Or how long her hair would be if he reached over and pulled out the bun.

"You're staring. Why?" She didn't look up, didn't make eye contact, as she turned the page to scribble something else.

"What else will I look at?" He gestured around the empty cinder block room, painted bile yellow. An interrogation room at a police station held little interest. *A pretty cop? A lotta interest.* He didn't say that.

She looked up, met his eyes, and gave him a smile. "We

searched the garage, you know. We didn't find a vase. How come?" Her voice was cloying, and he felt the makings of a trap.

He couldn't figure out how to answer. On one hand, he was pretty sure hiding the vase was a crime. On the other hand, was hiding it twice a worse crime? "I, uh, took it to work. Buried it in the warehouse. Then after all the searches were done, I took it home again."

She nodded, tapping her pen on her teeth. She gave him a werewolf grin, all white and gums, and wrote on the notepad.

"Hey, lemme ask you. Do you believe me?" Chris leaned in, his hands folded in front of him, and studied his knuckles. He turned his hands over. His palms were calloused and dingy gray, a working man's lifelong tattoo. Maggie had always claimed to like their roughness. She called them "man hands."

"I don't have all the information yet, Chris. I'd be a shitty cop if I said yes or no." She went back to her writing, and Chris deflated a bit. She glanced back at him and seemed to soften, just for a second. "I tend to believe you, yes. But there are... inconsistencies we still need to work out."

"So if I'm telling the truth, what will happen here? Will I go back to jail?"

"I can't tell you that. That's not up to me. That's up to Janice."

"Oh. She doesn't seem to be as fond of me as you are." Chris gave her a smile, half flirting, half self-deprecating.

She ducked her head, thumbing through her paperwork again, her mouth curved in amusement. "No, you're right, she's not."

***

JAKE, JANICE, AND RENNER TRUDGED back in, somber and puzzled, an hour and a half later. Their faces were drawn, and no one looked at Chris. Something wasn't right.

"What? What happened?" Chris stood, and Renner gave him a sharp look. He sat back down.

"There's no vase, Chris. Not in *Maggie College* or *Keepsakes* or *2010* or *Chris Probation*. We had two techs take that garage apart. Again. There's no vase." Jake's voice was gravelly and thick, as though he had mucous in his throat.

Chris wanted to cough, as if that would clear it. "What? That's impossible. I know I—"

Jake silenced him by placing *Maggie College* on the table. The room seemed to hold its breath. With reverence, Chris removed the lid. His hands pawed at photo albums and picture frames, a wine bottle with a hardened drip candle in it, an old calculus textbook, a tattered, dog-eared postcard that said simply *I love you.* He found Jake's lacrosse jersey. He pulled it out of the box almost delicately, and by the lack of weight, Chris knew there was no vase. As it unrolled, a photograph flitted to the table top. No one glanced at it. Jake turned his head to avoid looking at the swath of red, and all Chris could do was picture Maggie, bare beneath the netted fabric, wrapped in Jake's bedsheets.

He swallowed twice. "It was here. I swear, I put it here. I wrapped it in this so it wouldn't break and put it in the one box I thought no one would look through. Look, get Maggie in here. Maybe she knows what the fuck is going on." He pushed the jersey back into the box, covering what remained of *Maggie College,* and reached for the photograph. He was about to toss it on top and close the lid, but he stopped.

Maggie's face was pressed against the camera lens. Chris was behind her, blurry but still discernible. Farther behind them, even fuzzier, was a white horse. A scene Chris knew in memory, not from the print: a snowy Central Park night, the sound of laughter and a street performer's accordion, the smell of roasting chestnuts.

"This doesn't belong in *Maggie College*." His voice seemed to come from the other side of the room, not from his own body.

"What? Who cares?" Renner sat in the chair opposite Chris and talked to Small in a hushed tone, his head turned away from them.

Chris turned to Jake, who had flipped open his briefcase. *What the fuck is going on?* He knew that Maggie would never put a picture from their engagement night into her box of college memories. He certainly hadn't done it when he'd stashed the vase there. Chris tugged on Jake's arm. "Hey, Jake, something is wrong here. Have you seen Maggie?"

"Yeah, she was at the dig site yesterday morning."

"Have you seen her since then? Just now, was she at the house?"

"I didn't see her. But, Chris, settle down. She could be anywhere. I left her a message a while ago to come to the police station. I'm sure she's on her way."

"No. This is going to sound crazy, but I think this picture is a message from her." Chris shook the picture, his thumb creasing the center, cutting Maggie's open-mouthed smile in half.

Small and Renner stopped their small talk and stared at him.

"You think that... this... this photograph is a message from your wife? Like a code or something? What do you think it means?" Renner spoke slowly, the way one would talk to a child. Or a crazy person.

"I know it sounds insane, but you don't know Maggie. She's pretty organized." Chris looked at Jake, who nodded slowly. Heat rose on his neck at having another man vouch for the quirks of his wife. "Our engagement night picture wouldn't be in her college box."

"But couldn't it have been a mistake? Just got stuck

there by accident?" Renner asked.

"No. I mean, theoretically yes, but no. I *know* her. And it was wrapped up in that jersey, where the missing vase used to be." Chris tossed the photograph on the table. It skittered across the smooth surface and flipped over.

Renner snatched it. "Missing vase? So *you* say." He studied the picture for a minute. "Well, there's something written here. Can't tell you what it means though. Seems harmless enough." He handed it to Chris.

As Chris read the two sentences, he felt his limbs grow cold. Renner, Small, Farnum, and Jake looked skeptical, and the protest died in his throat. He put his head on the table and laughed. After everything, after all of it, she was going to screw him over. No one would or could see that but him.

Small plucked the picture out of his hand and read the back. "What? I don't get it. What does this mean? Seems like it could have been written a long time ago, when the picture was taken."

Chris couldn't stop laughing. "It's something we said. I just... can't explain it."

"I gotta say, Stevens, this seems pretty innocent. Kind of a reach to say it's a message, don't ya think?" She handed the picture back to him.

He studied the handwriting. Maggie's beautiful, perfect, loopy cursive. Her last love letter to him.

We'll never be old married folks. Promise you'll love me forever?

CHAPTER THIRTY

CHRIS

JANICE STOMPED AROUND THE COURTROOM, pointing and self-righteous, while Detective Renner nodded. The two of them were finally cohorts in the great battle against Chris Stevens. Jake simply shrugged, his earlier aplomb slapped down by Judge Puckett's large white palm. *Criminal! Violent!* Janice called him, and when Jake stood to object, Judge Puckett waved him away as though he were a flea. Gone was the affectionate *Mr. Philadelphia.* The preliminary trial had become a farce.

Chris watched Jake unravel. He showed up for court disheveled, looking as though he'd barely slept. They met in the prison conference room every morning, and Jake would follow him to court. Leon had testified on Chris's behalf, but even his usually bizarre charm seemed deflated. That could have been Chris's imagination.

Chris spent his nights thinking of nothing but Maggie. *Maggie.* Who he'd loved once. *Maggie.* Who was about to screw him. All he did was reconstruct their last conversation. What did she say? *What if they arrest you later? Or me?* And then what had he said? *Maggie, I thought of everything.* What had been genuine? Any of it? That was what kept him up until the wee hours of the morning. When he finally slept, he had gauzy hallucinations of Maggie leaning over him, her hair tickling his cheek. He woke up punching the air.

"Chris, think, what did Maggie say to you?" Jake had Chris's file spread open across the table. His hair stood up where he'd run his hand through it.

"I have no idea, Jake. Have you seen her?"

Jake shook his head. That was their script.

"She's gone, man."

Jake flipped through his pile of documents, searching for clues. "Gone, where? We need to find her, Chris."

"I don't think she wants to be found."

By the third day of that routine, Chris felt deflated. He'd had faith in Jake. Jake would succeed because Jake never failed. But for the first time, Jake was coming unhinged. Chris didn't know what to make of the fact that he would finally be the thing that brought The Great McHale to his knees. He had to appreciate the poetic irony to that.

Chris accepted that they were screwed long before Jake did. Maggie was smart and, to him if no one else, cold. He'd lived in her frigid shadow for so many years, and he knew without question it would be years before he felt the warmth of the sun again. With that resignation came a graceful peace. While Jake insisted she'd come back, that she was just angry, Chris knew with unflinching certainty that Maggie's disappearance was permanent. He just had to wait for Jake to realize it, too.

<hr />

JUDGE PUCKETT TOOK LESS THAN two hours in his chambers to determine probable cause. Chris was pretty sure at least an hour and a half of that involved a cup of coffee and a nice long bathroom break. The postdecision pow-wow with Jake and Leon took place in the facility conference room. They spread out over the sticky coffee table, talking animatedly and saying things like *now the real work starts.* Chris shook his head, watching them. They had it all, the truth and then some. No way Chris was walking away with a *not guilty.*

"Maggie's absence might be the best thing for your defense, come to think of it." Jake scratched his cheek and looked at the ceiling. "We have another suspect now, someone to pin the whole thing on. And the truth to boot."

"Boss, I can still try to find her." Leon had torn the house apart. He couldn't find one sign that Maggie was missing. Her purse hung on the hook in the hall, her keys tucked in the inside pocket. Her car was parked in front of the house where it had always been. All her clothes hung in her closet, organized by color, nothing glaringly out of place.

"Maybe something happened to her," Chris offered, a half-hearted shot in the dark. Every once in a while, he felt overcome with desperation. A small, sick corner of his mind longed for it to be a mistake. He picked at the rubber sole of his shoe when he said that to avoid the pitying glance between Jake and Leon.

Jake expelled a huff of air across the table. "Chris, we gotta tell you something."

Chris kept his ankle over his knee and worked at the glue between the canvas and rubber of his shoe. He nodded for them to continue but stayed focused on his task. He swallowed once. Twice.

Leon spoke first. "She took the twenty-five grand, buddy." His voice was low, and Chris almost didn't hear him.

Chris nodded. It was one of those things he knew without being told, and only after someone told him did he realize he'd already known. His neck burned.

Maggie had been gone for six days.

LEON WORKED ALL ANGLES PREPARING for the trial. Their defense was mostly truth combined with Maggie's guilt by proxy and a bit of speculation. Who murdered Logan May? Maggie. Who buried him? Chris. They decided to present the truth in its entirety to the jury, including the setup. The missing vase, including Maggie's somewhat cryptic note to Chris. (Although even Chris had to admit to having doubts about that. Maybe she wrote the note years ago.) Maggie's disappearance cemented the facts, gave them a certain validity, that without her abandonment might have seemed too outlandish. Finally, the suspicion that Maggie planted Smith Hamilton.

"Are you sure you want to go this way?" Jake asked, enunciating each word. "You won't win any favor with the ladies on the jury. You're blatantly accusing your wife, who you claim was almost raped that night."

"It's not an accusation. It's the truth! She killed him. I can do this. I can testify and be sad. I'll be the jilted one. I think it could work." Sometimes, even Chris was uncomfortable with his level of insouciance.

A few months before the trial, Jake successfully petitioned bail. Chris was permitted to return to his home. He stood in the hallway, expecting Maggie to be in the kitchen, humming as she stirred a pot and tucked her hair behind her ear. Sometimes when she used to cook, she'd knot her long blond hair and tuck it into the back of her shirt to keep it out of her face. When they were happy, Chris would hold the silky knot and bring it to his nose. It always smelled like honey. But the kitchen stayed dark.

Jake slept fitfully in the guest room. Chris heard him toss and turn through the walls. Sometimes he heard low murmuring. Once Chris snuck down the hall, on the pretense of using the bathroom, and stood outside the guest room door. Jake's pleading and his repeated apologies gave him a perverted pleasure. Inexplicably, Chris still felt as though he'd scored the better Hall sister. He crept back to bed, feeling ashamed.

The next day, when Chris asked him about Miranda, Jake shrugged.

He gave Chris a cocky smile. "Ah, you know. She's pissed I'm still here, but I think Maggie bugging off may have helped my situation."

Chris bristled. The insinuation was obvious, but the still-existing competition was absurd.

<hr />

WITH THE TRIAL A MONTH away, Jake left for Philadelphia. Chris assumed he was going to beg in person. The house felt empty and too big. Chris spent more time than he cared to admit drunk, waiting for time to pass.

One Saturday, a knock at the door startled Chris. He'd just sat down to watch college football, a can of Miller Lite and a bag of Doritos in his lap. When he opened the door, Detective Small waited on the other side.

He cocked his head. "Do I need to call Jake back?"

"No, this is an informal visit. May I come in?"

Hesitantly, Chris opened the door, motioning for her to come in. He was conscious of his ratty gray T-shirt and old frayed jeans. "I'd be stupid to talk to you, Detective Small."

"I know. You can call me Stephanie."

She balanced awkwardly on the arm of the recliner, facing the couch where Chris's beer and chips waited. She wore jeans and a button-down shirt. The first two buttons were undone, showing a shadow of cleavage that he avoided looking at. Her hair fell in soft waves. Football players moved silently across the television, and Chris stood in the center of the living room, shifting his weight and not knowing what to do with his arms. He crossed them and thought that was too confrontational. He ended up jamming his fists in his pockets.

"So. What's up?" Chris asked.

"I've been, um, deselected from the witness list. I thought you should know."

"Why? What does that mean?"

"It means Janice and I no longer agree on the prosecution of your case. Which is fine—I don't have to agree with her. She's the A.D.A. But I probably won't be called to the stand."

Chris sat on the couch and faced her. "I'm confused."

"I guess I'm saying that I believe you. I believe that Maggie killed Logan and you buried him. I believe that she set you up and skipped town."

"So why is Janice insisting I killed him?"

"Because to admit that Maggie killed him means a loss to her. A check in the wrong column. Unless the D.A.'s office gives her the resources to find Maggie and prosecute her. Which they won't do."

"Why not?" Chris grabbed onto that idea and resisted the urge to rub his palms together. *Yes, let's find the bitch.*

"Well, a few reasons, most of them political. But basically, Logan May won't be deemed worth it. There's no political pressure to catch his killer. No one *really* cares. And then..." She sighed. "They have you. For the small amount of pressure there is to close the case."

"So what now?"

"Well, I thought you might want to know that I'm no longer a witness for the prosecution. I wouldn't make a bad witness for the defense though..." She traced circular patterns in the arm of her chair with one slim finger.

"Can Jake call you?" Chris felt dumb for having so little understanding of the law, considering how much time he'd spent in the courtroom.

Stephanie smiled. "The cop on your case? I'd be a killer defense witness."

Before she left, she kissed his cheek. Chris found himself touching the spot she'd kissed for hours afterward.

A WEEK BEFORE THE TRIAL, unable to sit still any longer, Chris found himself digging through Maggie's things. There had to be a clue somewhere. He pulled apart her bookcase and her nightstand drawer. *When had she stopped taking the pill?* Not that it mattered; they hadn't had sex in months. With a jolt, he realized that it was likely they never would again. He thumbed through every photo album they had, reconstructing all the major milestones of their life together. Engagement, wedding pictures, new house, the few months they'd fostered a cat until Maggie had deemed them not "cat people" and he'd been adopted by a family down the street.

By Sunday, Chris felt consumed with and by Maggie. He did a final sweep through the closet and opened up a large shoebox, made for holding boots he'd bought Maggie once for Christmas. Inside was a small pine box with a broken brass clasp. The lid was labeled "Little Things," and it contained a hodge-podge of small trinkets of their life. A dried rose, a Hallmark "I'm sorry" card, a subway pass—city unknown.

As he pushed through it all, his stomach twisted with regret. At the bottom of the box lay a small stack of pictures. He thumbed through them—a self-portrait of them kissing that Chris didn't recall, a profile of Maggie, her hair being whipped in the wind, and one that Chris recognized with a thudding heart. Another self-portrait. Maggie's hair was splayed out on crisp white hotel linens, the sheets pulled tight across their nude bodies. Chris and Maggie smiled widely. Chris recognized the bed from the Plaza. On instinct, he turned the picture over and wasn't surprised to see blue ink scrawled in a crisp, clean message. There was no doubt.

It's time to move on. You won't find what you're looking for.

CHAPTER THIRTY-ONE

CHRIS

ON THE FIRST DAY OF jury selection, Jake explained Chris's ideal juror. "An African American male, age thirty to fifty. We're going to push hard the belief that the police focused on you and didn't look elsewhere due to your record. Second to that, we're looking for, basically, you. A blue-collar guy. Not the slickest, smartest guy. Again, thirty to fifty. They'll be sympathetic to your truth: Maggie killed Logan, you buried him to protect you both, and then she skipped town."

Chris was stung by Jake's depiction and the ease at which he threw it out. *Not the smartest guy. Nice.*

"Either guy would be sympathetic to your jilted status," Jake said.

"I'm jilted?"

"Yes, you're jilted." Jake tapped his pen on his legal pad and studied Chris's face. "The only hang-up is you're a little too good-looking. Men pretend not to notice when another guy is good-looking. Jurors notice. We'll see if we can do something about that."

For the first time, Chris understood why people hated lawyers.

Jake used all his exemptions on women in their early thirties and female senior citizens. Apparently, those would be the least sympathetic to his affair with Tracy and wouldn't forget it. The few women on the jury were in their mid-fifties.

Jake said they were "the perfect age to have lost the idealism of marriage, but not old enough to view it with the rosy lens of hindsight."

Chris hated the categories, the boxes Jake so easily slotted people into. He wondered more than once what box he would be put into had he been on the other side of the mahogany railing. *Not the smartest guy. Fuck-up. Good-looking.* He laughed inwardly at the irony. *Phillip put me in that box a long time ago.*

The final jury was mostly composed of their ideal jurors, with two over-sixty men Jake called wild cards. Both were retired, one a blue-collar mailman, but both had been married for over thirty years.

Jake just shrugged. "Depends on if they're happy or miserable, I guess. Married that long? Could go either way."

One of the women on the jury sat clicking her pocketbook open and closed, her lips pursed with disapproval. Her flame-red hair was patchy and thin, her spine straight with reproach. Chris wasn't surprised when she was selected as jury foreman.

<hr />

THE TRIAL COMMENCED ON THE coldest day of the year. The courtroom was alive with chatter, as if the cold had brought people to life. Lawyers, bailiffs, and police blew into their raw hands, their red cheeks puffed as they talked about the blistering weather. *The groundhog saw his shadow! Spring is right around the corner.* Chris shook his head— only in Pennsylvania.

The trial was a stark contrast to the hearing. The hearing had been pulsed and energetic, with a rally team feel that

Chris both abhorred and missed. The trial plodded along, steeped in ritualism and formality. Jake seemed almost bored. He barely jotted a note, when he used to fill pages during court sessions. He tapped the table and stared out the window.

Even Judge Puckett's jokes had waned. He referred to Jake as Mr. McHale. The February cold seemed to seep in through the windows and cover the courtroom in a thick gray blanket. Only Janice seemed energized, her small, wiry frame ricocheting around the courtroom. During Detective Renner's testimony, Chris looked over to find Jake texting Miranda.

Detective Renner, Officer Davis, and Mika all testified, exact replicas of their testimonies at the hearing. Mika retold the story of the night he punched her wall, and Chris felt no less shame. Jake asked him if he could *look sorrier,* and Chris wanted to ask how he should look sorrier than he felt. But he didn't.

When Jake stood for cross-examination, he pushed with a gentle prodding. "When was the last time you spoke to Maggie Stevens?"

Mika squirmed. "Back in July, right after the police came looking for Logan. I called her."

"You have no idea where she could have gone?"

"No." Mika's jaw jutted out, defying Jake to challenge her.

"Have the police questioned you about Maggie's disappearance?"

"No."

"Really? At all?" Jake feigned disbelief.

Chris knew it was feigned because the police weren't looking for Maggie. Detective Stephanie Small had been covertly using her police connections to perform a database search here or a flight scan there. To his knowledge, she hadn't found a trace of Maggie.

"I heard that she skipped town. It's pretty obvious that she's not really 'missing,'" Mika said.

"Skipping town can get you out of a murder rap these days, then?"

Janice stood. "Objection!"

"Sustained. Mr. McHale, please. Jury, please disregard that last statement." Judge Puckett waved his hand. Jake's charm had worn thin.

———⋘⋙———

TINY'S TESTIMONY WAS REDUCED TO the events of the night of Logan's death. All the mentions of Mickey Bricks or Emily Masterson were avoided. Even Smith Hamilton's testimony was abbreviated, shortened to only the parts Janice felt she could substantiate, including, of course, the location of Logan May's body. Elsewhere, Janice focused on Chris's predisposition toward violence. In the second-to-last testimony of the prosecution, she called retired police officer Michael Tanter.

When Jake had received the witness sheets, he'd studied them and showed them to Chris. "Who is this guy?"

The name hadn't rung a bell, but when Chris flipped the page and saw the red, corn-fed face of his past, his vision had wavered. He just shook his head. *Christopher Stevens is a violent-tempered kid who will be a violent man.*

Jake had taken the witness list to Judge Puckett's chambers and argued fervently that the events of twenty years ago had no bearing on the charges currently leveraged against Chris. Janice cited *pattern of behavior* and *violent tendencies,* and Jake left the chambers defeated and red faced.

Officer Tanter proved to be a stellar prosecution witness. He was a retired blue-collar boy with his crippled nephew slumped in the back of the courtroom. Chris watched his jurors, his ideal guys nodding in camaraderie and appraising Chris with new reproach.

"Can they do this?" Chris murmured.

"Yes" Jake said. "It's a sneaky trick. Sometimes called

the Silent Witness. They bring up the cop, but what they really want the jury to see is the guy in the gallery. They just use the cop to tell his story. Here, they have the best stooge imaginable—a helpless cripple. And *you* put him there." Jake shook his head in disgust, either at Chris or the situation. Chris couldn't tell.

Chris couldn't stop staring, couldn't stop turning around to watch Derek.

Jake pushed his knee into Chris's under the table and whispered, "You need to stop. Every move you make is being scrutinized."

Chris couldn't stop. Derek was thin and blond and tilted slightly to the left, his expression unreadable. He avoided eye contact.

During recess, Chris ate a takeout roast beef sandwich while Jake scribbled on what had to be his third, possibly fourth legal pad. Chris brushed the crumbs from his hands and made his way to the men's room, his head bent low. The halls were crowded, a bustling din that Chris welcomed. His life seemed filled with silence. Even Jake didn't have much to say anymore. Their silence in Chris's living room was permeated only by the television and the pop-hiss of opened beer bottles. He was struck with an intense longing for the high, giggling sound of Maggie laughing at one of his jokes.

Chris pushed open the door to the men's room and stopped. Derek Manchester sat ten feet from him, across the swarming hall of the courthouse. Without thinking, Chris let his hand drop and fought his way across the crowd until he stood awkwardly in front of Derek. They hadn't spoken since that fateful night, and possibly the last thing Chris had said to him was *asshole.* Twenty years later, Chris felt compelled to say one thing.

"I'm sorry." The words fell between them, flat and dead.

Derek only shook his head, giving a snort of disbelief. "Do you feel better now? Will you sleep at night?" He tilted his head, and Chris was surprised by his clear, deep voice.

"Maybe? Probably not." Chris pulled at the knot in his tie.

"You can rest easy, I guess. I'm fine. I'm married. I've got a kid and one on the way." Chris must have looked shocked because Derek laughed softly. "Yeah, crippled dudes still have all the right plumbing. Listen, I'll never forgive you, but I let go of my anger years ago. Had some help. You can probably let go of the guilt."

"How?" Chris asked, and the question startled him. He hadn't planned on asking it.

"I can't help you there. But it seems like you have bigger problems."

"Derek." Officer Tanter stood at the door to the courtroom, motioning Derek in and eyeing Chris warily. Derek gave Chris a small wave and wheeled away.

When Chris turned around, headed back to the conference room and to Jake—the men's room forgotten— he spotted the jury foreman standing in front of the ladies' room door, watching Derek's retreating back with a small frown. In her hands, her purse went *click, click, click.*

———◆———

THE PROSECUTION RESTED AFTER MICHAEL Tanter. Jake called Chris as the first defense witness, and Chris sat in the witness chair recounting the events of murder with Jake's voice in the back of his head. *Be contrite, but not too contrite; you didn't kill him. Be humble, be sympathetic toward Maggie. Be emotional, but for heaven's sake, don't cry. Whatever you do, don't ever, ever get angry.*

Jake's questions were open, giving Chris free rein to talk. Chris worked to keep his face the right balance of apologetic and principled. He started with the night of the murder, creeping down the steps to find Maggie holding the vase, and his blind panic, his absolute certainty that he would be blamed. He snuck a glance at the jury and saw the mailman nodding. Jake's gentle questioning was the easy part.

Janice was ruthless, angrier than necessary, and Chris kept one eye on the purse-clicker. Janice pushed at all the holes, but Chris was honest. He hid nothing. He didn't know where Maggie was, and he didn't kill anyone. Janice's hair seemed more wild than usual, the red, wiry strands standing in all directions, her eyes narrowed as she pointed in outrage. The mailman tilted his head, his eyebrows knitted, and Chris couldn't help but think that Janice was the personification of their defense. She was the overzealous A.D.A. pursuing Chris at all costs, regardless of the truth or shades of gray. When he stepped down, Jake had nodded once.

"Janice came off as brittle and desperate," Jake said later as he wiped the mouth of his beer bottle on his shirttail.

As the trial wound down, Chris dreaded the end of their comfortable nighttime routine. Either outcome held countless hours of solitude. He tried not to think of it, focusing instead on the television. The hockey game flickered with just the right amount of distraction. In the darkened living room, Jake looked ten years older.

JAKE CALLED DETECTIVE SMALL TO the stand. Chris hadn't seen her since the day she'd come to the house, offering to testify. As a witness, she hadn't been allowed in court. She pushed her hair behind her ears as Jake approached the witness stand.

"Officer Small, let me get this straight. You're testifying on Mr. Stevens's *behalf?* Why is that?" Jake asked.

"Because after a full investigation, I believe that Mr. Stevens didn't kill anyone. I believe his account."

"What have the consequences been for you?"

"I was removed from the case. I was told my conclusions

were no longer aligned with my partner's and the assistant district attorney's."

"What do you believe happened?" Jake asked.

"I think Maggie Stevens killed Logan May accidentally, in self-defense, and Christopher Stevens feared repercussions from his past, so he buried the body instead of calling the police."

"How did you come to this conclusion?"

"After Maggie disappeared, it became somewhat of a no-brainer."

"How so?"

"There was no real reason for her to empty their bank account and skip town, unless she's running from something. If Stevens killed May and Maggie truly knew nothing, she'd still be here, trying to figure out what happened. She has family in the area; it's a significant hardship for her to run away."

"Are the police looking for Ms. Stevens?"

"Not officially, no."

"What does that mean, unofficially?"

"I've done some querying on my own time. I'm not using the resources of the department but my own common sense," Small said.

"Have you found anything?"

"No. Maggie Stevens seems to have vanished."

"To your knowledge, did she take anything with her?"

"Judging by the Stevens's financial records, nothing but twenty-five thousand dollars."

———◆———

THE JURY DELIBERATED FOR A day and a half. When they filed back in, Jake gave Chris a quick nod.

"Ladies and gentlemen, have you reached a verdict?" Judge Puckett asked.

The purse-clicker stood, holding her folded verdict. "We have."

The bailiff took the paper and handed it to Judge Puckett. The judge read it, nodded once, and passed it back to the jury. "Go ahead."

The foreman said, "On the count of murder in the second degree, we find the defendant, Christopher Stevens, not guilty. On the count of manslaughter, we find the defendant not guilty. On one count of desecration of a corpse, we find the defendant not guilty. On three counts of obstruction of justice, we find the defendant guilty."

Chris sagged in his chair. *Unbelievable.*

Jake turned to him and gave him a big toothy grin. "You're free to go. Only capital crimes result in immediate incarceration. We'll be back for sentencing."

His hand clasped Chris's shoulder, but Chris felt only lightness. He was free.

JAKE TOOK CHRIS OUT FOR a beer to celebrate. They laughed and shared stories of college. They didn't talk about the trial. They didn't talk about the murder. They didn't talk about Maggie.

Jake came back to the house to collect his stuff. He packed quickly, and Chris walked him to the door. "I should get back to Miranda," Jake said.

"Yeah, probably. Fix that mess, I guess?"

Jake shrugged. "Nothing new. I'm used to it." He gave Chris a hug, walked to his car, and lobbed his bag in the backseat. "Hey, if you hear from Maggie, let us know okay? Miranda is worried."

Chris paused, giving Jake a pointed look. "Oh, wait up, hold on a second." Chris ran back into the house and up to his bedroom, taking the steps two at a time. When he returned to the front porch, Jake was standing against the passenger-side door. Chris tossed him a swath of fabric, which Jake caught easily in one hand.

"What's this?" Jake asked.

"I found it under my bed. So I guess if *you* hear from Maggie, maybe you let *me* know?"

Jake unfolded the fabric and studied it. It was a man's dress shirt, cobalt blue.

<hr />

AT NINE THAT NIGHT, THE doorbell rang. Chris approached the door cautiously, thinking it could be the media. When he looked through the peephole, he saw Detective Small, bundled in a pea coat and scarf. She held a pizza in one hand and a six-pack in the other. He opened the door, and she gave him a hesitant smile. He noticed for the first time that her right front tooth was lightly chipped in the corner. Her blond hair fell around her shoulders, and when she tilted her head, he noticed a small mole near her left ear.

"Detective Small?"

She gave him a small shrug. "Call me Stephanie. I thought you might want to celebrate?"

Chris held the door open, and she turned sideways through the entryway, giving him a sly grin as she balanced the pizza and beer. Chris led her through the living room and into the kitchen. He watched her unpack the pizza and fish around the island for paper plates while opening a drawer and pulling out a knife. He was struck by the disconcerting thought, *She knows where everything is.*

She noticed his surprise and gave an embarrassed shrug. "The search warrant execution."

They settled in the living room with their pizza. Chris was surprised by how comfortable he was.

She caught his eye. "So do you think you'll look for her?"

Chris didn't ask who; he didn't have to. He nodded. "Yeah, I will. I don't expect to find much, though. Maggie was... determined about a lot of things. I expect this is one of them." He chewed and took a swig of beer. "Will the police or Janice look for her?"

Stephanie wiped her mouth with a napkin and sat back, pulling her feet up on the ottoman. "I don't know. Probably not. I mean, here's the thing. Janice put *all* her eggs in your basket. She found that Smith kid and didn't want to listen to anyone that he wasn't reputable. Even if she puts all her efforts into finding Maggie and brings her back, the first thing her defense attorney will say is, 'How can you make a case for reasonable doubt against Maggie when you were convinced you had an airtight case on her husband not even six months ago, and especially when there's no new evidence?'

"Janice knows this, her boss knows this, and frankly, no one is pressuring the D.A.'s office to find justice for Logan May. People have moved on. I can't see anyone forking out money into looking for your wife. The FBI won't even get involved because there's enough evidence to suggest she left. Do you know an acquittal still counts toward the P.D.'s case closure rates?" She shrugged. "It's all politics at this point. I'll help you though, if I can."

"I guess I don't blame her for splitting. But still, it'd be nice to know she was okay. Or that she cared if I was okay?" He felt foolish admitting it.

"Well, to be honest..." Stephanie sounded uncertain about whether to continue or not. "Probably the reason you're here is because she left. Had she stayed and confessed, Janice would have turned it into a three-ring circus and called her a liar who was 'defending' you. I saw that done once. Worked, too. The jury thought the wife was lying at the last minute to save her husband."

"What happened?"

"The D.A. did a good job with it, and the husband was found guilty. Later they discovered her fingerprints on the bullet with new technology, and that was the end of that. Anyway, my point is, I started coming around to your way of thinking around the time she skipped town. It didn't sit right with me. The *only* way it made sense was if you were telling the truth."

"I wish Janice thought that way," Chris said. "My life would have been so much simpler these past few months."

"Oh I'm sure she does. Not that she'd admit it. You'd find Maggie before Janice did, trust me."

"I have no idea where to start. She's probably halfway to Mexico."

"I was married for ten years," Stephanie said. "I'm willing to bet if you think about it hard enough, you'll come up with something. At least a starting point."

Chris thought about that as he chewed. About five years earlier, they watched a show about the capture of a then-famous serial killer who had been hiding out in Los Angeles under an alias. While walking down the street, he'd been caught on film during the recording of a documentary on the homeless population in America. A film editor who had a special interest in wanted serial killers made the connection and called the crime show before he even called the police.

Maggie had clucked her tongue, gesturing toward the television with the remote. "That's the problem with these guys. They gravitate toward the bright lights, big cities. There's a populated city in almost every state in this country, but everyone thinks they can hide in New York or L.A., where every other person is filming some movie or documentary. But what happens in, say, Minneapolis or Jacksonville, Florida? Still plenty of people, but no one will look there. It's anonymously low profile."

Chris gave Stephanie a grin, his first real grin in what seemed like years, and passed her another beer. "You know, I bet I could come up with something."

CHAPTER THIRTY-TWO

MAGGIE

Six Months Earlier

MAGGIE PRESSED HER FOREHEAD AGAINST the window. She smelled the city before they crossed the bridge. It was the odor of garbage and fast food, a beacon of opportunity.

They'd stopped in Hoboken, and her silent seatmate, a sullen teenager plugged in at the ears, had gathered his things and exited. Only after she was certain no one would take his place did she pull a small envelope from the front pocket of her backpack. She examined the seal—it was intact, the stamp over the seam unbroken—and thought of that skittish kid at the diner. She ran one lacquered fingernail under the flap, the paper tearing easily along the fold. Not that she was that concerned about the tweaker. She doubted he even remembered her name. Meth ruins the mind and the body. She remembered his name, though: *Smith Hamilton.* The man with two *last* names.

She felt some guilt about setting up Chris. Had they just called the police that night, none of this would have happened, and if someone had to pay, Chris would point to her. But the moment she'd sat in the bathroom, staring at that purple positive sign, something inside of her had snapped into place. The concept of running away, once the idea occurred to her, stuck in her mind like a briar bush, needling and intrusive. She imagined the baby tightly ensconced in the red, pulsing cushion of her abdomen. She felt certain that the baby would live. She heard Chris's voice in her mind. *You always think that.*

That had been true. With every positive test, she'd told Chris, "This time will be different." A never-ending hope.

When she flipped through Jake's files, Smith's name had leapt off the page. It hadn't been difficult to find Smith. She'd met him at the diner and given him a thousand bucks and the location of the body. He'd grinned with his furry, green teeth and taken the envelope of cash with greasy hands. He smelled like dirty hair. She needed Smith twice, once to testify and once to point her in the direction of a new identity. As tenuous as it was, he was her only connection to the criminal world. *Yeah, I know a guy that could help.*

Chris would be fine. Jake was a smart, capable lawyer who was pointing the finger at her. He would pace the judge's chambers, declaring that her disappearance was indicative of guilt. They could come after her. Her heart galloped at the thought.

Maggie scrunched down in the bus seat and removed each item from the envelope. A dark blue, leathery book, her picture embossed on the inside, was stamped with the U.S. seal. A plastic card with a different picture and the word Minnesota across the top. A dog-eared two-by-four-inch piece of card stock, directly from the department of Social Security, with an unrecognizable nine-digit number. All with the name of a stranger. She studied the name, rubbing each item like a toddler rubs the silk on the edge of a blanket for comfort. *I am invisible.*

How long until they noticed she was gone? A day? Maybe four? She catalogued all the things that would tip them off. The depleted bank account, gone from twenty-five thousand dollars down to a hundred bucks in a single day. The picture in the *Maggie College* box—if they even noticed that. The only person who might pick up on that would be Chris, and she doubted he knew her well enough to even think twice about how the picture had ended up there. If Jake came back to their house, he would notice she had not. Would he care? Unlikely. She'd left the house in the early morning, skimming the shadows, and called a cab from a disposable cell phone, eleven blocks from her house.

The loudspeaker crackled an unintelligible message, followed by a deafening squeal of brakes. She stuffed the items back in their envelope, back into her backpack, and filed out of the bus. Port Authority was hub of activity, and the heat from the sidewalk swallowed her with a fetid gulp. She started sweating as soon as she hit the street.

"Luggage, ma'am?" the driver had the luggage compartment open.

She shook her head, turned, and faded into the bustling crowd. Everyone, it seemed, was going the opposite way. She swam upstream. There were eight blocks between Penn Station and Port Authority. Maggie walked six of them before she felt fatigued. She leaned against a corner post, her shoulder digging into the *Press to cross* button.

Under an abandoned storefront, a homeless woman arranged a selection of glass bottles—purples and greens and blues, wine bottles whose labels had been painstakingly removed, square amber whiskey bottles, chipped and broken beer bottles, a glittering rainbow city within a city. Maggie watched her arrange, then rearrange, then reflect on her placements. With only the vague notion of an idea, she unzipped her backpack and removed the Lennox vase. She'd bleached it and scrubbed it clean of blood and fingerprints, and she gripped it with the corner of her T-shirt. Keeping her head low, she set the vase down in front of the woman, who had slunk down against the soaped up windows. She offered it to the woman without speaking, only a general gesture of giving. Without making eye contact, she scurried away, hitting the *cross* button with purpose.

"Oooeee, child, this is 'spensive! You wanna trade me for somethin'? I gots a pretty purple one yas can have!"

But the walk sign lit up, and Maggie hurried across Eighth Avenue as though she was being chased.

At Penn Station, Maggie boarded a bus to LaGuardia Airport, and at LaGuardia, she bought a Delta ticket to Minneapolis-Saint Paul International Airport. No one glanced twice at her new shiny license. The only small hiccup was when the attendant behind the ticket counter called her Ms. McKinnon. Maggie turned around, looking behind her for someone else. She laughed it off with a wave. "Just married, takes forever to get used to!"

The attendant looked at her strangely because what kind of newlywed buys a one-way ticket to Minnesota?

After boarding and finding her seat, Maggie's fatigue consumed her, and she couldn't keep her eyes open. She drifted to sleep before the plane took off, her chin resting on her clavicle. Even in sleep, she was careful to remain self-sufficient—she wouldn't be one of those lean-on-the-shoulder-of-the-guy-next-to-you passengers. She dreamt of Tiny's gleaming head.

She jerked awake hours later, convinced she'd forgotten something. She stood and looked around the cabin, certain she'd see Detective Renner or Small. When she sat, sighing, her heart pounded too hard to drift back to sleep. She cracked the window shade. The clouds rolled by like billowing white sheets taken straight from the dryer, and she wanted to wrap herself in them, smother the guilt with something clean and fresh.

She thought of Isaac and Rebecca, their small cherubic faces, asking for her at Christmas, and she felt the only stab of regret. She thought of Charlene and Phillip or Miranda and Jake and felt nothing. She closed her eyes and tried to summon some emotion. She imagined her mother crying and wiping thick streaks of mascara from underneath her eyes with red acrylic nails.

Phillip would stand behind her, patting her shoulder. "It's so typical of Maggie, Charlene. She's never cared about anyone but herself. Are you surprised? She'll come back when she needs money."

If Charlene cried, it would be for Chris. "How could she leave him right now?"

Miranda would play the part of the "good daughter," stopping to check in on broken-hearted Charlene. Maybe she'd bring a casserole that no one else would eat. She'd cluck and clean Charlene's immaculate kitchen, and they'd speculate how far Maggie could get on Phillip's twenty-five thousand dollars.

Maggie felt nothing but ice-cold relief.

⋖◆⋗

IN MINNEAPOLIS, MAGGIE FOUND AN apartment in a converted Victorian, a bit southeast of Lowry Hill. At the end of the summer, the temperatures plummeted to the thirties, breaking all records, and Maggie invested five hundred dollars in a winter wardrobe. She was careful with her money. Twenty thousand dollars would help, but it wouldn't last forever. She cut her hair into a nondescript bob, a plain Jane in a busy, unremarkable city where no one would think to look. *I am invisible.*

She followed the trial obsessively, scouring the Internet for any mention of Chris Stevens or Jake McHale. Most days, Chris was on the front page of the local section of the Harrisburg *Sentinel.* He looked good, his dark curly hair cut short for the trial. He'd grown gray at the temples, and Maggie touched the computer screen. Then, like a defense mechanism, she'd think of Chris, his head tilted back and his mouth open, with Tracy splayed on his lap. She'd think of his eyes, glittering and angry, when she insisted on calling the police. Then she'd remember his face when he grabbed her arm and said, "This is all your fucking fault."

That Small cop, the pretty one, testified on Chris's behalf, and Maggie wondered if he was sleeping with her. She imagined the two of them in her old bed, but the picture slid from her mind. She tried to conjure jealousy and found she couldn't care.

Janice, that wiry woman-child of an A.D.A., had it out for him, her frizzy red hair and pinched face splashed on every article about the trial. The article about Chris's testimony showed her close to the witness box, pointing at Chris, her lips pressed in reproach.

Maggie functioned on autopilot. In the mornings, she'd walk around Loring Park, circling the pond sometimes two or three times. Her stomach was permanently twisted in some combination of dread and guilt, and her appetite dwindled down to nothing. She'd gnaw on dry toast in the morning and force down a frozen dinner at night. Her weight plunged to the lowest it had ever been, despite the pregnancy. How could she raise a child when she couldn't even seem to be pregnant properly?

She spent the evenings online, searching for anything related to Chris or Jake or the trial. On one of these nights, at two a.m., she saw it. On *findthemissing.org* was her name, her picture. She scrolled down to a snapshot of her laughing into the camera. Bright pink and purple balloons floated behind her at Rebecca's fourth birthday party. *For information, contact CJS95@gmail.com.* Ninety-five had been Chris's lacrosse number in college. He was looking for her.

When the verdict was announced, *not guilty, not guilty, not guilty, guilty* (for the one and only thing he was truly guilty of), Maggie struggled to right her spinning head. She felt an initial stab of fear. Would they find her? Possibly. All she could do was hope. She was truly relieved. She hadn't wanted Chris to spend his life in prison. Then again, he'd gotten them into that mess. The guilt washed off of her, easy and loose. She was free.

MAGGIE GREW ROUND, HER BELLY taking the shape of a beach ball. Her face filled out and freckled. She doubted that Miranda could have picked her out of a crowd. She daydreamed about Jake, ways she could initiate contact: surreptitious notes from a post office box or a call from a disposable cell phone to his office. It was never a real idea; she'd come too far for that. Jake would remain in Philadelphia, miles and light-years from her present life. When the pregnancy brought surging hormones, she thought of little but touching his bare back again. Every second of their last night together was burned in her memory, and her fingertips buzzed with the desire to touch hot flesh. Jake was a real regret.

Around six months, she started to believe it was real, that she might actually carry the baby full term. She consulted a midwife, a superstitious departure from her previous pregnancies fraught with medical monitoring. Luna was an ample, wobbling woman with a long gray braid, thickset cheeks, and large, capable hands. Luna carted a portable Doppler and a stethoscope in an oversized quilted bag to Maggie's house twice a month. Her appointments all ended with a massage. Maggie had never felt so loved.

Maggie waited for the inevitable cramping and blood, the searing pain and the trip to the emergency room. With every ache and stab of discomfort, she held her breath, knowing that could be the moment, just like with all the other babies. But it never came. *Sometimes the body just figures it out.*

Quinn Aurora arrived one cold night in March, and Maggie pushed through the birth alone. When Luna quietly asked if she could call someone for Maggie, Maggie just shook her head. Luna gaped at her with raw pity, and Maggie looked away. Outside her window, snow fell in round, chunky snowflakes, like pennies from heaven.

Later, Maggie traced the features of little Quinn's face, her perfect mouth, button nose, her gassy smile, and sea-green eyes. Maggie felt whole for the first time in her life. She felt warm. She felt needed. She felt *human*.

I am no longer invisible.

EPILOGUE

May 1st

Five Years Later

THE WARM SPRING BREEZE LIFTED the sheers, bringing in the light, sweet fragrance of blooming peonies. Lucy Westing fidgeted with the cut daisies in the ceramic vase on the table. The sunroom was her favorite room, a bright welcoming committee first thing in the morning or a light airy retreat as the sun dipped low on the horizon. She ambled around the house, her heart thumping in her throat. She checked the time. *Two hours!* What could she possibly do for two hours?

"You need to relax is what." Clive appeared behind her, reading her mind. His arm snaked around her burgeoning middle, the baby giving a blunt kick in protest.

She closed her eyes and leaned back into him, letting his solid frame absorb her worry. She turned to study his ruddy complexion, stubbled cheeks, floppy strawberry blond curls, and deep brown, heavy-lidded eyes. On impulse, she kissed him, her tongue running along his bottom lip.

He laughed. "This is how you want to kill the next two hours?" His faded Irish lilt was sexy as hell.

"Can we? Call it stress relief."

He held her out at arm's length, gripping her shoulders.

"Relax, darlin'. This is no big deal. Quinnie will love it. Look at all this purple! For God's sake, I've never seen so much damn purple. It's like we've literally moved into the belly of that dinosaur thing."

"It's her favorite color..." Maggie had to admit Clive was right. The entire house was covered in purple balloons, purple streamers, purple plates and forks and napkins, purple, purple, purple.

"It's not like she's expecting a birthday party months after her birthday."

They'd planned a surprise party to celebrate Quinn's fifth birthday two months after her real birthday so that she could celebrate with Clive's family. His parents, sister, and brother were visiting from Ireland for a cousin's wedding. She and Quinn had been so lucky that Clive's family accepted them as their own. Initially Lucy had been protective of her heart, but the Westing clan acted as though love was bottomless, and they forced their love on her like a pack of unruly wolves. In the beginning, their loud bickering and laughter, their singing, and his mother's constant need to touch had terrified her. She felt consumed by them, all of their emotions out there for the world to have.

She remembered saying to Clive, after meeting his family for the first time in their small, painted brick row in Dingle, Ireland, "Is it possible to literally be suffocated by love?"

His mother, Pearl, was round and earthy and wore long, shapeless dresses. His father, Finn, was red faced with a shock of white hair and lewd jokes. She watched Finn pat Pearl's behind through her layers of skirt and apron. She waved him off with an eye roll, but also a coy smile and a surreptitious wink. Lucy thought, *I want that.* She never felt suffocated again.

They'd all be there in—she checked her watch again—one hour and forty-two minutes. Lucy sank into the couch, plopping her swollen, tired, achy feet on the coffee table. With Quinn, she'd never felt like that. But she was five years older and twenty pounds heavier. She traced the voluptuous curve of her calf. *Like her sister's.* She watched Clive through the doorway, whistling as he emptied the nearly full dishwasher. She rarely thought about the past except in shadowy terms like *before and after.*

Clive appeared, holding two ice packs. She motioned to her feet and giggled as he knelt and wrapped her ankles with them. It felt amazing. He stood and dropped a lingering kiss on her lips. He tasted like peppermint. He trotted out the front door and returned with a stack of mail, which he dropped on the coffee table at her feet. She squawked a protest as he took the steps two at a time.

"I don't do the mail!" he called. "I can be talked into dishes and laundry, and I'll temporarily rub your feet and get your ice and massage butter or what the hell ever into your belly. You're right, I should really do more around here..." His laughter faded as he entered the bathroom. The pipes groaned as water rushed under the floor and up the wall.

She grinned as she picked up the stack of envelopes. *Junk mail, bill, bill, flyer, party invitation.* She sorted out the items to open and flipped them over, running her short, raggedy nail under each flap. She made a short stack by her side that she'd take up to her desk before the party.

She needed to call Kim, her best friend and neighbor down the street, and tell her to stop by later for cake and singing and drinking. Clive's brother Kaelan never traveled anywhere without his guitar, even if it meant dragging it through customs... *What the hell?*

She stared at the photograph. Her arms and legs went numb and cold. Her heart thudded so hard she thought it would fly out of her chest. She lurched forward, pushing her face between her knees. *What the fuck?*

When her vision cleared, she studied the picture again.

It was an extreme close-up of her *before* face, a shiny strand of long blond hair blown across her face. Absently, she touched her brown bob. In the background was a man. A man whose face she knew as well as her own, whose face she saw almost every day in their daughter. Farther behind that, although indiscernible in the picture, was a white horse-driven hansom cab, the feel of cold drifting snowflakes, and the smell of burnt chestnuts. *Shrimp and butter. Twelve-hundred-thread-count sheets, soft as silk under her back.*

She was going to be sick. She lurched up, ran to the toilet, and holding her belly, retched into the bowl. Her hair stuck to her cheek, and her ribs ached. She leaned back against the bathroom wall, sweat beading on her forehead. Only one person would have that picture. He'd found her.

How? The tweaker? Smith Something? *A man with two* last *names.* She rocked back on her heels. Or maybe Leon helped. *Leon has a gift. He can find out anything about anyone. I don't know how, and I don't ask.* How he'd tracked her down was of no consequence.

"Luuucy!" Clive's heavy footsteps bounded down the stairs.

Lucy's legs went numb with panic. *Oh God, Clive.* She shoved the photograph under her thigh just in time. The bathroom door cracked open.

"Y'alright, love?" The half of his face that she could see was creased with concern, his mouth bowed in a frown.

She nodded, her tongue crowding her throat.

He ducked his head and softly shut the door. He hovered on the other side for a moment. "Give a shout if you need anything."

Lucy was hot. Her skin felt stretched and feverish. She pulled off her shirt, and she leaned forward until her belly rested on the cold tile. She breathed and thought about her options. *Options. Think. Think.* Her heartbeat drowned out rational thought. All she could focus on was Chris.

Chris. Leaning against the door jamb in the kitchen, watching her cook with a small lopsided smile on his lips. *Chris.* The incandescent moonlight dancing across his sleeping face. *Chris.* The crease in his forehead as he spit venom at her, his fist pounding the filthy visitor's room table. *Chris.* Who had tracked her down instead of moving on with his life. Instead of dating, remarrying, having children, she envisioned him poring over the Internet late at night, the glow of the screen illuminating his face as he *clicked, clicked, clicked.* Her name echoing in his mind, a driving relentless force. God, would they ever move on?

At that moment, she knew she'd never be free. The thought struck her right below the breastbone, and her mouth tasted tangy, acrid. Maggie stuck to her like a spiderweb, clingy and invisible. No matter how she flailed, she couldn't lose those whisper-thin remnants of her *before* self—what she'd done, who she'd hurt, what she'd run from. She'd always be bound to her past. *Waiting.* At the bank, in the grocery store, in the pick-up line at the elementary school. She'd check her rearview mirrors, question every waiter, eye every cop.

Beyond the bathroom door, Clive whistled a bouncing, lilting rhythm. His life, untouched. If she could help it, it would remain that way. *He can never know about Maggie.*

She heard the back door open and Quinn's racing footsteps, followed by boisterous voices talking over one another. She heard raucous laughter, backslapping hugs, and loud smacking kisses. The voices faded into the kitchen.

Lucy pulled the picture out from under her thigh and studied it, tracing her eyes, her lips, her cheeks. The horse. The shadow of a man she used to know. Used to love. She flipped it over, knowing what she'd see.

We'll never be old married folks. Promise you'll love me forever?

OTHER BOOKS BY KATE MORETTI

Thought I Knew You

ACKNOWLEDGEMENTS

Thanks to my beta readers, Rachel, Audrey, Emmie, Betsy, and Becky.

Thanks, Mom, for "helping" me plot (write your own damn book), and thanks to Sarah for spending hours talking about things that haven't actually happened to people that don't really exist. May we always gossip about imaginary things.

Thanks to Elizabeth for just about everything—support, advice, reading, feedback, frantic middle-of-the-night emails, and endless amounts of wisdom.

Thanks to Matt Banks (Banks Law Group, LLC) for reading this novel in its entirety and providing pages and pages of encouragement and feedback. (Some of which I ignored for the sake of fiction, so don't blame inaccuracies on him. He tried.)

Thanks to Gary Asteak for providing guidance and entertainment while in the outlining stages, and helping me to understand the inner workings of criminal law.

Thanks to the folks at RAP: Michelle, Cassie, and Streetlight Graphics. For the second time now, I'm floored by the final product.

I'm eternally grateful for the widespread support from my family and friends who read my books, my sporadic blogs, tell their friends, rent billboard space, and share in my excitement. I can't tell you all what it means to me.

Finally, thanks to Chip—my everything, always—for taking care of real life while I make things up and letting me into that scary little-known world of "how a man thinks." You're my best friend and partner in crime.

ABOUT THE AUTHOR

Kate Moretti lives in Pennsylvania with her husband, two kids, and a dog. She's worked in the pharmaceutical industry for ten years as a scientist, and has been an avid fiction reader her entire life.

She enjoys traveling and cooking, although with two kids, a day job, and writing, she doesn't get to do those things as much as she'd like.

Her lifelong dream is to buy an old house with a secret passageway.

Made in the USA
Middletown, DE
08 March 2016